Praise for the Novels
of Karen White

The House on Tradd Street

"Engaging. . . . The supernatural elements are not played for scares, but instead refine and reveal Melanie's true character. . . . A fun and satisfying read, this series kickoff should hook a wide audience." —*Publishers Weekly*

"*The House on Tradd Street* has it all: mystery, romance, and the paranormal including ghosts with quirky personalities. For me this is White's best work and I am looking forward to the sequel." —BookLoons

"White delivers funny characters, a solid plot, and an interesting twist in this novel about the South and its antebellum history." —*Romantic Times*

"Has all the elements that have made Karen White's books fan favorites: a Southern setting, a deeply emotional tale, and engaging characters. "
—A Romance Review

"The key to this quirky charmer is the depth of the lead characters, especially the heroine and even some of the ghosts. Fans of paranormal romantic suspense will want to read this wonderful tale as Karen White provides a fine treasure hunt mystery with a nasty spirit inside a warm romance in which readers will say yes that they believe in ghosts and in love."
—*Midwest Book Review*

continued . . .

The Color of Light

"[White's] prose is lyrical, and she weaves in elements of mysticism and romance without being heavy-handed. An accomplished novel."
—*Booklist*

"A story as rich as a coastal summer . . . dark secrets, heartache, a magnificent South Carolina setting, and a great love story."
—*New York Times* bestselling author Deborah Smith

"As lush as the Lowcountry, where the characters' wounded souls come home to mend in unexpected and magical ways."
—Patti Callahan Henry, author of *Between the Tides*

More Praise for the
Novels of Karen White

"The fresh voice of Karen White intrigues and delights."
—Sandra Chastain, contributor to *At Home in Mossy Creek*

"Warmly Southern and deeply moving."
—*New York Times* bestselling author Deborah Smith

"Karen White writes with passion and poignancy."
—Deb Stover, award-winning author of *Mulligan Magic*

"[A] sweet book . . . highly recommended."   —*Booklist*

"Karen White is one author you won't forget. . . . This is a masterpiece in the study of relationships. Brava!"   —Reader to Reader Reviews

"This is not only romance at its best—this is a fully realized view of life at its fullest."   —Readers & Writers, Ink

"*After the Rain* is an elegantly enchanting Southern novel. . . . Fans will recognize the beauty of White's evocative prose." —WordWeaving.com

"In the tradition of Catherine Anderson and Deborah Smith, Karen White's *After the Rain* is an incredibly poignant contemporary bursting with Southern charm."
—Patricia Rouse, Rouse's Romance Readers Groups

"Don't miss this book!"   —*Rendezvous*

NEW AMERICAN LIBRARY TITLES
BY KAREN WHITE

The Girl on Legare Street

The House on Tradd Street

The Lost Hours

The Memory of Water

Pieces of the Heart

Learning to Breathe

The Color of Light

On Folly Beach

KAREN WHITE

NAL Accent
Published by New American Library, a division of
Penguin Group (USA) Inc., 375 Hudson Street,
New York, New York 10014, USA
Penguin Group (Canada), 90 Eglinton Avenue East, Suite 700, Toronto,
Ontario M4P 2Y3, Canada (a division of Pearson Penguin Canada Inc.)
Penguin Books Ltd., 80 Strand, London WC2R 0RL, England
Penguin Ireland, 25 St. Stephen's Green, Dublin 2,
Ireland (a division of Penguin Books Ltd.)
Penguin Group (Australia), 250 Camberwell Road, Camberwell, Victoria 3124,
Australia (a division of Pearson Australia Group Pty. Ltd.)
Penguin Books India Pvt. Ltd., 11 Community Centre, Panchsheel Park,
New Delhi - 110 017, India
Penguin Group (NZ), 67 Apollo Drive, Rosedale, North Shore 0632,
New Zealand (a division of Pearson New Zealand Ltd.)
Penguin Books (South Africa) (Pty.) Ltd., 24 Sturdee Avenue,
Rosebank, Johannesburg 2196, South Africa

Penguin Books Ltd., Registered Offices:
80 Strand, London WC2R 0RL, England

First published by New American Library,
a division of Penguin Group (USA) Inc.

 REGISTERED TRADEMARK—MARCA REGISTRADA

ISBN-13: 978-1-61664-474-1

Set in Bembo
Designed by Ginger Legato

Printed in the United States of America

To my parents, Catherine Anne and Lloyd Sconiers.
Thank you for your love and guidance.

Acknowledgments

I would like to thank the generous and gracious residents, past and present, of Folly Beach, South Carolina, especially Mary Rhodes, Bill Bryan, Ruth Rahaley, and Beth Lamm, for helping me with my research for this book. I would also like to extend a huge thank-you to the indomitable Marlene Estridge, city clerk for the city of Folly Beach, for the kind generosity of her time and information and her enormous patience with all of my questions. Now I know why there was a song written about her.

Thanks also for all of the lighthouse information provided by Carl Hitchcock of Save the Light, Inc., the organization working to restore and preserve the historic Morris Island Lighthouse for future generations. For more information or to learn how you can help, visit www.savethelight. org.

Great appreciation also goes to my readers, especially Sandra Popham and Mary Kelly, whose enthusiasm for my books is as flattering as it is inspiring. Thanks for all the kind words—I couldn't do what I do without you!

And thanks, as always, to my friend and fellow author, Wendy Wax, and my family—Tim, Meghan, and Connor—for enduring yet another deadline and ending up relatively unscathed. You make all of this possible!

The ocean is the same ocean as it has been of old;
the events of today are its waves and its rivers.

—Sayyid Haydar Amuli
FOURTEENTH CENTURY

On Folly Beach

PROLOGUE

Noblesville, Indiana
January 2009

Emmy awoke to the song of the wind in the bottle tree, to the black night and the winter chill, and knew Ben was gone from her the way the moon knows the ocean's tides. She'd been born with what her mother called *the knowing*, and until this night Emmy had never been afraid of it. But now the keening of the wind through the colored bottles bled through her bones and flashed behind her eyes like a newsreel, illuminating the one thing she'd never wanted to know.

Lying awake in the stillness, Emmy began her grieving, missing already the way Ben's laugh started as a rumble in this throat, and the warmth of his hand on her hip as he slept while she stayed awake to count her firsts and her lasts.

She'd started this on the night Ben had kissed her for the first time all those years ago, tilting her face to his as a sunflower turns toward the sun, and as he lowered his head toward hers she remembered thinking that this was the last time he'd kiss her for the first time. Emmy had assumed that everything with Ben would always be a litany of firsts, and for the most part, they had been. Except for saying good-bye. Since that first night, they'd made it a game between them, promising never to say good-bye to the other. It was insurance, Ben told her, that they would see each other again.

Slowly, Emmy rose from her bed and walked out of her childhood bedroom, where she'd moved when Ben left her for his second tour of duty. Then she went through the living room and the kitchen door to the backyard, ignoring the snow against her feet and the way the wind penetrated Ben's flannel shirt. The shirt was a poor substitute for his arms, and wearing it in Ben's absence was something her mother had told her was like swimming with a raincoat. But it was the one thing Emmy could hold on to.

She flitted like a ghost past her mother's sleeping herb garden, to the back of the picket fence to where the bottle tree stretched itself out through a dusting of snow, howling its unease to the brutal climate. The tree was the only thing her mother had brought from her South Carolina home, as if to bring more would make her exodus too permanent. Although it had been. Except for the funerals of both of Emmy's grandparents, her mother had never been back.

The tree itself was an artist's rendition in metal of a tree trunk and multiple branches, upon which each end had been topped with a glass bottle in various rainbow hues. Slaves from the Congo had brought the tradition of the bottle trees from their homeland to the American South, their intent to catch evil spirits inside the bottles before they could make it into their homes.

The bottle tree had stood in the backyard since before Emmy was born, and she'd asked only once why after so many miscarriages her mother had still believed in its power to turn away bad spirits, and never given up and taken it down for good. The obvious answer—*because then you were born*—had never formed on her mother's lips, and Emmy had stopped asking.

Still, the tree had become a point of refuge for her—a tie to a place she knew only in old photographs of her mother as a young girl, a place with an entirely different color palette from the flat Indiana farmlands of her home. Emmy had never seen the ocean, but as a child she'd liked to pretend that it was the sound of the ocean that lay trapped within the bottles, and if Emmy ever found the courage to lift a bottle from its branch, she'd finally learn what it was that made her mother miss a place so much.

A new moon bathed the frozen yard with a veil of blue light as Emmy closed her eyes and tried to block out the sound of the wind and the truth it wrapped around her head. *Ben is gone.* She closed her eyes tighter, trying to feel him again, to see him as she had the last time at the airport, when he was wearing army-issue fatigues with the name HAMILTON stamped on the pocket and saying everything but good-bye. But even her gift failed her, answering her only with bitter cold and utter blackness.

The screen door slammed shut, like a shout in the dark, but Emmy didn't turn around. "Mama?"

Her mother's voice came out as a sob. "Is it Ben?"

Emmy nodded, her words frozen. She turned in time to see her mother's knees begin to buckle. It was Paige's prerogative; she knew grief. She'd never allowed the birds of sorrow to hover above her, but instead had invited them inside to nest.

Emmy reached her mother before Paige fell into the snow, and found herself again being the comforter, the adult. She welcomed it. If Paige fell apart, Emmy wouldn't have to think about her own grief, of how she was barely thirty and already a widow. Or how she'd have to find a way to say good-bye to her husband for the last first time.

CHAPTER 1

The buzzing from the B-24 bomber approaching Center Street started like nothing more than that of a sand gnat, but soon the noise filled Maggie's ears to the exclusion of everything else. She ran out onto the front porch as Jack McDonough buzzed his hometown on one of his regular flybys. She waved, not sure if he could see her, then ran back inside and up the stairs to her sister's bedroom, recently relinquished to their widowed cousin, Catherine.

"Damn that Jack!" came a woman's voice from inside the bedroom.

Maggie opened the door without knocking and fixed a reproving look at her cousin. "Watch your language, Cat. There are young ears in this house."

Catherine stood on a chair while Maggie's nine-year-old sister, Lulu, used an eyeliner pencil to draw a line on the back of Cat's long tan legs. Lulu sent a worried glance toward Maggie. Lulu never liked to take sides, but usually ended up with Cat, anyway, whether she wanted to or not. It was hard to say no to Cat, no matter who you were.

Catherine waved her left hand with the gold band winking on the third finger. "I'm an adult now, and I can say what I want. And look, he's made Lulu mess up, and now she's going to have to start all over." She wiped her forearm across her forehead. "Damn, it's hot in here, considering that it's January. I need to open this window right now."

She stepped off the stool and perched herself on the wide windowsill of the casement window. Squatting, she lifted the lever while pushing into the window with her hip.

Maggie bit her lip but when she couldn't stand it anymore, she said, "You're going to get yourself killed, Cat, if you lean on the window while you open it. Why don't we just wait so I can call somebody to get it fixed?"

"And die of heat prostration first? I'd rather not, but thank you very much. Besides, I've been practicing, and I know how to do it now." As if even mechanical things couldn't argue with her, the window gave way at the same moment Cat leaned in to prevent herself from toppling out of the second-story window. "See?" she said, grinning as she stepped from the sill and back to the stool.

Maggie sat on the edge of the white chenille-draped bed in front of the open window and shrugged out of her sweater. "It's only sixty degrees, Cat. Hardly what anybody would qualify as hot and certainly not enough to warrant putting your life in danger to open a window." A cool ocean breeze flipped the eyelet curtains into the room as if to accentuate her point. She noticed for the first time the tight white blouse and red skirt her cousin wore. "Are you going somewhere?"

"Out. I don't care where, just as long as I'm out. Because of all the soldiers coming in, they're having dancing on the pier, even though it's not summer. I swear I can hear the music, and I don't see why I can't have fun just like all the other girls." Cat sent her a petulant look that only made her look more dangerous. Before her death, Cat's mother had always hoped some Hollywood producer would discover Cat and make her a star. With blond hair, green eyes, and a body with curves in all the right places, she was sometimes mistaken for Lana Turner—a mistake Cat rarely corrected.

Maggie bit her lip, not wanting another row. But a promise made on her own mother's deathbed dictated that she had to try to rein Cat in, if such a thing were possible. After a deep breath she said, "It's too soon, Cat. What will people say? We only just buried Jim, and his death deserves his widow's respect."

Cat remained where she was like a golden statue, eerily silent. Lulu, sensing the upcoming battle, scooted away into a corner, hugging her knees to her chest.

In a deep voice that didn't even sound like hers, Cat said, "Jim's dead, Maggie. Not me. I'm only nineteen years old, for God's sake! I've got my whole life ahead of me, and I'm much too young to be buried next to a man I was only married to for three months."

Lulu began to cry, the sound like a whimpering puppy. She'd loved Jim as only a nine-year-old girl could. It was because of her that Jim had come into their lives. She'd fallen at the roller rink and hurt her leg, and Jim had carried her home like a knight in shining armor. Maggie had thought so, too, warming to his easy grin and gray eyes, touched by stories of his own little sister he'd left behind in Louisiana. He'd taken her dancing twice, and had kissed her once. But then he'd met Cat, and there had been no more dances or kisses.

She stared at her cousin now, the old promise rubbing her like a new shoe. They'd been raised together, their mothers being sisters and Cat's father having deserted his family long before Cat was even born. Maybe it was because only Maggie saw the desperation in Cat, the hunger and loneliness that dogged her as she hunted for love. And it would have bothered Cat greatly to know that most of the time Maggie only pitied her beautiful cousin.

"You don't mean that, Cat. I know that you don't."

Cat stared out the window. "I want to live. I want to dance." She turned around, her eyes hopeful. "Come with me, Maggie. You can be my chaperone, although it should be the other way around since you're single and I'm the widow. It'll be fun. Just like old times."

Maggie looked down at her freshly dyed black dress, and her frayed fingernails and stockingless pale legs. Going dancing with Cat was never fun. Maggie would slide into orbit around Cat's sun, cast in shadow from her light. She wondered sometimes if Cat needed her to go so Maggie could witness that Cat was desirable and wanted, as if to prove that her father's leaving and her mother's death had nothing to do with them not wanting her enough.

Cat stepped down off the chair, taking off the high-heeled pumps that she'd badgered Jim into buying for her instead of paying rent. She stood in front of Maggie, her green eyes pleading. "Come on, Maggie. I can't go by myself—what would the neighbors say?"

Maggie turned away, shaking her head at Cat's use of Maggie's own argument. "You're a recent widow, Cat. You're not supposed to want to dance. Or be in the company of other men." Her heart tightened a little as it always did when she thought of Jim, of the way his eyes crinkled in the corners when he smiled, or the way he looked at you when you were speaking as if there was nothing more important in this world than what you had to say.

Cat turned slightly to catch her profile in the cheval mirror in the corner, smoothing her blouse and skirt to accentuate her figure. "In case you hadn't noticed, Maggie, there's a war going on. All bets are off. Things that weren't okay before are perfectly acceptable now." She lifted her left eyebrow in the way she'd perfected after she'd seen *Gone With the Wind*. "I'll let you borrow my blue dress—the one with the pretty collar—and my mother's brooch. I'll do your makeup, too. I can make you look like Bette Davis in that movie you like so much. You're just as pretty, you know, if you just put some effort into it. Don't you want a husband? There're men everywhere now. And it's up to us women to do our duty before they head off to do theirs."

"Jezebel," Maggie said, saying the title of her favorite movie, which Cat could never seem to remember, along with Maggie's favorite ice-cream flavor or how she was shy around men. At least she had been until she'd met Jim and forgotten to be shy.

"What?" Cat asked distractedly, still studying her reflection. "Oh, right. The movie. Anyway, I can make you look just like her if you'll let me." She grabbed Maggie's hands and squeezed them, looking right into her eyes, and Maggie knew what Cat was about to say before the words were out of her mouth. "You owe me, remember?"

Of course she did. Cat had been reminding her since Maggie was eight years old and on a dare had left the safety of the sand and dove headfirst into an oncoming wave. Maggie supposed it had never occurred to either of them that she couldn't swim, but Cat, with her strong and steady strokes, had made it to her side and hauled her out back onto the sand like a beached whale before another wave could drag her out into deeper water. And even though she reminded Maggie often that it had been she who saved her, Cat never did once mention that she'd also been the one who'd dared Maggie to do it in the first place.

"Fine," Maggie said, giving in to the inevitable, silently wishing she could stay home again with Lulu and their books, slipping away into other worlds where she was confident and beautiful like Cat and men were honorable and worthy like Jim.

"Great," Cat said, beaming. "You won't regret it."

Maggie smiled back, halfheartedly knowing that she already did, and watched as Lulu turned her face away and began to cry again.

ß

FOLLY BEACH HAD LONG SINCE been considered the wilder sister of her barrier-island siblings. The cottages with their trademark weathered paint and rickety steps, the dirt roads and general air of don't-give-a-damn made the tiny slip of island outside Charleston Harbor a haven to those who loved her, and an object of derision for those who didn't know her well enough to love her.

Maggie loved it because it was the place where the memories of her mother lived in each shell she plucked from the sand, and each marsh sunset she watched settle over the Folly River. Their home on Second Street, with its broad porch and flaking yellow paint, was the house her father, a Charleston lawyer, had built for her mother for a summer escape from the heat of the city right after they were married. Everything about the house had her mother's touch, from the eyelet curtains in the two bedrooms and the large picture window in the front room that faced the street, to the baskets of sand dollars and collection of sea glass that dotted the windowsills.

Seeing them and touching them each day brought her mother back into her life again, somehow making Maggie feel less lonely and wanting. It was why, when her father died, she'd moved here permanently with Lulu, waiting for the next phase of her life to start.

She found Lulu in the backyard, nearly hidden by the bedsheets hanging on the clothesline. Cat was supposed to have folded up all the linens and brought them in before the evening chill made them too damp to fold, and Maggie sighed inwardly as she stepped forward.

The sheets whipped in the unseasonably warm air, hiding and then uncovering Lulu in quick succession, and bringing to mind the end of a movie reel. Maggie's hair whipped around her head, ruining the curls Cat had spent an hour ironing into her hair. Trying to tuck the loose strands behind her ears, she marched toward her sister, preparing to scold her for not being ready to leave.

She stopped suddenly on the other side of a white cotton flat sheet, the yellow thread used to mend a hole flashing at her like a skittish cat. Peering around it, she saw Lulu kneeling in the sandy grass where she'd stuck a slender tree branch, its bark darkened and slick from being underwater for a long period of time. Maggie watched as Lulu lifted a green Coca-Cola bottle and inverted it before sliding the open end onto the stub of a severed limb; then Lulu sat back on her heels to admire her handiwork.

Wind whipped sand up from the ground, stinging Maggie's legs and smudging the black line Cat had insisted on drawing on them. But Maggie didn't move, entranced instead with the sound of the wind in the bottle, a keening of depth and otherworldliness—a sound that spoke to the naked part of her that she'd never shown to another human being. Except once.

"Lulu?"

Her sister turned abruptly, knocking the branch and making it lean.

Maggie lifted the sheet and stepped under it before kneeling in the sand in front of Lulu. Lulu's hazel eyes were wide with surprise and something else that Maggie thought might be anticipation.

"Did you hear it, Mags?"

Maggie nodded. "Yes, I did." Out of habit, she brushed a strand of light brown hair behind Lulu's ear, a losing battle with the wind. "What's it for?"

"It's a bottle tree. Jim told me about them. He said that African slaves used to put bottles on the trees outside their houses to scare away evil spirits."

Maggie wrapped her hand around the damp branch and straightened it, using her other hand to pack sand firmly at the base. "I didn't know that Jim was superstitious." She avoided looking at Lulu, afraid to see in Lulu's eyes the same eagerness she felt to talk about him.

"He wasn't. Not really. He said that he'd been listening to bottle trees his whole life, on account of the people that worked for his mama and daddy on the farm. He said that it wasn't really important if you believe in it; it was important just to have that little piece of something that reminded you of some place or someone you loved."

Lulu pursed her lips the way she did when she was debating saying something more, and Maggie knew to stay silent. Finally Lulu said, "Keeping away bad spirits is a good thing just in case, don't you think?"

Maggie stared into Lulu's eyes. "You don't really believe in bad spirits, do you? Because if I think you're serious about all of this, I'm going to take you to see Father Doyle tomorrow for confession."

Lulu kept her gaze down for a long moment, but when she looked up at Maggie again, her eyes were dark. "If Cat's going to live with us now, we're going to need this bottle tree, don't you think?"

Maggie opened her mouth to chastise the young girl but found that she couldn't say anything without lying to both of them. Instead, she rose and reached her hand out to help Lulu stand. They stood looking at each other while brushing the sand from their knees. Without saying anything else, Maggie took Lulu's hand and pulled her away.

"Come on. You're staying at Amy's tonight because Cat and I are going to the pier. I want you to help Amy and her mama take care of Amy's little brothers, okay? It's hard for them with their daddy gone. Just promise me you won't talk about the war like you did last time. It really upset Mrs. Bailey."

Lulu kept her head down. "But you always told me to speak the truth, and that's what I did. Soldiers die every day. Jim did. Maybe Mr. Bailey will, too."

Maggie's heart rattled in her chest as she wondered if Lulu's bleak outlook was due to the fact that her parents had died or just to the bitter wind of war that had blown sand into all of their lives. She squeezed Lulu's hand. "Yes, Lulu, soldiers die every day. But the people they've left behind don't want to think about that. They want to think about the time they'll be coming back. We'll add Mr. Bailey to our prayers tonight, okay?"

Lulu stopped walking and looked up at Maggie. "Cat never prayed for Jim, did she? Maybe that's why he died."

"Oh, no, sweetheart. That's not why . . ."

Lulu wasn't listening. "I'm going to make a bottle tree for them instead, and give it to them as a present. Maybe that will keep Mr. Bailey safe."

They had reached the back door, and both stopped to see Cat standing in the doorway, an annoyed expression doing nothing to make her less beautiful. She carried her shoes in one hand, not wanting to ruin them on the dirt streets, but her feet were moving restlessly. "Come on, you two. I can hear the music already, and all the best guys will be taken before I get there."

Lulu brushed past her, her brows nearly knit together. "I can walk to Amy's on my own."

Maggie watched her go, knowing her worrying over her little sister would be minor compared to the friction between Cat and Lulu if they walked together. Maggie called out, "Good night, Lulu. I'll pick you up first thing. And don't forget what we talked about."

Lulu's shrug was the only indication that she'd heard a single word.

Cat frowned after her departing back. "What's got into her?"

Maggie didn't answer, but led the way through the house to the front door, remembering to lock it. It was something they'd never thought to do only a month before, when the navy yard and Charleston Air Base weren't brimming over with men.

They made their way down Second Street toward West Ashley with the older, bigger houses of the year-round residents giving way to the shacks and whitewashed cottages of the summer visitors. After crossing West Ashley, they walked on the beach with their shoes in their hands, avoiding getting their feet wet by the chilly Atlantic.

Near the pier, they passed members of the new Folly Beach Mounted Patrol. Maggie wasn't quite sure what they were looking for since the Japs were off the West Coast and the Germans were three thousand miles across the Atlantic. But she figured it made the men feel as if they were contributing somehow. She knew that after each patrol they'd head to McNally's for a beer, storing their submachine guns in a closet while they drank. Maggie wondered if she was the only one who thought that residents had more to fear from drunks with machine guns than from spectral Germans.

As they approached the pier, they passed more and more people, on foot and in cars, heading toward the pavilion and pier for dancing or roller skating or whatever eatery or entertainment was still open in the wintertime. January was usually pretty slow on Folly, but with the influx of military personnel, the locals tried to accommodate the newcomers with as many diversions as they could.

The long pier, constructed mostly of palmetto logs, jutted out into the water, its roof painted a dark green with a red Coca-Cola sign emblazoned on the side. It was a South Carolina icon, as evidenced by the fifteen thousand people who'd shown up there for the Fourth of July celebrations just five years before. Cat had just turned fourteen but had been allowed to go, and had danced every single dance while Maggie held her cousin's shoes and fetched water for her all night.

People were beginning to park their cars on the beach next to the pier, cheating the tide for the time being. With all the light and gaiety, it was hard to believe there were larger concerns than finding a dancing partner or a cold beer. Only the men in uniform, present in more and more numbers as the weeks went by, reminded everyone that America was at war.

Regardless of Cat's pleadings, Maggie had kept on her black dress, and when she saw the sailors and airmen in uniforms, all of them with their heads turned toward Cat, she wished she'd changed. It wasn't that she wasn't used to being ignored when standing next to Cat; it was more that she hadn't even tried. Jim had told her that she had a beautiful smile and that she shouldn't hide it from the world. Wearing her stay-in-the-background dress, she almost felt as if she were dishonoring him. She shivered as a cold breeze pushed in off the water, making her tighten her coat around her throat.

Cat stopped before they reached the wooden boardwalk that connected Center Street to the pier and the site of the summer carnival, and turned her back to the crowd. Maggie stopped and watched as she opened her purse and drew out a tube of red lipstick. Maggie waited while Cat expertly applied it to her full lips before willingly allowing Cat to put some on herself. Maggie knew she didn't look like Bette Davis, but she thought of Jim and what he had said about her smile, and she forced herself to let Cat paint her lips red. When she was finished, Cat grabbed Maggie's hand and led her to the Folly pier, where a band had already started playing on the large stage. "Come on, Mags. Let's show them how it's done."

The crush of people and the kerosene heaters strategically placed around the perimeter managed to warm the space and allow Cat and Maggie to remove their coats.

Maggie's earlier bravado faded as she spotted the girls with their brightly colored dresses and high heels, with big earrings and seam-painted legs, and she suddenly felt like a crow in a sunflower field. Uniformed men and civilians stood in groups drinking Pabst beer and eyeing the ladies under a revolving crystal ball suspended from the ceiling.

"My treat," said Cat as she opened her purse again and paid the cover charge.

The tide was rolling in under them, crashing onto the sand beneath the pier as the first dancers of the evening began to crowd the dance floor. Spanish moss had been draped from the rafters, giving the entire space a magical air of whimsy. Maggie saw the heads turn as Catherine, tall and sleek like a lioness, slinked to a table and sat down, settling her skirt prettily around her crossed legs before pulling out a cigarette and a lighter.

Maggie sat down next to her and grabbed her arm. "Cat, don't. It makes you look cheap."

Cat shot her an annoyed glare. "It makes me look older. More sophisticated. That way those young guns won't bother. I'm looking for an officer."

What about Jim? The words sat useless in Maggie's mouth as she sat back in her chair. A waitress approached and they ordered two beers, although Maggie would have preferred a Coca-Cola.

"Loosen up, Mags. We're here to have fun. To forget about work, and the war, and all the things we can't control." Cat took a drag from her cigarette and kept her lips puckered as she blew out a long, sinuous string of smoke.

Resigned, Maggie tried to relax, but left her beer untouched as she began to count to see how long it would take for the first guy to approach their table. She'd reached only twenty-five when a young man who had a broad face and sparkling eyes and wore the dark blue Crackerjack uniform of an enlisted man flipped back a third chair and straddled it backward to face Maggie and Cat.

"Seaman William Findley, Summit, New Jersey. Now that I've got that out of the way, could I interest either one of you ladies in a dance?" Although he'd addressed both of them, he didn't take his eyes off of Cat.

Cat peered at him through a cloud of cigarette smoke. "I don't dance with anybody younger than me."

"I turn nineteen next week. Don't need no license to dance, neither."

Maggie noticed he was swaying in his seat and wondered how many beers he'd already had. She started to ask him when a large hand appeared on his shoulder. Maggie looked up to see a khaki-clad officer, his dark brown hair combed neatly down despite the wave that threatened to sweep across his forehead. His eyes were gray and sharp, but Maggie knew not to look too closely, that Cat had already claimed him for her own.

"I think it's time to say good night to the ladies, sailor."

Seaman Findley looked up to argue but stopped when he realized he was addressing an officer. With swaying reluctance, he stood and would have tripped over the chair if the officer hadn't steadied him before sending him on his way back to his barracks.

"I'm sorry, ladies. I hope he didn't bother you."

Cat sent him a brilliant smile. "Not at all. But I'll say he was only so I can thank you for coming to our rescue." She indicated the seat next to her, and he sat down without missing the chair, a remarkable feat to Maggie since he never took his gaze off of Catherine.

He introduced himself but Maggie couldn't hear him from the noise of the band and because he was facing Cat as he spoke. She caught his first name, Robert, and that he was a second lieutenant from Savannah and stationed at the new Charleston Naval Air Station, and Maggie decided that was all she needed to know about Cat's current distraction and stopped trying to listen. Both Cat and Maggie introduced themselves, but his eyes alighted on Maggie for only as long as it took her to get her name out before returning to Catherine.

He ordered another round of beer as they made small talk, and Maggie tried to be as unobtrusive as a third wheel could be. Robert took a long swig of his beer and turned to Cat. "I've been looking for a local to tell me what kind of music this is that they're playing. I've never heard anything like it."

Catherine's long, unvarnished fingernails were tapping on the table, the only part of her casual demeanor revealing her eagerness to dance. "I don't know what it's called officially, but we call it beach music. It's sort of a mix between swing and Colored music. It makes a person want to dance, doesn't it?"

Maggie blushed. The way that Cat said "dance" hinted at everything else two people of the opposite sex could get into, and it was obvious from the expression on the lieutenant's face that he was thinking the same thing.

"Do you think you could show me how to dance to it?"

With a voice sultry enough for Hollywood, Cat said, "It would be my pleasure. Just follow my lead."

He stood and pulled Cat's chair out for her. "It'll take some getting used to but I'm sure I can learn how."

Without looking back at Maggie, they walked to the dance floor with the lieutenant's arm around Cat's waist. Maggie sat at the deserted table staring at her untouched beer bottles until her attention was dragged back to the dance floor when the tempo of the music changed and she recognized one of her favorite dance songs, "In the Mood" by Glenn Miller. She hadn't felt sorry for herself when Robert appeared and paid attention to Cat instead of her. She hadn't even felt it when the two of them left her to disappear onto the dance floor. But with her favorite song playing, she felt cheated somehow, mourning a man who hadn't been her husband and wanting nothing more than someone to dance with.

The sound of two bottles being thumped on the table made her turn her head away from Cat and Robert. She looked up and saw a tall, light-haired man standing next to her table and scrutinizing her. He was a civilian, and wore a tan wool suit with a crisply folded pocket square.

She'd think later that her first thought was that he wasn't particularly handsome, but he wasn't ugly, either. His face was long and narrow, his hair dark blond. Sharp cheekbones and a strong jaw jutted from his face like those of a sculpture of an ancient Greek warrior. But it was his eyes that saved his face from being too harsh. They were amber-colored, like a cat's, and outlined in black, which made them almost mesmerizing. He smiled, and his teeth were even and white, but even then she couldn't help the first word that sprung to her mind. *Dangerous.*

"You're not drinking your beer so I thought you might enjoy a Coca-Cola instead." He sat down in Cat's vacated chair. "Do you mind if I sit?"

She did, but she didn't say anything. It was in the way he looked at her, as if he knew her sadness and saw beauty there instead.

He reached his hand out to her. "I'm Peter Nowak. My friends call me Pete."

She couldn't imagine anybody calling him Pete and knew if she spent more than five minutes with him, he'd forever be a Peter to her. He spoke with an almost imperceptible accent she couldn't place but her question died on her lips as his fingers touched hers to shake. They were soft as she imagined a poet's would be, and almost too hot to touch. She wanted to jerk away, but he held on. "And your name must be something regal, like Anne or Elizabeth."

Maggie managed to pull her hand away, feeling scorched. She started to speak and was embarrassed that it took her two tries to find her voice. "It's Margaret, Margaret O'Shea, but everyone calls me Maggie."

A "v" formed over his nose. "I think I'll call you Margaret. It suits you better. To call you 'Maggie' would be an insult to a woman like you."

His flattery didn't sound as empty as it should have. She wanted to leave, but not because she found his company unlikable. It had much more to do with the irrational way he made her thoughts jumble and her skin prickle. She stayed and fought to find her voice again.

"You're not from around here, are you?" Maggie asked.

He tilted his head. "What makes you say that?" His eyes sparkled.

Maggie smiled reluctantly. "I guess it's your accent. But mostly it's because I'm local and know everybody here. And I own a shop on Center Street, Folly's Finds. We sell books, but other things, too— like newspapers, magazines. Candy and some drugstore items. But just about everybody stops by at some point during the week, even newcomers, so I get to meet just about everyone."

"Except me." He leaned back in his chair and crossed an elegant leg over his knee while pulling out a gold cigarette case. He offered her one before choosing one for himself and lighting it. After a deep drag, he said, "I'm most recently from Iowa, where I've lived since I was fifteen. Before that, my family was from Warsaw."

Maggie leaned forward. "Poland?"

"Yes." He raised an eyebrow at her unspoken question. "We emigrated to the United States nearly eleven years ago. My father is Christian, my mother Jewish. They decided my brother and I would be safer and have more opportunities here."

She nodded, intrigued. She'd never been out of the state of South Carolina, but her favorite pastime was to study the atlases in the store and pretend she might actually one day visit the places on the maps printed in bright colors with exotic and unpronounceable names. "Why are you here on Folly? You're not in uniform." She was looking for a reason not to like him—a reason to get up and walk away from the unsettling way he made her feel.

"I have terrible asthma." He held up the cigarette with a rueful smile. "I know this doesn't help, but I can't seem to stop." He took another puff to prove his point. "I've had it since childhood and couldn't pass the physical for the armed forces. But I do my part."

It was her turn to raise an eyebrow.

"My father owns a leather-goods factory back in Iowa. We make shoes, belts, boots, that sort of thing. We retooled most of the factory to supply our brave soldiers. It's my job to visit with different military bases around the country to determine if our quality is good enough and what other needs are not being met. And to find new markets for our products." He smiled yet Maggie wasn't warmed by it; it made her feel like she was standing in the surf, sensing the sand being sucked away from beneath her.

"So, Margaret, what about you?" he asked with a lopsided smile as he stubbed out his cigarette in the glass ashtray on the table. "What

are you doing for the war effort besides doing without nylons and collecting foil?" He sat back and rested his long fingers on the arms of the
chair. "And dancing with the soldiers, of course. A beautiful woman
must consider it her duty, right?"

His trivializations made her angry, and she'd been about to excuse
herself when he'd called her beautiful. She hated herself for feeling
flattered, especially since she knew it was a lie. She was passable, but
not beautiful. Growing up with Cat had taught her that. But this elegant man was looking at her, and not Cat, and calling her beautiful.

Maggie stifled her unease and took a sip from her Coca-Cola
bottle. "Well, I run my store. I wanted to work at the navy yard in
Charleston but I'm the sole caretaker for my younger sister, Lulu."

"You have no other family?"

"Just my cousin, Catherine. She's a recent widow. She helps me
sometimes at the store and with Lulu. I think it's too soon for her to
be working."

"How sad. And you left her at home tonight?"

Maggie's lips tightened. "Actually, she's here. She . . . thought it
might help if she danced."

"Ah," he said, lifting his eyebrow again. "The grieving widow."

Maggie was unsure how to respond, recognizing his sarcasm but
feeling loyal to Cat. "My cousin is very beautiful. The men enjoy
being in her company. She's the tall blonde you probably saw dancing
with the lieutenant."

He didn't even turn, keeping his strange eyes focused on Maggie,
and something flickered in her chest. "I don't think I noticed."

She turned away from his penetrating gaze, finding it hard to
breathe. A familiar rhythm pounded from the stage, and she felt her
feet tapping an accompaniment. Cat and Robert were in the center of
a circle of spectators watching them dance, their arms and legs flying,
their faces slick with sweat. They were beautiful together, like mating
birds in midflight.

Maggie thought of Jim again, and how he'd thought she was beautiful when she smiled, and she felt a longing to be free of the sadness

that dogged her like a sand fly. Turning to Peter, she smiled brightly. "Do you know how to dance to beach music?"

The elegant eyebrow lifted again, making Maggie wonder if she'd said something wrong. "I'm a fast learner."

Dancing was the one thing she could do as well as, if not better than, Cat. Feeling emboldened, she stood and held out her hand. "Come on, then. Let me show you how it's done."

He stood and smiled, then grabbed her hand in a strong grip. "It will be my pleasure."

His voice covered her like a silk stocking, easing her into his arms. She glanced back at their abandoned table and spotted the two empty Coke bottles. Pulling away from him, she ran back and stuck one bottle under the table so the waitress wouldn't throw it away. She wanted to save it for Lulu and her bottle tree.

It didn't occur to her until much later to wonder why she was contemplating capturing evil spirits on the same night that she was finally considering letting them go.

CHAPTER 2

Emmy sat on the floor in the backroom of Paige's Pages, the bookstore her mother had owned since Emmy was a baby, opening boxes and logging titles into the store's computerized inventory system. It had been six months since Ben had returned in a flag-draped coffin from Afghanistan and been laid to rest next to his father and the faceless ancestors who'd loved the land they'd farmed for more than one hundred years. To Emmy, the passing of days had gone unnoticed, marked only by the flipping of a calendar page. Even the change of seasons had gone unmarked until Paige had insisted Emmy take off her winter sweaters and start wearing cotton and short sleeves.

Her grief was a silent thing—an invisible virus that gnawed at her from the inside but somehow managed to leave the rest of her unscathed. Her reflection was a surprise each time she saw it, expecting to see something withered and gray, or a black hole where her face had once been. Grief became to her like breathing; she couldn't rise or go to sleep without the pressing feel of it against her heart, the weight of it like a suitcase she didn't know how to unpack. Her sleep was dreamless, yet upon waking she'd be sure she'd heard fading footsteps in her bedroom, unsure if they were returning or going away.

And each dawn she'd force herself to lie in bed with her eyes closed, hoping to see Ben one last time; hoping he'd tell her which way the footsteps were leading.

Emmy found fleeting relief in the stacks of books in her mother's store. The silent words on the written page comforted her just as they had when she was a child, and she welcomed the forced solitude of sorting and shelving books. She left the customers and sympathy sayers to her mother, finding solace in the dusty back room office. The pain and emptiness couldn't find her there, where she kept her mind too busy to think.

Every once in a while, Emmy would consider resuming the life she'd planned before she met Ben. With her master's in library science, she'd once dreamed of being a curator for a museum or university with a large manuscript and rare-book collection. Her joy of dissecting the past through the study of fading words and brittle paper had come as a surprise to many in her small town, but not to her mother. Paige had named her only daughter after the author of her favorite book, *Wuthering Heights*, after all.

Following graduation, Emmy had chosen to work in her mother's store while waiting to find a job in her field, anticipating what corner of the world she'd end up in, when Ben Hamilton had walked in one afternoon in search of a book for his niece. Emmy had been in the process of rereading Austen's *Pride and Prejudice*, and she'd been almost convinced that her Mr. Darcy had entered the shop. Newly minted from Officer Candidate School, Ben was tall and blond and in uniform. He invited her to have coffee with him, and then dinner. Within the month they were engaged, and six months later, they were married. And it never occurred to Emmy to wonder where her dreams had gone. It wasn't that she hadn't loved the idea of them; it was simply that she loved Ben more. Now that he was gone, those dreams were like the stuffed animals and faded corsages that still decorated her childhood bedroom; remnants of her life before Ben.

The bell rang over the store's front door, but she didn't get up to see who it was. It was only seven thirty in the morning, before the store opened, and she knew it was her mother coming to argue with her again about not sleeping, or working too hard, or not eating enough. She wanted to tell Paige that as soon as she figured out the right way to grieve, she'd stop doing all those things that seemed to irritate her mother.

"I brought you breakfast," her mother said from the doorway.

Emmy didn't look up, but continued typing. "I already ate. But thank you."

"They're your favorite—honey wheat bagels from Crandall's Bakery. They're still warm."

Emmy paused and looked over at her mother. "Maybe later. Just leave them behind the counter."

Instead of leaving, Paige stayed where she was, watching Emmy closely. For the first time in a long while, Emmy really looked at her mother, noticing the fine lines around her eyes and mouth, the way her frown seemed almost permanent. And how the sadness Emmy knew she carried with her always seemed to be closer to her skin now, showing through in small patches like a molting snake. It was as if the sadness had grown too big for her mother, finally surpassing Paige's capacity to hold it in anymore.

Emmy also noticed that Paige wasn't carrying the expected bakery bag, but instead held a glass mason jar. The glass was fogged and blotched as if handled a great deal, and the metal lid had long since darkened. Curious now, Emmy stood and walked toward her mother.

"What's that?"

Instead of answering Paige held it out, and after hesitating for a moment, Emmy took it. It shifted in her hands, a soft rolling like an ocean wave, and when she lifted the jar to eye level, she saw what it was.

"It's a jar of sand," she said, knowing as she spoke that it was more than that—that somehow the sand was part of her mother, as much as her green eyes and curly hair. It was the part of her mother that she'd never shared with Emmy before.

"From Folly Beach. My mother scooped it up and put it in this jar and gave it to me on my wedding day. She said that way I'd never forget where I came from."

But you did, Emmy wanted to say, but remained silent because the sand in the jar had become warm under her touch, as if it were remembering the South Carolina sun.

Instead she asked, "Why are you giving it to me?"

Paige leaned against the doorframe, her face reflecting her exhaustion. "Because. . . ." She was silent for a moment. "Because this"—she indicated the room and the Indiana world outside the walls—"isn't all there is. It's safe and familiar, but it's not the rest of your life."

A bubble of anger erupted in the back of Emmy's mind. "I'm happy here."

"No, you're not. You think you are because you don't know any different."

Emmy squinted her eyes, trying to recognize the woman who sounded so much like her mother—the mother who'd given Emmy a roof over her head, good food to eat, and clothes on her back, but nothing that could have been called guidance. Emmy had always thought it had grown from her mother's heart being broken too many times with the deaths of her babies; there simply hadn't been enough remaining to hold another child.

Emmy thought of the attic stocked with folded-up easels, dried-up and clotted paints, and half-finished canvases. It was the attic that had been off-limits to Emmy during her childhood, making it an irresistible temptation that she'd succumbed to many times following arguments with her mother. The paintings were the part of her mother she didn't know—the part of the girl Paige had been before she'd married Emmy's father. Paige had caught her up there once, but instead of anger, Emmy had seen only resignation, like accepting a diagnosis long after the tumor had been excised.

Her mother had told her that the paintings had been part of her application to art school in Rhode Island, but that had been before she'd met Emmy's father, Bill. They had never spoken of it again, but every once in a while, when she saw her mother staring out a window or holding a forgotten cup of coffee until it got cold, she pictured the girl with dreams of being an artist carefully hidden inside the face of a woman who chose to paint the colors of her walls beige.

Emmy stood to face her mother, feeling defiant, the jar in her hands still warm. "But you do know different, and you're still here."

As if Emmy hadn't spoken, Paige said, "Do you know why coyotes are found in almost every state now? Because they adapt. They find that what they really wanted isn't what they need, that there's something just as good someplace else. It's how they survive." She paused a moment. "It's been six months, Emmy. I've held my tongue while I've watched you stumble through your days like a drunk woman, but it's past time that you pull yourself together. You need to make a change or you will never get over this."

Emmy's anger felt muffled, as if she sensed that her mother might be right. "Maybe I don't want to get over Ben. He was the best thing that ever happened to me. And this is my home, Mama. Leaving would be like leaving Ben, and that would be like him dying all over again."

Paige pressed the back of her head against the doorframe and closed her eyes as if summoning strength. "Sometimes, just when we think we can see our lives on course and we can settle back and get comfortable, a new path opens. Some people just keep going, too scared to veer off the familiar path. But others, well, they step off into the unknown, and find that maybe that was where they were supposed to be all along."

Emmy tasted salt on her lips and realized that she was crying. "You don't know what you're talking about, Mama. There is no other path. This is my home."

Paige stepped forward and cupped her hands over Emmy's as she clutched the jar. "I do know. I've never veered off course. But you've been given a second chance. And you"—she pressed a finger gently against Emmy's chest above where her heart beat—"you're one of those other people. I think I've known that since you were little." She sighed, her warm breath reminding Emmy of being rocked as a child. "Maybe that's why there's this distance between us. You were going to leave me eventually, and I didn't want it to hurt too much."

"I'm not going to leave at all." Emmy turned around and placed the jar of sand on the desk, but found to her surprise that some of the sand had managed to stick to her fingers, lingering like an unwanted thought. This was not the heart-to-heart conversation she'd always imagined other girls had with their mothers, or the one she'd always wanted to have with her own. This was a conversation that could culminate only with one of them saying good-bye, and after all the years of waiting, it was still too soon. "I can't. You need me here, in the store. And Dad, too." She thought of the morning coffee and newspaper she delivered to her father every morning, how she reminded him when it was time to cut his hair or put on a sweater. She didn't say it because it had long since become obvious that he allowed her to do those things to make her feel needed.

Paige smiled faintly, as if reading Emmy's thoughts and agreeing with them. "Life should be a question, Emmy, and you're way too young to think you've already found all the answers."

Emmy wanted to protest, to tell her mother that she was wrong, but she recognized the grain of truth in Paige's words, heard them in her heart as if she'd always known them to be true but had denied them anyway. She tried a new tack. "I can't go to South Carolina. I don't know anybody, and how would I support myself?" She tasted the loneliness already, like a bitter candy slow to melt.

Paige moved into the room toward the stack of boxes brought in the previous day by the UPS man. Paige sorted through them, sliding off a smaller box to reveal a large square one on the bottom of the pile. "I was on eBay a couple of weeks ago, looking for used books for our new trade-in section of the store. I've found that boxes from estate sales give me the best deals because usually whoever packs them up has no idea what's in them and is just too happy to get rid of them and prices them accordingly."

Bending over, she wrapped her arms around the big box and slid it closer to Emmy. "And that's how I found this."

Emmy tilted her head to read the shipping label: FOLLY'S FINDS. "Is that a store?"

Paige nodded. "It is. Or used to be. Apparently the owner is retiring and selling inventory. I used to love the store. It was run by two older ladies. The younger one had a sort of side business crafting bottle trees and selling them from the back of the store. It's where I got mine from, actually. Their last name was Shaw or O'Shea or something like that. It was more of a general store at one time, but the book section kept growing, so that became their main focus after a while. They carried all of the great classics, and they had a pretty extensive travel section. But they had an entire back corner of the store devoted strictly to romances." A look of whimsy passed over Paige's face, surprising Emmy. "I've tried to reconstruct that atmosphere here, although I don't know if I've got it quite right. It was a magical place to be, which is probably why I thought to open up my own store."

Emmy reached over to the desk and took a pair of scissors from the pencil holder and sliced through the line of tape that covered the top of the box but didn't move to open the flaps. "I don't understand. What does any of this have to do with me?"

"When I realized where the books were from, I called the store. The current owner is an Abigail something-or-other, who is apparently the daughter-in-law of one of the two women I remembered from the store. She's been unable to sell the business as is and thought that if she sold the inventory she'd have a better chance of selling the building for a different kind of business." Her eyes narrowed as she closely considered her daughter. "She also told me that in recent years they've become well-known for their rare books and manuscripts—although that's mostly online, with her acting as a broker of sorts."

Despite herself, Emmy felt a flutter of interest. But then she thought of Ben, and how this was the place she'd known him and loved him. As if somehow all of her memories of him were tied to this one spot in the universe and would disappear without her there to hold them down.

She turned back to the computer and sat down. "I can't afford it, even if I wanted it." Emmy swallowed, waiting for the flutter to disappear, and for her mother to agree.

"But you can, Emmy. You have the money from the house, and from Ben. His final gift to you."

Emmy felt overwhelmed suddenly, with grief and loss and the glimmer of possibility. It scared her, made her feel like a small child letting go of her mother's hand in a crowded place.

"I can't," she said again, sounding halfhearted even to herself.

"Yes, you can. You will. Ben chose you because of your strength. Don't disappoint him."

Emmy looked up at her mother with surprise. "He told you that?"

Paige shook her head. "He didn't have to. I've known it since the moment you were born. You didn't try to focus on my face like most babies; you were already looking behind me to find what else was out there."

Emmy brought her eyebrows together. "You didn't want me to marry Ben, did you?"

Paige closed her eyes for a moment and shook her head. Finally, she said, "This isn't about him anymore. You can choose to unpack your bags at the detour sign and dig a trench for the long haul, or you can make your own detour."

She retrieved the jar of sand and placed it in Emmy's hands again. "You can always come back, you know. You'll always have a home here with us. But that would be a lot like planting a rose in the desert; you'd survive but you'd never really bloom."

When she started to move away, Emmy grabbed her hand. "Why are you doing this?"

Paige pulled away and moved to the door, stepping over a small corrugated box. Without turning around, she paused and said, "Because you're my daughter. Because you're the me I never let myself be." She shrugged. "I've never known how to love you, Emmy. You've always been so damned independent. Maybe I've finally figured out that to love you means letting you go."

Emmy let her head sag as she spoke, her voice thick with tears. "I loved him, Mama. I loved him more than I ever thought possible, and I can't just make that go away. I don't want it to. And I can't help thinking that the best thing that's ever happened to me has already happened."

Her mother sighed and turned her head to look at Emmy. "Just think about it, okay?"

Paige left, leaving Emmy clutching the jar of beach sand from a place she'd never been. Emmy closed her eyes, feeling the warmth of it again, imagining she smelled salt air and some other nameless thing: a heavy, pungent odor of sun-warmed earth and stagnant water. And she imagined something else, too: a shimmering in the air that hinted of unsaid good-byes and unpaid guilt. Or maybe it was the scent of new beginnings. The thought sent a shock of fear and anticipation through her that lifted the skin from her neck. It reminded her again of the wind in the bottle tree the night she'd become a widow, and as she sat down in front of the box of books, she began to think in possibilities.

$\mathcal{B}$

EMMY AWOKE TO THE SOUND of diminishing footsteps—too heavy to be her mother's and the sound of her father's snoring from their bedroom down the hall told her that they weren't his. She sat up, straining to hear them again, but heard only the night sleeping around her.

A sliver of moon spilled through her window shade, illuminating the jar of sand she'd inexplicably placed on her bedside table. She stared at it, imagining it had become liquid swirling inside the glass in tiny waves.

Emmy leaned over and switched on the lamp, relieved to see the jar of sand exactly as she'd left it. Her gaze traveled to the floor where the box of books from Folly's Finds sat. She wasn't entirely sure why she'd brought it from the store, only that she'd been looking for something to do when she invariably woke up in the middle of the night with no hope of further sleep.

Sliding from the bed, she knelt in front of the box and pried the flaps back before lifting away crumpled newspapers. Peering inside, Emmy smelled the comforting scent of old books, the indefinable mixture of worn leather, ancient glue, and the passage of years. She reached inside and lifted out a thick hardbound book coated in bubble wrap and placed it on her lap.

Buying boxes of old books was something her mother had begun to do on a regular basis as she'd expanded their store to carry used as well as new books, and it was Emmy's job to sort through them. Every once in a while, Emmy would find something rare and valuable tucked in amongst the dog-eared doctor romances of a previous generation, or the coverless sagas from the eighties with food and coffee stains decorating the tattered pages. They invariably came from an estate sale, the unwanted books belonging to somebody's grandmother or great-aunt inherited by a family member who wasn't going to be the one to throw them away.

Emmy wasn't sure if she'd been given the sorting task because of her degree and expertise or because her mother knew that all she had to do was place her hands on a box to determine if anything of real value was inside. She wasn't always accurate, but accurate enough to warrant being the official sorter.

She flattened her hands on the book in her lap and felt the familiar heat against her palm, the slight tingling behind her ears, and she knew there was something in the box that warranted further inspection. She carefully removed the bubble wrap, then held the book at an angle to read the fading title better. *Romeo and Juliet.* Glancing inside to the front pages, she noted the copyright date of nineteen thirty-nine before placing the book on the floor beside her.

Methodically, she began unwrapping each book, disrobing it of its bubble-wrapped cover, revealing each book. She noted with interest that the majority of the books was travelogues or atlases, with a few classic novels—nothing autographed and no first editions to make them valuable—thrown in. Emmy spotted Austen, Fitzgerald, Tolstoy, and even a German translation of Shakespeare—all familiar friends, and she found herself smiling. It seemed a deliberate collection of books, almost as if they'd been in somebody's personal library rather than on the shelves of a bookstore.

When she reached the bottom of the box, she peered inside to see if she'd missed anything. She'd been almost positive that something wonderful had been lurking within the corrugated walls of the box, but she must have missed it.

Too awake now to even contemplate sleep, she sorted through the books again one by one to see what she might have missed. When she'd finished, she sat back on her heels and regarded the piles in front of her with narrowed eyes. Her gaze fell upon the first book she'd held, *Romeo and Juliet*, the one that had made her skin prick. Leaning over she plucked it from the top of one of the stacks and flipped it open again to examine it more closely.

She'd already studied the copyright page, so this time she flipped immediately to the back of the book. Holding the book up to her nose, she wondered if it was her imagination that made her smell salty air. For the first time, she noticed the warped bottom edge of the book as if it had at some point in its life been in contact with water. Flipping the book over, Emmy realized the bottom of all of the pages showed water damage. She began to turn pages, looking for rot or mildew, and when she didn't spot any, she surmised that the book had most likely been in contact with water for only a short while and then been properly dried instead of being left closed on a shelf.

Emmy was about to close the book again when it slipped from her hands, landing on a corner of the spine before toppling over splaybacked. Carefully, Emmy picked up the book, holding it fixed to the place where it had fallen open, and held it up to the light again. In the top right margin of the right-hand page was handwriting, the black of the ink now a bruised shade of purple.

The broad, thick strokes of the letters were undoubtedly made by a male and as she brought the book closer to read it better in the dim light, she found herself blushing at the intimacy of his words.

A great man once wrote, "Absence diminishes small loves and increases great ones, as the wind blows out the candle and blows up the bonfire."
   If only I were as eloquent as Mr. de la Rochefoucauld . . . I miss you, I miss you, I miss you. And I want you. And I need your kiss. And your touch on my skin like a man needs water. Always.

Emmy's mouth went dry, as if an unknown lover had whispered in her ear. *Who was he? Who was he writing to?* She flipped through the rest of the book twice until she was satisfied that there were no more notes in the margins. Curious and fully awake now, she pulled the next book off of a stack and began to thumb through it before hastily putting it aside when she didn't find anything. It wasn't until she'd reached the fifth book, a tattered copy of *Wuthering Heights*, that she found another note handwritten in the margin. The black ink was small and faded, eluding discovery until Emmy's third perusal of the book. She might have missed it, too, if she hadn't been so dogged about it, like a child searching for a lost favorite toy. The search had become almost like a lifeline thrown to her in the darkness, something to hang on to.

The handwriting was different in this book, softer, more feminine, and all thoughts that it was another random note fled as Emmy read the neatly printed words.

I saw you last night on the pier and I know you saw me, too, but your eyes wouldn't meet mine as long as she was around. I understand it and am glad you are not so bold in her presence as to acknowledge me too openly. But then I saw you touch her hand, then place your arm around her shoulder, and I had to look away. And when I lay awake all night, I kept seeing your hand on hers and I died a little inside. How long can we do this? How will this end? I'm like a bird flying into a glass window again and again, trying to reach the unattainable yet willing to die trying. I must be with you again. Where?

Emmy sat back, her breathing loud and her forefinger pressed against the page. *Who are these people?* The books were old, and the handwriting faded, which made her fairly positive that whoever had written these notes hadn't done so recently.

A clock struck four times somewhere in the house, and Emmy closed her eyes. She needed to at least try to get some sleep if she didn't want to be a complete zombie later that day. Reluctantly, she began stacking the books back into the box, being careful to stick bookmarks into the books she'd found with notes, and to separate the stack into books she'd searched through already and those that she hadn't. It would give her something to look forward to, and she felt the old flutter of anticipation.

She reached for a short stack of books, accidentally flicking open the back cover of the one on top, a dog-eared copy of Hemingway's *A Farewell to Arms*. As Emmy bent to close it, her skin pricked again, and she knew with absolute certainty that something was about to happen—some change or shift in her universe was going to take place and there was nothing she could do about it. She paused, realizing she'd reached such a dark place in her life that she no longer even cared.

Peering down at the book in the dimly lit room, she found herself holding her breath. Staring out at her from the opened inside back cover was a hand-drawn picture of what appeared to be tall sticks dug into the ground to give the resemblance of a tree. On the tip of each limb, inverted so that the openings could fit onto the tips, were bottles of different shapes and sizes, all colored in shades of black ink.

Emmy sat on the edge of her bed, the book open on her lap to the picture of the bottle tree. She felt an odd compulsion to laugh but instead fell back on the bed, the book clutched in her hands. Ever since Emmy's mother had given her the jar of sand, everything had taken on an air of inevitability, as if she were slipping on ice and unable to right herself.

It's time to go. She wasn't sure if the voice came from inside her head or if it was just a memory of Ben's voice. She listened to the silence for a moment, then, feeling bolder, said the words out loud: "It's time to go." She didn't know who had written the messages in the books, or who had drawn the picture of the bottle tree, but they had managed to shake her awake. They'd given her something to look forward to: unanswered questions in a life that she'd begun to assume wouldn't have any more. Folly Beach was unknown to her, but it seemed to be as good as any other place without Ben. She'd done the equivalent of spinning the globe and pointing her finger, but she couldn't help the feeling that the box of books had nudged her hand toward the small barrier island off the coast of South Carolina.

She closed her eyes again, listening for the footsteps but heard instead the soft sighing of a summer wind whispering inside the glass of her mother's bottle tree.

CHAPTER 3

Maggie kneeled in front of the bookshelf in the back of Folly's Finds, reshelving the atlas she'd borrowed to take home the previous night. She was always careful not to leave fingerprints on the covers or bend the spines, and since the atlas was one of the more expensive books she had in the store, she'd been extra careful. She normally limited her selection to a classic romance, but she'd taken the atlas on impulse, wanting to learn what she could about Poland.

She eyed the shelf critically, noticing how some of the books had been wrongly shelved and began pulling them off to reorganize. She gritted her teeth as she wondered if Cat had done it deliberately so that she wouldn't be asked to do it again or if she really was incapable of shelving books alphabetically by author. Sitting back on her heels, Maggie called out, "Lulu, could you please open that small box behind the counter—the one that arrived yesterday? It's toothpaste and shaving cream, and needs to go on the shelves."

Lulu didn't answer right away and Maggie pictured her sitting behind the counter out of view, her nose buried in yet another Nancy Drew mystery. Or drawing inside the back cover in ink. The first time she'd caught Lulu drawing in a book, she'd been angry until she'd seen how good it was. She'd held her anger in check and instructed Lulu to contain her drawings to her notepads, but every now and then she'd find an ink drawing tucked into the back cover of one of her precious books, like Lulu's signature.

With a halfhearted voice, Lulu called out, "Where do you want them?"

"On the front shelf to the right, third row down. Next to the soap if we have any left."

Maggie listened as Lulu let out an exaggerated sigh, followed by the sound of a box being shoved across the wood floor. She was about to call out again to tell Lulu to pick up the box because she was scratching the floor when the sound of a man's voice, slightly accented, stopped her.

"May I help you with that, young miss?"

Maggie felt her cheeks heat as her hands went to her hair to smooth it quickly. She bit on her lips to color them and stood, hastily untying her apron and shoving it on the shelf behind her. With what she hoped would be a calm and mildly interested smile on her face, she walked to the front of the store.

Peter wore a dark blue suit with a neatly pressed white handkerchief stuck inside the pocket. He finished moving the box before straightening and smiling when he saw her, making Maggie blush. "Margaret," he said, taking her hand and bringing it to his lips in a decidedly old-fashioned way.

"Peter," she said. "What a nice surprise to see you here." Peter had escorted her home the previous evening since Cat had pulled another disappearing act, but when Peter had kissed her hand and wished her good night, there had been no promises and she hadn't expected any. Most of the men on Folly were here only temporarily, and her experience with Jim had taught her to not look beyond the present.

He raised an eyebrow. "But you told me about your store. I presumed it was because you'd like for me to see it."

She appreciated his efforts to save her from embarrassment and found herself smiling back. "Yes, of course. And you're just in time for the morning paper. We just received our *News and Courier* delivery."

He nodded as his gaze traveled over the well-worn oak counter that had been there before Maggie had acquired the store and probably been there since the store's existence. He noticed without comment the candy baskets at the foot of the counter, the short shelves of cigarettes and the bowls of matches, the magazine racks of *House and Garden* and *Good Housekeeping*, the Coca-Cola ice cooler.

"It looks like you're not having any shortages here."

"Not yet. We've only been at war for two months. But I have a feeling things are going to change pretty soon. Already I'm finding it difficult finding ladies' hosiery. All the silk seems to have been requisitioned by the military."

He nodded and was silent for a moment as he continued to peruse the shelves. "You have a very nice store here," he said as he walked to the back, where the bookshelves stood. Lulu and Maggie followed him. "Ah, books." With reverence, he slid a volume from the shelf and examined the cover.

Maggie leaned over to look and read the cover, *Porgy and Bess.* Feeling the need to impress him, she said, "The author, DuBose Heyward, had a cottage here on Folly. He invited George Gershwin to stay in it while writing the music for his opera based on the book. I was only a little girl—about Lulu's age, I think—but I saw him a few times."

She knew she was rambling with nervousness, but when he looked at her with a raised eyebrow, she took it as encouragement and continued. "When he first got here, he was all New York and very formal with suits and proper shoes. It didn't take him long to go 'native,' though. He was going barefoot and had a beard within the first few months." Maggie's smile faded as she noticed that Peter didn't seem as enthusiastic as she was about the renowned musician.

His eyebrows knit together as he slowly flipped through the pages. "I'm familiar with the book although I can't say it was one of my favorites." He turned to Maggie. "George Gershwin—he's a Jew, isn't he?"

Maggie's eyes widened. "I have no idea. I love his music, probably because I was raised on it. My mother played piano and *Rhapsody in Blue* was her favorite. Why do you ask?"

Peter closed the book with a solid thud before reshelving it exactly where it had been, making sure it was lined up with the edge of the shelf. "Just an observation. In Europe everyone knows who the Jews are, yet here in America, they've been assimilated into the culture so much that it seems as if it's merely an afterthought."

Maggie turned back to the bookshelves with a shrug. "I can't speak for the rest of the country, but here on Folly, we're pretty accepting. We have our own little melting pot here, with people of different races and religions rubbing along with very little friction."

A smile tightened the corners of his lips as he let his index finger drift across the shelves. "I suppose that's what makes America so charming—your little 'melting pot' concept where everybody is equal."

Maggie looked at him sharply. "But that's exactly why you're here—why your parents were welcomed here and allowed to succeed in business. Because here a man's measure is determined by how hard he works, not by who his father was or what religious faith he practices. I would think that would make you proud."

Lulu, apparently bored with the conversation, returned to the front of the store, and they both watched her go. Peter's voice was gentle when he spoke. "And you are absolutely correct, of course. I was merely making a social commentary. We have a war raging in Europe seemingly against a single race of people, whereas here it's not even a concern. I am very proud of my adoptive country, and very thankful that my family and I are here now instead of over there."

His tone indicated that he was finished with that line of conversation, and he turned back to the books. Maggie watched as he slid his index finger along the shelves, silently reading the titles. He paused at *Romeo and Juliet* but continued without picking it up. She still wasn't sure why he was in the store, and she began to interpret his silence to mean that he was there to look for a book. But she stayed near him while he browsed, telling herself it was because she was unsure how to leave without being rude. She found herself studying his hands, noticing that his fingers were long and elegant like the rest of him, and it made her wonder if he played the piano. On the third finger of his right hand, he wore a gold insignia ring. Leaning in closer, pretending to line up the spines of books on the shelf, she saw the ring bore the letter *K*. He looked at her suddenly, catching her staring at him, and she stepped back, mortified at having been caught.

He surprised her by smiling. "It was my maternal grandfather's. He was killed in the First World War, so I never knew him. I wear his ring to honor him."

Maggie held up her arm, displaying the slim gold chain with the single pendant of a sand dollar. "This was my mother's. I wear it to remember her."

Peter's eyes softened. "Were you very young when she died?"

"Fifteen. My little sister was barely three."

He was silent for a moment, his expression closed. "Losing a mother is always hard, especially for one so young. My own mother passed away two years ago, and I still miss her every day. We had the same eyes, you see. So whenever I look in the mirror, I'm reminded of her."

Maggie was embarrassed to find tears stinging her eyes, but his voice had been filled with sadness, reminding her of her own loss, which never seemed to get easier to bear. "Two years isn't that long. It's been six years for me, yet it still feels like yesterday." She raised her hands, splaying the fingers wide like a starfish. "We had the same hands, and I inherited her love of books. That's why I bought this place. It was always the first stop we'd make when we came to Folly. My mother and I would spend hours on the beach reading each morning. Those were the happiest days of my life."

Maggie blushed, embarrassed that she was telling this virtual stranger her life's story. But his eyes were warm and understanding, inviting her confidences.

"We have a lot in common, it seems," he said softly before turning back to the bookshelves. After a moment he pulled another volume from a shelf and opened it, and when she leaned forward, she saw the title printed on the top of a page. *The Great Gatsby* by F. Scott Fitzgerald. "Ah, yes," he said. "The tragic story of Jay Gatsby. I was never sure if I should admire him or pity him. Regardless, it's one of my favorite books."

It was one of Maggie's favorite novels, too, and she felt herself flushing again. "You may borrow it, if you like."

He raised an eyebrow in question.

"These were all my mother's books, which I brought from the house in Charleston when I sold it following my father's death three years ago. I didn't have room at the cottage but I didn't want to get rid of them, either. They're all so much a part of her, and so much a part of what we shared together. So I keep them here, and allow people to borrow them. We do have a library here on Folly. I'm just another option. And instead of issuing library cards, I use the honor system." Maggie pointed to the old coffee can on a bottom shelf. "When you take a book, you place a nickel in the can, and when you return it, you take one."

"But what if I want to purchase a book for my own pleasure?"

The way he said the word "pleasure" reminded Maggie of the way Cat spoke, emphasizing certain words so that the listener was left wondering at the speaker's true meaning. Flushing again, she said, "Then I can order one for you. You don't even need to pay me until the book arrives."

He nodded as he opened the book and began to flip through the pages before examining the spine. "This book—has it been borrowed before?"

Despite Maggie's extreme care while reading her books, this copy was dog-eared and well read by not only her but by every customer who asked her for a recommendation. "Quite a bit. And I've read it at least five times, although since I own it that wouldn't really be considered borrowing it, would it?"

Peter's smile broadened. "No, I suppose it wouldn't." He reached into his pocket and pulled out a nickel before dropping it into the can, the sound very loud in the quiet store.

"Are you sure you wouldn't want another book . . . one you haven't already read? Or at least one in better condition?"

He studied her, his gaze intent. "It doesn't matter which book I borrow. My aim is really just to have an excuse to return."

Maggie flushed yet again, but was spared from fumbling for a response by Lulu emerging from the front of the shop. She eyed Peter suspiciously. "I finished with the toothpaste and shaving cream. Can I go back to reading now?"

Maggie put her arm around Lulu's shoulder. "Thank you, Lulu. And you may go back to reading as soon as you allow me to introduce you to my new friend, Mr. Nowak."

Lulu eyed him in silence before raising her hand and allowing Peter to shake it just as Maggie had taught her. "It's a pleasure to meet you, sir." Her sullen tone belied her words. "You talk funny. And why aren't you in uniform?"

"Lulu!" Maggie warned, squeezing Lulu's shoulder.

Peter put a gentle hand on Maggie's arm. "That's all right. The young should be rewarded for being inquisitive. . . . It's how they learn. To answer your questions, young lady, I'm originally from Poland but emigrated to the United States when I was a boy. As for my lack of uniform, it is because I have asthma. I seek only to do as much as I can for the war effort without donning one."

"Jim wore a navy uniform. He died at Pearl Harbor defending our country."

Peter sent Maggie a questioning look.

"Jim was Cat's husband. We . . . we were very fond of him."

Peter raised an eyebrow. "It's hard to say good-bye to those we love, isn't it? He must have been an admirable and honorable man to have won the respect and admiration of three beautiful and intelligent women."

Lulu's face softened for a moment and Maggie gave her shoulder another squeeze. "He was."

Peter knelt in front of Lulu and reached inside his jacket. "Because of my travels and position, I am sometimes able to acquire items that are a little more difficult to find these days. When Margaret told me that she had a younger sister, I knew just the thing that I had to bring if I had the good fortune to meet you today."

He pulled out a cream-colored lace hair ribbon. "Handmade in Brussels, Belgium. I bought just a few last time I was in New York looking for fabrics. And I can't think of a lovelier young lady more deserving than you."

When Lulu hesitated to take the proffered ribbon, Maggie nudged her. Slowly, Lulu extended her hand and took the ribbon. Fingering it gingerly, she looked up at Peter, her face serious. "Thank you, sir."

Maggie wanted to suggest that Lulu place the ribbon around her ponytail as a proper form of thank-you, but she didn't. Lulu was always slow to warm up to people—except for Jim—and some people never did break through her reserve. It would take more than an exquisite hair ribbon to win her over.

Peter stood and faced Maggie again. "If I'm not being too forward, Margaret, I was wondering if I might ask you to accompany me tonight to dinner, and maybe some dancing afterward."

"I . . ."

Maggie's answer was interrupted by Lulu, who blurted out, "She can't. She needs to watch me in the evenings because I'm only nine years old."

Maggie sent her sister a warning look. "I would love to. I just need to arrange for someone to stay with Lulu. What time were you thinking?"

"Seven o'clock?"

"I close up here at five, so that should give me plenty of time."

"Wonderful. And since you're a local, I'll have you suggest a place."

Everything Cat had ever taught her about playing hard to get or never giving away how she really felt by her facial expressions evaporated from all conscious thought. Without even trying to hide her enthusiasm, she said, "Do you like fried shrimp? Best place around here is Andre's. It's nothing special, just an old frame house, but you can't beat the food. It's close to the riverbank, so it's rather lovely around sunset—although the sun sets around five o'clock this time of year."

The door opened, and Cat stood in the entranceway with her cheeks pinkened by the return of a chilly January wind, her green eyes sparkling against her wool coat, which was nearly the same shade. Maggie saw instead her own brown hair and her pale gray eyes, which weren't dark enough to be called blue, and she felt the familiar disappointment squeezing her heart. She turned away to straighten the cigarette boxes and to avoid watching Peter's face as he noticed Cat.

Cat spotted Peter right away and her smile broadened. Slowly closing the door behind her, she leaned against it, her posture jutting out her chest. "Well, hello. I don't think we've had the pleasure of being introduced."

Maggie wanted to blurt out that they had looked for her on the pier the previous evening so she could introduce them then, but couldn't find her, and that she'd lain awake until three o'clock waiting until she heard Cat's footsteps on the bare wood of the risers as she climbed the steps to her bedroom. But then Maggie would have to tell her that she had worried about her, and that would have been a lie. Because all Maggie could think about as she'd lain awake was how alive she'd felt for the first time in a long while, and how warm Peter's hand on her waist had felt as they'd danced. And how maybe Lulu had been right about her bottle tree, and that bad news was finally finished with them.

Keeping her eyes on Cat, Maggie made the introduction. "Cat, this is Peter Nowak, a businessman from Iowa. Peter, this is my cousin, Catherine Brier, otherwise known as Cat."

"It's a pleasure meeting you, Mrs. Brier," he said.

Maggie forced her gaze back to Peter when she noticed that he hadn't moved to take Cat's hand. He was simply smiling as if he met beautiful women every day and had somehow become immune to them. His hands remained clasped behind his back as he bowed his head slightly.

"And now, if you ladies will excuse me, I have business to attend to. Margaret, I'll see you at seven?"

Maggie nodded and watched Cat as she waited until the last moment to move away from the door, brushing herself against Peter's arm. He pretended not to notice as he turned the doorknob and opened the door. Facing them once more, he slid on his hat, winked at Lulu, and said good-bye again before closing the door softly behind him.

Maggie's feeling of satisfaction faded quickly as she caught the look on Cat's face, her expression like that of an osprey sighting its prey. The three of them turned toward the window to watch Peter striding away to a car parked on the street. And when Maggie turned back from the window, she saw Lulu carefully tying the crème lace ribbon from Belgium in her hair.

*

As soon as Maggie let her leave, Lulu ran home as fast as she could. Martha, the housekeeper, was there mopping the kitchen floor when Lulu rushed in the back door, tracking footsteps on the damp linoleum floor.

Seeing Martha's arms on her hips, Lulu did an abrupt about-face to toss her shoes onto the back steps before racing past Martha again with a hurriedly shouted "Good afternoon."

Lulu ran up the stairs, her sock-clad feet slipping on the risers; then she raced into her bedroom, slamming the door behind her. She quickly opened it, yelled downstairs, "Sorry, Martha," then closed the door more gently.

After leaning against the door to find her breath, she hurried to the window to draw the drapes, then moved to the opposite wall before kneeling in front of the chifforobe. Even though she'd given up her room to Cat, her clothes had remained in the chifforobe because Cat had claimed the downstairs hallway closet as her own.

From the bottom drawer, on the right-hand side underneath her petticoats and nightgowns, Lulu pulled out the small jewelry box that had once been her mother's. It was made of dark, shiny wood with small metal hinges and had come from a place in Italy where her mama and daddy had gone on their honeymoon. She didn't remember her mama, but she did remember going to her mama's room in the house on Broad Street in Charleston and sitting on the bed when nobody was looking just so she could see if any part of her mother was still left.

The empty jewelry box had sat on her mama's dressing table, and after Lulu found the guts to open it, she'd seen a dark stain on the bottom. She'd pressed her nose into the box, and it made her cry since it smelled so much like her mother. She'd forgotten the sound of her mother's voice, and the feel of her hair, but Lulu still remembered what she'd smelled like. It wasn't until Lulu was older that she realized that her mama must have spilled some perfume into the box, but it didn't matter. It was still a part of her mama that belonged to her.

Carefully taking the box from its hiding place, Lulu placed it on the braided rug between the twin beds and opened the lid. The smell of perfume was hardly there anymore, only a whiff of memory, but it still made Lulu's eyes tear. She tilted the box to see all the treasures she'd collected since she was old enough to collect things, all the things that meant the most to her. Briefly she touched the penny that her father had given her, minted the year of her birth in 1933, and a pair of earrings with tiny sand dollars dangling from them that Lulu had found in the bottom of the chifforobe and liked to think had once belonged to her mother. She spotted the tortoiseshell barrette Cat had given her but Lulu didn't wear because an old boyfriend had given it to Cat. That meant it wasn't a true gift from the heart, but because it was so beautiful, she kept it and sometimes wore it when she was alone in her bedroom. Cat never asked her about it, and Lulu knew it was because she'd forgotten about giving her the barrette as soon as it was out of her hand.

Using her index finger to sift through the items, Lulu found the most precious treasure of all: a roller-skate key. She picked it up and held it in her hand, then closed her eyes and smiled. It was the key to the roller skates she'd been wearing the night she'd twisted her ankle and Jim had saved her. He'd carried her home and made her feel better with his smile and his laugh. It was the only time in her whole life when she'd wished she was older because she'd decided right then and there that she wanted to marry Jim and she would wait for him for as long as it took for him to look at her the way he looked at Cat.

Slowly, she untied the ribbon in her hair and wound it around her hand until it was as small as her fist. She picked up the barrette and used it to keep the ribbon from unraveling and then placed both in the jewelry box next to the skate key.

She wasn't putting the ribbon in the box because she liked Peter Nowak so much. She wasn't sure she even liked him at all yet, although she liked the way her sister blushed when he was near and how her eyes darkened so that she looked almost as pretty as Cat. No, her reason for saving the ribbon in her special box had less to do with her sister and more to do with the fact that it would always remind her of the first time Cat had ever lost. She'd been waiting for Peter to ask Cat to join him and Maggie for dinner, and when he didn't, Lulu had found something to like about the stranger that his accent and gifts hadn't done.

Lulu had just finished placing the box back in its hiding place when she heard Martha calling up the stairs. "Miss Lulu, you get yourself down here right now!"

Lulu jumped up and ran to the door, flinging it open so hard that it hit the wall behind it. Lulu knew better than to disobey Martha; Maggie had given the older woman permission to use the switch on Lulu's behind if she felt Lulu needed it, and more often than not, Lulu apparently did.

The back door stood open and Lulu ran though it, almost running into Martha's broad back, her dark skin gleaming in the winter sun like an omen. The laundry had been taken down from the lines, making the bottle tree a beacon in the backyard like the Morris Island lighthouse.

Lulu tucked her chin into her neck and clutched her hands behind her to make her look sorry. "Yes, ma'am?"

"I don't need to be asking who put that thing up there in the yard. Miss Maggie works too hard and Miss Cat's too lazy to make time for something like that."

Lulu felt a finger on her chin raising her head so she could meet Martha's troubled eyes. "We don't mess with things we don't understand, you hear? You don't know what things you're letting into your soul when you fool around with this bad stuff. It ain't Christian, and it don't belong here."

Lulu made her lower lip tremble. "But it's only bad if you think of it that way. I just see something pretty. And . . ." She hesitated long enough to make Martha start worrying.

"And what, sugar?"

"And mostly it reminds me of Jim. He told me how they had the bottle trees in Louisiana where he was from. It makes me think that he's nearby, and it makes me happy again."

"Oh, child," said Martha with a voice that didn't sound so angry anymore. She wrapped her arms around Lulu and squeezed. "Jim was a good man, and I know you miss him. But you shouldn't use something evil to remember him by."

Lulu rested her chin on the mound of Martha's stomach and looked up at the dark face of the woman who'd known her since she was born. "This is the one thing I have left of him, Martha. Please don't take it away. I don't think I could stand to lose one more thing."

Martha's eyes softened and Lulu knew she'd won. "And I promise to make two of the branches into a cross as a more fitting memorial to Jim, if that would make you feel any better."

Lulu felt Martha's hands loosening around her. "Well, I figure if you do that, it should be all right. You just do it right away, you hear? Before anybody else sees it."

"Yes, ma'am," Lulu said solemnly before walking out into the backyard, being careful to keep her head down. A small smile appeared on her lips as she thought how easy that had been. She turned her head back to Martha, unable to hide her grin, but her smile dimmed on her lips as she saw that Martha wasn't smiling, too. The older woman was looking at her with narrowed eyes and tight lips, shaking her head.

Lulu reached the tree and knelt in front of it, wishing very hard that it did have magical powers despite what she'd just told Martha. They all needed a little magic in their lives right now. Everything seemed so off-balance, like being on the Ferris wheel and getting stuck at the top, the sickly-scary feeling you got in the bottom of your stomach when you knew what was going to happen but you couldn't stop it.

She felt that way now, and all the praying in church hadn't made it go away. But her bottle tree, with its colored glass and breathless sound, comforted her as no one could, making her believe in things you couldn't see. She'd change it if that was what Martha wanted her to do, but she wouldn't stop believing. Sitting back on her heels, she closed her eyes and listened to the winter wind sing inside the mouths of the bottles and tried to remember what Jim looked like when he smiled.

CHAPTER 4

FOLLY BEACH, SOUTH CAROLINA
July 2009

The interstates between Indiana and South Carolina had been laid out in the 1950s at the direction of President Eisenhower as part of a national defense system for the entire country. Emmy knew this from the hours of meticulously poring over the atlases she'd found in her mother's store, her fingers pressed to the spidery veins of roads and byways, through places that sounded familiar and others, like Enka Village and South Congaree, that seemed as if they belonged in an entirely different part of the world.

By mapping out every turn of her journey, Emmy felt more in control of the whole process instead of the more familiar feeling of being like a marble dropped on the floor, rolling in whatever direction offered the least resistance.

Her parents had helped her pack her car—Ben's Ford Explorer— and after kissing her forehead, her father had reached in to latch her seat belt as if by doing so he could protect her from every danger down the road.

"I want you to stop every couple of hours and give us a call on your cell phone. You've got your phone charger, right? And an extra battery just in case?"

"Yes, Dad. And I've got cash hidden in three different spots, bottled water, and my Mace."

"You got a full tank of gas, too. I filled it up this morning."

"Thanks, Dad. I appreciate it."

He leaned in again and kissed her lightly on the forehead. "Don't forget to call."

He stepped back and Paige filled the space inside the open door but she didn't lean in. "You got all those books from Folly's Finds?"

Emmy patted the box sitting on the passenger seat next to her, feeling almost as if they were old friends. "Yes, thanks. And I wish you'd let me pay you for them."

Paige smiled. "I figure you need them more than I do. Consider them a gift." She looked away for a moment, the blue sky reflected in her eyes. "You felt something when you touched them, didn't you? I'm glad. Because I don't think I could have convinced you to go on my own."

Paige stepped back and shut the door with a solid thud, more final than any parting words could have been.

Emmy swallowed twice before she could find her voice. "I left your jar of sand on the desk in the office. Guess I won't be needing it where I'm heading." She tried to smile but it faltered when her lips began to tremble. "Mama—" she began but Paige cut her off by placing both of her hands on the open window.

"Don't forget to call or your daddy won't be able to sleep. Be careful."

Before Paige could pull her hands away, Emmy grabbed them and squeezed. "Good-bye, Mama."

Paige squeezed back, then let go, and Emmy's hands fell useless to her lap. "Good-bye, Emmy."

Emmy started the engine and raised the window before following the long gravel-and-dirt drive that led away from her parents' house, watching her father wave to her in the rearview window until the cloud of dust obscured them. Focusing on the road ahead, she flipped the radio on and turned up the air conditioner, listening to the tires roll over the road and trying not to think about how long her journey was going to be.

THE SUNSET SKY BLUSHED IN reds and purples by the time Emmy drove through Charleston nearly thirteen hours later. She was hungry and tired, and her jaw hurt from clenching her teeth so tightly, but she wasn't ready to stop yet. She was so close and she couldn't help but feel that if she stopped she might not find the courage to continue.

Crossing over the Ashley River Bridge, with the pastel Charleston skyline punctuated by church steeples behind her, she turned the radio off and rolled her window down. She breathed in the scented air that smelled green and wet to her; a smell as foreign to her as a stranger's kiss. The road hummed beneath her tires and she found herself tightening her jaws to the rhythm of the road.

Feeling anxious now, she flipped the radio back on, then fiddled with the dial on the old car radio before stopping on the first clear station. It was an oldies station playing music from the big-band era, and Emmy found herself relaxing. Although her parents were from the hippie generation, they loved to dance to the old music and had a cabinet full of records they'd take out from time to time and slow dance to in the living room. They'd been doing that ever since Emmy could remember, usually after she'd been sent to bed. But as soon as she'd hear the trumpets sing and the softer wail of the saxophone, she'd crawl to the top of the stairs and watch as her parents held each other tight, kissed, and spoke softly, reminding Emmy that there had once been a them before there'd been an us.

She'd watch for a short while, and when she returned to her bed, she'd lie on her pillow with a lump in her throat, wondering if it was from resentment that she wasn't the center of their world or from a distant hope that one day she would find someone who liked to dance in the living room and who would look at her as if she was loved best.

Emmy flipped the radio off again as the silent fist of her grief squeezed her heart. She marveled that the entire time she'd been in the car, she hadn't thought of Ben. She was angry with herself yet relieved, too, thinking this might be part of the recovery everybody had been promising her yet had remained as elusive as catching sand in the wind.

She glanced down at her lap to the map her father had drawn for her and took a left on Folly Road, the long, straight road that would take her over two small bridges before spilling her out on the little knife shape of land her father had labeled Folly Beach. Her car passed churches, strip malls filled with nail salons and realty offices, and a large Piggly Wiggly. Emmy hesitated only a moment before bypassing the entrance to the parking lot of the grocery store. If she didn't have food and supplies, it would be that much easier to turn around and head back to Indiana if what she found on Folly wasn't what she was looking for. Whatever that was.

She was nearly lulled to sleep by the heat of the sun through the window until her attention was caught by a brightly painted wooden boat off to the right of the road with *The Luv Guv* and *Don't cry for me, Argentina* spray-painted in white against a spatter of bright colors splayed over every flat surface.

Emmy nearly ran off the road as she craned her neck to get a better look at the locals' attempt at a billboard commentary about the South Carolina governor's extramarital exploits recently making the national news. She wasn't sure if she liked it or not, but it sounded just like what she'd heard about the people of Folly Beach, whose physical exertions and attitudes were directly related to the intensity of the heat from the Southern sun.

After crossing over the first bridge, Emmy sat up straighter to take in a better measure of where she was headed. Off in the distance to the left was a large blue water tower with FB in large black letters inside a white oval announcing that she was at least going in the right direction. Traffic slowed as the road narrowed approaching the Folly River Bridge, the docked shrimp boats announcing the proximity to the Atlantic Ocean. A salty breeze filled the car—a new smell that was strange yet oddly familiar, too. Maybe her mother's childhood memories had been transferred to Emmy during infancy, as if the memory of warm sand between your toes were as tangible a thing as nourishment and security.

Red-flowered bushes Emmy had never seen before waved from each side of the road like spectators at a welcome parade, easing the tightness in her chest just a little. *The Edge of America,* she thought, recalling the Folly Beach nickname her mother had told her, an appropriate name for a destination for someone with nowhere else to go.

Glancing at her map again, she headed straight where Folly Road became Center Street, the only street on the island with a stoplight. In the old days, her mother had explained, if you stayed on Center Street, you'd run right into the ocean. Now, though, a monolithic cement Holiday Inn blocked access and the view, forcing all vehicles to either turn right or left on Ashley Avenue.

The light turned red and Emmy stopped. Perspiration trickled down her back and forehead, but she still resisted rolling up the window and turning on the air. The voices of the tourists and locals filling the sidewalks, shops, and restaurants, and the sound of blaring music from passing cars was the sound track to her new adventure, and she was afraid she'd miss something—miss a clue telling her that she was doing the right thing.

She turned left on East Ashley, the holiday weekend traffic heavy on the two-lane street, each side of the road packed with cars parked bumper to bumper. Everyone wore bathing suits, even the babies in strollers, and coolers and surfboards were the ubiquitous accessories as beachgoers unloaded them from cars, trucks, and minivans and lumbered toward the beach accesses.

Emmy passed old, paint-peeling houses that were nestled side by side with larger and newer beach mansions. Most of the houses, big and small alike, had names like Banana Cabana and Height of Folly posted on painted wooden signs by the driveways. All the houses sat on pilings, their one commonality apparently being a fear of the sea. Entire streets had been taken away by hurricanes in past years, according to Paige. While Emmy was no stranger to tornadoes, she felt a certain dread when she thought about the force of a tornado coupled with the strength of the ocean and wondered if mere pilings would be enough.

She looked down at the map one last time for the address she'd written at the bottom for the house she'd rented, sight unseen. Not that doing such a thing surprised her anymore; she'd agreed to purchase a business without ever having seen it either, much less even visited the state of South Carolina. Her chest filled with a silent sigh. *Mama, what have we done?*

The traffic thinned as she drove toward the east end of the island, and she slowed, checking the house numbers on mailboxes and posts, and even a painted surfboard stuck in the yard, as she passed each one before finally pausing in front of the correct address. Slowly, she turned into the shell-and-sand driveway with two cement tire runners and stopped, staring at the house in front of her through the windshield.

The house belonged to the son of the bookstore's owner, Abigail Reynolds. The son was a developer in Atlanta who'd had the house built for his fiancée a couple of years before. Abigail hadn't elaborated and Emmy was left to speculate that both the son and the fiancée lived in Atlanta and used the house only sporadically, renting it when they weren't living in it.

Not that Emmy had been expecting to live in a mansion, but she was relieved that the house in front of her couldn't by any stretch of the imagination be called a shack, either. It was painted in a bright yellow with two stories sitting atop the pilings, the hip roof sporting a windowed turret on one side. A wide wooden staircase led up to the raised first floor, where the double doors lay nestled under a rounded portico protruding onto a wraparound porch. Bright white rockers sat on the porch, the strong ocean breeze making them wave like a greeting. Several piles of two-by-fours lay in the sparse grass of the front yard; a circular saw and sawhorse sat near them with tufts of sawdust lying in the grass and flitting in the air on the breeze. Emmy frowned at the scene for a moment, trying to remember what, if anything, Abigail had mentioned about any new construction on the house; then she moved her gaze back to the front doors, and her eyes widened.

Slowly opening her car door, she exited without taking her eyes off the doors, not really sure if she was seeing clearly. She removed her sunglasses and squinted in the bright light, feeling the brunt of the South Carolina sun for the first time like a heavy slap on her bare shoulders.

Ignoring the heat, she trudged across the lawn and up the front steps to what had caught her attention. The doors had been stained a dark cherry, but inset in the wood were two large windows nearly as long as each door, each bearing one half of the etched depiction of a bottle tree. Emmy studied the willowy stems and random bottle shapes for a long moment, making sure she was actually seeing what she thought she was, feeling the familiar pinpricks against the back of her neck.

The heat seemed to hit her again, and spots danced in front of her eyes. Leaning forward she pressed her forehead against the cool glass to see inside, and saw instead a reflection in the glass that wasn't hers. It was an old woman, with two long braids but the image was gone as soon as Emmy realized she was seeing it. With a stifled gasp, she pulled back and blinked before pressing her forehead against the glass again. All she saw this time through the glass was a large, sparsely furnished room but one that was blessedly empty.

Emmy stumbled to one of the rockers and sat down, allowing the breeze to wash over her. It must have been a shadowed reflection of a passing cloud she'd seen. Either that or the heat was playing tricks on her mind. She closed her eyes as a strong breeze lifted her hair, cooling her neck and cheeks as relief coursed through her at the logical explanation of the reflection in the window. She felt foolish. She was used to heat in the summer, and even humidity. But it was more than that, and she knew it just as she'd known Ben was gone all those months ago. It was a feeling that this place was expecting her and that she was supposed to be here.

Feeling better she stood and looked over the railing, noticing for the first time that she had a view of the ocean through the empty space between the two houses across the street. She was too far to hear it, but she could see the ripples of waves outlined by sun and shadow, see the line at the edge of the world where the ocean met the sky.

She felt a tug somewhere near her heart, as if this strange new place meant something to her, as if the pull of the ocean was one more thing she'd been born with and she'd always known this place. It didn't matter that she'd never seen an ocean before; she already knew what it meant to be able to see the ocean from your front door.

Slowly, she walked down the steps and began looking for a path that would lead her to the back of the house. Abigail had told Emmy that her son had picked a spot between the Folly River and the ocean as the perfect spot for his house but that she'd let Emmy figure out the reasons why by herself. Abigail had left a key in the lockbox on the back door, and Emmy had memorized the combination from saying it aloud many times on the long trip from Indiana.

She passed under the house, where there was space for two cars to park in tandem, and emerged into a grassy clearing, where wooden steps led up to a screened porch and, presumably, the back door. Slapping her leg as something bit her, she began to hurry up the steps, pausing on the landing to unlatch the screen door. Another strong breeze ripped the door from her hand, causing her to look up to see a darkening sky. Her gaze dropped to the view from the back of the house, the expanse of lawn giving way to tall, spider-leg-like grass and what looked like a wide wooden dock leading into the middle of it. Shades of browns, greens, and yellows lay like a spotted cat, leading to deeper water and a clear view of a lighthouse in the distance. The lighthouse appeared stranded in the middle of the sea, its rust and white stripes leading up to a darkened light.

The back of Emmy's neck prickled again as she grabbed the door more firmly this time but stopped as a familiar sound crept across the lawn toward her. The door banged shut again as Emmy realized she'd let go of it, her legs already leading her back down the steps toward the sound of wind through the glass lips of empty bottles.

She found herself in the middle of the yard and closed her eyes to listen for a moment, then followed the sound to a hidden corner behind a large palmetto tree. The bottle tree stood as tall as Emmy, its metal trunk as thick as her arm. Delicate branches reached out toward the sky in no apparent pattern, their randomness adding to its beauty. Bottles in rainbow hues sat perched on each limb, affixed permanently on their branches, allowing the wind to visit without disruption.

It was just like the one in her mother's garden and her homesickness hit Emmy with the suddenness of a clap of thunder. Reaching up, she touched a green bottle, amazed to feel it solid and real beneath her fingertips, as if to assure herself that this figment of home wasn't just in her imagination. Emmy walked around the tree, admiring its artistry, stopping when she'd gone three-quarters of the way around. Staring at a wide-lipped amber-colored bottle that had been placed nearly perpendicular to the branch, she saw something that seemed to have been caught inside.

Leaning closer, she gingerly pushed on the bottle watching as its position on the branch allowed it to move. She ducked beneath it to peer inside, and spotted a rolled-up piece of paper. Her well-honed curiosity regarding old writings and their histories overrode the twinge of conscience as she managed to roll the piece of paper to the edge of the bottle lip before plucking it out of its prison.

The paper was damp, but not yellowed, telling her although it had been in the bottle for a while, it wasn't that old. Her academic curiosity now firmly swatted away her conscience as she unrolled the piece of paper to reveal a single sentence written in bold, spidery strokes: *Come back to me.*

"You're trespassing."

Emmy dropped the note in surprise as she turned toward the woman's voice. "I'm sorry." She stooped to pick up the paper, hoping the old woman couldn't see too clearly through the thick glasses she wore perched on her pert nose. Holding the paper low, Emmy began to roll it up as she spoke. "Actually, I'm Emmy Hamilton. I'm renting this house for a few months."

"Exactly. You're renting the house, not this tree. So you're trespassing." The woman's sharp hazel eyes followed Emmy's hand as she moved to return the note to the bottle. "I suppose you never heard about curiosity and the cat."

Emmy fumbled with the rolled piece of paper, and it fell to the ground again. "Oh," she said for lack of anything better before she squatted and retrieved the note. "I'm sorry. I really didn't mean to pry."

"Really? Then what do you call messing with other people's things?"

As Emmy stood there searching for an answer, she got a better look at her interrogator. The woman was short, probably no taller than five feet, and probably somewhere in her seventies. Her long hair was more gray than brown and worn in two braids, which fell over her shoulders. She wore a sleeveless white blouse tucked into the top of a pair of elastic waisted jean shorts. Ugly brown sandals covered small, squat feet devoid of toenail polish. But that detail, Emmy noted, went with the rest of the woman, who was adorned with neither jewelry nor makeup.

Emmy swallowed, embarrassed and angry at the same time yet also somehow relieved that she was still capable of feeling something other than just grief. "Look Ms. . . . ?" When the woman didn't interject her name, Emmy continued. "You're right. I was prying. I suppose it's my nature—I sort of specialize in old documents, so any stray piece of paper always seems to snag my attention. I'm sorry. But as I mentioned, I'm renting the house, which, I assume, includes the grounds, so I don't think I can rightly be called a trespasser."

Without a word, the old woman turned around and began to walk away toward the driveway. Emmy hurried after her. "Wait. Are you Abigail?"

"Nope."

Emmy paused, confused for a moment. She hadn't thought Abigail had sounded that old. "Are you her son's fiancée, then?"

The old woman let out a loud harrumph, which could have been a laugh, and kept on walking.

Feeling winded from the unaccustomed exertion, Emmy finally caught up with the stranger in the driveway. She stopped while the woman kept walking, a stray thought solidifying in her head. "Wait . . . please. The bottle tree makes noise, but none of the other ones I've seen do except for the one my mother has in her backyard. Are you the artist who made them?"

The woman stopped and slowly turned around, but didn't say anything, as if waiting for Emmy to say something else.

Emmy continued. "The sound reminds me of the ocean, although until today I'd never even seen the ocean before. It's like a song, isn't it? Sad and haunting, but full of memories, too. And possibilities. Is that what you want people to hear?"

Something flickered in the woman's eyes, but she gave no other indication that she'd heard anything Emmy said. "I'm Lulu O'Shea. My nephew owns this house." She spoke through thinned, tight lips, as if they were used to having words pried out of them. Before Emmy could ask her anything else, Lulu turned without another word and started walking away.

Come back to me. Remembering the rolled-up note, Emmy again jogged toward the older woman, who was walking faster than any septuagenarian had a right to. "Wait. Is that your note in the bottle?" Emmy didn't think it was, since the writing was definitely that of a male, but she wasn't ready for Lulu to leave, either.

In answer, Lulu called over her shoulder, "Don't you go scratching those wood floors in the house. They're Brazilian cherry, and my nephew went to a lot of trouble to get them here."

Breathing heavily, Emmy watched the woman's departing back before a large dog pulling a teenager on a skateboard down the street captured her attention. The boy flashed her a peace sign as he sped by, leaving her alone except for the noise of the wheels on asphalt.

A fat raindrop hit her on the top of her head as she opened her trunk, and by the time she'd reached the back steps with her suitcases, she was completely soaked by the sudden downpour. "Welcome to Folly Beach," she said under her breath as she struggled up the steps to the screen door, managing to thrust it open and throw herself and her suitcases onto the covered porch. She listened to the patter of the rain on the marsh, feeling more lonely than she'd ever felt in her life, and realizing that she'd forgotten the combination for the lockbox.

She slid to the floor, not even bothering to find a chair, and rested her forehead on her knees, and wondered how long it would be before the rain stopped and she could shove her suitcases back into the trunk and leave this place far behind.

CHAPTER 5

Lulu sat on the edge of her bed and watched as Maggie got dressed for her date with Mr. Nowak. She called him that, even in her head, though she'd only ever thought of Jim as just Jim. There was something grown-up about Mr. Nowak, and she couldn't even picture him as a little boy. He was nice and all; he just wasn't Jim.

Lulu wondered why Maggie had suggested Andre's even though it had been Maggie's favorite place for fried shrimp ever since Maggie was little and their parents had taken her there for special occasions. But Lulu knew, too, that it had been the first place Jim had taken Maggie, and she couldn't understand why Maggie would ever want to go there with somebody else. Lulu thought maybe it had just popped out of Maggie before she had had time to think, the way Lulu sometimes still announced to the world that she needed to go to the bathroom before realizing she'd said it out loud.

Still, as Lulu watched Maggie choose her second-best church dress instead of her best—which she'd worn when she'd gone with Jim— she figured that maybe Maggie hadn't forgotten after all.

"Have you seen Cat?" Maggie asked as she stared at herself in the mirror with her head tilted in the way she did when she couldn't decide about something.

"She's been in her room since we got home. I think she's pouting."

Maggie raised an eyebrow at Lulu but didn't argue. "She has such good taste. I'd really like her opinion."

Lulu imitated her sister's tilted head, wondering if a person really did see things differently when not looking straight at it. She saw the Maggie she loved with all of her heart, the sister she'd always thought was beautiful. But now, with her head to the side, she saw the Maggie that Cat probably saw when she called Maggie a frumpy housewife. "You need dark red lipstick like Cat. It'll make you look prettier."

Maggie screwed up her face as she stared at her reflection. "I don't have any," She seemed to think for a moment. "I guess I could go ask Cat if I could borrow hers."

Their eyes met in the mirror, and as Lulu noticed how the gray dress fit too loosely over her sister's body, and how the fabric looked more like a bedspread than something somebody should wear on a date, she had an idea. As she slid off the chenille bedspread, she said, "I'll go ask."

She crept across the hallway and gently turned the doorknob of her old bedroom to peer inside. The curtains were drawn against the dying light of day, and Cat lay under the bedcovers on her back with a black silk mask over her eyes.

Being as quiet as she could, Lulu crept over to the chifforobe and pulled out her secret box. With a quick glance over to her sleeping cousin, she reached inside and pulled out the sand-dollar earrings and tortoiseshell barrette before returning the box to its secret location.

After shoving her treasures into her pockets, she tiptoed silently across the room to the dressing table where Cat's "secret potions," as she liked to call them, lay scattered across the lace doily Maggie had made by hand, which was now stained with makeup. She searched for the tube of lipstick she'd seen Cat use and found it in the back corner, the top lying to the side.

Very carefully, Lulu picked up the tube and its lid before quietly tiptoeing back to the door. As she stuck her fingers in the crack of the door to pull it open, Cat spoke from behind her.

"What are you doing?"

Lulu turned around, her hands at her side and her fist closed tightly around the lipstick. Cat was leaning on her elbow, her eye mask pulled up to her forehead. "I was just getting some of my stuff."

Lulu began to back toward the door but stopped when Cat spoke again. "What's in your hand?"

"Nothing."

Cat sat up in bed and slid the mask the rest of the way off. "Show me nothing."

Knowing that if she didn't open up her fist Cat would force her to, Lulu slowly opened her fingers, one by one, to reveal the tube of lipstick.

"I hope you weren't planning on playing dress-up with my lipstick. That's my favorite shade and I can hardly find it anymore."

"I wasn't going to waste it," said Lulu, feeling insulted. She'd never played dress-up like the other girls, preferring instead to read or draw. "I was getting it for Maggie so she could wear it tonight on her date with Mr. Nowak." She realized she'd made a mistake before the last word came out of her mouth.

"You little thief," Cat said, springing from the bed and marching toward her. "Give it back. Now." With one hand on her hip, she held the other one toward Lulu, palm up.

Lulu clenched her fist again. "But Maggie doesn't have any lipstick to wear."

"Well, now, that's her problem, isn't it? Give it back."

Lulu realized that her hand was shaking as she lifted her arm to allow the tube to drop into Cat's outstretched palm.

"If you steal something from me again, I'll throw you over my knees and take a switch to you—just see if I won't. You're not too old to be spanked, no, sirreee."

Lulu felt the heat in her cheeks not only at the prospect of some-body like Cat spanking her, but at knowing that she'd let Maggie down. Before she started to cry, she faced the door again and began to pull it, but paused when it was only halfway open. She was breathing heavy, as if she'd been swimming for miles, and she wasn't really sure what she was going to say until she'd already said it and it was too late to pull it back.

"You should let me have that back, Cat." She swallowed, try-ing to be as brave as Maggie always told her she was. Somehow, thinking of her sister did make her braver. With a stronger voice, Lulu continued. "Or I'll have to tell Maggie that I saw you at the pavilion kissing that soldier when you were still married to Jim. Or that you told Jim that Maggie didn't like him anymore and wanted him to stop calling on her. I didn't figure out that it was a fib until after you were already married and it was too late to tell Maggie, but I bet that if I told her now, she wouldn't let you live here anymore."

It was real quiet for a minute, and all she could hear was her breathing. But she could smell Cat's perfume, so she knew her cousin was still behind her, and she flinched, waiting. Then she heard Cat's bare feet padding against the wood floors, followed by the bedsprings squeaking and the unmistakable sound of something small and hard hitting the ground and then rolling for a short distance.

Slowly, Lulu turned and met Cat's eyes. They reminded her of an alligator's as it waited near the banks of a pond pretending to be a log. Cat smiled, but her teeth didn't show. "You're a good sister, Lulu. Loyal. That's a good way to be. And you don't miss a thing, do you?"

Lulu darted her gaze to the floor, searching for the tube of lipstick until she found it just under the dressing table by one of the legs. Scrambling on her hands and knees, she stuck her hand under the dresser and pulled it out before running out the door. She'd reached the hallway before she remembered that Cat had asked her a question.

She stopped, then slowly returned to the bedroom, where Cat still sat on the edge of the bed, which had once been Lulu's.

"Nope," she said. "I don't." Then she put her hand on the door-knob and gently pulled the door shut.

PETER SHOWED UP PROMPTLY AT seven o'clock. Maggie sent Lulu downstairs to open the door when he knocked since Cat hadn't left her room. She wanted to go herself, but Lulu reminded her that a lady always kept a gentleman waiting so that the lady didn't appear over-eager. The words were repeated verbatim from one of the many lessons Cat had been attempting to drill into her for years, proving that at least one of the O'Shea sisters had actually been paying attention.

Maggie did pause to consider why Lulu was being so accommodating about her going out. She'd not put up a single fuss, even when she'd learned that she'd be alone with Cat all evening. It was too early for Lulu to have become accepting of Peter, much less fond of him. But as soon as Cat had shown her disapproval of Maggie having an admirer, it had suddenly made Lulu Maggie's advocate. While the sisters had never been close because of their ages, their relationship had definitely disintegrated since Cat had come to live with them, and while Maggie never knew the reason, she suspected it might have had something to do with Cat's taking over Lulu's room and, in many ways, their lives.

After staring at her watch for the required five minutes, and only checking herself in the mirror two more times, she walked out into the hallway, pausing for a moment outside Cat's door. She raised her hand to knock, then let it drop. She wanted Cat's approval on her appearance, and to thank her for letting her borrow the red lipstick. But she knew, too, that Cat was in one of her moods and was best left alone. When she got all worked up like that, she said hurtful things that Maggie was sure she didn't mean, but words nevertheless that Maggie didn't want to hear right before leaving with Peter.

As Maggie began her descent down the stairs, she looked back at Cat's closed door. The last time she'd been like this had been right after Jim had died. Maggie had made the mistake of trying to swallow her own grief to comfort her, only to be told to go away. And in an ugly voice that Maggie had never heard Cat use before, Cat told Maggie that she could never understand what Cat was feeling because Maggie was used to being ignored by men but Cat wasn't and that now that she was a widow, she'd never have the chance to meet anybody else. It had taken the bond of the promise Maggie had made to her mother to keep her from asking Cat to leave then.

It had turned out not to be true, after all, but the words still stung. Not the words she'd said about Maggie, but what Cat had implied about Jim. So in the weeks that followed, Maggie had said extra prayers for Jim at church, grieving doubly for him since his widow didn't seem to be able to.

Maggie continued her descent, swinging her head to feel the sand-dollar earrings jostle beneath her ears, and pictured how pretty the tortoiseshell barrette made her hair look. She found Lulu and Peter in the small front room. Lulu sat on the edge of the love seat while Peter examined their mother's collection of sand dollars. He held one between two long fingers as he turned to greet Maggie.

"Margaret, you look beautiful."

She blushed, knowing he was just being kind, but still flattered because he sounded so much like he meant it. "Thank you, Peter." She walked to stand next to him, smelling his cologne and noticing the fine tailoring of his light gray suit. His overcoat and hat had been placed over the arm of the love seat. "Sorry to keep you waiting."

His strange amber eyes tilted at the corners as he smiled. "The anticipation made it that much more exciting. Plus, I had the added pleasure of Lulu's company. She was explaining what these are." He held up the delicate shell, his signet ring reflecting the light from the lamp.

"Sand dollars," Maggie said, gently taking it from his lifted hand. "Did Lulu tell you the story about them?"

He shook his head, his eyes never leaving her face.

Maggie continued. "It's something our mother told us. The story goes that sand dollars were left here by Christ to spread the faith."

Peter raised his brows. "How so?"

Stepping a little closer, she placed one side of the shell flat in her hand to show him the other. "These five holes show Christ's wounds on the cross, and this in the middle is a blooming Easter lily surrounding the star of Bethlehem."

Maggie lifted her eyes and saw that Peter was staring at her instead of the shell. Quickly she averted her eyes and turned the sand dollar over. "On the other side is the Christmas poinsettia to remind us of Christ's birth. They say if you break the center five white doves will be released to spread goodwill and peace."

"That's lovely," Peter said, and when Maggie raised her eyes again, he was still looking at her.

She turned back toward the window, placing the shell in the basket with the others. Forcing her voice to sound steady, she said, "These were our mother's. She collected them all on the beach here on Folly."

"Ah," he said. "Even more reason for them to be precious to you."

She smiled at him, feeling again that he truly understood her. She liked him for that, regardless of whether he really thought she was beautiful.

"Are you ready?" he asked.

"Yes, let me get my coat and hat." Maggie moved toward the hallway and the hall closet but Lulu raced past her, returning with Cat's green cashmere coat and matching hat instead of Maggie's own dull brown one. The green coat had simply appeared one day, and when questioned about it, Cat had claimed only that it had been a gift from an admirer. She hadn't explained anything else, and Maggie had been reluctant to ask, not sure she wanted to hear the answer.

She gave a slight shake of her head, trying to catch Lulu's eyes but not wanting to make a scene in front of Peter. Instead Lulu held the green coat out to her. "The brown one's missing a button. I'll fix it for you tonight if you like."

Maggie stared hard at Lulu, trying to figure out why she was lying and why it was so important to her that she wear Cat's coat. Peter took the coat from Lulu, then held it open for Maggie to slide her arms into. "Maybe I should go ask Cat for permission before borrowing it," she said, looking pointedly at Lulu.

Lulu smiled up at her, appearing so innocent that for a moment, Maggie thought that maybe her brown coat really did have a missing button. "I already did and she said it was okay."

Maggie narrowed her eyes but Lulu had run back into the hall and was pulling open the front door. Maggie waited as Peter put on his own coat and hat. Then he held out his arm for Maggie before leading her out the door and down the porch steps to his late-model Ford sedan.

Despite the fact that summer visitors wouldn't be coming for several more months, Andre's had a nice crowd mostly due to the influx of servicemen in the area. Maggie greeted the people she knew, introducing Peter each time, before being seated at a booth by a window overlooking the marsh. Peter took time to repeat each name as he was introduced, as if committing it to memory, asking questions and taking a genuine interest in the answers. He was a salesman at heart, she knew, but she couldn't help but be impressed by how likable he made himself to all of her friends and neighbors.

From the corner of her eye, she watched Peter take in the wide wooden-plank floor, the colorful murals of shrimp boats and other scenes from the area, and the shrimp nets hanging from the ceiling. She felt a little twinge of nervousness as she saw it all through the eyes of a man whose parents were European and who'd traveled a bit and who was more sophisticated than most of the men she knew in Folly—a man perhaps more suited to a fine Charleston restaurant than to a beach dive with the best fried shrimp anywhere.

She leaned forward, touching his arm. "If you don't like it, we can go somewhere else. There're lots of nice restaurants in town."

He placed his hand over hers. "No, this is perfect. I want to get to know the local flavor. And I've never had fried shrimp before. Besides, when I'm with a beautiful woman, nothing else really matters, does it? I could eat grass and I doubt I would notice."

She smiled at his easy laugh, reassured that she hadn't made a blunder. Relaxing back into her seat, she studied the menu without really seeing anything as she searched for a wise and witty reply, almost wishing Cat were there to coax the right words from her. Instead she said, "I recommend the fried shrimp, of course, but you need to try the hush puppies and the coleslaw. I get that every time I come here. I should probably try something new, but then I'm afraid I'll just be disappointed that I didn't get my shrimp and hush puppies." She felt herself blushing, embarrassed to be rambling about food so much.

He closed his menu. "Then I will trust your expert guidance and order exactly what you're getting, too. I'm going native."

He smiled, but still managed to look so worldly and sophisticated that his words made her laugh.

"What's so funny?" he asked, feigning a hurt look.

She was spared from answering by Robin Henderson, an old schoolmate of hers from Rivers High School, who arrived to take their order. She'd married while they were still in high school and had four kids one right after the other. Her husband, Dave, worked at the navy yard and Robin worked part-time at Andre's waitressing, saving her tip money, which kept her in lipstick and stockings so that Dave didn't have to know how much she was spending.

Maggie watched as Robin blushed and played with her blond hair as she spoke to Peter, realizing that he had that effect on most of the women they'd spoken with. Even Cat. But for some reason, he'd picked Maggie out of the crowd on the pier that night. She still thought that if Cat had been sitting with her, Peter wouldn't even have afforded her a second look. But here she was at a worn booth in

Andre's, sitting across from him as the other women in the room kept stealing glances, and wondering why he had chosen her.

With a final lingering look at Peter, Robin took their menus and retreated to the kitchen, looking back over her shoulder twice. He didn't appear to notice.

When their food arrived, Maggie realized how hungry she was. The anticipation of her date had made her unable to eat much all day, and she had to force herself not to grab a handful of hush puppies and shove them in her mouth.

Instead, she took her time explaining to Peter what everything was and watched with amusement at his confusion as she explained what the sauces on the table were. He picked up his knife and fork and cut into a deep-fried hush puppy, the aroma of the sweet corn bread making Maggie's mouth water. He blew on it slightly and put it in his mouth, closing his eyes as he chewed.

"So, what do you think?"

He paused as if to give himself time to think. "It's swell," he replied as he turned his attention to the fried shrimp and prepared to cut off a bite.

Maggie laughed, not sure if it was because the word "swell" seemed so incongruous coming from his mouth or because of the way he was preparing to eat his fried shrimp with a knife and fork.

With utensils suspended over his plate, he looked at her with a bemused expression. "What's so funny?"

"Don't they eat with their fingers in Iowa?"

A dark look flashed over his face so fast that for a moment, Maggie thought that she'd imagined it. Then, after gently placing his knife and fork back on the table, he smiled at her. "Of course. Corn. We eat a lot of corn on the cob in Iowa, and always with our hands. I just thought the shrimp might be too hot to touch, that's all."

Gingerly, he picked up one of the shrimp and delicately dipped it into the red sauce as Maggie was doing, before biting into it and chewing heartily. "Delicious," he said, dabbing at the corners of his mouth with a napkin.

"Not swell?"

He raised an eyebrow. "Better than swell—that's why it gets a delicious."

She laughed again, reassured that she hadn't said the wrong thing even without Cat there to guide her. She pictured how she looked right now, with her lips a deep red and a tortoiseshell barrette in her hair, sitting across from Peter and laughing in the way other couples did at a private joke. The same way she and Jim had that one time they'd come here. Maggie eagerly pushed that thought away as she picked up another shrimp, focusing on Peter instead of old memories of a man who'd never really been hers at all.

It was after nine o'clock by the time they left the restaurant. The moon sat with its pregnant glow over the marsh, coaxing the high tide through the winter-bleached spartina grass. A winged night hunter flittered over the water near their car as Maggie snuggled into the cashmere of Cat's coat, watching her breath rise in the moonlight. She felt sated and content for the first time in a long while, and unwilling for the evening to end. Even Peter seemed to feel the same way as he drove much slower on the way home than he had earlier. She was about to suggest that he come inside the house for a cup of coffee when he turned to her inside the darkness of the car, the wash of the moon tinting his face a ghostly blue.

"Come walk with me."

It wasn't a question, and she didn't bother with an answer as he pulled in front of one of the false-fronted buildings on Center Street and turned off the ignition. He opened the car door for her and placed her gloved hand in the crook of his arm and began to lead the way. Her ears tingled from the cold, and she wished Cat's hat was more than just decorative. They headed in the direction of the pier, following the pull of the moon like turtle hatchlings, moving mindlessly toward the sound of the sea.

Maggie was relieved when he turned to the right, away from the pier and from the sound of people, and headed toward Arctic Avenue instead. The street had once been the beachfront thoroughfare, running almost all the way down the west side of the island. But following the storm of 1939, only four houses remained on the west side of Arctic, and two of them, now abandoned, were stranded over water during high tide, their pilings nearly halfway covered with water.

As if he knew where he was going, Peter led her to the first house, its pilings and peaked roof skeletal against the winter moon. In the daylight, the sun turned the salt-sprayed shingles silver, making it a magical place for children to explore the large, empty rooms. But at night the house cast a different light: a reflection of moon and ocean, outlined with the shimmering anticipation of the unknown. The tide was coming in, reaching about halfway under the house but leaving a path of beach to the front of the house.

Maggie shivered as Peter took her hand to help her across the sand to the steps that led to the front door of the house, and didn't argue when he opened the unlocked door and led her inside. They moved in silence through the old house and out another door to stand on a back porch suspended over the rushing ocean below. For a brief moment Maggie felt airborne, as if nothing held her to the earth anymore except the moon and the sound of the waves crashing against the pilings. She was small again, and her mother alive, and there were no such things as storms and war and death, and all that the vastness of the ocean held was dreams.

"Margaret, are you too cold? Do you want to go back to the car?"

Peter's voice brought her back to solid ground, and she could almost feel the air rushing back into her lungs. She turned to face him and realized how close he was standing by the smell of his cologne and the sound of the bristles on his chin against the collar of his coat. "I'm fine," she answered, her voice airy. "Just a little cold, I guess."

He put his arm around her and drew her close to his side so that they were looking out over the ocean together. The house had been built higher than its neighbors, affording a clear view of the small cottages nestled behind the dunes and clusters of palmettos. They watched the lights sparking from the pier in the distance and the yellow beacons of porch lights from the houses on the west side of the island.

Peter's voice was close to her ear as he spoke. "What is this place? I've passed it so many times and wondered."

Maggie relaxed into his embrace, staring at the moon and stars as if she'd never seen them before. "It used to be a family home, but after the storm the year before last, nobody's moved back. There used to be a whole street here, but most of it's underwater."

"So nobody owns it anymore?"

Maggie shrugged. "I suppose they still do. But it would be foolish to move back in. When they built the jetties to protect Charleston Harbor, Folly started losing a lot of her beach. The erosion is especially bad after a storm. I can't imagine that the remaining houses will last through the next big one."

He nodded slowly, his eyes reflecting the moonlight as his gaze scanned the water. "Lots of lights. I thought that after Pearl Harbor all the coasts were blacked out." He looked down at her, half of his face shadowed by the brim of his hat.

"Well, sure, but that's all on the West Coast, since it's closer to Hawaii and Japan. But we're three thousand miles across the ocean from Europe. We have our mounted beach patrol—we might even see them on the beach now, but I think that's just because people need to feel as if they're doing something for the war effort. The Germans can't cross the Atlantic without us knowing about it. Everybody knows that."

"True," he said, his teeth a pearlescent blue in the moonlight. "You should be safe here." He pulled her a little closer. "That makes me feel better, somehow, knowing that you're safe."

"Really?" She tilted her head, her lips almost touching his.

"Really."

Maggie wasn't sure when the word ended and his kiss began. All she knew was that she felt suspended in time and space again, the rocking of the waves beneath them and his breath on her skin as elemental as air.

He pulled away suddenly. "I'm sorry. It's just . . ." He stopped for a moment and she could feel his eyes on her. "I couldn't stop myself."

Their breath mingled in white smoky puffs between them. She watched their breath rise and spread, wishing that he hadn't stopped, but knowing he was right. Cat would have kissed him back and asked for more. But it wasn't Cat he wanted.

Maggie put her gloved finger to his lips. "Don't say anything else. Just keep me warm and keep talking, and everything will be fine."

He wrapped his arm around her shoulders again, pulling her closer as they both looked out over the railing again. "Tell me what you see from here."

Pulling on his hand, she led him through the house to a large picture window and pointed. "This is the west side of Folly. The street names are the same on both sides of Center Street, except here they're west and over there they're called east. Like West Ashley and East Ashley—that's the street one block from the ocean on the east side but it's now oceanfront over here where Arctic Avenue stops."

He studied the pinpoints of light in the darkness as she pointed and continued. "My street, Second Street, runs perpendicular to the ocean. Nearby on West Ashley is a hotel everybody calls the Beach House. Rumor is that the coast guard is thinking about using it for barracks."

Peter nodded, and they stood in silence for a long moment before he spoke again. "The people who live in these houses—where do they work? What do they do?"

"Well, we've got our library and chief of police and post office—that sort of thing, but most of the men work at the navy yard in North Charleston. But those are the permanent residents. In the summer it's different with all the visitors, and our population just about doubles. And now, of course, we'll have all sorts of military personnel since Charleston is just swarming with bases."

Peter surprised her by touching her chin gently. "Smart and beautiful. What an attractive combination."

Before she could stammer out a response, he spoke again. "What's on each end of the island?" He put his hand over hers and directed it to the end of the island, where the dark ocean seemed to swallow all the light.

"Nothing but forest at the tip. It gets really narrow at that end, with houses perched right between the ocean and the Folly River, it seems."

He placed his chin on the top of her head, and she relaxed into his embrace, allowing her head to rest on his chest. "Is it a good place to swim?"

"Pretty much. Really nice beaches. Not so much on the east end of the island. You can't see it from here, but that's where you can see the Morris Island lighthouse. The light's automated now because it's surrounded by water, but it's a pretty view. The currents are real bad so no swimming. But at low tide you can get a boat out there and still go up inside to the top."

Peter faced her. "Have you ever been? All the way to the top?"

She looked away, remembering. "Yes. It's higher than it looks." She ducked her head, not wanting him to see her eyes and the memories of Jim she'd shared with no one.

"Maybe you can take me sometime." He smiled gently, as if he understood.

"I'd like that." She glanced down at the water, where the moon seemed to be reflecting off bigger waves. "We'd better go before the tide strands us."

Taking her hand, he began to lead her toward the front door. Looking down at the bottom of the steps, he said, "We're a little late. I'm going to have to carry you."

He lifted her in his arms, just like her favorite scene in the book *Gone With the Wind*, and carried her through the shallow water to the shifting sands on the shore. He hesitated for a moment, holding her in his arms before gently placing her on her feet again.

"Thank you," she said, feeling breathless and grounded at the same time.

He cupped her face in both hands and leaned forward, softly touching his lips to hers. "Thank *you*," he said, pulling back and tucking her hand into the crook of his elbow again.

It wasn't until much later that night, as she lay in her bed next to a sleeping Lulu, that she thought to wonder exactly what he'd been thanking her for.

CHAPTER 6

A close-up jingling sounded as something wet slathered its way across Emmy's nose and cheek, but Emmy lay still, not sure if she were still dreaming and unwilling to awaken yet. She'd heard the footsteps again, but this time instead of approaching or going away, they'd simply stopped, and in a half-awake state Emmy had held out her hand. *Come back to me.*

The smell of wet dog hit her as something tickled her hand. Slowly she became aware that the rain had stopped and that what she felt on her hand and inner arm was definitely a warm breath. Her eyes shot open, revealing a large mud-colored dog of indeterminate breed wearing metal tags and a jaunty red bandanna, and a man wearing flip-flops, cargo shorts, and a T-shirt sitting on a chair with his elbows on his knees, watching her very much like what she pictured Baby Bear had when he discovered somebody sleeping in his bed.

She sat up abruptly, nearly falling out of the chair she seemed to be slumped into. After finding her balance, she stood, blinking rapidly at the stranger and the dog, who now sat at her feet.

"Who are you?" she asked, wondering why she wasn't worried. The man was tall and slim, and certainly bigger than she was, but the expression in his light brown eyes was more confusion and a little bit of annoyance rather than anything threatening.

"You were crying in your sleep," he said matter-of-factly.

She used her forearm to wipe her face. Embarrassed, she repeated, "Who are you?"

Putting his hands on his thighs, he pulled to a stand, effectively towering over Emmy by almost a foot. Ben had been tall, too, and she had the irrational feeling of being protected while standing next to this stranger. She took a step back and crossed her arms over her chest.

"I was about to ask you the same thing," he said, his accent nearly hidden as if he'd spent a lot of time out of the South. Or maybe he'd just spent a lot of time trying to erase it.

Keeping her arms tightly crossed, she said, "I'm Emmy Hamilton. I'm renting this house for a few months."

He raised sandy-colored eyebrows, which matched his sun-streaked hair. His hair touched his ears and brushed the collar of his shirt. She'd once found longer hair on men attractive. But then she'd met Ben with his military haircut, and she couldn't remember what she'd found so alluring about longer hair. Especially on this man, with his casual stance and untucked shirt, she found the longer hair almost an affront.

"I'm Heath Reynolds. I own this house. I came over today to work on the dock and saw your car. I wasn't aware that the house had been rented."

Emmy blinked. "Oh. But it has. I have the rental agreement in the car."

He waved his hand at her. "Don't sweat it. My mom's been pretty busy with selling her bookstore and getting everything ready for her retirement. It must have slipped her mind, and she just forgot to tell me."

Emmy allowed her hands to fall to her sides. "So your mother is Abigail."

He nodded, then tucked his hands into his back pockets. Again, she found herself slightly irritated at his casualness, thinking that he'd look a whole lot better if he'd tuck in his shirt and put on a belt. *You were crying in your sleep.* Had she really? And why would this man point it out to her? Her irritation and embarrassment grew.

Without thinking, she blurted, "Oh, so that Lulu woman is your aunt."

A hint of a smile framed his eyes. "Actually, 'that Lulu woman' is my great-aunt. My father is her nephew—her sister's son."

Emmy's analytical mind began trying to catalog the information, putting all of it in organized slots. "So her sister would be your grand-mother. Does she still live on Folly, too?" Emmy pictured another short and squat woman who looked and acted just like Lulu, and hoped that the answer was no.

He shook his head. "No. She died in 1989. During Hurricane Hugo."

His answer surprised her. "I thought they did forced evacuations for big storms."

"They do. But she hadn't left the island in more than forty-five years, and she said a storm wasn't enough reason to make her go."

Emmy flinched, not really sure why. "It must have been hard on her family to leave her behind."

He leaned back against a charcoal grill that looked like it had never been used. "I was only eleven at the time, so I don't remember much, except being excited about getting out of school so we could evacuate. But my mom and dad and Aunt Lulu were pretty upset. Nothing they could say would persuade her, and there was nothing legally they could do to make her go. She kept saying she was waiting for some-one, and that if she left, she might never come back and then he would never find her. Aunt Lulu later told me she was waiting for someone who was never coming back."

Chill bumps erupted at the base of Emmy's neck as she recalled al-most the identical words that her mother had said to her—something about burning days while waiting for someone who was gone forever.

"Who was she waiting for?" She tried to act casual, as if the answer wasn't important to her.

"I don't know. You could ask Aunt Lulu. She'd probably know."

Emmy shuddered, preferring to walk barefoot over broken glass than to ever voluntarily speak to the old woman again. Unable to leave a factoid alone, she continued to prod. "But you're her nephew. I would have thought that you'd have asked at some time, found some answers at least."

His brown eyes hardened momentarily. "First, I'm a guy. It doesn't always occur to us to dig into the reasons behind people's behavior. We just sort of act on the behavior, you know? Second, I've learned not to live in the past. It's already gone, and there's nothing you can do about it. I'm not going to spend my life worrying about something I can't change."

His tone had changed from casual to almost angry before he'd recovered his nonchalant attitude, ruining her initial, safer impression. Emmy watched as his gaze traveled over what was surely her slept-on and humidity-frizzed hair, then to her suitcases and finally to his dog, who was still sitting on her feet. He patted his leg. "Come on, Frank. Give the lady her space." The dog trotted over to the back door, where Heath pulled a ring of keys from his back pocket and unlocked it.

When he turned back to her, a small smile lifted his mouth, showing white teeth against his tanned face. "There're three bedrooms inside, you know. No need to sleep on the porch." He threw open the door and the dog bounded inside as if he were on familiar terms with the house.

Emmy frowned, then lifted her two suitcases, forgetting that she hadn't planned to bring them inside at all. "I forgot the combination, that's all. And then it was raining so hard that I decided to wait instead of getting everything drenched. I guess I was just tired from driving all day and fell asleep."

He walked toward her, his brows creased, and again she couldn't help but wonder why she wasn't afraid of him.

"I'll take those and bring in the rest." He moved to take her luggage from her hands.

She continued to hold her suitcases, although they seemed to get heavier by the second. "I'm perfectly capable of carrying my own suitcases, but thank you."

"I didn't say you weren't capable. It's just that if my mother finds out that I let you carry your own suitcases, she'll take a switch to me. And no, I'm not kidding."

His face was serious but his eyes weren't. She was tired, and she was in no mood to argue. Besides, it would be nice to have somebody else carry her baggage for a change. "Fine, if it means that much to you." Emmy relinquished her hold and allowed him to follow her inside the house.

The first thing that Emmy noticed was the light. Even on a cloudy day, the neutral walls glowed from the floor-to-ceiling windows that flanked the front door and were echoed on the opposite side of the house that overlooked the marsh. The open floor plan boasted beautiful cornice moldings and dark wood floors, but very little furniture. It was as if the builder's dreams of light and air had ended with construction and with no real plan for the interiors. She saw a winding wrought-iron staircase that led to a catwalk that bisected the main living area and presumably led to the two upstairs bedrooms. The third bedroom, the master, was on the main level, and when Heath walked past her toward a door on the other side of the kitchen, she followed.

The master bedroom filled the entire width of the house and boasted views of both the ocean from the front and the marsh from the rear with large fan windows. The room held only a large bed, a dresser, and a night table, again striking Emmy as odd. In the far corner of the room was an arched alcove, and as Emmy approached, she realized she'd found the turret she'd seen on the outside of the house.

As Heath settled her suitcases on either side of the dresser, she stuck her head through the opening and nearly shouted with surprise. Winding up the walls like the painted stripe on a lighthouse were shelves of books, stacked three and sometimes four deep, going all the way to the top of the window-filled apex and accessed by an equally winding spiral staircase. The books were held in place by wrought-iron doors that allowed a view of the book spines while keeping the books from tumbling down the stairs.

"You like books?"

Emmy jerked around at the sound of Heath's voice, almost hitting her head on the edge of a shelf.

"You could say that. I have a master's in library science, and have worked at my mother's bookstore off and on since I was a girl."

"Master's in library science, huh? So you're a librarian."

She crossed her arms across her chest again. "Technically, I suppose I am, but I'm not *just* a librarian. I'm qualified to be a museum curator handling historical documents, or to procure historical letters for a university. That sort of thing."

He nodded as if contemplating her words. "Interesting. But you work in your mother's bookstore instead."

Anger, lingering loss, and the unnerving thought that he'd struck a chord she didn't want to hear bombarded her simultaneously so that no words came from her open mouth as she stared at him, unable to reply.

As if sensing he'd stepped into forbidden territory, he turned his attention to the winding shelves. "These came from my grandmother's store."

Emmy swallowed, searching for her voice. "Your grandmother's store?" she repeated, confused. She held up her hand, her mind clearing. "Wait. Abigail's mother-in-law, right? She left Folly's Finds to your mother when she died. What was her name?"

"Maggie. Maggie O'Shea Reynolds. Lulu's sister, and my grandmother."

Emmy nodded, wanting to move out of the small space, but Heath blocked her exit. She was stuck staring up at him, unable to move unless she touched him. "Right. It makes sense now. So Maggie was the one who was lost in Hurricane Hugo."

He looked upwards, the light from the turret window turning his brown eyes white. "Yep. And this was her personal book collection, which Lulu and my mom rescued before the storm. We stored them in my parents' attic, which, by some miracle, retained its roof. Their house is farther from the ocean than Maggie's, so they figured the books would be safer there. We moved as many as we could here when this house was built, but they didn't all fit, so the rest stayed at my parents'. My mom started selling some of the boxes on eBay when she decided to retire and put the store up for sale until Lulu found out and made her stop."

"Why didn't Lulu keep them?"

He looked down at her, then took a step back as if realizing how close he was standing. "She lives with my parents. She used to live with Aunt Maggie, but after Hugo, she moved in with my parents and has lived with them ever since."

"Doesn't she have any other family?" She couldn't imagine any person putting up with the old woman for any length of time, but the thought of her being alone nipped at Emmy's conscience.

He shook his head. "She never married. But she was always close to my father, so it made sense."

"Your poor mother," Emmy said under her breath as she squeezed past Heath and back into the bedroom. She stood in the middle of the room with her hands on her hips, noticing the dog had found a spot in the middle of the bed.

"She works at Folly Finds, you know."

Emmy turned back to Heath. "You mean she used to. I own the store now—or will as soon as all of the papers are signed. I'm assuming that means I get to hire who I want."

Heath raised his eyebrows, but didn't comment. "Let me show you the rest of the house." He slapped his hand against the side of his hip again, and Frank jumped from the bed and followed them out of the room.

The kitchen, dining area, and remaining bedrooms were as meticulously designed and as full of light as the rest of the house, but just as devoid of furnishings. The only evidence of any interior design was the large black-and-white photographs that had been framed and hung on every wall surface or that sat on the few occasional tables in the various rooms.

Emmy walked toward one of the larger ones hung on the wall behind the dining table. It was a photograph of two women and a small boy about two years old. They sat on the front steps of a weather-beaten clapboard house four windows wide, with a covered front porch and two dormers on the second floor. They were all dressed in styles from the nineteen forties, the women wearing skirts below the knees and fitted blouses buttoned up to the neck and the boy in a short sailor suit complete with a sailor's hat. All three stared into the camera, squinting into the bright sun.

The boy sat on the lap of the slimmer woman, who had a face that, Emmy decided after regarding it for a long moment, wasn't exactly pretty, but was what people probably once referred to as handsome. She had medium brown hair and light eyes with regular features that might be forgotten as soon as you walked by, except for something about her that made Emmy do a double take. Was it the eyes? Emmy leaned forward to get a better look. No, it was something else, something that had to do with her expression. There was sorrow there, sewn into the lines between her brows; but her eyes held so much hope and possibility that it was impossible to look at her and not believe that something better was around the corner.

Emmy's gaze moved to the shorter, younger woman sitting next to the woman holding the boy. On second glance Emmy realized that it wasn't really a woman, but a girl of about thirteen or fourteen years old. She had bad skin and wore her hair in two braids with a severe and unflattering part down the middle. She neither frowned nor smiled into the camera, as if she were still deciding what her take on life should be. She wore saddle shoes with ankle socks over thick legs in contrast to the slim legs of the woman next to her. The towheaded boy held a small American flag, its stars blurry from rapid movement as if held in strong wind.

"That's my grandmother Maggie and Aunt Lulu with my father. It was taken on D-day, 1944. That's why he's holding the flag. That was their house on Second Avenue, the one that was destroyed by Hugo. I own the lot, but it's still vacant."

Emmy focused on the little flag, her throat constricting. It did that every time she saw an American flag, remembering the tightly folded one she'd been given at Ben's funeral, now carefully packed in her suitcase.

Clearing her throat, she said, "It's a great picture. Was your grandfather in the war?"

He squinted at the photograph. "Yes. In the navy. He died before I was born, but I don't know exactly when. Nobody really talks about him, so that's about all I know."

She blinked her eyes, horrified that she might start to cry. Since Ben's death, she'd been subject to periods of irrationality, and even near strangers were fair game. Turning to Heath, she said, "I would think that if you had a war veteran in your family, everyone should know about it and celebrate it. It's a little ungrateful not to, don't you think?"

His eyes widened as he stared at her for a long moment. Then, to Emmy's surprise, he said, "You're probably right. My mom would know. When you meet with her to sign the papers, you can ask her about him." His eyes narrowed slightly. "Has she gone over all the stipulations regarding the purchase of the store?"

A cool chill settled into Emmy's spine, making her shiver. "Most of them. I'm sure she'll go over all the details with me."

Heath just nodded, although it looked like he wanted to say something but thought better of it after regarding her militant stance with her arms crossed tightly over her chest. Which was fine with her. His abrupt arrival had made her forget about returning her suitcases to her car and leaving immediately, but she still wasn't sure she was going to stay. The purchase of the store wouldn't be finalized until the closing, after all, and maybe all she really needed was a vacation at the beach.

Still, the feeling she had when Heath mentioned the store had her intrigued. It was the same feeling she'd had when she'd opened the box of books and found the notes in the margins. She needed to see Folly's Finds. And maybe, after that, she'd be ready to leave.

She spotted another photograph, this one about eight by ten inches, in a frame on a table behind an overstuffed sofa. It was another black-and-white photograph, but there was only one subject in this one. A tall and slim woman in a nineteen-forties-era bathing suit stood in a Hollywood pose facing away from the camera with her hands on her hips and her head turned back over her shoulders toward the photographer with a demure smile.

Unlike the two women in the other photograph, this woman was beautiful by anybody's standards. Her blond hair shone like spun gold in the sunlight, her facial features perfectly proportioned and her left brow doing an excellent Scarlett O'Hara impression in arched surprise. Her legs were long and lean with trim ankles, and she had slim hips tapering up to a tiny waist. A glimpse of an ample bust could be seen peeking through the triangle of her arm, her skin nearly pearlescent against the sandy beach of the background.

Emmy's curiosity made her reach for the frame to get a better look. This time she noticed the espadrilles tied at the ankles and the slim bracelet with a sand-dollar drop the woman wore on her left wrist. Emmy held the photograph up to Heath. "Who's this?"

"That would be my grandmother's cousin, Catherine. That's all I know. All of these photos used to be in one of my grandmother's photo albums that my mother took with her when they evacuated before Hugo. It was her idea to have them blown up and framed for my house. Said every house needs a personal touch."

Emmy wanted to ask him where the rest of the furniture was, or why the only personal touch came from the framed family photographs that his mother had given him. Except for those, the house definitely lacked the feminine touch, and if he'd built the house for his fiancée, why was there no sign of her ever being here? Regardless, she was glad to have the photographs. She'd left all of hers, including her wedding photos, at home. Her mother had suggested that, but had also told her that she'd send them as soon as Emmy was ready for them.

Heath interrupted her thoughts. "I'll go and bring everything else in. You stay here and get acquainted with the place and don't argue. The neighbors will call my mother if they see you hauling anything inside."

Without waiting for her to argue, he opened the front door and, with Frank offering encouragement, brought the rest of her belongings in from the car.

After piling everything up in the middle of the living room, he said, "Look, I'll wait to work on the dock so you can get settled in without listening to the hammering. But feel free to call me if you need anything." He handed her a business card, and she took it.

"Thanks, although it looks like your mother has pretty much covered all of the bases." Emmy offered him a tentative smile, and tried not to feel too eager to see him leave. But there was something about him that irked her—something that felt as out of place as a biography shelved in the fiction section.

"Yeah, except for not telling me I had a tenant." He scratched the back of his neck. "Well, then, I'd better get going and let you unpack."

After Emmy thanked him again and they said their good-byes, she let him out of the front door. She watched him through the window as he took a bike leaning against the tall palmetto tree in the front yard and rode away with Frank jogging next to him, and wondered absently if his fiancée was now his wife and if she'd come with him to Folly Beach.

Emmy turned away from the door and realized she still held his business card in her hand. Holding it up, she looked at it, seeing for the first time the embossed drawing of a bottle tree, an identical replica of the ones etched into the front-door windows. *Bottle Tree Building and Design. Heath Reynolds, FAIA LEED AP.* There were an Atlanta address and two phone numbers, both starting with area code 404, which wasn't South Carolina.

Emmy stuck the card into her back pocket, knowing she wouldn't call him. He irritated her in the way sand in a shoe did, not overtly annoying until you realized you'd created a blister by ignoring it. She pushed aside thoughts of the bottle tree in the backyard, and the note inside, and of his grandmother Maggie, who'd been lost in a hurricane because she'd been waiting for somebody who never came, and she tried very hard not to think how much she and Maggie had in common.

IN THE YARD BEHIND FOLLY'S Finds, Lulu clutched her pruning shears in one hand as she straightened from the cherry laurel bush she'd been grooming. She stood back and admired the way the dark green leaves were a perfect backdrop for the scarlet-colored bottles on the tree next to it. She loved this garden, loved tending it as if it were a child, and in many ways, it was. John was long since grown, and so was his son. But her garden remained. The living plants came and went, but her bottle trees were always there. Tourists and locals alike came to see her garden, and quite unexpectedly, she'd created a flourishing business in custom orders, ultimately shipping her trees up and down the Eastern seaboard.

Jim's tree was long gone, taken like so many other things by Hugo, but she still remembered the spot on the vacant lot where it had stood. She still visited it, leaving a handful of sand each time she went, just so he'd know she'd been there. Prickly blackberry vines had consumed the back and side fences of the old lot, claiming more and more ground each year, no matter how much Heath tried to beat it back. She liked the vines and the sweet dark berries, remembering how Jim had liked the blackberry jam she and Maggie had made.

Lulu touched a bloodred bottle on a low branch of a tree, feeling the hum of air inside of it as if it were a living, breathing thing. It gratified her to be doing something useful that allowed her to stay on Folly Beach, where the cycle of the tides and the influx of summer people came and went, leaving things pretty much the way they'd always been after they were gone. Lulu didn't like change; it messed with the natural order of things.

She thought about the woman in Heath's house and pursed her lips. She didn't like her. She was an intruder just like all the summer visitors, except that this one wasn't planning on going away again. Lulu wanted to think that it wasn't personal, that she'd dislike any newcomer threatening to stay longer than the summer season. But this Emmy Hamilton was different. There was something familiar about her. Not familiar in the way one would recognize an old friend, but familiar in the way a person recognizes the scent of the air before a storm. Maybe it was the haunted look that bracketed the woman's eyes that made Lulu think of Maggie. Or maybe it was the prodding inquisitiveness that reminded Lulu too much of herself.

She remembered how excited Abigail was to have found someone to buy the store so she wouldn't have to dismantle it and sell it piece by piece. But, Lulu knew, memories couldn't be dismantled like a jigsaw puzzle. Memories were like pilings on a house; once you started sawing away at one of them, the house would fall.

She turned back to the cherry laurel bush she'd been trimming, admiring the dark blue fruits that suddenly seemed as precarious as her past. Yes, most memories were meant to be kept intact. And, she thought as she lopped off a thick stem, the bright green leaves and cluster of fruit falling at her feet into the sandy grass, some secrets were never meant to be shared.

CHAPTER 7

Maggie rested her elbows on the front counter at Folly's Finds and watched Lulu finish her after-school snack and drain the last drop from her Coca-Cola bottle. She knew it would find its way to the box in the storeroom, where Lulu's growing collection of empty clear and colored bottles was kept. She'd made a tree for Mrs. Bailey, her friend Amy's mother, and two other people who'd seen it had asked Lulu for one, too. Lulu hadn't thought about charging for them yet, except in Coca-Colas and other bottles, but Maggie would have to step in if she thought that people were taking advantage of her sister's generosity and artistic bent.

The bell over the shop door rang, and Maggie looked up with a smile, expecting to see the deliveryman who brought their gallon jugs of drinking water every week. There was no drinking water on the island, which was one of the reasons why her father had never stayed more than a week at a time while her mother had been alive and the main reason he cited why he rarely returned following her death.

Maggie's heart lurched as she recognized Peter's broad shoulders in a herringbone swagger coat, the slicked-down brown hair as he took off his hat.

"Margaret, it's good to see you again." He held his hat in his hands, his eyes piercing.

"Peter," she said, trying not to sound as overjoyed as she felt—one of Cat's rules. But he'd gone for two weeks back to Iowa and his father's factory, as well as too many other places for her to remember, according to Peter, and she'd missed him. She could even admit that she was so happy to see him that she forgot to be angry that he hadn't written to her, nor given her an address to be able to write to him. He'd left suddenly, with only a short note telling her he'd gone tucked into her front door.

He placed his hat and gloves on the counter and took both of her hands in his before squeezing gently. "How are you?"

Ignoring all of Cat's advice, she blurted out, "Better—now that you're here." They'd been out exactly four times, yet his absence had made her feel as if she'd known him forever.

His eyes warmed, and for a moment, Maggie was sure that he was going to lean across the counter and kiss her. But then he spotted Lulu sitting on her stool and watching him carefully, and he dropped Maggie's hands as he focused his attention on Lulu.

"Just the young lady I was looking for." Reaching inside his overcoat, he said, "I've been to New York and found something I thought you might like." He removed a brown-paper-wrapped package and handed it to her.

Lulu slid from the stool and hesitantly took a step forward. "What is it?" she asked without smiling.

"Lulu, your manners." Maggie frowned at her little sister, wondering when Lulu's reticence had turned into rudeness.

"Thank you," Lulu added quickly. "What is it?"

Peter laughed, apparently charmed by her youthful honesty. "Open it and see."

Lulu accepted the package and, after contemplating it for just a second, ripped at the paper, letting it fall to the floor. When she'd unwrapped the package completely, Lulu's habitual frown gave way to a lopsided smile. *"The Quest of the Missing Map,"* she read out loud. Then, holding it up to Maggie, she said in a much louder voice, "Golly, Mags. It's the brand-new Nancy Drew—I haven't even seen it yet! Can I go show it to Amy?" She looked up at Maggie with an expression of unbridled joy, a look that Maggie hadn't seen on Lulu's face since Jim died, and all of Maggie's reasons for not being left alone with Peter fled.

Forgetting to remind Lulu of her manners, Maggie said, "Sure. Come back before four so you can do your chores before closing."

Lulu grabbed her navy blue wool coat from the coatrack and ran to the front door. But before she reached it, she raced back and stopped in front of Peter. "Thank you, Mr. Nowak. I really like my book."

Then she flew out the door, not even bothering to put on her coat.

Maggie smiled at Peter. "Thank you. I haven't seen her that excited about something in a long time. Her smile is the best gift you could ever give me."

He reached into his other inside pocket and pulled out another small package also wrapped in brown paper, and slid it in front of her on the counter. "Don't speak so hastily."

"What is it?" she asked, and then they both laughed as she realized that she sounded just like Lulu.

"Open it." His amber eyes were lit from within, and she shuddered involuntarily, remembering something Cat had told her about how a man could make you feel when he touched you without any clothes on. Maggie figured she now somehow knew what Cat had been talking about. She tried not to think of Jim and his chaste kisses, or the way he was afraid to hold her too tightly.

She grabbed a letter opener from the mason jar by the cash register, then used it to gently open the package, sparing as much of the paper wrapping as possible so she could reuse it. She peered inside and found neatly folded tissue paper. With her forefinger, she tentatively moved the tissue aside and stopped. A blush suffused her cheeks as she raised her eyes to Peter's.

"I hope it's not too personal a gift, but a good friend assured me that in these times, it's perfectly acceptable for a gentleman to provide a lady with any items that she might have use for but is unable to find."

Feeling slightly mollified, she looked inside the package again, where two pairs of neatly folded silk stockings lay nestled in tissue paper. At least he hadn't included a garter belt because then she would have just died of mortification.

"I haven't seen silk stockings in a while." She held the package to her chest, feeling wanton, and beautiful, and desired by a handsome man. "Thank you, Peter."

He put his elbows on the counter, leaning toward her. "It's the least I can do. You've made my time on Folly something to look forward to." His eyes darkened as he regarded her, and she found herself frantically trying to think what Cat would do, yet every answer only deepened her blush.

Peter smiled as if reading her mind. "You can wear them tonight. Thought we could go to the Folly Bowling Center. They've got the biggest juke box in town, so I hear, and there's going to be dancing. I'd love to be able to show you off."

"I'd love to." She smiled back at him, their faces close, and wondered if tonight would be the night he'd kiss her again. The bell over the door jangled, followed by a blast of cool air and high, shrill laughter. Maggie looked up to see Cat and her officer standing much too close, the officer's hand resting possessively on Cat's hip. Cat wore her green coat, the one Lulu had given to Maggie for each of her dates with Peter, and as Maggie watched his expression, she could tell he noticed it, too.

"Good afternoon, Lieutenant. Hello, Cat." She smoothed a pleasant smile on her face as the handsome couple entered the store, the light suddenly gone from the small space.

Cat's expression gave no indication of her mood, making Maggie wince. It was easier to deal with her cousin when she knew for sure what to avoid saying.

"Have y'all heard the news?" Cat's tone was almost giddy. Robert dropped his hand as the two of them moved forward.

Peter nodded his head slightly at Cat in greeting. "Mrs. Brier," he said quietly, stiffening almost imperceptibly.

After introducing the two men, Maggie turned to her cousin. "What news?" Folly's Finds sold both the *News and Courier* and the *Charleston Evening Post*, and she read them cover to cover to be well informed despite what Cat told her about men disliking women who knew more than they did. The papers were full of the war in Europe, but Maggie knew that Cat's news would probably have a more local interest.

"The Hendersons have cousins from North Carolina staying with them for a couple of weeks, and they're saying that there're German submarines in the water off of Cape Hatteras, where they live. Isn't that exciting?"

Maggie's eyebrows furrowed. "But that's impossible. All the newsmen have been saying that it's too far for submarines to come all the way over here."

Robert seemed to be studying Peter's face before he spoke, as if measuring how much detail or how candidly he could speak. "Actually, that's not completely true. The German U-boats are more than capable of crossing the Atlantic. Whether or not they've made it to the eastern coast of the U.S. is conjecture at this point."

Cat squeezed herself in between Peter and Robert at the counter. "Well, Sally and Katie Henderson are saying that a bunch of stuff has been washing up on shore—stuff that could be coming from ships—and the fishermen are complaining of oil slicks killing fish. They're saying that they've even seen bodies in the water. And that the Germans are planning on landing somewhere on the coastline."

Maggie turned to Robert. "Do you know if that's true?"

"I can only tell you what I know. At this point, there is no real evidence that any boats have been sunk by a German U-boat. It's wartime and rumors are everywhere." He glanced at Peter as if for reassurance that Maggie and Cat were strong enough to hear the rest. He continued. "I have heard that the new German subs have extended range because they store their diesel in ballast tanks, giving them enough fuel to make it here and back." He smiled reassuringly. "I'm sure there's no need to worry. And if there is, you'll be the first to know."

Cat squeezed his arm and pressed herself against him, but Maggie caught her throwing a glance at Peter to see his reaction. Cat must have been disappointed as Peter seemed to be more focused on the headlines in the newspapers stacked in front of him.

As if sensing eyes on him, Peter looked up and smiled. "Well, I'm thinking it's a bunch of talk. When I was in New York recently, I read a newspaper article asking the people to stop spreading rumors. Seems the whole Eastern seaboard is saying they've heard of somebody else who's seen a U-boat, but nobody can find firsthand witnesses. Besides, we don't have to worry about it here in Folly. We have the horse patrol keeping an eye out, right?" He gently touched Maggie's arm, as if to remind her of the evening on the beach when they'd gone into the deserted house, and her face flamed again.

Robert cleared his throat. "Of course not. Especially with all of the servicemen here and the nearby airfield in Charleston, it wouldn't make sense for the Germans to pick on Folly. And if they're blowing up ships off of Cape Hatteras, it's because that's where northbound ships ride up the gulfstream; we don't have that so close to our coastline here in South Carolina. But a tanker sure would make a real easy target sandwiched between a German sub and a well-lit coastline."

Peter skewered him with a look. "So you're saying it's possible there's some truth to the rumors."

Robert looked chagrined as he put his arm around Cat. "I suppose it's possible. It's just that nobody's actually seen one of the U-boats.

And it appears that Washington doesn't believe it either since no official blackouts have been ordered for the eastern coastline."

Peter leaned forward. "But you're with the navy. Surely you could tell us if there are more patrols being sent out to keep these ladies safe."

Robert paused for a brief moment before answering. "I'm not at liberty to say, sir, but I can assure you that the United States Navy and Coast Guard will do their duty to protect the coastline. These ladies and all their neighbors can sleep soundly at night knowing that."

"Good," Peter said before stepping back, his arm brushing Maggie's as he turned to look at her, and all she could do was remember to breathe.

Robert glanced at his wristwatch. "I'm heading out to Florida with some new recruits, so I need to leave." He took both of Cat's hands in his and looked at her in a way that made the room seem much warmer. Quietly, as if for her ears only, he said, "I'll see you in two weeks."

Without kissing Cat, doubtless because of Maggie and Peter being there, he said his good-byes and left. Cat stared after his departing back, and for a brief moment, Maggie believed that Cat might actually be sad to see him go.

Cat faced them again and walked back to the large oak counter. "What's this?" she asked, picking up Maggie's package without waiting for an answer.

Before Maggie could take it away from her, Cat had already opened it and pulled the stockings out of the tissue paper. Touching them with her fingertips as if to make sure they were real silk, she said, "What a lovely gift. Not exactly appropriate for a gentleman to give a lady, but I promise not to tell." She sent Maggie a reproving glance before stuffing the stockings back into the bag and dropping it on the counter.

Cat kept her head down and sighed heavily. "It must be nice to have a man looking out for you." Cat looked up at Peter with tear-filled eyes that almost fooled Maggie. Cat placed her hand on his sleeve. "I don't know what I'm going to do without Robert. He's really been helping distract me from my grieving over Jim." She frowned, even managing to look pretty with her furrowed brows pointing in a "v" over her delicate nose. "And he promised to fix my window but he didn't get a chance to. Now I'm going to have to try to fix it myself, and I just hope that I won't get hurt."

Peter remained stiff and unyielding despite Cat's hand on his arm. "Can't you wait until he returns?"

She sniffed. "I would, except on warmer days my room gets so stifling that I feel as if I'm going to suffocate, or that the stale air will make me ill. And then what sort of help would I be for Maggie?"

They both looked at Maggie, who'd begun to feel the same way she did when she was in a boat and the wind suddenly changed direction. "You could come sleep in my room, Cat, at least until Robert gets back—or until I find somebody else to fix it. I'm sure Lulu won't mind sleeping in her old room again."

Cat shook her head. "I couldn't possibly do that to poor Lulu. She needs fresh air, too." She peered up at Peter through her thick, dark lashes. "I was hoping that Peter would be able to help me. Surely you could spare him for a couple of hours."

Maggie wanted to shout no, to grab Peter and run as far away from Cat as she could. But she wasn't a young girl anymore, and she couldn't behave like one. And if she couldn't trust Peter, wasn't she better off without him? She tried not to think of Jim and how she'd trusted him, too.

Maggie found herself nodding. "Of course. I need to unpack a few boxes that arrived today anyway. Y'all go on."

With a look of disappointment that sent Maggie's heart soaring, Peter turned to her. "All right. But I'll pick you up at six o'clock, okay?"

"Great," she said, sounding much more upbeat than she felt. She focused on her breathing, moving her lungs in and out as she watched Peter escort Cat through the door, the bell jangling as the door slammed shut.

ℬ

LULU RAN AS FAST AS she could down the dirt streets littered with sand and shells to her friend Amy's house on Third Street. Her lungs hurt from the cold air, but sweat dampened the back of her blouse despite the cooler temperature. She clutched the book in her hand, already feeling the anticipation of curling up in whatever room Martha wasn't cleaning and reading the book from cover to cover without getting up once.

But first she needed to show it to Amy, if only to make her a little bit jealous, and to promise to lend it to her friend once she had finished reading it.

She bounded up the cracked and peeling front steps to Amy's house and pounded on the outside screen door, which was missing most of its screen. When nobody answered right away, Lulu flung the door open and banged on the wooden front door, cutting her knuckle on a faded chip of red paint that crumbled under her fist.

"Amy!" she called, stepping back so that her voice would carry up to Amy's bedroom. When she saw no movement in any of the upstairs windows, she slid her gaze down and saw that somebody had replaced the blue star in the front window with a gold one. Carefully, Lulu let the screen door shut and walked over to the gold star, raising her hand to the glass.

She swallowed down the lump in her throat. She knew what a gold star was, of course; they had their own, hung in the window by Maggie when Jim had been killed. It hadn't occurred to Lulu before to wonder why it hadn't been Cat to do it.

Slowly, she walked down the steps before turning around to stare at the empty house, wondering if Amy would be back. Not really paying attention to where her feet were taking her, she crossed the yard and went around the house to the backyard, where the bottle tree she'd given Mrs. Bailey was. She and Amy had started a club, although they hadn't come up with a name yet, but they'd started leaving secret notes to each other in the bottles to discuss their secret meetings and ideas and even the names of other girls they might want to invite to join the club.

Lulu stopped short as she came around the corner of the house. The tree lay on its side where a strong wind must have knocked it over, the bottles intact yet scattered around the thin tree branch. Lulu moved closer to study it, almost relieved that her tree couldn't be blamed for Mr. Bailey's death. It could only keep away the bad spirits if it was standing up, the mouths of the bottles open and ready for the bad spirits. She had a picture in her head of Jonah and the whale when she thought about her bottles, which made her think that her bottle trees couldn't be evil if they made her think of a Bible story.

Carefully placing her Nancy Drew book on the ground, Lulu set about restoring the bottle tree to where it should be, using her feet to pack the sandy soil up against the base of the trunk. Then she replaced the bottles on the upturned branches, liking the way the house and yard changed when she looked through glass, like she was being taken to a distant place where men who went off to war always came back.

She stepped back to admire her artwork, realizing too late that it wasn't the same tree she'd made before. But maybe that was better, because this house and the Bailey family weren't going to be the same, either.

After laying her coat on the ground, she knelt beside it and dug into the pockets until she located the broken pencil she'd found on the school playground. Then, after thinking about it for just a minute, she picked up her Nancy Drew book and carefully tore the bottom off of a blank page next to the back cover. It made her a little sick to do it, but she didn't have anything else to write on and it was important that she do this.

Using her leg as a writing surface, she wrote a note to Amy.

I'm sorry about your daddy. I liked him a lot and I know you will miss him like I still miss Jim. My bottle tree is to help me remember him, and I hope if you come back you will think of this tree in the

same way about your daddy. I'm thinking our club name can be
the Bottle Tree Memories Club, if you want.

I hope you come back. I've got a new Nancy Drew book and
I'll let you read it as many times as you want.

Without signing the note on purpose, thinking it wouldn't be much of a secret club if she put her name on everything, she rolled the paper up lengthwise and stuck it inside the wide mouth of a mason jar, making sure the note was wider than the mouth so it wouldn't fall out.

After standing back to make sure everything looked good, Lulu picked up her coat and her book and began the slow walk home. She was kicking large shells and rocks and had just started to think how angry Maggie would be when she saw the scuffed toes of her new saddle shoes, when she turned the corner onto her street and stopped in surprise.

She watched as her cousin Cat walked in that swishing way that she did whenever there was a man around, moving her hips so that her dress would swing around her legs. Lulu ducked behind a palmetto tree so she wouldn't be seen and continued watching as Peter and Cat strolled up the walk to the front door. Cat made an obviously fake stumble, but Peter didn't seem to notice that Cat wasn't really hurt because he let her lean heavily on him before he seemed to give up and just lifted her under her legs like Jim had done to Lulu after her fall at the skating rink.

Lulu looked around to see if Maggie was coming, but didn't see her. She didn't think she would be or else Cat wouldn't be acting that way in front of Peter. Peering around the tree trunk, she saw Peter fumble to turn the doorknob while holding on to Cat, who'd wrapped her arms around his neck and seemed to be whispering something in his ear.

Peter pushed the door open and stepped inside, but not before Cat lifted her head and turned in Lulu's direction as if she knew somebody was watching them. Lulu ducked back behind the tree and didn't look back until she heard the front door slam.

Then she slid down to the base of the tree and opened her book, and began to read, making sure she had a good view of anybody entering or leaving the house. Because even though Cat was wrong about a lot of stuff, she'd been right about something: Lulu never missed a thing.

CHAPTER 8

FOLLY BEACH, SOUTH CAROLINA
July 2009

The glowing numbers of the clock by the side of the bed read three twenty-eight when Emmy awoke suddenly. She wasn't sure what it was that had startled her awake; it was this still and dark at her parents' house, too. But as she lay there staring toward the ceiling, she wondered if it could be the liquid feel of the air in the house where it lay between river marsh and ocean, taunting both with its existence. It made her feel vulnerable, as if the house's pilings were no more than matchsticks, the water a crouching tiger.

Emmy closed her eyes, smelling an unfamiliar detergent in her sheets, the white starkness giving no hint of anybody's presence but her own. She sat up, sleep as lost to her now as Ben's scent on her pillowcase, and then slid from the bed. The sky had cleared and the full moon bled from the ocean-side windows, casting a pale veil over the room. Slowly, Emmy walked to the French door that led to the back porch and walked through it to stand outside.

She took a deep breath, the salty air seasoned with another more foreign one—one that reminded her of the jar of sand she'd left behind with her mother. The air felt heavy, full of something Emmy couldn't understand but, as she'd thought before, seemed to be as much a part of her memory as her mother's face.

A strong, humid breeze pushed past her and into the house, creating a ruffling sound behind her. Emmy turned and spotted the opened box of books she'd had Heath carry into the house. She'd have to transport them back to Folly's Finds at some point, but hadn't wanted to leave them in her car where the heat and humidity would play havoc with the delicate pages.

She returned inside, shut the door to the odd and unsettling scent of the night, and carried the box back to the bedroom. After flipping on the bedside lamp, she knelt beside the box and started taking out the books again, sorting them into three separate stacks—those she'd gone through already and didn't have any writing in the margins, those that did have writing in the margins, and those she'd yet to check. Piling the latter onto the bed, she crawled on top of the sheets next to them and eyed the stack in front of her.

Her eyes alighted on an old familiar gray-blue cloth binding halfway down the pile. She'd forgotten it was there after her initial discovery of the margin writings had redirected her attention, but now, with a surge of excitement, she carefully removed it from its position. *"The Quest of the Missing Map,"* she read out loud. Her mother had given her the entire Nancy Drew collection, most of them first editions, but Emmy was fairly certain that she didn't have the first edition of this particular one.

Almost giddy, she flipped open the book to the front to find the copyright date, and paused. There was an inscription inside, almost illegible as if it had been written in a hurry, with broad black strokes from a pen. *To Lulu, Please accept this small token of my esteem. Stay good and sweet, Peter.*

Lulu? *Sweet?* Surely it couldn't be the same Lulu. Then again, the store had been owned by Lulu's sister. And who was Peter? The handwriting was unusual, with feet on the capital letters, and the lowercase "g" written like a typewritten letter.

Quickly, Emmy flipped to the title page and saw that the book was, indeed, a first edition. And it was in excellent condition, as if it had been read very gently and carefully stored. Emmy felt her excitement fade when she realized she'd probably have to ask Lulu if she wanted it back before she could decide to sell it or keep it for her own first-edition collection.

Curiously, she flipped through the pages, looking for more notes in the margins, not really surprised when she didn't find any. The copyright on the book read 1942, and judging from Emmy's own calculations, Lulu would have been about ten years old at the time, much too young to be writing love notes. Emmy turned to the last page and stopped when she spotted a jagged tear at the bottom where about one third of the page had been ripped off. It was too even to have been made accidentally, but it was odd, too, seeing in what good condition the rest of the book was.

Emmy twisted and stuck the book on her nightstand, resigned to the fact that she'd have to find Lulu and offer the book to her. She even considered asking Heath to do it, but quickly dismissed the idea, as she had no interest in speaking with him again, either.

Facing the stack, she began pulling each book from the pile, painstakingly checking every page for any kind of marking, going through half of the books without finding anything. Frustrated, she stood and stretched, then retrieved a notepad from a pile of her belongings in the corner and began to make an inventory of the books in the box she'd already examined. At least that way she could feel she was being productive.

When she was finished with that, she stood and stretched again, then yawned. It was still dark outside and dawn was a few hours away, so she figured she could at least grab some sleep. But as she began to stack the books she hadn't yet explored, she paused. There were so few left that it would be silly not to just finish up. That way, she could bring the entire box and inventory with her when she met Abigail at Folly's Finds the next day.

She sank back down on the bed, crossed her legs, and reached for the first book. As she'd done previously, she turned each cover and each page methodically, looking for any markings. She found the selection of books eclectic, yet all seemed to yield a nod to travel or romanticism, or both: Shelley, Keats, Wordsworth, D. H. Lawrence, Henry James, Hugo, Verne, Kipling. The names were all familiar to her, and holding the books in her hands and rereading favorite passages were a little like visiting old friends. She felt a kinship to the person who'd assembled this collection, wondering what else they might have in common.

Emmy had nearly reached the end of the pile before she found the first note. It was inside a leather-bound copy of Tolstoy's *Anna Karenina*, the spine well creased from frequent use. She smiled to herself, remembering the first time she'd read the book in tenth grade, being forced into secrecy so she wouldn't take any ribbing from her schoolmates. Again, she thought of the anonymous owner, Emmy's affinity for her growing with each book she plucked from the pile.

Emmy opened up the front cover, then began the tedious task of examining each page in what was definitely the thickest book in the entire box. She'd reached page 623 when she finally found what she was looking for.

Soul meets soul on lover's lips. Percy Shelley's familiar words jolted Emmy out of a half sleep, her skin tingling from the intimacy of the words, and making her feel almost like an intruder. The words were written by a woman, the loops and curves of the cursive light and delicate. The squeezing pain around Emmy's heart surprised her, as if to remind her that broken hearts were ageless and not her private domain.

Wanting to hear the man's response, she rapidly flipped through the remaining pages, finding nothing else. Hurriedly now, Emmy picked up two more books before she found anything else. It was a single word, written in pencil, the pressure from the writing instrument so firm that an impression of the word traveled through the next two pages. The words were block-lettered and traced over so many times that it was hard to tell if a man or woman had written it: *WHEN???*

Emmy quickly searched through the three remaining books, nearly giving up until she reached the very last book in the pile, a late edition of *Madame Bovary*. At first glance, she was fairly certain that this one had been written by the same woman who'd written some of the other notes.

In our house in the sea, time waits in a bottle. At first, Emmy thought the writer was referencing more current music titles, but she couldn't be sure. These books had presumably been packed up from Folly's Finds in 1989 and stored in Abigail's attic ever since. Although they were all editions from the nineteen forties or earlier, it was still possible that someone more recently had made the marks in the margins.

She studied the words, mulling them over again and again, trying to make sense of them. She didn't recognize them, nor could she guess which famous author, if any, had penned them originally.

Yawning heavily, she dropped the book and inventory list next to the other books before crawling back into the bed and flipping off the light. She lay wide-awake for a long time, trying to make sense of everything she'd read in the margins so far. There seemed to be no rhyme or reason to their order, but from what she'd found, it was apparent to her that there had once been a stream of messages and responses back and forth, and invitations to clandestine meetings. There was no proof that they were secret, of course, but Emmy figured that to go through the trouble of putting messages into book margins meant that there had to be some reason for keeping them hidden.

She watched as the sky over the marsh illuminated the walls of her room, infusing everything with a peach glow like the inside of a shell. Emmy closed her eyes just as the sun rose on her first full day on Folly Beach, and in the moments before sleep found her, she wondered if she'd even stay on Folly long enough to figure out who the mysterious lovers were, and who the book collector was who had so much in common with Emmy's own taste. Lulu's name popped into her head, jarring her momentarily awake as she considered the possibility, before closing her eyes and drifting into sleep in her new bed without Ben for the last first time.

THE FOLLOWING MORNING, AFTER HAVING fortified herself with an entire pot of coffee, Emmy threw on a skirt and blouse, loaded the box of books into the Explorer, then headed for Folly's Finds.

With the holiday weekend over, she was relieved to see that most of the cars that had lined East Ashley were gone, leaving behind garbage cans and recycling bins brimming over with beer cans, wine bottles, and other evidence of a good time.

Before she left, she walked to the bottom of the driveway to look for the mailbox to mail home a postcard of South Carolina that she'd purchased at her last stop for gas on her trip over. It had pictures of palmettos, and stately homes, and the shoreline, which she hadn't even seen yet, but she'd wanted to let her parents have some physical reminder of where she was. She even pictured her dad pulling it out of the mail stack on the counter and sticking it to the same refrigerator door where her art projects had once hung.

She looked in vain for a mailbox on her side of the street, and then across the street, then ran up the front steps to see if maybe she hadn't noticed a letter box stuck to the side of the house, but all of her efforts were in vain. Confused, she placed the postcard on her dashboard, then headed off to Center Street.

When she'd asked Abigail for a street address to help her find the store, Abigail had just told her to head down Center Street and take a right at the Planet Follywood restaurant onto East Eerie, then go down about a block, right past the Folly Beach Crab Shack on the right. Emmy brought her map just in case.

It was a lot easier than she'd expected, finding the pale pink stucco building within five minutes of leaving her house. She pulled into one of four grassy parking areas in front of the store, wondering how she'd get out if it ever rained.

The store had apparently once been a small cottage, judging by its large bay picture window out front displaying a variety of books and the single front door with a small overhang and simple columns on either side of it.

An ancient Volkswagen Beetle, its paint a barely discernible yellow, sat parked under a rusty carport. A bumper sticker, of perhaps only a slightly newer vintage than the car, read in bleached-out letters: *Where's the Beach?* Emmy figured it was most likely referencing Hugo's visit twenty years before. On the other side of the rust-speckled bumper was a newer sticker, the words making Emmy smile: *Life Begins on Folly.* She was about to turn away when she noticed the South Carolina license plate MRSDRCY.

Emmy stepped back, assessing the store. Like everything else she'd noticed so far about Folly, it appeared to be well used, and not overly concerned about what people might think. Bright orange lettering on a wooden sign above the door had the words *Folly's Finds* and *No Shoes, No Shirt, Come On In!* painted on it while two large pots overflowing with flowers guarded each side of the door. The flower beds in front of the cottage were littered with unrecognizable flowers and broke through their boundaries by spreading riotous cover over the front steps and sparse yard. Freshly painted shutters in glaring white bracketed the picture window, and rainbow-striped streamers ran across the top of the window inside, dancing around in the air-conditioning. Despite Emmy's initial impression of unkemptness, her second look made her think more of a well-loved teddy bear, proud of its exposed stuffing.

She climbed the two short steps to the front door and paused for a moment to read the stickers on the window: *Reading Is Sexy* and *Eat. Read. Sleep.* Her mother had the same stickers at Paige's Pages, and they made Emmy feel a little homesick at the same time that they brought her a sense of familiarity. With a deep breath, she turned the knob and pushed the door open.

A bell jingled over the door as a sweet fragrance from a pillar candle on a nearby table wafted over to her. A large counter covered with displayed books, small items for sale, and a stack of newspapers dominated the far-right corner of the store. Emmy walked toward it as a dark-haired woman in her early sixties wearing cat's-eye glasses on a chain looked up from a computer.

The older woman smiled warmly as she came around the counter, lowering her glasses to hang on the chain down her chest. "You must be Emmy," she said before enveloping the younger woman in a hug. Surprised, Emmy held her arms stiff for a moment before bringing them down to pat the woman on her back.

"Are you Abigail?" Emmy asked hesitantly, remembering asking Lulu the same question.

The woman pulled back. With a thick Southern drawl, she said, "I sure am. I feel like I'm the only one who hasn't met you yet." She wore a sundress and flip-flops, and her deeply tanned face spoke of years in the sun. "Heathcliff said he found you sleeping on the porch." Her face sobered, and Emmy could see the pale lines at the corners of her eyes, where the sun never reached, as if Abigail smiled a good deal.

"Heathcliff?"

The smile was back and the lines disappeared again. "My husband let me name our only son after my favorite fictional character, God bless him. But I'm the only one who calls him that—everybody else calls him Heath."

"He didn't mention that."

"No, he wouldn't."

Emmy noticed a small table by the counter filled with books by the Brontë sisters and Jane Austen. "I guess he's lucky you didn't name him Fitzwilliam," she said, indicating a copy of *Pride and Prejudice*. Pointing to a leather-bound copy of *Wuthering Heights*, she said, "My mother named me after Emily Brontë."

Abigail clasped her hands together. "Isn't that wonderful! I knew your mama and I were kindred spirits."

Emmy looked at her closely. "I didn't know you knew each other."

"Well, we've never met—although she went to high school with my husband. But we've talked on the phone quite a bit since she bought that box of books from me and decided that you buying the store would be even better!"

Without waiting for Emmy to question her further, Abigail grabbed her arm. "Come on, let me show you the place so you know what you're getting into." She took Emmy through a small alcove on the other side of the store. "This is Folly's Playgrounds—our little coffee shop, which I added on about five or six years ago. It even has its own side entrance. I lease it to Janell Stephen, who owns and operates it so you don't have to do anything with it, and I hope you'll continue with the lease. We get a nice cross-traffic between the store and the coffee shop, with a good solid local fan base as well as a bunch of tourist traffic since we're so close to Center Street."

A tall, slender woman was opening a large box beside the counter but straightened as Emmy and Abigail approached. "Emmy, I'd like you to meet Janell. Janell, meet the new owner of Folly's Finds."

Janell smiled, her green eyes warm as she shook Emmy's hand. Emmy noticed beautiful square crystal drop earrings dangling from her ears, and a matching crystal and beaded necklace worn on a leather rope chain. Her short brown hair was a perfect backdrop for the jewelry, and as they shook hands, Emmy noticed the counter displays of bracelets, rings, and earrings.

"It's very nice to meet you, Janell. I love your jewelry."

"It's nice to meet you, too. And thanks." She indicated a small standing rack of necklaces on the counter. "I actually make all of this jewelry myself. It used to be a favorite hobby of mine until I was getting so many requests from people that I decided to make it a business. Abigail gets a small percentage of everything I sell in the store, and I hope you and I can continue with the arrangement. At the very least, I want you to select something to wear each day as a sort of walking advertisement. Abigail always tells me that knowing she can accessorize once she gets here cuts down her getting-dressed routine from six minutes to five."

Laughing, Abigail gave Janell a light slap on her hand. "Oh, quit." Turning to Emmy she said, "You'll soon learn that people around here think you're going to meet the governor or going to a funeral if you wear much more than flip-flops." Eyeing Emmy's skirt and blouse, she added, "Don't worry. You'll learn. And that's what I'm here for."

"And me, too," said Janell as she went back to the box she'd been emptying.

Abigail continued to show Emmy around the quaint store. There was a small children's section, a new-releases table, and a used-book section for out-of-print books. Across the walls that weren't covered in bookshelves were painted quotations from famous books as well as golden stars and whimsical books made to look like flying carpets.

Emmy looked at them with delight. "Did you do that yourself?"

"Actually, Lulu did. She's very artistic."

"Lulu? Heath's great-aunt?"

Abigail laughed again and Emmy realized she probably did that often. "The one and only. It takes her a while to warm up to strangers. But, as I told your mother, with the two of you working together, you'll figure out a way to rub along just fine."

Emmy stopped walking. "I'm sorry—what did you say?"

Abigail continued past Emmy to a display of young-adult vampire books with corresponding action dolls, and began straightening them. As if Emmy hadn't spoken, she continued. "Don't think you have to take everything in right away. As I explained to your mother, I'll stay on as an employee for a couple of weeks—more or less depending on what you want—to introduce you to the locals and make sure you know the lay of the land."

"Thanks. I appreciate that. But what did you say about Lulu and me working together?"

"Come here," Abigail said, indicating a door at the back of the store. "Let me show you something."

Emmy followed, a crease between her eyebrows. Abigail threw open the door and walked outside into the bright sun, and Emmy followed. She found herself on a small wooden deck with two steps that led down into what would have been a compact backyard of the cottage, but had instead been transformed. Emmy stood, mesmerized, sure she knew how Alice felt when she'd fallen down the rabbit hole.

Metal bottle trees of varying widths and heights stood at attention in soldierlike rows, their brightly hued bottles like flashy military epaulettes. Interspersed along the wooden fence that bordered the yard and in between the trees were flowering bushes and plants in every color, giving the yard the appearance of a multinational flag.

"These are Lulu's."

Emmy continued to stare out at the yard, not able to formulate her question.

As if sensing her confusion, Abigail said, "Her story is a lot like Janell's. She started making a few for friends and family; then others started noticing them and would order one or two until word just spread. She actually makes a pretty decent living doing it, and I also take in a percentage of the proceeds in return for the space. As I explained to your mother, continuing the arrangement isn't negotiable, but should also be a no-brainer. Lulu brings in revenue—lots of it. And she really is a wonderful person once you get to know her."

"My mother knows about Lulu?"

Abigail turned to look Emmy in the eye. "Paige and I spent a lot of time chatting on the phone while you were preparing for your move. Although we never knew each other, we're of the same age with the same hopes and dreams for our children." Her face was serious again, showing the elusive white lines, and for the first time, Emmy saw a shadow in her eyes. "She knows this store is the opportunity you need right now. But she also understands how I can't retire and leave Lulu adrift." With her smile returning, she looked back over the glass bottle garden. "She creates such beauty, as I think only those who've known great sadness can do. She needs this little spot on earth as much as you do, I think."

Emmy opened her mouth to speak, to explain to Abigail that she had enough sadness to deal with and wouldn't welcome the burden of the older woman, but stopped when Abigail placed a hand on her arm. "You don't need to make your decision right now. I'll call the lawyers and postpone our meeting until tomorrow so you have time to think about it." She winked. "But your mama told me what a smart girl you are, and I know you'll make the right decision."

Abigail jerked open the door. "Come on, let's get out of this heat. Can't think much about anything with your brain frying in the sun."

Emmy led the way, closing her eyes at the blast from the air-conditioning. Her blouse stuck to her skin, and she began to understand the idea of loose cotton clothing.

The old-fashioned bell over the front door jangled as Emmy blinked her eyes in the dim interior of the store, making out the outline of a person standing inside the door.

"Well, speak of the devil. We were just talking about you," Abigail said as she brushed past Emmy to envelop Lulu in a hug and plant a kiss on her withered cheek. Emmy watched, surprised, as Lulu returned the hug and even forced her thin lips into a smile.

Abigail stepped back and indicated Emmy with her hand. "We were just admiring your garden. You remember Emmy Hamilton, don't you? She's staying at Heathcliff's house."

Lulu looked exactly as she had when Emmy had last seen her, except this buttoned-up blouse she wore today was a blue-and-white-checkered pattern. Unsmiling, she regarded Emmy. "You being careful with those wood floors, like I told you?"

"Yes. That is, I haven't done anything to scratch them, if that's what you mean." Emmy wasn't sure why the woman made her feel like a scolded teenager.

Lulu turned to Abigail. "She favors Jolene, don't you think? 'Cept Jolene's prettier and got a bigger chest."

Emmy stared at the old woman, trying to figure out how to respond to such an unveiled insult.

Lulu walked past them to the back door. "Hope you didn't touch anything back here and ruin it. If you're going to work here, you're going to have to remember to stay away from my garden. Can't stand intrusions."

Emmy started after her. "What do you mean if *I'm* going to work here?" She was answered with the back door slamming in her face.

Abigail touched her arm. "I'm sorry, Emmy. Sometimes she gets in her moods; I promise she's not always like that. I know you'll find this hard to believe, but Lulu is probably one of the most loyal and trustworthy people I have ever met. She would give her life for any of the people she loves without even thinking about it." Abigail offered an encouraging smile. "She's just a little suspicious of strangers, that's all. But you won't be a stranger for long."

With any luck I will be. Even the thought of having to speak to the woman again sent a shudder of revulsion through Emmy. "I have something of Lulu's that I found in the box of books I left in the car. Let me go ahead and get it." *So I don't ever have to be in her presence again.*

She left to go to her car and retrieve *The Quest of the Missing Map*, her hair damp with perspiration and sticking to her forehead as she made her way back into the store. Abigail and Janell were nowhere to be found, and for a moment, Emmy contemplated just leaving the book on the counter in the hope that somebody would read the inscription and give it to Lulu.

But, being an organized and methodical librarian at heart, she knew she couldn't do that without losing sleep. Steeling her resolve, she clasped the book in one hand and marched out the back door, squinting in the bright sunlight as she searched for Lulu in the garden.

She saw the old woman crouched by the fence near a climbing vine that dripped with clusters of berries. Emmy paused as she watched, amazed at how delicate the short, blunt fingers were as Lulu carefully pulled off dead stems with the attention of a mother pushing back the hair from a child's eyes.

Squinting against the bright sunlight, Emmy made her way down the short steps and moved to stand in front of Lulu. "I found something that belongs to you, and I wanted to know if you still wanted it."

Bracing both hands on her thighs, the old woman stood slowly, her hazel eyes large behind her thick glasses. Wanting to get the scene over with as quickly as possible, Emmy held out the Nancy Drew book. "I found this in a box of books that Abigail sent to my mother's store. It has an inscription to someone named Lulu, and I was wondering if that was you."

Lulu stared at the book for a long moment before taking it from Emmy with both hands and clutching it tightly as if she were afraid that Emmy might take it back. "Yes, it's mine." Her voice was gentle, almost like that of a young girl, and when Emmy looked into Lulu's face, it had softened, as if a hot iron had been pressed against the crease of years. It reminded Emmy that Lulu had once been young, too, before the hurts and disappointments of growing up had found her.

"It's a first edition," Emmy said, trying to distract herself from humanizing thoughts of Lulu. "I have an entire collection of first-edition Nancy Drew books, which is why I wanted to know if you still wanted it. I'd give you fair market value if you didn't."

Quietly, and without raising her eyes, Lulu said, "I want it." She paused for a moment as if the next words might hurt her. "Thank you for bringing it back to me. A lot of people wouldn't have bothered."

Their eyes met, and for the first time, Emmy didn't feel any animosity from the older woman. With a tentative smile, Emmy said, "I have enough experience working with libraries to know the pain of a missing book."

Emmy thought she saw the glimmer of a smile in Lulu's eyes, but wasn't sure. She turned around, ready to leave this woman and her odd garden and, she'd already decided, the entire store and island, when Lulu's voice drew her back.

"Where's your husband?"

Emmy turned to see Lulu looking at the gold wedding band Emmy still wore on her left hand. Emmy wasn't going to answer at first, but she'd begun to feel the creeping pulse on her scalp—the warning sign she always got when she was about to learn something important. Lifting her chin, she said, "He was killed. In Afghanistan."

"Soldier?"

Emmy nodded slowly, surprised at Lulu's interest.

The softening appeared in Lulu's face again, rounding the edges of her frown into a look of compassion. "War is never easy, especially for the women left behind." She paused, measuring her words like flour for a cake. "They don't give medals for that kind of bravery." Her eyes seemed distant, as if seeing another place in time, and for a moment, Emmy thought Lulu had forgotten she was there. Then Lulu jerked her head back to Emmy, and pursed her lips together. "I'm sorry for your loss."

Emmy stood there, blinking her eyes rapidly and trying not to cry as she began to understand that somehow this woman, with whom she shared no connection and didn't even like, comprehended her loss, and really was sorry that Ben was gone and Emmy was alone.

"Thank you." Emmy wiped at her eyes, embarrassed to find them wet.

Lulu bent down and picked up another cluster of fruit and began working in silence. Emmy was about to walk away when Lulu spoke. "You can stay and work here at Folly's Finds if you want, and I won't mind. I won't like it, but I won't mind."

Emmy wanted to laugh out loud at the incongruity of the old woman's words—as if *she* had a choice in the matter. But something about Lulu O'Shea intrigued Emmy—something about their shared love of books and maybe even how they both knew what it was like to be left behind. And Lulu had called her brave, which was the first time somebody had ever called her that.

There was a story there, just like between the covers of every book. And if Emmy left now, she'd never know it, would never know how it began or how it ended. Or what evil spirits Lulu was trying to chase away with all of her bottle trees.

Without a trace of sarcasm, Emmy spoke to the back of Lulu's head as the older woman continued to deadhead the fruit clusters. "Thank you."

When Emmy entered the store again, Abigail was back, looking at her expectantly. "I called the lawyers to postpone our meeting. They want you to call them back to tell them if ten o'clock tomorrow morning works for you."

Emmy shook her head, trying not to think too hard about what she was going to say. "Call them back and tell them that we're coming over now. I've made up my mind. I'll buy Folly's Finds, and Lulu can sell her trees from the back garden for as long as she wants."

"Are you sure?"

Emmy nodded. "Let's do it."

As Emmy watched Abigail pick up her cell phone and start entering the phone number, her scalp began to tingle again. She felt out of breath suddenly, the need for fresh air propelling her to the back door again and the odd little garden. Exiting the building, she leaned against the closed back door and took several deep breaths. Slowly, she opened her eyes, surprised to find herself alone in the garden, and Lulu nowhere in sight.

She walked down the steps again, toward the first bottle tree in the row in front of her. Leaning forward, she studied the twisted metal and the graceful limbs, noticing how most of the bottles had a metal ring around their necks that soldered them to the branch. But one bottle the color of spring grass was loose, inverted on a short limb with only gravity holding it in place. Just the perfect spot for a person wanting to hide a note. After Emmy glanced at the other nearby bottles, it appeared that all of them had a loose bottle, and she smiled to herself, wondering if this was Lulu's trademark.

She was about to go back inside and return to Abigail when she spotted the Nancy Drew book on the top step, placed neatly in the corner as if it had been put there deliberately so that that Emmy would see it.

Emmy stooped and retrieved the book, absently flipping pages as her gaze searched for Lulu between the bottle trees. Her fingers stopped at the back cover and Emmy glanced down, surprised. The first page, the one with the inscription to Lulu from Peter, was missing, cleanly torn off as if it had never been there.

Emmy looked around again for Lulu in case she had missed her, before clutching the book and returning inside, the door snapping shut behind her.

CHAPTER 9

Cat sat at the kitchen table, her legs crossed and a shoe dangling from her toes. Maggie watched as she flipped through the Sears catalog, pen in hand, circling any item that caught her interest. Maggie said good-bye to Martha, who for the third time had threatened to stop cleaning Cat's bedroom if she couldn't find the floor; then Maggie moved to stand behind Cat just as she was making a large black-ink lasso around something in the catalog.

Leaning closer, Maggie saw the silver foxtail jacket that had caught Cat's interest. "That's seventy-four dollars and fifty cents, Cat! Where are you expecting to get the money?"

Thumping the pen against the page, Cat said, "Oh, don't worry about me. I've got my widow's pension from Jim. As well as a few other . . . sources."

Maggie felt a little sick, thinking of what the other "sources" might be, and knowing they were nothing a good widow would involve herself with. "I hope you'll be respectful of Jim and not do anything to cheapen yourself just for something pretty to wear."

Cat let out an inelegant snort. "All the pretty girls are doing it, Mags. Those navy and coast guard men are just crawling all over the place, looking for a little company. Why shouldn't I get rewarded for it?"

"What about Robert? I thought you two were an item now."

Cat shrugged and flipped to another page. "I like him just fine, but he can be a real stick in the mud sometimes. His father owns a paper mill in Savannah, and he's going to help him run it after the war's over. He doesn't like asking for handouts from his dad, though, and insists on living on his military pay—and we both know how little that is."

"Then he certainly can't afford to buy you a fur coat."

"Nope. He certainly can't." As she spoke, Cat circled another fur jacket in a different style for $52.50. Turning the page, she tapped her finger on the lower-right-hand corner. "I'm going to order this leg makeup. Look right here." She pointed. "It's by Max Factor. It says 'Used by the stars in Hollywood for greater leg appeal. Lends a smooth, silky appearance to your legs. Easy, quick to apply. Leg makeup for that silk stocking glamour.' I swear I'm sick to death of not having stockings. And they're saying that they're going to start rationing sugar and gasoline soon, too."

"Where did you hear that?"

Cat jostled the shoe on her foot again. "At the post office today. There were all sorts of people there, and I heard a lot of news—one tidbit about somebody we both know."

Maggie refrained from acting too excited to hear, knowing her interest was inversely proportional to Cat's speed in telling her. Nonchalantly, she settled herself on a chair opposite her cousin and folded her hands on the table. "What'd you hear?"

Cat continued to thumb through the catalog with her pen, licking her finger every once in a while to turn the pages. When she was ready, she said, "Freddy Jameson's sister was there and she was bawling her eyes out and telling everybody that Freddy was killed last week. He was on a navy destroyer right off the coast up north somewhere—New Jersey, I think—and they're saying it was torpedoed by a German submarine."

Maggie looked down at her hands, remembering the shy young man who had always come into the store looking for adventure books and who had given her her first and only cigarette when she was thirteen and visiting for the summer. It had burned her throat and made her cough so badly that he'd run home to her father to get help, landing them both in trouble. Freddy had joined the navy right out of high school, and every once in a while, she'd gotten a postcard from him, and he'd always sign them with his name and a drawing of a cigarette, which made her smile.

"I can't believe it. He was here at Christmas. I saw him at church, and he told me he'd met a girl in Norfolk and was thinking about asking her to marry him."

Cat paused in her perusal of the catalog for a moment. "Pretty soon there won't be any eligible men left. Better get busy, Mags, or you're going to be an old maid, for sure."

Cat's eyes held a challenge in them, as if waiting for Maggie to say something about Peter. She wanted to; wanted to tell Cat how she'd let Peter kiss her and how he'd held her so tight, like he never wanted to let her go. But even so, she wasn't sure she wanted to hear Cat's response.

Instead, she focused attention on straightening the fruit in the centerpiece bowl. "Were they positive it was the Germans?"

"The survivors are saying that's what they saw, but the newspapers are reporting that it could have been mines. Mrs. Ellsworth at the post office has a bunch of newspaper clippings friends have been mailing her. There's one from Norfolk, Virginia, that says that sightings of German submarines are just rumors and that people spreading rumors should be put in jail for the rest of the war."

Maggie frowned. "I wish Robert were here—he'd know, wouldn't he?"

"I suppose. But he's down in Florida again and he's not sure now when he can come back. They're also talking about making us use blackout shades at sundown and painting the top half of our headlights so the beams can't be seen by German subs." A sly smile formed on her lips. "They're looking for members for the Ground Observer Corps to be airplane spotters. I think I might volunteer for that. It would mean not being able to help you as much at the store, but I think I should do something for the war effort."

Surprised at Cat's enthusiasm, Maggie nodded. "Maybe we both can. We could always alternate our schedules."

A look of annoyance flitted across Cat's face before she returned to the opened catalog. "I suppose you could, although you'll have to find somebody to watch Lulu." She flipped a page. "Oh, I picked up the mail while I was at the post office. It's on the counter by the coffeepot."

With excitement, Maggie turned to look for it, positive something must have arrived from Peter by now. He'd remembered to say good-bye this time, and at night when she closed her eyes, she could still taste his kiss. Jim's kisses had been sweet, so sweet that she'd always kissed him with her eyes wide-open. But Peter's kisses made her close her eyes so she could better see the things he made her want to do.

She spotted the stack of mail, mostly bills and a few letters, sitting on top of a small brown-paper-wrapped package. When she picked it up, a new book that still smelled of paper glue slid out of the opened end, and she caught it, holding it up to read the cover. She ran her hand across the title, *The Great Gatsby,* remembering Peter telling her how it was his favorite book, and how he'd borrowed her own dog-eared copy.

Focusing on the package, she frowned, realizing that someone had neatly cut the string and sliced open one end, allowing the book to slide out. "Do you know how this got opened?" Maggie turned around and held out the package to Cat, the cut string dangling from the bottom.

Without looking up, Cat said, "I opened it."

Maggie took a step closer but didn't say anything, waiting for Cat to look up. When she didn't, Maggie asked, "Why? It's addressed to me."

Cat finally looked up, her green eyes bright from the slanting light coming in from the kitchen window. "Because Peter might have been sending something to me, too, and stuck it in the package. I just wanted to check."

An icy chill swept down the back of Maggie's neck. Her mother had once told her that when you felt like that, somebody was walking over your grave, and for the first time, Maggie finally understood what she'd meant. "Why would he be sending something to you?" She hadn't wanted to ask that question, but it was too late to pull it back.

"Because he's my friend, too, Mags. You can't monopolize him just because you found him first, you know. He's actually the one who thought I'd make a good spotter."

"When did you talk to him?"

Cat shrugged, but it didn't mask her look of self-satisfaction. "I suppose you were working in the store. He was actually on the way there when I spotted him and asked for his help in carrying Jim's things to the car. I finally decided to get rid of Jim's clothes, what with storage space being what it is, but I needed a strong arm to help me. So I asked Peter."

A memory of Jim flashed in Maggie's mind; it had been his wedding day and Maggie had faced him in the receiving line on the front steps of the church. She'd pressed forward to kiss his cheek, surprised to find it as cold as her own hands despite the heat of the day. When she pulled back, he'd grabbed her arms and the look on his face made her think of a man who'd just discovered that his new and expensive shoes were too tight.

Maggie fell back into her chair, her fingers gripping the package so tightly that the tips turned white. "No, Cat, please. Don't."

"Don't what?" Cat's gaze faltered, her eyes slipping back to the splayed catalog.

Maggie put the book down on the table and reached across to grab Cat's hands in hers, not allowing Cat to pull away. "You're my family, Cat. I love you. Jim loved you. Isn't that enough?"

Cat didn't respond right away, but Maggie held on, not willing to give up. Finally Cat sniffed, and Maggie watched as a tear slipped onto the catalog page, the small drop spreading with greedy fingers, mutilating the face of one of the fur-clad models. Cat shook her head as if to clear it, and when she faced Maggie again, her face was twisted with an odd mixture of remorse and defiance.

"No, it's not. It will never be enough."

Maggie dropped Cat's hands as her cousin pushed back from the table, then ran from the room, and with a tightening in her chest, Maggie felt the truth of Cat's words.

"Maggie?"

Maggie swung her head around to where Lulu stood inside the back door holding a dark amber narrow-necked bottle that might have once contained some sort of tonic. Lulu's face was unreadable as always, leaving Maggie unsure of how long she'd been standing there. Forcing a smile, she said, "Yes, Lulu?"

She held out the bottle to her sister. "I think Amy left me a note but I can't get it out of the bottle."

Maggie took the bottle and held it up to the light, seeing the corner of a torn piece of paper that had been shoved into the neck. "How do you know it came from Amy?"

"I put a note in a bottle on Amy's tree, so I think this must be her answer. I went over to their house again, and their neighbor told me they'd been back a couple of days ago for just a few hours to collect the rest of their things, and then they left again. I figure Amy couldn't find me, so she stuck a note in this bottle—but she didn't roll it up like I did, so I can't get it out."

Gently, Maggie placed the bottle on the table. "I've got tweezers in the medicine cabinet in the bathroom. Why don't you run upstairs and get them and we'll see what we can do?"

When Lulu returned, Maggie easily plucked the scrap of paper from the upturned bottle before handing it to her little sister and waiting while she read the note to herself. Slowly, she raised her eyes and handed the note to Maggie. Squinting to read the tiny writing scribbled across every available space, she read:

we're going to live with my grandpappy in Greenville maybe
forever. I wish I could read your book. I wish we were staying in
Folly. I wish my daddy wasn't dead. But Mama says wishing is like
bailing out a johnboat with a thimble so I'd just better quit. I'll
miss you but Mama says it's okay to bring the bottle tree so I
can remember you just like you remember Jim with your tree.

   your best friend, Amy

Maggie gently squeezed Lulu's arm. "I'm sorry, Lulu. Amy was a
good friend to you."

Lulu stared back at her, her hazel eyes dry and somber. "Did you
mean it when you said you loved Cat?"

Surprised, Maggie nodded, struggling very hard to separate obliga-
tion from true affection. "I suppose I do." She stopped for a moment,
trying to think of a way to explain to a nine-year-old the complicated
feelings she had for Cat. Continuing, she said, "She and I were raised
more like sisters than cousins by our mama, so we share that bond.
And Mama taught me that I can still love a person while not always
loving their actions." Maggie sat back, satisfied with her answer, and
decided not to tell Lulu that Cat looked like their mama or how Cat
had been the one who'd let her scream and cry when Maggie's mother
had died because she understood what it was like. Or that Cat hadn't
started out so needy but had changed after her own mother died, and
Cat had begun to act as if she'd been cast adrift on the ocean. Maggie
had read about survival stories at sea, and how sailors turned to canni-
balism to stay alive. She'd pictured Cat that way, clinging to whatever
life had left her.

It was all of these things that had made Maggie say yes when her
mother made her promise to look after Cat, to understand how Cat
was different from most people and deserved love even when it appeared she was incapable of giving it. And Maggie had agreed because
of all of those things, but mostly because she was the only one left
who could.

Lulu continued to gaze at her for a long moment until she finally turned away and picked up her note from the table. "I guess I'll go collect scrap metal all by myself then." She began to walk away, but then stopped to turn around and face Maggie. "If you ever stop loving Cat, would you let me know?"

Maggie studied her younger sister as she would a stranger, noticing the short, squat body, the mousy brown hair and deep, mournful eyes, and wondered not for the first time what toll so many losses would take on Lulu as she grew into womanhood. It was times like this that Maggie missed her mother the most, wishing to have her back just for a moment to find out if she was doing things right. But like Amy's mother had said about bailing johnboats with thimbles, wishing would get her nowhere.

Straightening her back against the chair, Maggie said, "We never get to choose whether we love someone or not, Lulu. It's not like a gift you can give and take back. It just is."

Lulu continued to study her sister with those eyes that seemed too old in her face before nodding and turning away. "I'll be back by suppertime."

Maggie turned back to the empty bottle on the table and the small scrap of paper that had been hidden inside, and thought about poor Amy and her mother, and Cat, and the desperate measures people sometimes took just to survive.

CHAPTER 10

When Emmy pulled her Explorer into the driveway of the house, the sound of steady hammering was coming from the backyard. She leaned back against the headrest and closed her eyes. She didn't want to see or talk to anybody—she'd already had a day full of people as she'd struggled to find her way around the store and learn how it ran, in addition to learning how to operate the antique brass cash register that Abigail told her had been there since the store opened in the nineteen twenties. Silently, Emmy promised to herself that one of the first things she'd do would be to replace the antiquated register with a computerized inventory system.

Wearily, she shut the car door behind her and headed toward the hammering. She paused by the bottle tree, admiring the artistry of it and imagining Lulu bending each metal twig and placing each colorful bottle into a pattern pleasing to her eye and her artist's heart. Emmy still couldn't quite reconcile the Lulu O'Shea she knew in person with the woman who created the kind of inspired beauty that managed to touch the soul.

She spotted the amber bottle and dipped her head to peer inside. The rolled note remained near the neck of the bottle where she'd left it. *Come back to me.* She shivered, not knowing why, then looked up when she realized the hammering had stopped.

Heath stood on the partially completed dock wearing sneakers, socks, shorts, and nothing else. He held a hammer, looking at her expectantly, as if the sweat wasn't pouring from his face and down his tanned and, Emmy had to admit to herself, well-muscled torso. She forced her gaze up to his face and tried not to think about how his mother had named him after Emily Brontë's Heathcliff. His eyes traveled from the bottle tree back to her, reminding her that she'd been snooping. Blushing, she stammered, "I didn't mean to disturb you. I'll just go into the house. . . ."

He tossed the hammer down on the wooden boards. "You're not disturbing me. This is your house right now, so I'll stop making noise since you're back." He picked up a towel and wiped his face. "Let me go jump in the ocean to cool off. Then we can talk about some sort of schedule so I'm not always invading your space."

"Like right now? Don't you need a bathing suit?"

He smiled and the wrinkles at the corners of his eyes reminded Emmy of his mother. "Don't need one." He walked past her, then stopped when he realized she wasn't following him.

"I'll wait here."

"I'll keep my shorts on, promise."

She frowned at him to hide her blush. "It's not that. It's just, well, I don't have a bathing suit."

This time he almost laughed. "I wasn't asking you to jump in with me—just have a chat. But now that you mention it, it might not be such a bad idea for you to hang out at the beach for a while. You have the skin of a librarian."

Without waiting for her to respond, he began walking again down the driveway to the street, passing his bike leaning against the tree.

She caught up to him at the end of the driveway. "I told you already. I'm not a librarian."

"Right. You told me that."

A push of wind from the direction of the ocean lifted his hair, revealing a straight white scar that ran from his temple and disappeared into his hairline. His smile faded when he saw her looking at it, and he began to walk away again. "Are you coming?"

His dog, Frank, who'd been resting in the shade of the front porch, ran up to her and jogged by her side as they crossed the street and approached the sandy trail that was labeled as a beach access.

She could now hear the ocean and the cries of strange birds, and she stopped. "Wait."

Heath stopped, but Frank kept going, running faster.

"I've never seen the ocean before."

He looked at her expectantly as if waiting for her to make a case for stopping.

Feeling foolish again, she said, "Is there . . . I mean, should I be afraid of alligators or anything?"

He smiled as he walked toward her, but it wasn't mocking. "Alligators don't usually like salt water, so you're pretty safe from them on the beach." He glanced down at her kitten-heel pumps. "The sand's pretty deep next to the dunes; you might want to take those off."

He waited while she slipped off her shoes, then began to walk again. Looking behind him, he said, "Hey, if I were in a cornfield in Indiana, I'd probably be watching out for killer crows or something."

She bit the inside of her cheek to keep herself from smiling. "Yeah, right." She stopped again at the rise of the dune, where wooden steps had been placed to guide beachgoers down to the water.

"But we do have sharks," Heath shouted as he and Frank started to run toward the water, sand flying behind their heels until they'd reached the water's edge, man and dog quickly disappearing beneath the waves.

Emmy held her breath until both heads, shiny and wet, appeared above the surface like those of dark seals. Heath looked up at her and waved her forward, but still, she hesitated. She'd seen oceans in movies, and in her mother's photographs, but now, standing in front of the great Atlantic, she felt the pulsing of the waves, felt the power and breadth of the water as it bled out into the horizon, endless and liquid like the earth's lifeblood. It made her feel alive, unlike anything she'd felt under the broad, flat skies of home. As she stared out at the dark blue vastness, her veins seemed to pump with the ancient rhythm of the waves, giving her kinship to every person who'd ever lived by the water, yet at the same time making her feel very, very insignificant.

Emmy moved forward, the hot sand burning the soles of her feet as she looked out across the expanse of sand and saw the haphazard placement of large umbrellas scattered across the beach like brightly colored starfish. Children with buckets and shovels sat in clusters sculpting mounds of sand decorated with blobs of shells and other beach debris. Nearly naked sunbathers with bronzed and lobster red skin lay sprawled on chairs and towels like sacrificial victims to a sun god. She looked down at her own pale skin and remembered how Ben had loved touching it, marveling at its unblemished whiteness, which had never been exposed to the sun. What she'd once loathed, she'd begun to feel proud of, taking extra care of her skin with expensive lotions and sunscreen. She still did, out of habit, and quickly crossed her arms across her chest trying to hide the exposed skin from the sun.

Emmy stopped where the sand became smooth and wet, yet she was just out of reach of the encroaching waves. It was almost as if she believed that if she felt the ocean, she would understand what her mother loved and what she'd missed all of those years, and she wanted nothing to tie her to this place of strangers—this place that Ben had never been.

Heath and Frank emerged from the water, both shaking their heads in synchronicity and flicking water over each other and Emmy. She stepped back, wiping the water from her face. "Careful!"

"Sorry," said Heath, although his smile told her he wasn't really. "The water feels good—you should give it a try."

"I should actually get back inside or find a hat and sunscreen. My skin's not used to the sun."

Water clung to his lashes, making his eyes appear star-kissed. "The beach is really nice at sunset, especially since most of the tourists have packed up and gone home by then. You should come back then." He paused, looking at her intently as if he wasn't sure she'd come back on her own, as if it were important that she love this place. "I'll bring you sometime," he added.

She wasn't sure how to respond, so she said, "Were you serious about sharks?"

He began walking down the beach and she kept abreast of him, being sure to keep him on the ocean side and her feet dry.

"Yep. I've even caught a few from the pier. Have to throw back the babies, but you can keep the ones that are over a certain size. There used to be hammerheads and bull sharks, but nobody's seen those for almost twenty years. Now it's mostly sharp-nosed and black tips, with the occasional tiger shark and a few others."

She gave a wary glance over at the water. "Are they man-eaters?" Scenes from the movie *Jaws* flashed through her head, and from Heath's amused expression, it seemed that he was reading her mind.

He kept his gaze focused straight ahead. "Some of them." He let the tension build while they walked a little farther down the beach, and she found herself jogging to keep up with his long strides. "But mostly they leave people alone. You know, you have a much greater chance of being struck by lightning while standing in a cornfield than you do of getting eaten by a shark."

Emmy raised her eyebrows, still keeping a close eye on the shoreline for any telltale fins. "That's reassuring. Thanks."

"No problem."

They continued to walk, the salty breeze off the water a welcome respite from the sweltering heat. Frank continued to run in and out of the water, occasionally racing up to people on the shore, who greeted him by name and gave him a scratch behind the ear or a treat.

They'd passed several other people with dogs, all of them on leashes. "Isn't there some kind of dog-nuisance law for the beach?"

"Sure. No dogs allowed on the beach after ten in the morning or before six in the evening, and only on a leash."

She watched as Frank jogged up to a group spread out on blankets;

apparently they were getting ready to have supper on the beach. They greeted Frank with pats and food offerings, and Heath waved to all of them, giving Emmy a running litany of names and occupations as if she would remember any of them. The jumble of names she'd learned from Abigail that morning was already forgotten.

"And Frank is excluded from the rules?"

He sent her a sidelong glance. "Until somebody complains, I guess. He's actually pretty well behaved, and only goes up to people he knows. Otherwise, he pretends he's on a leash and sticks next to me."

She hid her smile as they picked their way across lines of large rocks that stretched like arms from the shore into the ocean, which Heath explained were groins placed there long before Hugo to help with the constant erosion of the beach. "The jetties in Charleston Harbor and these groins probably did more damage to the ecosystem than protect the shore. We actually have a beach renourishment project, where every eight years we get sediment pumped onto the front beach, but that's only temporary. And, unfortunately, it attracts more development."

"I would think that as a builder who owns some property here, you'd see it as a good thing."

"One would think. But Folly has been my family's home for generations. It's a little annoying to see the landscape changed so drastically by a few outsiders." With a shrug, he said, "I guess in the last few years, I've begun to think a little differently than I used to—altered my focus, you might say. Which is one of the reasons why I've been spending more time on Folly than in Atlanta."

She wanted to ask him what had changed to alter his focus, but he'd moved forward, as if to deliberately avoid any questions. His words irked her, bringing back memories of Ben and his sense of duty and love of country, which had sent him to the other side of the world and away from her and all that he loved.

She was still brooding when they turned around to go back the way they'd come and Heath asked, "So why are you here, Ms. Media Specialist with a master's degree in library science?"

She turned to look at him, seeing again the tanned skin, the longer hair, the careless posture in his shoulders—shoulders which had never carried a rifle or traveled in a convoy over mine-ridden roads and belonged to a man whose life's ambition now seemed to center on playing in the surf. She didn't want this man, who was made, it seemed, of sea and sun and sand, to question her motives or to attempt to know her loss. But his eyes were kind and not mocking, and her answer was a lot easier than she'd thought it would have been.

"My mother loved the beach." Emmy realized how stupid that sounded, and tried to clarify. "She grew up here and loved Folly, although I don't think I realized how much until recently. And she loved Folly's Finds from when she was a little girl. She patterned her own store in Indiana after it, actually."

He stopped and she stopped, too. "But what made you come here?"

She looked past him toward the ocean, feeling the pull and tug of the tide as if it were trying to take her someplace she didn't want to go. With a deep breath, she said, "I recently lost my husband, and my mother thought this place would be good for me."

They turned at the sound of a sharp cry behind them, and for a moment, they watched a gull circling something still and dark in the sand, flying down to peck at it before swooping up with a cry into the air again. It reminded Emmy of her grief, of the way she continued to live and breathe and eat, but every so often she would return to the dark speck inside, and renew her sorrow.

"I'm sorry. Was it expected?"

Emmy faced him again. "He was a soldier. I guess I would have been naive not to expect it, but I don't think it really ever occurred to me that I would never see him again."

He picked up a shell from the sand, then reached back and threw it as hard as he could into the rushing waves before turning back to her. "I hope you find what you're looking for here. I think you will."

There was something in his voice, as if he knew what she needed, and the memory of the note in the bottle tree flashed through her head. *Come back to me.* It was unlike her to hold back any questions when she wanted answers, but Heath Reynolds made her hesitate. And then it was too late because he bent down and pulled something out of the sand before holding it out to her in his palm. She stepped closer and saw what looked like a dark brown seed shell with two thin antenna-like protrusions from the top and bottom.

"It's called a devil's pocketbook, although they're actually skate egg sacks, and in May they're all over the beach." He handed it to her and she took it, feeling the slickness of the waterlogged casing against her fingers. "There're always surprises to find here in the sand. When I was a boy, my mother told me that what you found on the beach was just reminders that we're not alone in the world. That you'll always find what you need if you look hard enough."

Emmy began walking again, unable to answer because of the old familiar feeling teasing the back of her neck. They passed a woman who was at least in her sixties wearing a bikini and a baseball cap with two long gray braids dangling from each side of her head. For a brief moment, Emmy thought it was Lulu before she realized that what she knew of Lulu did not include exposing any skin on the beach. Thinking of Lulu, she turned to Heath. "I meant to ask your mother this, but I figure you would know as well as she does—was Lulu ever married?"

With a soft grin, he said, "Definitely not. There's never been a man good enough for her, I think."

Emmy studied him for a moment, unsure of whether he was joking.

Heath continued. "I think when she was younger, she fell in love, but I don't know what happened to that relationship."

"Was his name Peter, do you know?"

He thought for a moment, then shook his head. "I don't think I've heard that name mentioned before. You can ask her, though."

"I'd rather not." She said the words without thinking, then quickly looked up to see if Heath had taken offense and was relieved to find him smiling.

"Where did you come across the name?"

"In the box of books your mother sent to Indiana. There was a 1942 edition of a Nancy Drew mystery book and inside someone named Peter had inscribed it to Lulu with the words, 'Be good and stay sweet.' I gave it to Lulu today, but she tore out the inscription page before giving it back to me. I thought it odd, but she doesn't seem that open to questions."

"I can ask her myself if you like."

Emmy wanted to say no, reluctant for him to be more involved in her life. But the alternative was even less appealing so she nodded. "If you wouldn't mind. And I have one more request, and I promise it will be my last. The books in your house—the ones that once belonged to your grandmother Maggie—can I sort through them and rearrange them in some sort of order? They look as if they were just thrown haphazardly on the shelves, and I thought you might like to know what you have."

He grinned. "That really bothers you, doesn't it?"

"Yes," she admitted without blinking. "It really does."

"Sure—have at it. And if you find something that you really want, it's yours."

"But not if it's valuable. I'll be happy to give you fair market value for anything I find."

"No, really. I don't care. You can take all of them if you like. Or sell them at the store—it doesn't matter to me. I've learned to believe in not holding on to things anymore. They're only things."

Emmy stopped abruptly, thinking about the tightly folded flag and Ben's Medal of Honor, which she kept in her bedside drawer, and of Ben's clothes still hanging in the closet in the bedroom at her parents' house. If she had her purse with her, she could reach in and show Heath the nail clippers that had once been Ben's, and the dog tags he'd been wearing when a roadside bomb exploded near his convoy. They were only things, true; but they were all she had left of what her life was supposed to have been.

She forced the words out of her constricted throat, feeling dizzy enough to faint. "Don't say that. Don't." She sucked in a wheezing breath. "You don't know." She swallowed, trying to force the hot, humid air into her lungs. "You don't know what it's like." She stared at him, his image shimmering in the heat like a mirage. "Or you'd know how precious things can be."

The wind lifted his hair again, revealing the scar. She waited for him to protest, to tell her she was wrong, but he just stared at her with somber light brown eyes.

"Maybe," was all he said before turning his attention back to the water, where the waves were creeping closer to shore, each bubbling finger grasping more sand than before.

"I know my way back from here," Emmy said abruptly, stumbling up into the thicker sand, and not caring that they hadn't talked about scheduling his work time on the dock. "Good-bye." She didn't turn around as she headed toward the first beach-access walkway she could find. She passed the same gull they'd seen before, still in its macabre dance as it swooped and swirled over its find in the sand. She stopped and watched, remembering what Heath's mother had said about the treasures buried in the sand. *You'll always find what you need if you look hard enough.*

Turning away, she headed toward the dunes, with their bald pates covered in sparse grassy hair, the sound of the gull like laughter behind her back.

CHAPTER 11

A heavy Sunday afternoon downpour darkened the sky and the watery world around the house, creating a cool oasis from which Emmy didn't want to emerge. She'd spent most of the morning lugging books down from the turret, dangling from the circular staircase again and again to grab hidden and stacked books, refusing to let a single book go unrescued and uncataloged. She then hefted them into the living room in haphazard towers, creating a tiny city of leather and paper.

Her goal had been to have this job done in a week, but she'd quickly found that she didn't have as much free time as she'd originally thought. Although helping at Paige's Pages had prepared her for a lot of the work at Folly's Finds, it was a far cry from the responsibilities of actually owning a store. Handling and anticipating the needs and requirements of the employees, Janell, Abigail, tourists, and locals overwhelmed her at times, in part because everything was new, and also because by nature she was more reserved than what was required of a business owner on Folly Beach. She was relieved that the residents didn't ask her about Ben, and wondered if that had been Abigail's doing.

She found herself calling her mother often, asking for advice on bookstore business matters. At least that was how the calls always started. But then the conversation would turn to other things, like the change in the color of the cornfields, or good books they'd read recently, or her father's health. Strangely, these were topics that were never discussed when Emmy lived with her mother, as if the lines between mother and daughter were placed in a minefield, too easily ignited. And now Emmy had begun to tell her mother about Folly and the people here, and Paige listened and asked questions with the intensity of an exile too far from home.

Thankfully Emmy hadn't had to deal with Heath, who, according to Abigail, had gone back to Atlanta for several weeks for business. Emmy had forgotten that he was a developer and architect in Atlanta, and found it curious that he would choose to spend so much time on Folly, away from his company and the root of his business. She thought often of their argument the last time she'd seen him, wanting each time to feel the anger she'd felt then. Instead, she kept seeing the scar on the side of his head and the guarded look in his eyes, which made her think of a funhouse mirror you found at arcades where what you saw was a distortion of what you thought you would see.

Best of all Lulu kept to herself, moving unnoticed to and from her bottle garden behind the store, miraculously appearing whenever a potential bottle-tree customer visited the store. Emmy was amazed at the sheer number of people who came to Folly's Finds for the sole purpose of buying a tree, as well as the letters she received from all over the country inquiring about ordering one.

Emmy stood and rubbed her back, sore from all the lifting and leaning, and wondered if she was too young to take a nap. She eyed the empty shelves, thinking of the next step that involved scrubbing the emptied shelves and lining them with the rolls of acid-free paper she'd ordered online.

Instead, she backed out of the alcove of the turret and left the bedroom, closing the door behind her so she wouldn't be reminded of what awaited her. Then she returned to the living room, feeling reassured that the stairs and shelves would still be there later after she'd gone through more of the books.

Before she started, she turned on the stereo and stuck in a Glenn Miller CD. She'd been surprised to find it amongst the REM, Foo Fighters, and Rolling Stones, but somehow big-band music fit her mood. Maybe it was the photos on the walls taken in the nineteen forties that inspired her, but it was to the brass notes of "String of Pearls" that Emmy opened up her laptop, where she'd already transferred her inventory notes from the books in the box onto an Excel spreadsheet, and flipped it on before seating herself next to it on the floor in front of the first stack.

As she'd done before, she began at the top, pulling each book from the stack and meticulously turning every page in search of any writing. She still had her pile of books in the bedroom with the margin writings she'd found previously, and she intended to add any more she found to that stack. It had begun to occur to her that the messages might make more sense to her if she figured out some sort of order for them, and had already started on her computer a document about the messages she'd found so far. She'd studied them for a long time, and the only thing she'd concluded was what she'd already known from the start—that they were love notes between a man and a woman. The clandestine aspect of the love affair was still mere speculation, but she hoped she'd find more in Heath's books, if only because they came from the same source—his mother's attic.

She'd reached only the fourth book before she found the first note. It was in a later edition of *Robinson Crusoe*, and in the familiar woman's handwriting in blue ink were written the words: *I miss you. It's cold outside and the pavilion is deserted.*

Feeling satisfied that this was more evidence to support her hypothesis of a clandestine affair, she placed the book on the floor next to her to start a new pile, and reached for another book. It was nearly an hour later that she found the next message, this one in a worn copy of Mary Shelley's *Frankenstein*. In the familiar broad strokes of the man's handwriting were written the words: *Nothing of him that doth fade / But doth suffer a sea change / Into something rich and strange.*

Emmy recognized the words from Shakespeare's *The Tempest*, but wondered at their meaning in the message. What sea change? And who was the "him" referring to? She turned the page, seeing the impression of the words on the next page as if the writer had again written with agitation.

The CD ended, and she got up to replace it with a Tommy Dorsey's greatest-hits album and poured herself a glass of wine as "In the Blue of Evening" began to play. Emmy's mother always claimed that music was a subliminal advertisement for dancing, and Emmy began swaying across the room, avoiding the stacks of books, as she recalled the steps from watching her parents dance.

She waltzed into the dining area, where she hadn't yet ventured, preferring to eat her meals on the bar stools at the granite kitchen island. She turned away from the windows and saw for the first time the wall arrangement of four more old photographs, matted in matching bleached and distressed wooden frames, and stopped. Taking a step forward, she took a sip of wine and began to study the people in the pictures, trapped forever in time in their wooden boxes like butterflies.

The photograph on the upper left was a wedding photo of a bride and groom standing outside on a boardwalk with the ocean behind them. The man wore the white uniform of a navy enlisted man, with dark shoes and a dark tie that crossed over his chest. He was tall and light haired, and while not what Emmy would call handsome, he had a charming smile and warm eyes that tilted up at the corners, which probably made him look like he was smiling even when he wasn't.

The bride looked familiar, and after Emmy had studied the photograph for a moment, she realized that it was the same woman in the bathing suit in the photograph from the living room, Heath's great-aunt Catherine. She was beautiful in her bathing suit, and even more so on her wedding day in a dress of white lace and clutching a tumbling bouquet of white roses. But whereas her groom's face was open and smiling, her expression was a little unsure: an arched eyebrow that looked almost victorious matched with eyes that seemed more surprised than joyful. It was an odd combination for a wedding day, as odd as the two individuals that seemed to be mismatched as a couple.

Her gaze strayed to the next photograph of the woman she recognized as Maggie standing outside a store that Emmy easily recognized as Folly's Finds. It was hard to determine the color in black-and-white, but it was lighter than the current pink, and the door was completely different, with only two large windowpanes devoid of any stickers.

Maggie wore peep-toe pumps and a prim checkered dress buttoned up to the neck. As Emmy had noticed before, she wasn't beautiful, but her face demanded attention from the sheer intensity of her expression and the light in her eyes. Unlike Catherine, Maggie was a person Emmy wished she could meet, if only to understand how a person could remain alone in the face of a hurricane.

The third picture was of the little boy, whom Heath had told her was his father, John. He stood in a striped shirt and overalls, holding a fishing line with a tiny fish dangling from the end. His face was split with a grin, the boy apparently oblivious to the size of his catch.

The last photograph made Emmy pause as she sipped her wine. A male in a dark-colored suit and tie stared out at the photographer with a questioning look, as if he wasn't sure why his picture was being taken. He was seated at a table and people were dancing behind him. He held a cigarette in one hand and a bottle of Pabst in the other, and his head was turned slightly as if he had been caught by surprise by the photographer. A gold signet ring winked from his finger, but the letter on the top of it was blurred, as if the photographer had caught the subject in movement. The man was young, about thirty, and undeniably handsome in an old-fashioned kind of way. But his eyes in the photograph were what made a person stop and pause; light and piercing, they conveyed much more than surprise. They were the eyes of a man unsure yet confident at the same time, a juxtaposition that Emmy presumed would break an ordinary man.

She stared at the pictures for a long time, making a mental note to ask Abigail more about them. Then she poured herself another glass of wine and returned to the stacks of books. Seating herself in her familiar spot on the carpet again, she reached for another book.

The rain continued its deluge outside, and twice she went to the window to check the level in the marsh, watching the tall grass sink lower and lower beneath water. She relaxed when the rain finally tapered to a persistent drizzle when the dock was still above the waterline.

Emmy sorted and inventoried and searched through pages of books for nearly two hours, switching from wine to an unbearably sweet tea that Abigail had sent home with her. Emmy had been assured it was a taste she'd become accustomed to, but she wasn't sure. Her mother had always made unsweetened tea for her father, which made Emmy wonder what other concessions her mother made when she moved out of South Carolina.

It was nearly seven o'clock when Emmy's stomach began rumbling, and she realized she hadn't eaten since breakfast. Emmy leaned back and sighed, then surveyed her progress. She'd inventoried about seventy-five books—out of approximately five hundred—and three of them were first editions of moderately valuable volumes. And she'd found three more books with notes—two from the man, and one from the woman. She'd ask Heath again about the first editions, and offer payment or at least a percentage of whatever she sold them for. She was thinking about moving the store's rare book and document business online, and these three would be perfect on the home page.

She picked up her laptop and opened the correct document and began to type in the appropriate columns:

Moll Flanders, *Page 105, Female—I saw you today at the Post Office. I waited across the street until you left so others wouldn't see the way I look at you. She complained to me that you are gone most nights, doing your civilian duty, and I told her she should be proud. I know that I am. I must see you.*

Huckleberry Finn, *Page 34, Male—Forgive me.*

Canterbury Tales, *Page 222, Female—Yes, yes, yes. You make it impossible to say no and I can no longer consider the repercussions. All's fair in love and war, and I cannot think how very true those words are.*

Emmy saved the document, then slowly closed her laptop's lid, not ready to stop but realizing she should to avoid this hunt for two unknown people becoming an obsession. She placed the laptop on a side table and stood, her knees stiff and cracking. As she stretched, she spotted a book about five volumes down in a nearby stack. Crouching next to it, she carefully pulled it out and flipped open the cover to Fitzgerald's *The Great Gatsby.*

Slowly she turned the opening pages, pausing when she reached the title page. There, in the same scrawl she recognized from Lulu's Nancy Drew book, were the words: *To Margaret, a woman of boundless beauty and substance. Yours always, Peter.*

Emmy stared at it for a long time before grabbing the copy of *Huckleberry Finn* to compare the handwriting. The crush of disappointment surprised her, making her realize that maybe it was too late to avoid an obsession. She wasn't a handwriting expert by any means, but it was clear even to her that the notes in the book margins hadn't been written by the mysterious Peter. The unidentified man wrote with the same bold scrawl as Peter, but the words were slanted to the left instead of the right, his L's and T's written with loops. Emmy was about to close the book when she noticed one similarity: in the P's and B's and D's, the legs of the letters stood alone, the ensuing curves not intersecting the lines at any point.

Still, the rest of the handwriting was different enough to convince her that there were two separate writers. At least she had a name, and she made another mental note to ask Abigail.

Slowly she closed the book and put it on the side table to go through later. She was walking toward the kitchen to grab a frozen dinner to stick in the microwave when she heard the distinct sound of a key turning the front-door latch.

Emmy was frantically looking for some sort of weapon when a tall, slender woman walked into the kitchen. They stood staring at each other, and Emmy wasn't sure who was more surprised.

"Can I help you?" she asked.

"I was about to ask you the same thing." The woman spoke with a Southern drawl, her voice deep. She twirled a set of car keys in her hand, and when they slipped from her fingers, she left them where they fell.

Emmy almost smiled, remembering a nearly identical conversation she'd had with Heath on her first day in the house. "I'm Emmy Hamilton. I'm renting this house from Heath Reynolds for a few months."

The woman raised an elegant auburn eyebrow, perfectly formed and set above a pair of large green eyes. Emmy noticed how incredibly beautiful the woman was at the same time she smelled the alcohol on her breath. The woman's words weren't slurred, making Emmy wonder if she'd had a lot of practice with that.

"He sure didn't waste any time. Is he here?"

"Excuse me?"

Ignoring Emmy's question, the woman walked over to the master bedroom and peered inside at the neatly made bed and the remaining stacks of books Emmy hadn't yet moved into the great room.

Joining her in the doorway, Emmy said, "If you're referring to Heath, no, he's not here. And may I ask who you are and why you're here?"

The woman looked down at Emmy, exaggerating the difference in their heights. Then she slid out of her high-heeled sandals and began to walk back to the kitchen, barefoot. Emmy couldn't help but notice how even the woman's feet were beautiful, the tip of each well-formed toe painted a crimson red.

The woman opened up a cabinet and pulled out a wineglass, then made her way back to the bar in the great room and helped herself to the opened bottle of wine. After taking a sip, she said, "I'm Jolene Quinn. This house was built for me."

"Oh," Emmy managed, watching as Jolene eyed the stacks of books along with the spare furniture and framed photographs hanging from the walls. She recalled what Lulu had said about Jolene, how they favored each other but that Jolene was prettier and with a bigger chest.

"I love what you've done with the place," Jolene said as she took another sip of her wine. "What is this—early librarian?"

Defensive now, Emmy said, "Actually I haven't done anything with the place. The furniture and books are Heath's, but Abigail framed and hung the pictures." She stopped herself from explaining more about the books. "You know, I don't think you're supposed to be here. As I said, I'm renting the house."

Jolene let out an inelegant snort, then stumbled, sloshing red wine from her glass. "How can that be? It's my house."

Emmy reached over and took the glass and carefully set it on a sofa table before leading Jolene to the couch. "I want you to sit here and rest while I call someone to come get you." She didn't wait for Jolene to protest, and doubted Jolene could pull herself off from the couch.

Emmy dialed Abigail's cell phone, and was surprised when Heath answered it.

"This is Emmy. I was trying to reach your mother."

"She's right here—she just picked me up from the airport. She's driving, so I answered the phone. Is there anything I can help with?"

Emmy paused for a moment, trying to figure out how to word her response. "Yes, actually." She stuck her head around the corner and spotted Jolene now horizontal on the couch, her red hair partially obscuring her face. Her eyes were closed, and she was snoring quietly. "Your fiancée is here, and she's passed out on the couch. I was wondering if you had any suggestions."

Heath uttered a muffled curse. "I'll be right there. I'll have my mom drop me off, and I'll drive Jolene home. I'm assuming her car is there."

"She had a set of car keys when she arrived."

"I'll be there in forty-five minutes. Call me if she wakes up before then."

Emmy hung up the phone and returned to the living room to keep watch on Jolene while she waited. Emmy sat down on the couch opposite the one Jolene was on and noticed for the first time the beautiful oval sapphire solitaire Jolene wore on her left hand. It was a cushion-cut stone, like Emmy's grandmother's ring, and Emmy wondered if it was an antique. Her eyes strayed to Jolene's face and found that the woman's eyes were open and silently contemplating her.

Jolene didn't lift her head when she spoke. "He wasn't so mean before the radiation, you know."

Emmy leaned forward, recalling with startling clarity the scar on Heath's temple. "What radiation?"

But Jolene had already closed her eyes again and resumed her quiet snoring.

It took Heath thirty-five minutes to get there, each minute an agony as Emmy tried to recall each word she'd said to him on the beach.

She heard the car outside and a door shutting. Running to the front door, she opened it before he could knock. After pulling it wide, she held her finger to her lips. "She's still sleeping."

He entered, and she saw he wore suit pants and a long-sleeved business shirt with an unbuttoned collar, making her picture him hastily unknotting a tie and discarding it as soon as he could.

He seemed pale and drawn, as if being away from the beach had taken a physical toll. He glanced over at the sleeping Jolene and took in the partially filled wineglass on the table and didn't seem to look too surprised. His eyes were tired when he spoke, and she tried not to stare too hard at his scar. "Why is she here?"

"I was hoping you could tell me. She told me that the house had been built for her."

He rubbed the stubble on his jaw, making a rasping sound. "It was.

But that was when we were still engaged." He sighed heavily. "Jolene has a drinking problem. I guess some people have a problem dealing with life when it doesn't turn out the way it's supposed to."

Emmy jerked her chin up, her defensiveness disappearing when Heath ran his fingers through his hair, exposing the scar. She wanted to ask him about it, but held back, unsure if she'd be willing to reciprocate. And maybe leaving messages in bottles was the same as speaking to empty rooms: impotent communication with the ghosts of what might have been.

"She can stay here tonight if that helps. I really don't mind and she's already on the couch."

He shook his head. "No, my mom said to bring her to their house—she went on ahead to put fresh sheets in the guest bedroom."

They both looked over at the sleeping woman, whose deep auburn hair spilled over the arm, making her look like a princess in a fairy tale. Then Emmy said, "I'll go get her shoes and car keys and open the car door for you."

As she collected Jolene's things, Heath spoke. "I asked Lulu who Peter was."

Emmy straightened, the high-heeled sandals dangling in her hand. "What did she say?"

"She didn't." He grinned slightly. "Once you get to know Aunt Lulu, you begin to understand what each of her silent stares means. The one she gave me was distinctly 'none of your business.' You might have better luck asking her yourself."

Emmy looked at him dubiously. "What makes you say that?"

"Well, she would never lay a switch on you, and some of us have very painful memories of that happening in the past."

Despite herself, Emmy smiled. "Ouch. Still, I'll have to think about it."

He seemed to notice the stacks of books for the first time. "How's the sorting going?"

"Not too bad. It's definitely a long project but I'm having fun." She glanced over at Jolene to make sure she was still sleeping. "I was wondering if anybody has ever noticed any messages scribbled in the margins of the books. There're quite a few, and I'm wondering who might have written them."

Heath raised his eyebrows. "Messages?" He shook his head. "Sorry to be so ignorant again, but I don't think so. Remember, those books came out of my grandmother's store in nineteen eighty-nine and have remained in storage for twenty years. The only person who would probably know more is Lulu."

Emmy grimaced. "I was afraid you were going to say that. And I don't think I'd bother, except . . ." She stopped, aware that she'd been about to tell him that these voices from the past were her main reason for getting up in the morning ever since she'd discovered the first one. That these unknown lovers had awakened emotions in her that she thought were long dead.

His eyes were serious, and again she felt as if he knew what she'd meant to say. "Sounds right up your alley—these messages from the past. Like talking to ghosts, isn't it?"

Her mother had said the same thing, except to Paige ghosts weren't just the dead; they were the spirits of what could have been. Emmy had always believed that the specters of her little brothers haunted her mother not because they had died, but because they represented the death of the life Paige had always dreamed for herself.

Heath moved to stand near the couch, where Jolene lay. Looking down at her, he said softly, "I don't believe in ghosts."

Emmy turned away and began searching for the car keys, finding them by the door, where Jolene had dropped them. Heath carefully lifted Jolene in his arms, then followed Emmy out the front door to the Audi sedan parked half sticking out into the street. He laid her in the backseat, using his rolled-up suit jacket as a pillow; then he gently shut the door.

"Thank you," he said, his eyes somber again, making Emmy wonder if what he'd said about not believing in ghosts was true.

"Anytime," she said as he walked to the driver's side door and opened it.

He started the engine and backed into the street, waving as he drove by, the tires loud against the wet pavement. When she could no longer see the taillights of the car, she ran to the back of the house and flipped the floodlights on before kicking off her shoes and stepping into the backyard.

The unfamiliar sounds of the marsh sang to her like a lullaby in a foreign language, the tune recognizable but the words untranslated. Her feet sank into the wet grass as she made her way to the bottle tree, her curiosity surrounding Heath and Jolene too piqued to wait until full daylight.

Emmy grasped the bottle in which she'd seen the note and held it up to the floodlight. She squinted her eyes and shook the bottle to be sure, but when she looked at it against the light, she saw that the bottle was totally and completely empty.

Come back to me. She started to cry, recognizing the words that she'd said to empty rooms long after Ben had gone, haunted by the ghost of the life they'd never have.

Carefully, she replaced the bottle, then stood for a long time in the wet, sandy grass under a starry sky. The scent of the marsh at night comforted her like a shawl as she wrapped her ghosts around her, not yet ready to tell them good-bye.

CHAPTER 12

M aggie searched for shells and rocks big enough to hold down the four corners of the blanket she'd placed on the sand as far from the surf as she could get it. They would be tucked away behind rocks and the scrubby brush that littered the less-inhabited side of the island, but in full view of the lighthouse on Morris Island.

Not that they would need to seek much privacy. Neither the season nor the currents on this end of the island were conducive to bathers or beachgoers, so they would have the beach to themselves. Large waves crashed against what was left of the section of Morris Island that had once contained not only the lighthouse but the lightkeeper's house and other outbuildings. The tides and time had long since separated Morris Island from Folly, leaving behind a small creek that ran between the two islands at low tide. But when the tides rose, the encroaching water erased the land around the light like a vengeful finger, drawing in the sand until all that was left was a small spit of land only slightly larger than the base of the lighthouse.

The lighthouse keeper had left and the outbuildings had been dismantled when the light was automated in nineteen thirty-eight, and the Army Corps of Engineers came in and built a steel bulkhead around the base of the lighthouse to protect it from erosion. It was a lonely place now, which was why Maggie loved it. It was always the place she'd go to think and be alone, knowing she wouldn't be interrupted. Locals knew that the undertow and currents were too strong here for swimming, yet the summer influx of visitors always meant an occasional drowning. Maggie had grown up believing that the erosion and the currents were simply reminders to those who would listen that man was temporary, the ocean eternal.

She watched as fiddler crabs rode in on a wave, then disappeared like miniature magicians into tiny holes. As a child, she'd spent hours on the beach, watching the crabs and the oddly elegant black skimmers with their red-and-black beaks as she and her mother searched for sea glass, turtle eggs, and other watery treasures given up by the sea. Her memories of her mother were strong here, the in and out of the tide like her mother's breath. The sound and sway of the ocean was so much a part of her that she couldn't imagine living anywhere else.

That was why she wanted to give Peter a picnic homecoming on the beach. His job had been keeping him busy traveling to accounts from state to state, marketing the products his father's factory had begun making for both the military and civilian sectors. He always sent her presents, mostly books, from his travels, and he'd started to include long letters about where they'd go once the war was over. His words thrilled her, made her think of the future, when the war would be relegated to the past and boys she'd known since birth wouldn't be dying in the killing fields of Europe and the Pacific. The picnic was meant to welcome Peter back as much as to ground him to her Folly Beach, so he'd understand that no matter how far they might travel together, this would always be her home.

Maggie shivered and pulled her sweater closer around her. It had been an unseasonably warm day, but here on the beach, with the wind blasting around this edge of the island, the temperature was much cooler. Just as she was placing the last rock, she heard her name called.

Whipping her head around, she spotted Peter approaching with a bare head, carrying his shoes and jacket.

Maggie started walking but she broke into a run as soon as she could see the smile on his face and the sun glinting off his hair. He ran toward her, too, then dropped his shoes and jacket in the sand to embrace her. Their kiss was long and sweet, his tongue tasting hers as his arms pulled her closer to his body. And then his hands were cupping her face, his lips kissing her closed eyes, her cheeks, and her neck, and she knew in her heart that she would never let him go.

"Why are you crying?" he asked.

Maggie opened her eyes, surprised. "I . . . don't know. I suppose it's because I'm so happy to see you." She buried her face in his neck and heard him sigh as he pulled her even closer to him. "I missed you."

Still clinging to each other, they walked back toward the blanket, the wind lashing at them in impatient bursts. She smiled shyly at him. "I wasn't sure you'd be here. Your letter said you'd be back on Folly at noon, but since I had no way of reaching you, I crossed my fingers and gave your landlady a message that I'd be here and hoped for the best."

He leaned over and kissed her, and she wanted to cry again. "And so here I am." He eyed the large wicker picnic basket. "I hope there's food in there because I'm starving. Missing you seems to deplete all of my energy."

She smiled up at him, chewing on her lower lip; then she knelt to begin unpacking the basket. "I made fried chicken and corn bread, but it's unsweetened on account of the sugar rationing. And no Coca-Cola, either, for the same reason. But I made blackberry tea, which I think is very tasty, if I may say so myself."

He reached for her hand and brought it to his lips for a kiss. "If you made it with your own hands, then it will be more than sweet enough."

She laughed at his silliness and handed him his plate of food, then watched as he ate it, her own plate untouched. She couldn't believe he was there, with her, after being away for so long.

He paused in his chewing and swallowed. "Aren't you hungry?"

Nodding, she took a bite of her chicken and washed it down with a sip of tea, not tasting a thing.

When they were finished eating, he rolled his jacket up for a pillow and lay back, pulling her up against him like nesting spoons. He kissed the back of her neck, and she thought she'd die from the pleasure of it. She reached for his hand, which was nestled at her waist, and squeezed it. "Don't go again. Please. It gets harder and harder each time."

"I know. I don't like leaving you. But this is war, and we all must play our part, although I feel sure that the war will be over soon."

She rolled a little to face him. "You sound so confident."

He shrugged. "With the United States now fighting with England and its allies, I can't imagine that it will go on much longer, that's all."

"I hope you're right. I really hope you are."

Leaning down, he kissed her nose, then lay back on the blanket. "So, tell me all the news from here. Don't leave out anything; I want to feel as if I've lived it all with you."

Smiling, Maggie snuggled into his chest. "I already mentioned the sugar rationing, and gas rationing is going to be right around the corner, I'm afraid. All lights have to be extinguished at midnight, and every house has mandatory blackout shades now. We've even started painting the top half of our headlights so no stray light can be seen out in the ocean."

She felt him rub his chin against the back of her head. "Are they really taking a German threat that seriously?"

"Yes. We've been hearing reports from North Carolina and Florida about people standing on shore witnessing ships being blown out of the water. And then, for days, wreckage will wash up on the beaches. Oil slicks are the only things left to show where the ship had once been."

"Is the coast guard doing anything about it?"

"All I know is what I hear on the radio or read in the newspaper—and that's not a whole lot because I can't stand hearing so much bad news, so I avoid it—but apparently we're fighting the submarines with only a few ill-equipped coast guard cutters—mostly because the navy seems to be focused on the Japanese in the Pacific."

"Coast guard cutters? Against German U-boats?"

"I don't know what good they can do, and Mrs. Ellsworth at the post office says not enough because it seems the Germans are sinking oil tankers every day. Mr. Ickes—he's the Secretary of the Interior and in charge of fuel resources—says that it will be a dire situation for the United States if we keep losing all that oil. Which is funny because the newspaper writer said that each tanker was just a small amount of our oil and would only temporarily affect a small section of the country."

He kissed the back of her neck again. "It's hard to know who to believe."

She sighed and nestled closer. "But they're taking the threat of an air attack pretty seriously in Charleston. They're sandbagging the roofs of hotels and publishing the locations of refugee and casualty centers in the papers. They've gone so far as to designate public bomb shelters—in Charleston! Even here on Folly, they've started doing an air-raid siren every Saturday at noon so people will know what to do just in case of an airplane sighting. It's all rather frightening."

Peter was silent for a moment "And all of this is on speculation? Or has someone actually seen something to make the area feel threatened?"

"Not that I know of. Except several people did see an explosion out at sea, but we never found out exactly what it was, even though the navy said they were investigating. I think everyone's just thinking it's better to be safe than sorry." A pair of sanderlings flew overhead, their pure white underbodies identifying them from their fellow shorebirds. "Cat's going through training to be an aircraft spotter for the Ground Observer Corps. I think it will be good for her, to give her a purpose. She's been so . . . lost, I suppose, ever since her mother died. It got worse after Jim was killed. I just . . ."

Peter squeezed her hand. "You just what?"

His voice was soft and reassuring, coaxing her into admitting something she'd never admitted, even to herself. "I want her to have a distraction that's not self-destructive. That doesn't involve . . . you." She closed her eyes, glad her face was turned away from his.

"Me?"

"Cat's very beautiful."

Peter leaned close to her ear. "And what does that have to do with me?"

Maggie swallowed, and continued to keep her eyes closed. "Men are very attracted to her. They can't seem to help themselves." She felt a gentle pressure on her chin as Peter tilted her face toward him again, and she opened her eyes.

"Sweet Margaret, are you so blind that you can't see your own beauty? I barely notice Cat when you're in the room. You fill a space in my heart, and there's no room in there for anybody else. Can you believe me, Margaret? Can you?"

She nodded, her throat too tight to speak. With his thumb pad, he wiped her cheeks, then kissed her gently on the lips. He lay back down beside her, and she sighed, losing herself in the warmth of his body beside hers.

"I was thinking about signing up to be a spotter, too, if only to keep my mind busy so that I don't have to miss you as much."

She felt his arms stiffen. "I know I have no right to say this, but I don't want you put in harm's way. When I'm away from you, I like knowing you are safe at home or your little shop, filled with books. I don't know if I could bear knowing you were out in the elements, making yourself a target for the enemy."

"But I really don't think there's any danger. Remember, nobody's seen anything off the South Carolina coast."

He squeezed her hand again. "Please, Margaret. I only ask this one thing so that I can continue to do my work for the war effort without worrying about you."

She was touched by his need to see her safe. "Oh, Peter, if you really feel that way, I could find another way to serve my country."

"You give discounts to the servicemen who buy from your store, don't you?"

Maggie nodded.

"That's a service right there. Besides, doesn't Lulu need you? She's a sweet girl, but I can see how much she looks to you for guidance. Losing a mother isn't easy, as we both know. Being around for her, and continuing to give discounts to those in uniform could be the best benefit you can give to our country."

His words did have a certain logic to them, and she found herself agreeing for now. It felt so good to be in his arms that she didn't want to argue and ruin the mood.

Peter must have felt the same way because he squeezed her again and asked, "Is there anything you need? Anything you can't get here that I can bring to you next time?"

She thought for a moment, then shook her head. His concern and care for her had made her feel confident and flirtatious. "Only you," she said, her lips smiling around the words.

His chest rumbled against her back as he laughed. "Did you save any of your old newspapers? I'd like to read them to catch up on the news I've missed."

"Actually, I have quite a few. Lulu has gone a little crazy collecting bottles for her trees, and she uses the newspapers to wrap them in so they don't get broken in storage." Tilting her face toward him, she said, "I've been prattling on and on, but you've barely said a word. Tell me everything you've been doing. Every place you've been. Don't skip anything. I want to be able to picture you living your life while we're separated. That way, it won't feel like we're apart at all."

He sighed heavily and pulled her closer to him. "It's just that it's all so boring, and to repeat it all to you would not only bore you to tears—it would also send me to sleep in the reliving of it. Suffice it to say that I went home to Iowa to meet with my father and discuss other products we might be able to make not just for the military, but for civilians, too. There's a huge market right now for blackout shades and curtain materials that he wants me to look into. Everything else is a blur—I get in my car and drive from city to city, visiting accounts and asking lots of questions." He kissed the back of her head. "Margaret, surely we can think of something else we'd rather do instead of talking about dull things."

Maggie smiled up at him, allowing him a long, deep kiss, and she realized she no longer felt the wind or the cold. Peter sat up on his elbow, and looked over at the lighthouse, which had dominated the landscape on this end of the island since long before she was born.

"Where does the lightkeeper live?"

"There isn't one anymore. Four years ago, they automated the light and dismantled all of the outbuildings so the debris wouldn't be a hazard to boats. It's kind of sad to know it's empty, isn't it?"

He studied the tall, striped structure for a long moment without speaking before turning back to her. "And you said people can still go inside, right?"

"Sure, although you only want to do it at low tide, or you'll get stranded. You're not supposed to, but you can climb all the way up."

"Have you been to the top recently?"

Maggie closed her eyes, glad she wasn't facing Peter. As a child she'd been in it many times, as one of the lightkeeper's daughters had been a friend of hers. But after she'd grown up, she'd been inside only once, and that was with Jim. He'd wanted to see the ocean from the top of the lighthouse, so she'd taken him. They'd run up the winding black wrought-iron stairs, emerging onto the deck at the top, breathing heavily and laughing at how absurd they were to run like children, nearly killing themselves in the process.

Then, without warning, he'd kissed her, and by the time he'd pulled back, she'd known her heart had been snatched by the wind and given completely to him.

"Yes," she said to Peter, "about a year ago."

"Is it still safe then?"

"Safe enough, I suppose. Once a month a lighthouse tender comes to check the lens and make sure everything's working, so he has to get up in the top. The door's locked now, but when I came here last, I was with Cat's husband, Jim. It was before he met her, and we . . . Well, it doesn't matter now. Anyway, his father was a locksmith in Louisiana, and he knew how to open just about any lock."

Maggie rolled over onto her back to look up at Peter. His face shaded hers from the murky sun as he looked down at her. "Did you love him?"

Maggie looked into Peter's eyes, which had seemed so strange to her at first and now become what she dreamed of at night. Slowly, she nodded, and then, before she could stop herself, she said, "But not as much as I love you."

The sky darkened as a black cloud moved over the sun, and Peter continued to stare down at Maggie, his expression unreadable. "Do you love me enough to wait for me?"

She sat up, leaning on her elbows. "What do you mean? Are you leaving again?"

Peter ducked his head and shook it. "Not right now. But later, I might have to leave suddenly and not have time to send word to you for a while. I just need to know that you'll wait for me to come back for you."

Maggie smiled nervously. "I don't understand. What part of your business would make you have to leave without word to me?"

His hand cupped her cheek, his fingers sliding into her hair. "If I succeed in obtaining government contracts for anything sensitive, they won't want me talking about it or letting anyone know where I've gone. It would be safer for you."

She lowered herself to the blanket again, then lifted her arms, placing both hands behind his head and drawing him down toward her. "I promise, Peter, I'll wait for you. Forever if I have to, but I'll wait for you to come back for me."

He lowered his lips to hers and pressed her against the blanket and the sand as the wind wrapped around them and the ocean continued its pulsing breath against the shore.

⌘

SITTING IN THE CLOSET, LULU flicked off the flashlight she was using to read when she heard the creak of the floorboard outside in the hallway. Cat's schedule for when she was supposed to be spotting planes was taped to the icebox in the kitchen, and tonight was definitely not on the schedule, and her spotter cards, with the silhouettes of enemy planes to make recognition easier, were on the bureau in her bedroom. Still clutching the flashlight, Lulu pushed open the closet door and tiptoed out of the bedroom without awakening Maggie. Pausing at the top of the stairs, she waited until she heard the front door softly open and close before heading downstairs, avoiding all the squeaky spots she'd known since childhood. After quickly grabbing her coat from the coatrack, she slipped outside, her bare feet chilled in the evening air. She spotted Cat already halfway down the block and knew she wouldn't have time to grab her shoes.

Navigating by the murky light of the moon, she ran behind Cat, being careful not to cry out each time she stepped on something sharp or stubbed her toe. Cat kept her flashlight aimed directly in front of her, but dipped low to the ground as if to light the way. She crossed West Ashley, then headed up toward Arctic, and Lulu realized they were moving in the direction of the pier and pavilion. It was too late for dancing, which just made Lulu even more suspicious.

They passed another pedestrian, and Lulu watched as Cat stepped back into the shadows to avoid being noticed. Lulu did the same, not really knowing why. She didn't recognize the man, which wasn't unusual anymore. It was odd to Lulu, who in the winter months had once known everyone. The summers had always brought strangers to Folly, but not now when the beaches were too cold and the wind could steal the hat from your head.

As Cat approached what was left of West Arctic, she began to slow and flipped off her flashlight. Lulu did the same, and immediately stumbled in the dark, letting out an accidental "Oomph." Cat stopped and turned around, and Lulu ducked behind a palmetto tree, holding her breath until she heard Cat's footsteps again crunching on sand and rocks.

Cat finally stopped on the beach in front of the abandoned houses, and Lulu stopped, too. They both stood like statues until Lulu started to shiver, her feet so numb she knew they'd be blue if she could see them. She squatted, not taking her eyes off of Cat; then she sat on her bottom so she could tuck her feet under her coat. Lulu figured it had to be about four o'clock in the morning, and her eyelids kept wanting to close over her eyes but she forced them open. Nancy Drew would never fall asleep while spying on someone.

After a while, a brief flare like a match lit up and then vanished, followed shortly by the smell of cigarette smoke. Lulu frowned, knowing that Maggie would be upset that Cat was smoking. Maggie had been giving Cat bubble gum to chew on whenever she felt like having a cigarette, but now Folly's Finds didn't even have any gum because the army needed it more.

Lulu searched around on the ground around her with frozen fingers until she found a nice-sized rock. She stuck it under her hip so that she'd be too uncomfortable to fall asleep, and then continued to watch as Cat stood against a fence post and lit another cigarette.

Despite the rock, Lulu must have dozed because she found herself waking with a start, and wondering what it was that had changed. She looked over to where Cat had stood and realized she was gone.

Struggling to stand on feet that were most likely frostbitten by now, she stumbled through the dark, afraid to turn on her flashlight and using the dim glow from the sky to light her way, being careful to stick to the shadows to avoid being seen. She spotted Cat near the waterline, looking up at the first abandoned beach house, and Lulu began to get worried. She'd secretly read Maggie's copy of *Anna Karenina* and knew what women sometimes did when they couldn't be with the men they loved. Not that Cat had shown any sadness when Jim died, but maybe Maggie was right and that was just a show that she put on for everyone when she was in public.

Lulu stopped abruptly, her mind spinning in circles. What if Cat was going to drown herself? Would it really be such a bad thing? She wasn't a nice person, and she made Maggie upset. Lulu breathed heavily, her breath a silent cloud rising above her until it disappeared. She stood still as she watched Cat stop to remove her shoes.

But then Lulu remembered what Maggie had told her about how you couldn't help who you loved, and that Maggie loved Cat like a sister and Lulu knew that she couldn't let Cat drown herself. She began to move forward quickly, her fingers so frozen that she fumbled with her flashlight, unable to turn it on. She stumbled and dropped it, hearing the sound of broken glass as the flashlight hit something hard.

Squatting, she picked it up and held it under her coat and forced the power switch by using her two thumbs. Not even a flicker of light appeared and Lulu knew she'd probably broken the bulb and that it would be no good to her tonight.

She stood, prepared to call out Cat's name, but stopped when a light shone from an upstairs balcony at the first house. It was a round, small spot of light, and it was gone almost as soon as she knew she'd seen it. Lulu's eyes searched the dark, wondering how Cat could have gotten inside so fast until she spotted Cat on the beach, unmoving as if she, too, had seen the light.

Again, the spot of light appeared on the balcony, except this time Lulu was looking right at it and could see more than she had before. Somebody was standing outside holding a flashlight, flipping it on and off in an uneven pattern.

Her eyes searched out Cat until she spotted her, moving into the dark surf toward the steps of the house. Lulu moved forward, creeping closer now that the ocean hitting the beach was making enough noise to hide behind. Her feet barely felt the cold water as she stood in the damp sand watching as Cat made her way up the wooden steps, stopping at the top for a moment before moving around the side of the house to where the light continued to appear.

It stopped so quickly, it was like a blanket had been thrown over it. From where she stood, all Lulu could see was two people facing each other on the upper balcony. They stood still for a moment, then began to move like dancing shadows. It looked like they were talking but the crash of waves against the sand erased any words before they reached her. And then, suddenly, they moved together, creating one single shadow. They disappeared for a moment, pressed against the side of the house, hiding in the darkness under the roof's overhang, before appearing again at the railing.

Lulu squinted, trying to see what was happening. And then, unexpectedly, the shadow broke into two again and one of them moved toward the door and opened it. The two figures melted into one again before disappearing completely inside the house. Lulu imagined she could hear the bang of the door as it shut, leaving the beach and the night dark and still again.

Blowing hot breath onto her hands to warm them in the way Jim had once shown her, Lulu turned around and headed home, hoping to be back in her bed before Maggie awoke. She'd already made up her mind not to tell her sister what she'd seen—not that Lulu even knew what she'd seen. But as she'd learned before, sometimes it was better to be quiet and listen, then wait until the time was right to reveal what you knew.

She continued to walk along in the dark, listening for Cat's footsteps behind her, while she thought about lights in the darkness, and all the secrets the night could hold.

CHAPTER 13

FOLLY BEACH, SOUTH CAROLINA
August 2009

Emmy emerged from the back office at Folly's Finds with a stack of paid bills to be mailed. She hadn't planned to hide in the office as long as she had, but she'd had to wait until the puffiness under her eyes had diminished at least a bit. The night before, she'd heard the footsteps again, but this time they seemed to be walking in circles, leaving her more bereft and full of questions than before. She'd spent the rest of the night lying awake and listening to the night sounds around her, waiting for the footsteps to return and point her in the right direction.

She lifted her hair off the back of her neck and sighed. It was only nine o'clock in the morning, but she was already sweating despite the air-conditioning. It got hot in Indiana in the summer, too, but nothing like the waterlogged air of South Carolina's Lowcountry. She stuck her fingers inside the neck of her short-sleeved cotton sweater and readjusted the belt on her skirt in the hope of letting air in to touch her skin.

Emmy spotted Janell behind the counter at Playgrounds, serving various coffee confections to a dedicated group of locals whose names and faces were finally starting to sink in. A man in his sixties wearing a loose floral shirt, a Bermuda bathing suit in a conflicting pattern, dark socks up to his knees, and sandals waved a greeting to her. "Good morning, Miz Hamilton. It's going to be another hot one."

"I'm afraid you're right, Mr. Bivens. I don't think I've ever felt this hot in my life."

His wife, wearing a strapless floral sundress and sneakers, approached with two cups. "You need to go get yourself something more suited to our climate, sweetheart. The saying here on Folly is that if you want to look like a local, dress like a tourist." She laughed at her own joke, and Emmy laughed with her, recognizing the truth of her words.

Turning to Janell, Emmy asked, "Has the mailman been here yet? I've got a stack of bills that I'd love to go out today."

Janell looked at her oddly. "Just put them on the counter where you usually do, and I'll make sure they get mailed."

"I hate to make you do that. If you'll just tell me where the mailbox is, I'll be happy to do it myself."

Janell laughed, her long, beaded earrings clicking. "We don't have mailboxes here on Folly, Emmy. Since the beginning of time, we've gone to the post office to pick up our mail. A few years back, they took a vote to see how many people wanted home delivery, and not enough people did. So we go to the post office to drop off and pick up our mail."

Emmy stared at her. "I'm so sorry. I had no idea. I just assumed I kept missing the mailman." She scraped her hair away from her face. "The heat must be frying my brain or something. Look, tell me where the post office is, and I'll take the mail this morning."

Janell smiled and slid a package across the counter toward Emmy. "Too late, I've already been. But you can go later if you like. It's an easy walk—just over on East Indian and right behind the Catholic church. Just don't go at noon—they close for an hour at lunch."

Emmy shook her head. "I promise to go from now on. Really. I can't believe I didn't figure that out. I've been trying to mail a post-card to my dad since I moved in. I was just too embarrassed to admit that I couldn't find the mailbox either here or at the house."

"Actually, I think you're going to have to fight me over that. It's sort of where we get all the news, if you know what I mean. On a slow day, it can be the highlight of my day."

"I see. Well, then, maybe we'll just have to take turns."

Janell laughed again, then greeted a customer standing behind Emmy. Excusing herself, Emmy picked up the package and took it behind the counter in the bookstore. She read the return address with some surprise, and wondered what her mother could be sending her.

She sliced the tape to open the outer box and found a translucent white gift bag from Zoey's Boutique in Fishers, Indiana. Stuck to the outside of the bag was a folded note written on Paige's Pages stationery. Being careful to untape the note without tearing it, Emmy opened it up and read:

I saw this and thought of you—a little something to help you beat the heat and perhaps feel a little more native.

Since you've left, your father has become restless and has started talking about traveling. Not sure if that will last, but maybe we can fit in a visit to Folly Beach while we're at it.

The note wasn't signed, but at the bottom there was a postscript:

P.S. Don't forget to drink plenty of water and wear sunscreen.

Putting the note aside, Emmy lifted the bag out of the box. After cutting the curling ribbon that had been attached to the handles, she pushed aside a swath of tissue paper and found a pale yellow cotton dress with tiny spaghetti straps, and a matching hat with a wide brim and strings that tied under the chin. When she lifted the dress, she discovered what looked like a scrap of material tucked beneath it. Curious, she placed the dress on the counter and lifted up the material, only to find that it was an improbably small black string bikini. Dropping it quickly back into the box, Emmy looked around to see if anybody else had seen it just as Abigail walked through the front door.

"Good morning, sugar," she called out to Emmy as she entered wearing the ubiquitous Folly uniform of a tank top and shorts with flip-flops. Turning her head toward Janell, she said, "I'm wearing red today—let me know if you have anything pretty to go with it."

Abigail stopped in front of the counter, scrutinizing Emmy's face before lifting her hand to Emmy's cheek, the way Paige had done when Emmy had been small and sick with a fever. "Ben been back visiting, has he?"

Emmy widened her eyes with surprise as Abigail tucked a strand of hair behind Emmy's ear. "He'll be there as long as you think you need him." She dropped her hand. "Maggie stayed with me for a while, too. I think it was because I was so worried about running the store without her, and not knowing what to do. But as soon as I began to feel more confident about my abilities, she stopped coming round."

"I don't . . ." Emmy shook her head. "I don't believe in ghosts. I'm just having bad dreams."

Abigail patted her hand. "And that's okay. I don't think I believe in ghosts, either. But whatever our minds create to help us get over a rough spot is a welcome thing." Her smile faltered a bit. "When Heath was so sick, I felt Maggie close by again, and it helped me get through it. She'd been a second mother to him, so I think it natural that my thoughts would turn to her. It made me feel not so all alone. Not that my family and friends weren't there for me. It's just that nobody else was his mother, that's all. It's the hardest thing in the world for a mother to see her child suffering."

She studied Emmy closely, making Emmy wonder if Abigail knew about her dead brothers and what the loss had done to her own mother. Maybe being so far from home, Paige had no one to conjure; no one to talk with when the night was at its darkest.

"I know Heath had radiation. If you don't mind me asking, what was it for?"

Matter-of-factly, Abigail said, "He had a brain tumor. By sheer accident, we found it very early. Heath was riding his bike—without a helmet, of course, because that's what fool boys do—and fell off and hit his head. He said he felt fine, but I insisted that he go see his doctor, and the doctor ordered a CAT scan of his head. And that's how they found it. No bigger than a peanut, but there it was."

"And it was malignant?"

"That it was. They were able to get all of it, but he had to go through radiation to make sure. That was almost two years ago, and to see him now, it's hard to believe. Except he gained a scar and lost a fiancée."

Emmy pictured her mother rolling her eyes at what Emmy liked to think was her intellectual inquisitiveness but what Paige had always referred to as just plain nosiness. Pushing away the image of her mother, Emmy asked, "So Heath broke off the engagement when he found out he was ill?"

Abigail shook her head and pursed her lips. "No. Jolene can't handle serious illness. Her mother died of breast cancer when she was twelve, which is why Lulu says she couldn't handle Heath being so sick. But sometimes I can't help but think that it was because Jolene couldn't take the fact that her very perfect life had reached a bump in the road. Some people are like that, you know: they just fall apart at the first hurdle instead of looking for ways to go around it."

Come back to me. The note in the bottle was beginning to make a lot more sense to her now. "But he still wants her back?"

Abigail shook her head. "Not anymore. Heath has never been the kind of person who can live with the broken pieces. Even if it's all glued back together, he'd still see the cracks. I'm not saying that he's still not just a little bit in love with her, since there has to be a reason why he hasn't asked for the ring back. It belonged to Maggie, and should stay in the family." She began absently straightening the racks on the counter, her gaze taking in the package from Emmy's mother. "Jolene stayed in Atlanta until recently, but has been driving up here just about every other weekend for the last few months to see if Heath will change his mind. It's exhausting for all of us."

"Because of her drinking?" Emmy bit her tongue, too late to pull the words back.

"Among other things." Abigail slid the package closer and lifted the bikini out of the tissue paper. With a lifted eyebrow, she said, "I was going to suggest you buy some new clothes that would keep you cooler, but I never expected this."

Embarrassed, Emmy explained, "My mother sent it—although I can't imagine why. I don't even own a bathing suit, and if I did, it wouldn't look like that. But she sent this, too." She pulled out the yellow sundress and held it up. It even appeared to be the right size.

"They're both nice, Emmy. Don't say no to the bikini so quickly." Abigail winked. "You've got the figure for it, although it's hard to tell with all that fabric you're usually wearing." Coming behind the counter, Abigail placed her purse in a drawer. "So, what's on the agenda today?"

Emmy smiled at the older woman, relieved that the subject of Abigail's retirement hadn't come up since Emmy had purchased the store. It was the proverbial pink elephant in the room, but neither one of them seemed in a rush to address it and the situation seemed to work out for both. Every other week, Emmy processed the payroll checks, and Abigail smiled and thanked her, and that was all. It was as if they each needed Folly's Finds for different reasons, and they accepted the status quo for the time being.

Emmy stepped around the counter. "Glad you asked. I've been separating our sales into categories, analyzing which areas produce the most volume and which ones don't. This huge wall here is dedicated to travel and maps. I agree that it's one of my favorite sections in the store, but it just doesn't sell enough to dedicate the square footage that we're giving to it. I would like to pare it down considerably, maybe to the bottom three shelves where we keep the classics, and use the space to introduce an out-of-print book section and maybe even a local interest or local author section, too. We could also use some of the space to increase our children's area and put in a bigger reading corner for weekly story hours. What do you think?" She held her breath, surprised at how important Abigail's nod of approval was to her.

Abigail stepped closer to the shelves, her hands on her hips, as she studied the space, her eyes narrowed as if picturing Emmy's changes in her head. After a long moment, she turned back to Emmy.

"I completely agree. I think the reason why I've kept this section so big for so long is because of Maggie. It was her favorite, and I suppose I just kept it because of that. But I was thinking, too. . . ." She crossed her arms over her chest and tapped a finger against her chin. "I've got a box of Maggie's travel books and her favorites somewhere. She wanted to keep them with her when we were packing up before Hugo, and only agreed to let Lulu take them at the last minute, which is why they were separate from the other books. And I'd totally forgotten about them until now." She was silent for a moment as she contemplated the shelves. "But if I could locate them, we could incorporate them into the new out-of-print section. It could be quite a collection because they're so old."

Emmy's eyes brightened. "And I've been thinking about starting a Web site, moving the rare-books portion of the business completely online—maybe even highlighting the old travel books. I'm sure there are collectors who browse the Web looking for that exact thing." She took a breath. "But first we've got to get rid of that cash register and move into the twenty-first century with a computerized system."

The creases around Abigail's eyes deepened. "Well, then, looks like we've got some work to do. And if it's all right with you, I'd like to ask Lulu if she wouldn't mind helping with the design of the children's corner. She's got a really good eye for that kind of thing."

"Hrumph."

Both women turned toward the back door, where Lulu had apparently been standing for some time. Abigail placed her hand over her heart. "You scared me, Lulu. I didn't hear you come in." She turned to Emmy. "Lulu once told me that when she was a young girl, she liked to pretend that she was Nancy Drew, girl detective, and would practice sneaking around undetected."

Lulu pretended not to hear and stepped forward, her hair in braids and wearing the same shorts and shirt Emmy had seen her wearing the first time they'd met. "Maggie wouldn't want you to sell her favorite books."

Abigail tilted her head to the side. "You know, I thought just the opposite. She loved sharing those books when she was alive, loved talking about different places with other people. Don't you think that making the books available to other readers would be a way of honoring her?"

Emmy moved to stand next to Abigail. "And we wouldn't have to make them all available for purchase. I'd be more than happy to let you go through them and pick out which ones you'd like to keep. But I agree with Abigail: sharing Maggie's books would be the best way to honor her memory."

Lulu's only answer was a snort. Ignoring Abigail and Emmy, she walked past them to the spot where Emmy had wanted to put the children's corner. "A story hour would be nice. Maggie had one during the war to keep the children's minds off of their daddies, who were off fighting. Watching me didn't leave a lot of time for her to contribute to the war effort, so she did what she could. Gave them books, too, which she couldn't really afford to do, but that was her way. Still, I don't think you should go selling her books."

Abigail said, "This whole argument might be moot if I can't find that box of books. You had them last, Lulu, but I don't remember evacuating with them. Do you have any idea what happened to her box of favorites?"

Lulu shrugged and shook her head, her eyes considering the space where Emmy wanted the story hour.

Abigail continued. "Well, I haven't run across it in twenty years, which makes me think that it might be lost forever."

Lulu crossed her arms over her chest, her hair and her stature making her look like an old Indian chief, and stuck out her chin. "I suppose I could decorate the children's corner for you. But it won't come cheap."

Emmy frowned. "Of course I would pay you for your work."

The corner of Lulu's mouth lifted in what Emmy guessed was a wide grin for her. "I heard what you were saying about the Web site. I'd like you to hire Jolene to do it, and I want a page on there for my bottle trees."

Emmy blinked several times, not sure she'd heard correctly. "Jolene? As in Heath's ex-fiancée?"

Abigail put a hand on her arm. "She's an interior designer in Atlanta, but she's developed an award-winning interactive Web site for her business. It's pretty innovative, which you young people think is the best way to be. You can build floor plans and place actual to-scale pieces of furniture that you find on her site to make sure it all fits."

Emmy forced a smile. "That sounds great and all, but . . . Jolene?"

Lulu stuck her chin out again. "Don't like her 'cause she's so pretty, right?"

Crossing her arms tightly, Emmy explained, "It's not that I like her or don't like her. I've only met her once, and she was drunk. Not a good first impression for a prospective employee."

"Maybe not," Lulu continued, "but it seems to me like you need a new project. Folly's Finds will get along just fine without being messed with, but you won't."

"Excuse me?" Emmy frowned at the older woman, half wanting her not to explain herself.

Abigail stepped in. "And Jolene can do the work in Atlanta, too. It might give her something else to focus on besides Heath."

Emmy looked from Lulu to Abigail, then back again; their matching expressions of hopeful anticipation would have been almost comical if the women weren't both so serious.

Unable to give them a flat-out no, Emmy stalled for time. "Okay. Fine. I'll talk to her. I'm not promising anything, though. And if she's too expensive, it's a definite no." She eyed Lulu, who was standing with a decidedly smug expression on her face. "And on one condition."

Lulu looked wary.

"I want you to be the one to read to the children. You're about the same height, so they shouldn't be intimidated."

Lulu's expression went from relief to amusement, surprising Emily and making her wonder what Lulu thought she might ask instead. "One more thing, Lulu." She reached under the counter where she'd stored the copy of *The Great Gatsby* she'd found in the turret. When her fingers touched the cover, the familiar electric pulse coursed up her arm, surprising her because she hadn't felt it before. Hesitating only a brief moment, she held the book out to Lulu. "This book is dedicated to Margaret, from Peter. Do you know who Margaret was?"

Lulu took the book and held it for a moment before opening the front cover, then slowly turning to the title page. She smiled softly as she read the inscription, her face softening like clouds after a storm. "Peter was the only one who called her that. She was known to everyone else as Maggie."

Emmy rubbed her arm, the memory of the static shock still fresh. "And who was Peter? He signed your book, too."

Lulu began to turn the pages slowly, keeping her head down. "He was Maggie's friend. He traveled a lot and always brought us gifts—mostly books since we all shared a passion for reading."

"Was he a soldier?"

"No." Lulu shook her head. "A civilian. He had asthma and couldn't do active service. But his father owned a factory out west, so Peter was sent out as a salesperson and to determine wartime needs of both the military and civilians."

Emmy watched Lulu closely, her years of scrutinizing small scraps of text and searching for relevance piquing her curiosity. "What happened to him?"

Lulu shrugged without looking up. "He . . . left. He was here one day, and gone the next. We never heard from him again. It was the middle of the war. We always assumed he must have been called into active service despite his asthma, or he was working on secret military contracts and couldn't let us know where he was."

Emmy lifted her hair off of her neck again, the store suddenly suffocating. "But what about after the war—still no word?"

Lulu slowly shook her head and closed the book before holding it against her ample chest. "No word. I figure he just got on with his life and forgot about us here on Folly."

Emmy continued to watch Lulu, convinced there was more to the story but just as sure that the other woman was not going to reveal it. She indicated the book. "You can keep that, if you like."

"Thank you," Lulu said, her words clipped.

The bell rang as the door opened again, allowing a blast of hot, humid air to invade the store. Emmy turned to see a tall, attractive, and very pregnant woman enter the store. Her hair was a sun-tinted light brown and her eyes only a shade darker, and she looked vaguely familiar. Abigail rushed toward her and enveloped her in a hug. "Lizzie sweetheart, what are you doing out in this heat?"

Grabbing the woman's arm, Abigail led her toward Emmy. "Emmy, this is my daughter, Elizabeth—yes, after Elizabeth Bennet in *Pride and Prejudice*. I know you're probably tired of hearing me talking about her, so here she is in person."

Lizzie appeared to be about Emmy's age, and as they shook hands, Emmy couldn't help but notice how much she resembled her brother, Heath.

As if reading Emmy's mind, Lizzie said, "Yes, we're twins. And I'm expecting a girl and boy twins, too, which is why I'm here today."

She seemed to notice Lulu for the first time, and gave her a huge hug and kiss on the cheek before turning back to Abigail. "Dr. Clemmens said she's going to induce me on Monday because I'm getting too big, and my ankles are now thicker than my waist. So I decided to come out to Folly and get everybody for dinner at Taco Boy to celebrate my last free Friday night without diapers and spit-up." She put her arm around Emmy's shoulders. "Mama's told me so much about you that I feel as if we're practically best friends. So please tell me you'll come, too."

Before Emmy could respond, Abigail said, "You know, Lizzie, only the Mt. Pleasant people eat at Taco Boy. Why don't we go to Snapper Jacks instead?"

Lizzie frowned. "Mama, I've lived in Mt. Pleasant for four years, so it's time to get used to the fact that your own daughter is now a 'Mt. Pleasant person.' Besides, it's my party, and I can have it where I want. And Taco Boy has the best guacamole anywhere, and I know I won't be able to eat that for a long, long time."

Emmy frowned to hide her relief that she couldn't go. It wasn't that she didn't want to, but crowds always made her nervous, and meeting new people always meant questions that she dreaded answering. "Thanks, but I'm scheduled to close tonight, so I don't think I can make it."

Lizzie waved her hand dismissively. "So close early—this is Folly Beach. People will understand."

As much as Emmy wanted to protest, she knew that Lizzie was right. Even though she'd only been on Folly for little over a month, it had become clear to her that Folly Beach time was fluid and flexible and on nobody's schedule. Assuming people had schedules here. And she hadn't quite decided if that was something to love or hate about her new home. Knowing Lizzie wouldn't accept no for an answer, she nodded. "Sure. I can be there. What time?"

"Five o'clock. My parents like to eat early like the other seniors." She rolled her eyes as her mother elbowed her gently in the arm. "Afterward, I thought we could go over to the pier. They're having one of the last Moonlight Mixers tonight, and I'd hate to miss it. Who knows when I'll get a chance to dance again?"

Emmy had no desire to dance in public but figured she could leave right after dinner without anybody noticing. They all glanced over at Lulu, and Emmy expected the older woman to decline because she couldn't picture Lulu in a social setting in which she'd be expected to be nice to people.

"I've got to finish up a custom order, but I guess I can be there."

Lizzie clapped her hands together and smiled as if Lulu's acceptance had been an enthusiastic one. "Great. Joe and I will see everybody then. Nice to meet you, Emmy. I'll look forward to getting to know you better over margaritas." She frowned, patting her swollen belly. "Well, one margarita and one glass of ice water."

Lulu allowed Lizzie to hug and kiss her good-bye, and then they all watched her leave. Abigail shook her head and smiled. "Having twins will serve her right. She and Heath just about killed me when they were younger." Her face softened slightly. "She and Joe didn't plan to have kids, but then Heath got sick, and it made Lizzie sort of reevaluate her life. And I sure am glad she did. I'm going to be a grandma! Still hard to wrap my mind around it, but there you have it."

Emmy forced a smile, and tried not to think about the plans she and Ben had made—the plans she'd shelved like a tissue-covered treasure while she'd waited for him to return. It was the thoughts of their own home and babies that had been her bedtime companion on the lonely nights without him—dreams that became for her living, breathing things. It made her grief harder now. Waiting to start a family had been her idea, and burying Ben had meant burying his unborn children alongside him. She wondered, sometimes, if that was why she still felt Ben around her, a restless spirit searching for what might have been.

Abigail touched her arm, and Emmy realized she'd asked a question while Emmy's mind had been gathering wool. "I'm sorry—what did you say?"

"I said that I still have some of Maggie's old photos. She wrote names on the backs of most of them, so maybe we'll find a picture of that Peter fellow. If he was a friend to Maggie and Lulu, we might have to stick him in a frame. I took the pictures out of the albums because the old albums they were put in weren't archival quality, and I didn't want the photos to disintegrate. I have them loose in a box now, waiting to be put in a new album or framed—I haven't decided yet. One of those things I thought I'd do once I retired."

Their eyes met at the forbidden word, and they both looked away at the same time.

Lulu still clutched Maggie's book, her fingers white at the tips. "I've got to get back to work. Just got a delivery of my tree limbs, and I've got to sort them." She stopped when she reached the back door.

Without turning around, she said, "Thank you for Maggie's book. It was her favorite."

The door rang as a woman with a young child entered the shop, and Emmy turned to greet them. By the time she'd turned back, Lulu was gone.

B

LULU STOOD IN FRONT OF the vacant lot where the old house had once been, and where the encroaching blackberry vines and the weathered white cross near the back fence were the only reminders that lives had been lived and lost here.

In the beginning, right after the storm and during the search for Maggie, Lulu had placed a bottle tree here in the hope that she'd find a message from Maggie in one of the bottles, or at least turn away the evil spirits that had managed to come into their lives. But the bottles kept getting stolen, so Lulu took down the tree, deciding that it was too late to ward away the bad spirits; they'd taken root here long before Hugo blew in on 135-mile-per-hour winds.

Lulu's fist hurt from clenching it so tightly around her handful of sand, but she'd been doing this ritual for twenty years and wasn't going to allow a little bit of arthritis stop her now. She moved slowly toward the cross and carefully got down on her knees in front of it, another painful and laborious process that she refused to concede to. Opening her hand one finger at a time, she allowed half of the sand to fall at the base of the cross. Maggie had loved the beach and the ocean, and even though they'd never found her body, it gave Lulu some consolation to know that she was buried under the blanket of her beloved Atlantic. And every once in a while, she wondered if Maggie's spirit knew that the waiting was finally over.

Using her other hand to help her stand, she began to pace twenty steps to the right before stopping and going through the process of kneeling again. Opening up her fist, she allowed the remaining sand to drift down to the ground. This memorial was for Jim, whose bottle tree had once stood on the spot. It was sacred to Lulu, for many reasons—reasons Lulu expected to take with her to her grave.

"Aunt Lulu, it's too hot for you to be out here without your hat."

She recognized Heath's voice before twisting around to see him standing there like a bronzed god, his hair now blessedly long after having it shaved off. She hadn't expected him to survive, had even seen his sickness as just punishment, and now to see him so fit and happy, it made her think that maybe she'd already atoned for her sins.

He took hold of her elbow and helped her stand. "I'm fine, just fine. Don't need you to be adding me to your worries."

He smiled his wonderful smile that so reminded her of Maggie, of her gentleness and resilience. "I don't have any worries, remember? I've finally taken Grandma Maggie's words to heart: live for the day in the best way possible, and everything else will work itself out. Seems to be working for me so far."

She frowned. "Yeah, except for the cancer."

"Now, now, Aunt Lulu, that's only because I hadn't embraced her philosophy yet. But while I was going through the radiation, that's what got me through. It changed my life—in a good way."

She looked up at him, thinking again of Maggie and if she'd died still believing in her own words of wisdom. "What are you doing here?"

Heath squinted into the sun, surveying the lot. "Just seeing if today is the day this place speaks to me and tells me what to do with it." He looked back at her. "You know, the land is much more valuable today than when you deeded it to me. I feel as if you've been taken advantage of."

Lulu shook her head. "It's yours, fair and square. Maggie would have wanted this to be yours, to do with it whatever you think is right. I don't have any use for it."

Heath moved away from her, taking in the riotous vines and scrubby grass, picking up a beer bottle somebody had thrown. "I don't know. I can't seem to get a clear picture here. It's like the whole place is restless and can't settle down." He sent a smile to Lulu. "And if you repeat any of this to anyone, I'll cement you in the foundation."

She snorted. "You and what army? I think I still outweigh you by fifty pounds. You got some catching up to do."

"I'm working at it." He kicked at the ground with the toe of his sneaker. "If I ignore my conscience, I could build a really huge house with lots of bedrooms and bathrooms and use it as a rental property." He glanced across the street at the modest bungalow that had been there since the twenties. "Of course, the neighbors would hate me and talk about me and complain to my mother, and I don't think I could stand that."

"Still a mama's boy after all these years." She gave him a half grin. "Oh, and, Heath? Don't put any more notes in the bottle tree. That girl who's staying over at your house is too nosy."

He almost grinned. "It was a stupid thing to do, anyway. I don't know why I let you talk me into doing that. But don't worry. I got rid of it."

"It worked, though, didn't it?"

"Well, that would depend. Jolene came back, but now I almost wish that she hadn't."

Lulu turned her head, imagining she heard the sound of the wind in a bottle. "But maybe you needed her to come back, even if it wasn't for the reason you thought."

His brows formed a questioning "v." "What do you mean?"

"Oh, I don't know. My bottle trees are a lot more powerful than even I ever imagined. Maggie might have had her strong beliefs, but I've always just relied on my trees. They've never let me down."

Heath watched her for a long time, mulling over her words much as he'd done with the baby cereals she'd fed him as a child. "So what are you doing here?"

Lulu craned her neck back to look up at the wide blue sky, smelling salty air. "Greeting old ghosts, I suppose."

He looked at her oddly. "Emmy and I were just talking about ghosts, too. I told her I didn't believe in them."

Wiping her sandy hands off on her pants, she began walking toward the street. "It's easy to not believe in something you can't see,

I guess." Stopping, she put her hands on her hips and faced him. "I think ghosts will show when they're ready to be seen. Or when they think you're ready to see them. Sort of like this lot. You'll know when it's ready to tell you."

He stared at her for a long moment, his face expressionless. "I think you need to get out of the sun, Aunt Lulu." He winked at her. "I'll save you a seat next to me at dinner, all right?"

She waved a hand at him dismissively. "Sure. See you tonight." Turning her head, she chewed on her lower lip. Lulu believed with her whole heart what she'd told Heath about ghosts; knew the truth of it in the same way she knew when a hurricane hovered on the horizon. And that was what scared her. She headed down the street without glancing back, hearing again the sound of the wind crying into the necks of open bottles, afraid of what she might see if she did.

CHAPTER 14

Summer weekenders had descended on the island with a vengeance, leaving no open parking spots along Center Street or the nearest surrounding blocks. Cranking up the air-conditioning, Emmy pointed the vents toward her face as she searched, realizing she'd have been better off leaving her car at the store instead of going home first to change.

The yellow sundress fit her perfectly, although she felt self-conscious exposing so much of her shoulders and back. She'd decided to complete the outfit with a pair of flip-flops she'd purchased from one of the tourist shops near the Holiday Inn. She'd left the hat behind, thinking she wouldn't be needing it for sun protection at five o'clock in the evening. Looking up through the windshield at the still-burning sun, she began to doubt her decision.

She finally found a spot in front of what she could only describe as a cement box on stilts, possibly a remnant of Folly's past when it was known as the poor man's beach. Most of the older structures had been removed by Hugo, but perhaps this owner had a strong nostalgia for the way things used to be.

As she crossed Center Street to reach Taco Boy, she was nearly run over by a Lincoln Navigator driven by a harried mom on her cell phone trying to make the yellow light. Emmy turned her head to read the license plate, knowing already it would be from out of state. "Damned tourist," she muttered to herself, stopping in the middle of the street and nearly getting run over again as she recognized the irony of her remark.

People spilled out of the popular eatery onto the sidewalk, waiting for a table. The combined scents of beer and cigarettes mixed with suntan lotion and perfume, making her wrinkle her nose at the foreignness of it all. It wasn't that it didn't get hot in Indiana, or that people didn't smoke or wear perfume; it was just that everything seemed *more* here: more hot, more pungent. Or maybe it was the simple addition of suntan lotion that reminded her of how very far from home she really was.

Emmy stood next to a group of long-haired, bushy-bearded, and tattooed men wearing Harley T-shirts chatting with what looked to Emmy like a group of soccer moms on a girlfriends' night out. Standing on her tiptoes, she peered through the crowd, hoping to recognize somebody and not relishing making her way through all the people.

She felt a hand on her arm. "Emmy."

Turning, she found herself looking into Heath's smiling brown eyes. "Hang on to me, and I'll lead you to the table. We got a nice big one on the patio."

She grabbed his arm and allowed him to lead her into the restaurant, then directly out again onto the patio eating area, which seemed more like part of the sidewalk despite the partitioning because of all the people milling around outside.

They stopped in front of two square tables that had been pulled together to accommodate seven chairs, three of which remained empty. She recognized Abigail and Lizzie, and was introduced to Lizzie's husband, Joe, who looked like a younger version of Jimmy Buffett with a loud Hawaiian shirt but with more hair. When Heath introduced the man at the end of the table as his father, John, she found herself staring. She wasn't sure if it was because nobody had mentioned that he was in a wheelchair or because she had expected to see him as a small boy in a black-and-white photo holding a small American flag.

She held out her hand and felt it clasped in a firm handshake; then she looked into deep-set eyes that called to mind the colors of the marsh outside her window. They were a mixture of brown, green, and gold—an unusual combination that was as arresting as the eyes were beautiful.

"It's a pleasure to meet you," she said as she took the empty seat on one side of him. Abigail sat on her left and Lizzie across the table. Heath seated himself in the empty chair at the foot of the table; the remaining vacant chair next to him was presumably for Lulu. Emmy knew it was uncharitable for her to think so, but she was glad Lulu was as far from her as possible.

"Abigail tells me that you lost your husband in Afghanistan."

Emmy's mouth went dry as she faced Heath's father.

John placed his hand on top of hers. "Sorry. I didn't mean to blind-side you. But I wanted you to know that I might understand more than most. I was in Vietnam." He patted the arms of his wheelchair. "It's the reason I get to ride this fine set of wheels." Squeezing her hand, he leaned closer to her and with a somber voice he said, "I appreciate your sacrifice and honor your bravery."

Bravery. Lulu had used the same word, and it still sat uncomfortably on Emmy's shoulders, especially coming from a veteran in a wheelchair. Bravery was facing enemy fire or parachuting behind enemy lines. Or staying behind with a fallen soldier so he wouldn't die alone. That was real bravery. Being left behind was hard; but it wasn't brave.

She looked into John's unusual eyes as he squeezed her hand, and she felt his sincerity. For a brief moment, just as she had while standing with Lulu in the bottle-tree garden, she could almost believe that a glimmer of truth hid behind the word.

"Thank you," she managed, keeping her eyes focused on their hands, and feeling somehow relieved that she'd survived another mention of Ben without bursting into tears or having to endure another extended conversation about the war. The other members of the Reynolds family were talking about other things—a reminder that life did indeed exist beyond the walls of her grief.

John patted her hand, then pulled his away. He turned toward the others at the table and cleared his throat. "Anybody thirsty?" he asked as he signaled for the waitress, who'd just turned from the neighboring table. "We'd like a pitcher of frozen margaritas all around and iced water for the pregnant lady, please."

The group nibbled chips and salsa while chatting easily about the store, the quality of fishing from the pier, the anticipated end of the tourist invasion, and the heat. Emmy found herself relaxing, due in part, she was sure, to the strength of the margarita she sipped. The Reynolds clan—with the exception of Lulu—was easy to like and to get to know. She found herself wondering if her mother had stayed on Folly if their family would be like this, if their conversations would be open and free, not halting like skipping stones on a river, avoiding the areas that would drown all words.

She turned to Heath's mother. "I'm curious, Abigail. You know so much about me, yet I've known you for over a month now, and I'm just finding out that your children are twins, and your husband is a Vietnam War vet. Why is that?"

Abigail took a long sip from her margarita. "I guess it's because I've lived in the same place for so long I just assume everybody knows everything about me already. As for me knowing so much about you, remember I had all that time on the phone with your mama before you even got here. Sort of a head start, I guess." She eyed Emmy over the edge of her glass.

There was a commotion near the front of the restaurant, and everyone turned their heads to watch as a loud and irate Jolene greeted everyone she saw as she was led by Lulu to their table on the patio.

Heath stood and waited for them to approach. Jolene wore a slim skirt and a halter top with high heels, looking even more gorgeous than when Emmy had first met her. She was weaving on her feet and relying on Lulu to keep her upright.

Heath pulled out his chair and indicated for Lulu to bring her over to it, but Jolene held up her hand. "No, I didn't come to intrude. Just wanted to say hi and to thank Ms. Hamilton here for offering me the job as webmistress for Folly's Finds." She fumbled in her purse and pulled out an elegant card case. After she dropped it twice, Heath took it from her, opened it, and gave a card to Emmy.

Emmy glanced at it without really seeing it, feeling almost as embarrassed as Lulu looked. Frowning and avoiding Emmy's eyes, Lulu said, "I told her only that she was in consideration. I thought it would . . . help things."

Jolene twisted her mouth in a look of exaggerated concentration. "I don't remember that." Leaning over, she tapped a manicured fingernail on the card lying on the table in front of Emmy. "Call me. We can do lunch and discuss your site."

She stumbled and Heath moved to catch her. "I'm going to take you home now before you break your leg."

"To our house?"

"It's not our house anymore, remember? I'm taking you back to my parents'."

Closing her eyes, she rested her head against his shoulder and allowed him to lead her back through the crowd. "I'll catch up with y'all later," he called back right as Jolene reached over and squeezed his butt.

Lulu stood abruptly. "I'm going to the ladies' room. And don't get me one of those damned fancy Mexican drinks. Get me a beer."

Emmy waited until Lulu was out of earshot before leaning toward Abigail. "Why is Lulu such a fan of Jolene's?"

Abigail watched as Lulu barreled her way through the crowd. "I asked her that same question when she defended Jolene right after she broke the engagement. All she told me was that Jolene reminded her of somebody she'd once known—somebody she owed an unpaid debt." Abigail shrugged and returned her gaze to Emmy. "It's all right. Jolene doesn't have too many fans, so I can't begrudge her Lulu."

Emmy nodded and took another sip from her margarita, remembering Lulu's calling her brave, and Lulu's face softening when Emmy had given her Maggie's book, and Peter's inscription *Be good and stay sweet.* She stared down into the bottom of her glass, and wondered what might have happened in Lulu O'Shea's life to make her into the woman full of contradictions she was today.

Despite the disturbance and Lulu's usual reticence to speak, they managed to have an enjoyable dinner. Lizzie and Abigail did a great job of carrying the conversation and bringing others into it, even Lulu, so that nobody was allowed to be left out. To her surprise, Emmy enjoyed herself. She was embarrassed to admit, even to herself, that she'd spent every night since she'd arrived alone with her microwaved dinners. It was almost as if she were planning not to like it here, to prove her mother wrong and finally show that the best part of Emmy's life had already happened.

Despite Emmy's protests, Mr. Reynolds paid for everyone's dinner, and as he was signing the bill, Abigail slid her chair back from the table. "Oh, before I forget." She pulled her large purse off the back of her chair. "I found those photos I told you about. Only one of them is marked with Peter's name, but the other ones look like the same person. I stuck in a few others that I thought you might be interested in seeing, too." She handed Emmy a large brown envelope. "Keep them for however long you need them."

Lulu also slid her chair back from the table. "I gotta go. Thanks for the dinner."

John smiled up at her from his wheelchair. "Got to go polish your broom?"

She snorted in his direction, but as she turned to leave, Emmy was sure she saw Lulu's cheek twitch.

Turning back to Abigail, Emmy took the envelope. "Thanks, I appreciate it. And next time you're near the house, please stop by—I wanted to ask you about several of the framed photos in the house. Heath said you'd know more about them than he would."

"I'd be happy to, although I'm not sure if I can offer much more. I married into the family, remember, and my husband is an only child.

He's also male, which means that studying his family tree wasn't a priority for him. Considering how near we are to Charleston, where they practically worship their bloodlines, it always struck me as odd that John would be so ignorant about his." She shrugged. "I asked him why once, and he said Maggie never really talked much about it, only that her mother and father died when she was still pretty young and that she practically raised Lulu."

Emmy thought for a moment. "I suppose I'll most likely end up asking Lulu, but I'd like to try you first."

"Lulu doesn't like talking about the past—that's for sure. Maybe John can offer some coaxing if you need it." She reached over and kissed her husband on the cheek. "He's her favorite, you know. She used to treat him like a doll when he was born, dressing him up in baby-doll clothes until he was old enough to fight back. Turned out all right in spite of it. Didn't you, sweetheart?"

"Yes, dear." He grinned, and allowed himself to be wheeled from the table, the crowd parting at his approach.

Once outside, Lizzie clapped her hands like a little child. "Let's go to the pier and do some shagging." She turned to Joe. "Honey, can you run to the car and get our fold-up chairs? We'll need somewhere to rest after cutting some rug."

Emmy held up her hand. "Don't worry about getting one for me. I'm not much of a dancer, and I've got work to do at home, so . . ."

"Oh, come on, Emmy," Lizzie cajoled. "It will be fun whether you dance or not. There'll be tons of people talking and dancing and a lot just watching."

Emmy shook her head but was spared from speaking by Abigail. "I think Emmy's trying to say that after all our yammering over dinner, she needs a little bit of quiet alone time."

Lizzie looked genuinely disappointed. "I understand. I really do. I've been jabbering at you all night long as if I've known you forever, and you must be plain sick of hearing my voice. And I'm sorry. It's a nasty habit I got from my mother, so you've been doubly tortured for one night, and you are free to go."

With an appreciative look, Emmy said, "Thank you for being so understanding. But would you please let me take a rain check?"

Joe came back with folding chairs under each arm. "Be careful what you wish for, Emmy. Lizzie won't let you forget it."

"Good," Emmy said, surprising herself. It had been too long since she'd allowed any kind of friendship in her life. Her high school and college friends had drifted away once she'd met Ben, and after his death, she'd felt years older than them, too far removed from their lives of husbands, children, and mortgages to care enough to resurrect their old friendships.

But there was something warm and genuine in Lizzie, and her entire family—with the exception of Lulu, and even Heath sometimes—that made Emmy long for the girlhood friendships she'd once cherished.

She turned back to Lizzie. "Good luck next week. Everything will be fine."

Still smiling, Lizzie wrinkled her brow. "You sound like you really know that for sure."

Emmy shrugged. "I'm not psychic or anything. It's just sometimes I . . . know things. I get this little buzzing in my head, and most of the time, I know what it's trying to tell me—like in this case. Other times, I just feel stupid because I have no idea what I'm supposed to know."

Lizzie gave her another hug. "You can't imagine how thankful I am to hear you say that. Thank you. I don't feel quite as anxious now."

"You're welcome. Glad I could help."

Joe leaned over. "Guess you couldn't tell us if they'll be good sleepers, huh?"

They all laughed, and Emmy said, "Nope, sorry. You're going to have to figure that out on your own."

John wheeled his chair over to their group. "When my mother was pregnant, the doctor prescribed beer for her. Said it was good for the baby's health. And all I can say is that I turned out fine."

"According to you and who else?" Abigail grabbed the handles on the back of his chair. "Come on, let's go do some dancing and leave Emmy alone."

They said their good-byes, and Emmy stood on the sidewalk watching them leave, one part of her wishing that she was going with them and the other part of her wanting nothing more than to dig into the stacks of books in her living room that she'd had very little time to go through. In the handful that she'd flipped through over the past few weeks, she'd found only three short, cryptic notes, all saying the same thing: *When?* It had been nearly impossible to determine who had written them with only a few characters to judge, but Emmy thought that one had been written by the woman and the remaining two by the man.

Sooner or later, she'd have to approach Lulu, and she dreaded it. For now, the elusive story of the unknown man and woman played out in the margins of the old books was Emmy's alone. She felt protective of them, and if she wanted to look closer, she was indebted to them for pulling her out of the shadowed existence she'd been in since Ben's death. And they had brought her to Folly's Finds in an indirect way. As much as she loved the store, even she couldn't deny that the two clandestine lovers were what kept her getting out of bed every morning, keeping her grief contained. She couldn't tell anyone, least of all her mother, that she still felt Ben's loss the way she imagined trees missed the rain. Folly's Finds and the people she'd met since moving to Folly were only a Band-Aid that hid the hurt and loneliness she felt every time she rolled over at night and found the space empty. Sooner or later she was going to have to rip it off and allow herself to let Ben go. But that would take a lot more bravery than she had, regardless of what John Reynolds and Lulu told her.

THE SUN HAD DIPPED LOW in the sky by the time Emmy made her way back to the house, the orange glow turning the tips of the marsh grass golden. She stood on the back porch, watching the shades of color shift like those on a chameleon, wondering what the true color of the marsh was. The lighthouse stood sentry in the distance, abandoned on its spit of land, caressed at each high tide by the same ocean that threatened its existence.

She'd yet to venture onto the dock to see the marsh up close. Like the ocean, it was an enigma to her, a place full of strange smells and sounds that at the same time seemed so familiar. She resisted the pull to move forward, content for now to view it only from a distance.

Despite the mugginess of the late-summer evening, she left open the French door leading to the screened porch, wanting to hear the night sounds of the marsh as a backdrop to the hidden notes between two lovers.

After grabbing her laptop, she settled herself between the stacks of books, then pulled the first book off the top and began her methodical examination. She'd gone through an entire stack and was halfway down the second one before she found something. In a copy of Edith Wharton's *The Age of Innocence*, on the last page of the book and written in a woman's handwriting, were Shakespeare's words:

"My love is as a fever, longing still
For that which longer nurseth the disease."

Oh, darling—this is wrong! But I must see you. Tell me when.

The ink was smeared, the paper warped as if it had been touched by water. Or tears. With renewed enthusiasm, she reached for the next book, a collection of poems by A. A. Milne entitled *When We Were Very Young*. It was an old copy, but in her enthusiasm to find more notes, she didn't bother to study the copyright page to determine if it might be a first edition.

Still, she turned the pages carefully, not wanting to accidentally tear one or bend a page, her patience rewarded in the very center of the book with a short line, written in the man's handwriting. *Sir Francis Bacon said it best: It is impossible to love and be wise.*

The doorbell rang, ending Emmy's time-traveling, leaving her confused for a moment as she regained her bearings. Glancing out the front window, she spotted a golf cart, then recognized Heath's outline in the leaded glass of the front doors. She had a fleeting thought of pretending she wasn't there so she could go back to her books and their secrets, but realized he'd already seen her car in the driveway and the lights she'd turned on inside the house.

She opened the door and stood in the middle of the doorway, blocking his view of the mess behind her. "Hi, Heath. Thought you'd be dancing."

"I thought so, too, until Lizzie told me you'd gone home. Figured I could make you reconsider."

Emmy shook her head. "Only if you want broken toes. I'm a terrible dancer." She waited for him to admit he'd given it his best try and leave. Instead, he smiled at her, an odd glint in his eye.

"I knew you were going to say that. That's why I came prepared with an alternative. The Perseids are visible tonight. There's going to be some cloud cover but we'll still get a pretty cool show. I bet Frank that you haven't been over to the east end of the island yet, so I figured we could kill two birds with one stone tonight."

"I'm kind of . . . busy," she said, unwilling to tell him what she'd been doing, somehow knowing he'd disapprove.

"With what?"

She frowned. "I'm organizing your books. It's a huge mess in the living room, and I'm trying to finish so I can walk in a straight line again."

"You're finding more messages, aren't you?"

She knew it would be pointless to lie. "Some."

"They'll still be there when you get back, won't they?" He leaned a hand on the doorframe, as if he was prepared to wait a while.

"Yes, but . . ."

He grabbed her arm. "Then come with me. I promise to only keep you out for a little while."

"Wait. I've got to shut the back doors."

A slow smile crossed his face. "You're liking the smell of the pluff mud, aren't you? Unless you're a native, most people can't stand it. Must be a sign."

She frowned, then went inside to close the doors and grab her keys, not pausing long enough to wonder how he'd manipulated her. With a last look at the books and her laptop, she closed the door and locked it behind her.

As they drove down the nearly deserted East Ashley, Heath turned to her. "Why do you always frown when you see me?"

She thought for a moment, realizing that he was right. "I don't really know. Maybe because you seem to always be okay with the world around you, despite the fact that I know you know better. Like you're one of those eternal optimists or something."

"An eternal optimist?"

"Yes. You're one of those people who always thinks good will come out of every situation, regardless of how bad it is." She thought for a moment, then asked, "Glass half filled with water?"

"Half full."

"A rainy day?"

"Great excuse for sleeping in and reading in bed all morning."

"A hole in your pants?"

"Time to go shopping."

She paused for a moment. "Losing someone you love."

He didn't answer right away, and kept his gaze focused on the street in front of them. "Feeling lucky enough to have had that person in your life, and to have known love at all."

Emmy turned away, forcing breath into her lungs. He had no idea; he couldn't know that sometimes she wished she hadn't been working the day Ben walked into her mother's store. That loving Ben had been the best part of her life, and losing him was far worse than never having known him. Before she could pull the words back she blurted, "What about Jolene?"

He remained silent, navigating the golf cart to the end of the street, where he parked it near the beach access. He stopped the motor and sat back. "I'm not going to answer that right now because you're in a snit. You're upset because I'm not like everybody else who leaves you alone to wallow in your misery. Life's too short, Emmy. Believe me, I know."

He hopped out of the golf cart and retrieved two lawn chairs from the backseat. Emmy crossed her arms, more angry than she wanted to admit. "And having cancer suddenly makes you an expert on life."

Leaning on the chairs, he met her eyes, not showing surprise that she knew. He was probably used to his mother and sister sharing his life with others. "Yeah, it does. Now come on. They close this part of the beach at eight o'clock, and I'm not in the mood to be arrested for trespassing."

"I want to go home."

"No, you don't. You wanted to see the Perseids."

He began walking away from her, and not knowing what else to do, she hopped from the cart and ran to catch up, the thick sand still warm under her feet and slowing her down.

"I don't even know what they are," she said, panting. "Please take me home."

He stopped to face her, his eyes serious. "Every year in August, the Earth passes through rock and dust fragments left behind by a comet. As these rocks and fragments collide with the Earth's atmosphere, they burn up, creating a bright streak of light across the sky." He paused as if waiting for her to say something, but all she could do was stare at him and wonder why he couldn't see that she was a ghost and not really there at all.

He continued. "So you see? Your life isn't over. You're about to see something wonderful that you've never seen before. The Perseids have always been there, every August up in the sky, since long before you were born, and they will be there long after you're gone. Doesn't that make you feel like you're part of this universe? Part of a story that hasn't been told yet?"

The wind shifted the hair off his forehead, revealing the scar that glowed white against his tan and the fine lines around the eyes that showed he was a man who laughed a lot. Who saw a hole in his pants as a reason to go shopping.

"Fine," she said, not really knowing why, while also knowing that if she'd really wanted him to take her back, he would have.

He smiled broadly, his teeth glowing in the dimming light. "Great. Let's walk quickly so we can see where we're setting up our chairs."

She followed him down a path that was part deteriorated road and part sand through scrubby grass and bushes, stumbling over rocks in the dimness. On their left, they passed the graffiti-covered remains of the foundations of buildings. "What's that?"

Heath didn't slow down, apparently eager to get to where he was heading. "Old coast guard long-range navigation station. Built around nineteen forty-five, I think. Was active through nineteen eighty but pretty much made obsolete by sonar. Now teens just use the area to make out and have a few beers."

Emmy stepped over a beer bottle and found herself wondering if Heath had ever been one of those teens. She started jogging to catch up, panting heavily with her dress sticking to her back, until the path ended on a rise, the wide expanse of beach and the Atlantic Ocean in front of them. Rocky groins stuck out like muscled arms into the water, while looming above them, the Morris Island lighthouse rose over the waves that slapped at it on all sides. She stopped while Heath kept going, the view of the defunct beacon as it stood in lonely isolation unsettling her somehow. The skin at the back of her neck began to prick, rising as if it had been brushed by a goose feather. She continued to stare as the sun began its descent, the sky already darkened by the growing cloud cover. Hurrying to catch up with Heath, she tried to shake the unsettled feeling she'd had.

Sparse groups of people dotted the beach, apparently planning to watch the meteors, and Heath headed toward a spot away from the others. He had already set up the two chairs and was motioning to her when the sky lit up with a shooting arc of light, quickly followed by another and another, making the sky blush in shades of gray and white. Ribbons of white light continued to illuminate the sky in rapid succession like a congregation of silent lightning bolts, reflecting off the swaying waves as they touched the shore and danced with the meteors.

Forcing her gaze from the sky so she could find her way to her chair, Emmy sat down and tilted her head back to stare upward. They sat like that for a long while, not speaking, taking in the cosmic light show as if it were being performed for their sole benefit. Eventually, she lowered her head because her neck had begun to hurt, and she realized that her face hurt, too, as if she'd been grinning for a long time.

"Pretty cool, huh?" His words held a smile.

"Why are they called the Perseids?"

"Because it appears as if they're coming out of the Perseus constellation, but they're actually only about one hundred miles from earth. And I'm sure you remember the story of Perseus and his love for Andromeda."

She did, but she enjoyed listening to him talk. She usually found herself alone in the evenings, and it occurred to her that she was probably starving for human companionship. "Tell me," she said.

"Perseus sets out to free Andromeda, the virgin who was chained to the rock to be devoured by Cetus, the whale. Before Cetus can eat his dinner, Perseus arrives with the head of Medusa in hand and shows the head to Cetus. On seeing Medusa, Cetus is turned into stone, leaving Perseus to marry Andromeda, and they live happily ever after."

Emmy shuddered, thinking of being turned to stone. "That's a harsh punishment for only wanting a meal."

"One of the worst, for sure," he said, watching her, his face serious.

She squirmed a little in her chair and looked back at the sky, eager to change the subject. "It's beautiful. I can't believe I've never bothered to notice them before. How come you're so familiar with them?"

He didn't answer right away. "I spend a lot of time outdoors, especially at night during the summers. There's a lot you can learn about the world and life in general just by being outside. A lot more than you can with your nose stuck in a book."

"My nose isn't always stuck in a book. I do other things." She paused, her mind scrambling, knowing that going through a room of books looking for hidden messages wasn't what he was looking for. "Like running Folly's Finds. We're starting a children's reading corner, you know. And I . . ." She thought for a moment. "I walk. Sometimes I'll walk around downtown Folly during my lunch break. But not for too long because then I'll get too sweaty to go back to work."

He stared at her without speaking for a long moment. "That's pathetic. You're so near to the beach, you should start running every morning. It clears the mind, and it's good for your heart. You'd get to find sea glass and cockleshells before the crowds show up."

"What's sea glass?"

"Come running with me and I'll show you. You can work on your tan while you're at it."

She turned away from him, frowning. "I like my skin a healthy white, thank you. I'll let you know about the running—but don't hold your breath."

"You do that."

They settled back into their chairs as the night glowed all around them, the background music of the ocean lulling her into an almost doze. She turned her head to face him, her curiosity erasing all filters once again. "How long have you been cancer-free?"

"Nine months, two weeks, and five days. So far so good."

His face was turned toward her but she couldn't see his eyes in the shadows. "Do you ever worry about it coming back?"

He didn't hesitate before answering. "No. I think worrying is a lot like chewing gum. Eventually it runs out of taste, and you've got to spit it out."

She laughed, then covered her mouth, embarrassed. "I'm sorry. I just . . . Well, I can't believe you'd compare chewing gum to cancer."

"No, I was comparing worrying and chewing gum. I figure if I take care of myself and get my checkups like my doctors say, then I'm doing all I can to stay well. There's nothing else I can do, and worrying won't help. I figure each day I have is sort of like a bonus, so I might as well enjoy each one."

The silence between them lay heavy, full of light and sand and water, threaded with loss, longing and regret. She'd once greeted each day with hope. But that Emmy was a ghost now, haunting her now with a dogged persistence, and she wasn't sure how to exorcise her. Or what permanent part of herself she'd lose if she did.

Tilting her head back, she stared up at the sky, pulsing like a heartbeat, and she tried to remember the last time she'd examined the world around her, realizing with a start that it had been long before she'd even met Ben. Sometime when she was still a girl, when she knew her mother saw only something she could lose whenever she looked at Emmy. She'd found her books to be her refuge, and in many ways, she supposed, she still did. They would never leave her, and she took no small comfort in that.

She threw a sidelong glance at Heath, mildly irritated with him for shaking up her equilibrium and with herself for allowing him to.

"I read your note in the bottle tree."

He turned his head to look at her. "I know. That's why I took it out."

"Did you expect Jolene to see it and answer it?"

Shrugging, he said, "Not really. It was Aunt Lulu's idea. She said that when she was little, she used to leave notes for a friend who'd moved away, even though she knew the friend would never see them. She said it brought peace to her soul—like sending a prayer directly to heaven—and I figured that's pretty much what I needed."

Emmy shook her head. "Your aunt Lulu is like Jekyll and Hyde. She'll give me so many reasons to dislike her, and then, wham, I hear something like that, and I can almost begin to understand why people love her enough to hug her and invite her to family gatherings."

His soft laugh carried to her in the night air. "Don't be so judgmental. She's had a hard life with lots of losses. But she's one of the strongest people I know. She's still standing and thriving despite it all."

Emmy threw a sharp glance at him, wondering if his words were meant to inspire her, as if he knew anything about her. She was about to let him know that she was just fine without him playing Freud when he spoke again.

"Maybe I'll teach you how to shag."

"Excuse me?"

"Shag. The South Carolina state dance. They call it a warm night with a cold beer and a hot date." He winked and waggled his eyebrows. "During the forties and fifties and even part of the sixties, the Folly Beach pier was the place to be. We had all the major performers—Glenn Miller, Tommy Dorsey, the Drifters. Big names. And where the Holiday Inn is now, there was a pavilion with an arcade and concessions, and next to that was Folly's Playground—the real thing, not a coffee shop—which was set up every spring and had a large Ferris wheel."

Emmy closed her eyes, seeing it all so clearly as if in a black-and-white photograph, the sound of big-band music hidden beneath the crash of waves against the shore. "What happened to it all?"

"Two fires—one in nineteen fifty-seven and the last in nineteen seventy-seven. But by then the playground was long gone, and the crowds had been staying away for a while. They rebuilt the pier and then built the hotel in nineteen eighty-five. Some even called that progress." He smiled as he turned to her. "But they still dance on the pier in the summertime."

She raised an eyebrow. "Maybe I'll just watch."

"It's not as much fun, trust me."

She gave a short laugh, then tilted her head back to watch the light show, her gaze straying to the lighthouse, which stood out in relief against the glowing sky. "Have you ever been inside the lighthouse?"

"When I was a kid. You're not supposed to, but you know how kids are. It's pretty cool up there. You can see all the way over to Sullivan's Island. There's a foundation now raising money for its restoration. There's actually a little mini-lighthouse replica near where we parked. You can pick up some information about the light's history and the foundation on the way out."

She nodded, focusing on the lighthouse again. "How do you get there—swim?"

"No, definitely not. These are some of the toughest currents around Folly. It's a strict no-swimming zone, but you occasionally hear about people drowning. Either they were stupid enough to wade out into the surf, or maybe they fell off one of the large rock groins. I don't even like taking my boat out there, and I wouldn't recommend it for beginners."

He stood and looked around, then glanced down at her. "It's almost eight o'clock—we should get going. I'm sure you've got books to go through back at the house."

She stood, too, and they both folded up their chairs. Heath took hers to carry, and they began walking back the way they'd come, the Perseids continuing to light the sky around them.

They were almost back to the road before Heath spoke again. "I almost forgot. I think I might have found out who your Peter is."

She stopped to look at him and he stopped, too. "Peter—as in Lulu's and Maggie's friend?"

"I think so. I own the lot where Maggie's house stood—Lulu deeded it to me some years ago, and I'm still trying to decide what to do with it. Anyway, I was going through some of my papers the other day, looking for something, and I came upon all the paperwork for the house, going back to when it was built at the beginning of the last century. While flipping through them, I found a sales transaction from May, nineteen forty-three where Maggie O'Shea sold the house to a Peter Nowak. For ten dollars."

Emmy raised her eyebrows. "Ten dollars? I know real-estate prices were much less then, but still, that sounds like a steal."

They began walking again toward the golf cart. "It was. It seems like it was more of a gift than anything else."

"Sounds like maybe he might have been more than a friend. Especially considering that Maggie still lived in the house at the time of her death in nineteen eighty-nine."

They reached the golf cart and stopped while Heath placed both chairs in the back. "I thought the same thing. Guess you have one more thing to ask Aunt Lulu."

Hoisting herself onto the front passenger seat, she groaned. "Yep. Might as well make a list and get it all over with at one time. Maybe you could come with me."

"Maybe," he said noncommittally as he turned the key until the motor purred.

As they drove down the street, Emmy asked, "I need to add some bookshelves to the store to accommodate our new design-and-greeting-card section. Do you know anybody to recommend?"

He looked hurt. "What am I, chopped liver?"

"You're an architect. I just need a carpenter I can pay at carpenter prices."

He pulled into the driveway and stopped before switching off the motor. The night became alive with the humming of thousands of invisible insects. "I'm a carpenter at heart, and it's what I used to do before I went to school to become an architect. I can build your shelves. I'm on a part-time status at the firm right now anyway, so I might as well be productive. I'll even bill you at a reasonable rate if that makes you feel better, but I'd be happy to do it for free. But only on one condition."

"What would that be?" she asked slowly.

"Tell me that watching the Perseids was one of the most wonderful things you've ever seen, and that you were glad you went with me tonight to see them."

She stared at him while the sky cheered behind him. She wanted to argue, to say that he was wrong, but she couldn't. Unable to resist smiling, she repeated, "This is one of the most wonderful things I've ever seen, and I'm glad I went with you tonight to see it. There, are you satisfied?"

He nodded. "Pretty much. And now I'll be building those shelves for you. I'll be there tomorrow morning if that works for you."

"Thank you. I get there at eight, so anytime after that is fine." She exited the golf cart and was surprised to see him getting out, too.

Seeing her confusion, he explained, "A gentleman doesn't leave a lady in her driveway but walks her to her front door. The neighbors, remember?"

"Right," she said and began walking toward the front steps with Heath close behind. She'd enjoyed herself far more than she'd expected to and was reluctant to end the evening. As she stopped at the front door to retrieve her keys, she looked at him, half tempted to ask for his help in sorting through the books and hunt for messages. She knew that he would if she asked, but still she hesitated.

"Thank you," she said after opening the door. When he didn't start to leave she said, "Would you like to . . . ?"

Her words stilled in her throat as a low ribbon of light streaked across the horizon, leaving a rainbow-colored trail behind it like a memory.

Heath had turned around, too, to watch it. "An earthgrazer," he said. "Those are the ones that get the closest, and you can see all their colors." He faced her with a half smile on his face. "Make a wish."

"What?"

"Haven't you ever heard that if you make a wish on a shooting star, it will come true? And a meteor shower could be considered a storm of shooting stars."

She shook her head. "I don't believe in that."

He considered her for a long moment. "That's a shame." He began heading toward the steps. "Thanks for the company. I'll see you tomorrow morning."

Emmy watched him leave, then went inside and closed the door. Crossing the house to the back door, she went outside and looked up at the sky over the marsh, the quivers of light still agitating the night. Then, closing her eyes, she tilted her head back, and for the last first time, she made a wish that didn't include Ben.

CHAPTER 15

Maggie stared at the emptied shelf on the top of the rack with some satisfaction before moving her step stool around the stacks of her travel books and atlases, stopping in front of the pile of books that Peter had given her over the period of the nearly four months since she'd met him. Her mother's books had been precious to her, but these had become more so. Which is why she'd decided to find them a place on the shelves where people wouldn't have easy access to them or ask to borrow them. They were hers, and she would share any other book she owned, but not those.

After she'd gone into the back of the store to find a soft cloth to wipe dust off the covers, she heard the bell over the door ring, followed shortly by the sound of a nickel being dropped in the borrowing library's can. Hurriedly walking out of the storeroom, she called out, "I'll be right there. . . ." Her words stilled as she saw Peter staring back at her, a lopsided grin on his face.

"Hello, Margaret. I've brought you some more books." His face was tight and drawn, but his eyes brimmed with an intensity meant only for her.

Forgetting about decorum or the real possibility that someone could walk into the store at any minute, she ran and threw her arms around him, almost knocking them both into the bookshelf behind him. He dropped the books he'd been holding and enveloped her in his arms so that no space separated them.

His warm breath tickled her neck, and she sighed. "Oh, darling. It gets harder and harder each time you leave."

"I know." He kissed her behind her ear, sending delicious shivers over her skin. "When this war is over, things will be different, I promise."

"But when? When will this all be over?" She pulled back to look into his amber eyes that always seemed to be backlit by a fire that burned inside.

"Soon," he said, kissing her gently. "Soon." He moved her to his side but kept his arm around her shoulders. Examining the piles of books and empty shelves, he asked, "What's going on here?"

Maggie smiled guiltily. "I'm being totally selfish and placing all the new books that you've brought to me on the highest shelf, where nobody can see what's up there. That way, I don't have to share them."

He raised an eyebrow but his smile gave him away. "How very bad of you, Margaret. But I can't say that I wouldn't do the same thing." Leaning over, he kissed her again, longer this time until they both had to come up for air.

"Can I see you tonight?" he asked.

Maggie tried to push back her disappointment. "They've opened the fairgrounds for the summer, and Cat, Robert, and I promised to take Lulu after I closed the shop a little early." She rested her forehead against his chest, smelling wool, aftershave, and salty air. It was as if Folly Beach had already claimed him, branding him with her saturating scent. "But I don't want to leave you."

He sighed deeply, his chest caving with the weight of it, and Maggie sighed, too, sure it was because he didn't want to share her. Pulling her away from him, he held her by her upper arms. "Well, then, you can't disappoint Lulu."

"Why don't you come, too? You know Robert and Cat, and Lulu

would love to have you there, too. It's not just for children. Adults and older kids love it, too—it's a real Folly Beach icon. Everything shuts down after dark on account of the mandatory blackouts, but if we get there at four o'clock, we'll still have a couple of hours to have fun." She grabbed both of his hands and squeezed. "It's something we don't get a lot of anymore." Rubbing her nose against his chin, she said, "And I think you need to have a little fun. You've been working too hard."

His eyes seemed to shutter themselves, dimming the light that she'd seen when he looked at her. "Sure," he said slowly. "I just need to get back to my lodging house to unpack and change, and I'll meet you at your house at four. How does that sound?"

"That would be perfect. And I know the others won't mind—especially Lulu. Did you bring a book for her, too?"

His lips turned up in a small smile that didn't completely diminish his exhausted state. "Of course. I thought she might like Sherlock Holmes. I know she's a bit young, but Lulu is mature for her age. Besides, Mr. Holmes is an Englishman, so nothing he does between the covers of a book can be too alarming." He smiled and raised his eyebrows. "I also brought you a pound of sugar."

Laying her head on his chest, she listened to his heartbeat beneath her ear. "You're so good to us, Peter. I think I'd rather starve than not be with you." She closed her eyes, shutting away her tears. "Remember that time on the beach when you told me to wait for you? I thought this was the time that you wouldn't come back. But I waited, didn't I? I didn't even go into Charleston because I was afraid that you'd come back and not find me."

He put his hands on the sides of her head and kissed her lightly on the lips. "And I came back, didn't it? I'll always come back for you."

Their lips met again as Peter's arms pulled her closer to him, and Maggie closed her eyes, wishing they were somewhere more private. The bell rang again as the door opened, and they broke apart quickly when Lulu rushed to the back of the store.

Lulu stopped abruptly when she saw that her sister wasn't alone.

"What are you doing here?" she asked. Then, after Maggie had given her a nudge on the arm, she said, "It's good to see you again, Mr. Nowak." Her gaze dropped to the floor, where the books he'd brought had fallen, and her face brightened.

Following her gaze, Peter knelt and scooped up the books. "Yes, of course. I had to bring books back for my two favorite girls."

Lulu blushed as Peter placed the book in her hand. With excitement, she held it up for Maggie to see. *"The Hound of the Baskervilles."*

Peter turned to Maggie. "There aren't any Nancy Drew books out that she hasn't already read."

"You're more than generous. Thank you." Maggie sent a pointed look at Lulu.

"Thank you, Mr. Nowak."

Maggie glanced at the clock on the wall, then gave Lulu a hard look. "And why aren't you in school? You don't get out for another two hours."

Lulu's impatience to leave and start reading was evident on her face and in the way she tapped the toe of her saddle shoe on the wood floor. "Cat was throwing up when I was getting ready to leave this morning and she asked me to stay home in case she needed me."

Maggie chewed on her lower lip. "I hope it's not the influenza."

Lulu moved a step closer to the door. "It's not. She's feeling much better. That's why she sent me here. To make sure that you remembered you have to close the store early today so we can go on all the rides. Robert promised to take me up on the Ferris wheel two times."

"Must have been something she ate, I guess. All right. Tell her I'll be home around three thirty to change. And tell her that Peter's back and he'll be coming, too."

Lulu was already skipping toward the door. "I'll tell her," she said, the last word cut off by the slamming of the door.

Maggie's smiled dimmed when she turned back to Peter, whose face was even more drawn than before. She placed the palm of her hand against his cheek. "You look exhausted. Why don't you go back to your room and take a nap and see if you feel better? You won't hurt my feelings if you're not up to going."

He placed his hand against hers, then moved her palm to his lips for a soft kiss. "I am tired. I'm sure all I need is a little rest. I promise to be there at four."

He kissed her again before retrieving his hat from the front counter, where he'd left it, and then he exited through the front door without glancing back.

When Maggie returned to the house, she found Lulu on the front porch with her nose stuck in her new book, taking advantage of the warmer spring temperatures. Maggie greeted her but Lulu didn't respond or even acknowledge that she was aware of the world around her.

Smiling to herself, Maggie opened the door to find Martha putting her coat on in the front hall. She was frowning, which made Maggie begin to worry. "Is Cat feeling better? You don't think it's the influenza, do you?"

Martha shook her head as she tightened her lips. "It ain't the influenza, so don't be worrying yourself about that." She stared hard at Maggie for a moment before moving past her to the door. "But whatever it is that's ailing Miss Cat, I don't think it's something you can fix." She shook her head, then pulled the door open. "I made some chicken soup and she ate a lot of that at lunch with some crackers, so she can't be feeling too poorly. I put the rest in the icebox for later."

"Thanks, Martha," Maggie said as the older woman left, shutting the door hard behind her.

Maggie ran up the stairs, pausing briefly outside Cat's closed door before knocking and opening it a crack. Cat lay on her side facing the window. It was closed, but the blackout shades were pulled up and the curtains open, allowing the sunlight to pour over the bed like a warm drink.

Softly, Maggie said, "Cat?"

Cat moved her head slightly and smiled. "I was just thinking about you."

"You were?" Maggie approached the bed and sat down on the corner. She placed the back of her hand against Cat's forehead, relieved to find it cool.

"Yeah. I was remembering when we were kids, before my mama died. Remember playing half rubber with all the neighborhood kids? None of the boys wanted to let you play because you weren't very fast. But I let Donny Rowe kiss me so he'd let you play on our side. He was right, though: you weren't very good. But I wouldn't let him kick you off the team."

Maggie smoothed Cat's hair away from her forehead. "I never knew that. I thought Donny was just being nice."

Cat turned back toward the window. "And I was remembering when your mama died, how your daddy and everyone was turning to you to take care of Lulu and everything else, but I could see you were torn up pretty much more than anybody else but nobody was letting you cry for your mama."

Maggie swallowed, recalling those dark days and the sadness that never really went away. "And you took me to the beach and made me run in the water with my bare feet even though it was freezing, and I got the hem of my dress all wet. The black dye ran all down my legs, and it looked so funny that I wasn't crying anymore."

Cat smiled and looked up at her cousin. "There's not a lot you can't do, Margaret O'Shea. It took me a long time to find something you needed help with."

Maggie smiled, too, relaxing in the warmth of the room and the old camaraderie between them that had somehow been allowed to pack its bags and move on. "What's made you think about all of this now?"

"I don't know. Maybe I'm just tired. But I just wanted to see if you remembered, that's all."

Cat moved over and patted the mattress next to her, and Maggie lay down just as they had when they were girls. She felt sad and happy all at once, remembering how things had been between them while growing up together, how things had been before Jim.

They lay there without speaking for a long time, and Maggie's eyes were beginning to drift closed until without warning Cat hopped out of the bed. Maggie sat up, watching her cousin cross the room to the window.

"That damned window. It's so damned hot and Martha couldn't get it open." She hopped up on the windowsill with her bare feet.

"I wish you wouldn't do that, Cat."

"Well, somebody's going to have to. I've had so many people look at it to see if it can be fixed, and everybody tells me no. I guess they just want me to suffocate or something." She lifted the latch and threw her body weight against the window.

"Please, Cat—don't! You're going to get hurt."

"I know what I'm doing. And apparently I'm the only person in the world who knows how to do it." Holding on to the latch, she threw her body against the window three times until it opened. Maggie jumped up and screamed as it looked like Cat was about to go through the open window, but Cat's hand had found purchase on the sill, her other hand still clasped around the latch.

With a brilliant smile, Cat said, "Told you," then gently hopped down onto the bedroom floor, brushing her palms against each other.

"You're going to hurt yourself one day, and then I'm going to tell you that I told you so." Despite her words, Maggie couldn't help grinning at her cousin. They were practically sisters, with the bond that went beyond shared blood—a bond that was even stronger than a deathbed promise. Regardless of the past few years, Cat was the one who'd always made Maggie laugh. The only person who could make her take herself a little less seriously. She'd needed this reminder, and she made a mental promise to herself that she'd never forget it.

Maggie glanced at the small clock on the bedside table. "It's almost four o'clock. Are you sure you're feeling all right to go to the carnival tonight?"

"I feel fine. Must have been a touch of a stomach bug. I'll stay away from the cotton candy—if they even have any with sugar being so scarce."

"Great. I'm going to go change. Robert and Peter will be here at four." She turned toward the door and opened it.

"Peter's coming?"

Maggie turned around slowly, not recognizing the note in Cat's voice. Facing her again, she replied, "Yes. He came to the store and I invited him. I didn't think anybody would mind. Lulu was supposed to tell you."

Cat smiled, putting Maggie at ease. "I guess she forgot. But I don't mind if he's coming. It'll be good to see him again."

Maggie smiled back, then left, closing the door behind her. Yet the entire time she spent getting dressed, a niggling worry dug under her skin like an unreachable bug bite—tiny and invisible, yet undeniably there.

Robert and Peter arrived promptly at four o'clock, and Maggie was ready to greet them. Cat kept them waiting for thirty minutes before descending the stairs, looking more stunning than usual and wearing a slim pencil skirt, alligator shoes with high heels and ankle straps, and a short fur jacket. Maggie recognized the shoes as new since they were alligator instead of leather, which had been designated for strictly military use. Cat had been evasive when Maggie asked where she'd got the money to buy them, and Maggie wasn't all that sure she wanted to know. It was too warm for fur, but Maggie could tell that the temperature had nothing to do with Cat's choice.

Maggie felt like a little girl in her cotton dress and cork-soled wedgies, and she realized to her horror that she was dressed a lot more like Lulu.

The men stood and Cat greeted Peter briefly before approaching Robert and taking both of his hands in hers. "Darling, I'm so glad you're back. I've missed you." Then she slid her hand into the crook of his elbow and smiled at Peter and Maggie. "Shall we go?"

Robert and Cat led the way while Peter and Maggie collected Lulu from the porch, linking hands with Lulu in the middle as they made their way to Center Street, with its assortment of bars and eateries. It was the first night of the carnival's opening for the season, and the streets were already crowded with men in uniform and women in heels and pretty dresses heading for the pier to dance. Maggie looked at them with longing and Peter caught her expression.

"Tomorrow night I'll take you dancing again, all right?"

"Oh, please, could we?"

"Whatever you want."

She blushed, unable to respond. Lulu looked up at her and said, "You should ask him for a million dollars, Mags." She giggled at her own joke, then let go of their hands and surged forward to chat with a few friends ahead of her on the street.

Maggie and Peter strolled close together, almost touching but not quite. The dirt street beneath her feet and the smell of the approaching ocean all disappeared, her world shrinking to only the space between his shoulder and hers. He turned to say something to her but stopped when Robert slowed and they caught up with him.

"I was hoping I'd run into you, Peter."

"Really? And why is that?" Peter asked with mild interest. His hands were shoved into the front pockets of his pants as they strolled casually down Center Street toward the carnival and the Ferris wheel, which loomed over the shoreline like a giant beach ball.

"One of the fellows in my unit is from Solon, Iowa. Isn't that where you said you were from?"

"Yes, it sure is. What's his name—perhaps I know him. Solon's a very small town."

"That's what he said, too. Nathan Haynes. I believe you're around the same age. Ring a bell?"

Peter continued walking, his forehead creased in thought. "No, I'm afraid it doesn't. But I didn't attend school in Solon. My parents sent me to a private boarding school in Chicago, so I didn't have a lot of friends my age in town."

Robert nodded. "He knew you. Or your family, I should say. The Nowak name is well known because of the factory and the number of people your father employs."

Peter smiled. "I hope it was all favorable, then."

"Oh, definitely. He did say that he went to school with your sister, but he doesn't remember her having a brother."

"Really? My sister and I aren't that close, most likely because we're six years apart and I was sent away to school and she stayed home. Maybe because of my absence, she felt more like an only child." He paused and they continued walking. "Or maybe your friend just doesn't have a good memory."

"Yeah, maybe," said Robert as they approached the ticket booth.

The sound of the carnival mixed with the band music coming from the pier, a heady concoction almost as delicious as the promise of the candied apples and roasted peanuts being sold at the concession stand at the entrance. Like hunting for shells on the beach, the summer carnival was a part of Maggie's childhood, and for a moment she wanted to take off running like Lulu, her head spinning from the lights of the giant Ferris wheel, unable to decide between the crazy mouse roller coaster or the tilt-a-whirl.

Cat and Robert disappeared in the crowd while Peter and Maggie wandered aimlessly, keeping an eye on Lulu as she rode various rides with her friends. Peter paused in front of a ball-toss booth and Maggie stopped, too. "How many tries?" he asked the attendant, an older man with a missing front tooth and skin as seamed as windswept dunes. Peter was already reaching for his wallet.

The man spoke without dropping the toothpick from between his lips. "A nickel buys you five tries to get it into the bull's-eye. Or for a dime I'll give you fifteen."

Peter pulled out a nickel and slapped it on the counter. "I'm not going to need more than two, I don't think." He winked at Maggie. "And what do I win if I get it in the bull's-eye?"

The man working the booth tapped a dirty fingernail on the glass-covered counter. "Your pick of any of these ladies' fashion rings."

Both Peter and Maggie peered at the cheap glass rings, then smiled at each other. Taking the first ball from the attendant, Peter said, "Go ahead and pick yourself a ring, Margaret, because you're going to be wearing one before I'm through."

Feeling silly, she held her breath while Peter took aim and tossed the ball. It bounced off the cup of the bull's-eye, ricocheting against the sheeting hanging in the back of the booth before rolling onto the floor.

"Four more tries," the man said without dropping the toothpick while handing the second ball to Peter.

This time, Peter tossed the ball a little higher than before, and it sank in its mark, barely touching the edges.

Maggie clapped her hands but restrained herself from throwing her arms around his neck. The attendant didn't look happy as he pulled the tray of rings out from the counter and dumped it on top. "Pick one. And do it quickly. Got a line of people behind you."

Maggie pretended to consider the choices for a moment before selecting a flower-shaped ring with five pink glass petals surrounding a pale blue center stone. Before she could slide it on the finger of her right hand, Peter stopped her.

"Allow me," he said.

Something cold and solid slid over the knuckle of Maggie's right-hand ring ringer, feeling a lot heavier than the cheap ring had looked. She gave a gasp of surprise as she straightened her hand out in front of her the way Cat had done with Jim's engagement ring. A single oval-cut sapphire winked up at her, catching the glowing lights from the giant Ferris wheel.

"It's your birthstone. I saw it and couldn't resist."

"Oh, Peter." She pulled her hand in, clutching it close to her chest. "I can't accept this. It's just not . . . It's not proper for me to accept such an extravagant gift from you."

He placed his own hands over hers. "Even if it's a promise ring?"

Her eyebrows knitted over her nose. "What do you mean?"

Peter nodded. "Remember our promise?"

Her eyes searched his. "Yes, of course, I do."

"I want you to remember it every time you look at this ring. The world is a complicated place right now, and I can't offer you any more than this. But things will change—that's the one thing we can bet on. And then we can make new promises to each other."

The air thinned suddenly, the carnival lights and sound of the ocean encircling Maggie's head like a time warp as the earth stilled on its axis. She paused, stamping each sight and sound in her memory, knowing that this would be the moment she'd recall always as the happiest moment of her life. She stood on her tiptoes until her lips were only a breath away from Peter's when she felt someone grab her hand.

"Mags!"

Maggie looked down to find Lulu looking at her impatiently. "You said you'd go on some of the rides with me." Her gaze slid to Maggie's right hand. She didn't say anything, which made Maggie fairly confident that she'd heard every word.

Before Maggie could respond, Peter said, "Let's go ride the Ferris wheel."

Their eyes met, and she swayed into him. "Oh, please let's! But I promised Lulu I'd go with her."

"We'll all go together." After waiting for Lulu's nod of approval, he took both their hands and led the way through the crowd to the end of the long line waiting for the Ferris wheel. Maggie couldn't remember being this excited before. Maybe it was the change in season, or even this small symbol of normalcy amid a world that seemed turned upside down. Or maybe it was simply that Maggie and Peter both knew that everything could change without their consent.

The three of them squeezed onto the seat with Lulu in the middle, their feet nestled against the footrest beneath them, and waited for the attendant to fasten the thin metal bar in front. They crept upward as the attendants unloaded and loaded each car. Then, with a loud grinding noise, the large wheel began to spin slowly.

Lulu kicked her feet with excitement as Peter met Maggie's eyes over Lulu's head. His intensity made her blush and look away toward the endless ocean, where it touched the sky's edge. It made her think of possibilities and of promises made. She placed her left hand over her right, feeling the shiny new ring.

When Maggie looked back at Peter, he, too, was staring out at the ocean, his face serious and unreadable, his gaze fixed on the horizon. But when he turned to face her again, his eyes were shuttered to her, as if they'd been looking at something completely different and what he'd seen had nothing at all to do with possibilities or promises. He looked away, down toward the ground, as if he couldn't wait to get off the Ferris wheel, and Maggie felt her world shift.

When the ride was over, Peter reached for Maggie, helped her out of their car, and smiled at her warmly. But as they walked away with the bright lights of the Ferris wheel behind them, Maggie couldn't stifle the feeling that she'd just missed a step on a long flight of stairs and found herself tumbling to the bottom.

CHAPTER 16

Emmy awakened at dawn, sure she'd heard footsteps. But when she opened her eyes, all she heard was the morning birds, whose names she didn't yet know. Like the marsh, they were to her another mystery of the Lowcountry—another unknown that made her feel more of a visitor than a permanent resident.

She sat up in bed and closed her eyes, trying to recall the footsteps again, remembering that they hadn't been in her bedroom but had come from the living room nearby. She shivered under the ceiling fan, afraid that the footsteps had been walking away from her.

After sliding from the bed, she went to the kitchen and started coffee, then stared at the mess around her. The new children's corner at Folly's Finds and the brand-new computer system and Web site had been taking up most of her time and energy, leaving little of either to go through the books scattered around the living room floor. There was only a small section left, probably only one or two days' worth of work. As she fixed her coffee, she tried to ignore the niggling thought that her reluctance to finish had less to do with time and more to do with her inability to say good-bye.

She considered going for a walk on the beach before showering and dressing, but quickly dismissed both thoughts. It was Sunday and she didn't have to leave the house at all, or even shower if she didn't want to. As comforting as the thought was, she bargained with herself to at least run to the grocery store later, if for no other reason than to see another human being.

After pouring herself a cup of coffee, she opened up her laptop, then settled herself behind the first stack of books and grabbed the one on top. She opened up the front cover and was surprised to find the first note, written by the unknown woman. The letters were small, John Dryden's words wrapping around the page: *"Love reckons hours for months, and days for years; And every little absence is an age." I need you, I need you, I need you. When? And please, make it soon. I love you.*

Emmy tasted the desperation and longing in her own throat, felt as if she'd written those very words. *Who was she?* For a brief moment, Emmy considered quitting, then putting all the books back on the shelves in the turret and closing the door. For months she'd known that it was a possibility she'd never know who'd written the notes or what had become of the two lovers. But now she found herself wishing that she wouldn't find out, knowing all too well that love wasn't enough to keep two people together forever.

In quick succession she found two more entries. The first, again from the woman, read: *You erase all doubts when we are together, and I cannot believe that we are doing wrong. Soon darling. Please.*

Emmy picked up her untouched coffee, only to find it had grown cold. With a shaking hand, she slid the last book in the pile, *Mansfield Park*, closer to her and opened the front cover. Slowly she flipped through each page until she'd reached page 141 and her hand stilled, the words, written in the man's handwriting, sending the old familiar chill down her back. *This must end. I am near desperation—the kind of desperation that can drive a man to murder. I've been lying awake at night, trying to think of a way out of this intolerable situation. I need to talk to you. Meet me. Murder?* The word sent a chill through her, giving her the feeling of eavesdropping on a conversation she was never meant to hear.

The doorbell rang and Emmy jumped up, knocking the cup and spilling coffee over its sides. She looked down at Ben's old T-shirt, which went to her knees, then pictured her unbrushed hair and the dark circles that hovered under her eyes. For a moment, she thought about pretending that she wasn't there, but she caught sight of Abigail's car in the driveway through the front window.

With a lingering glance back at the books, she made her way to the front door and opened it. Her welcoming smile faded when she spotted Lulu standing behind Abigail and looking about as happy to see Emmy as Emmy was about seeing her.

"Good morning." Emmy looked expectantly at Abigail.

"It's afternoon," said Lulu, her gaze focused on the bottle tree etched into the window glass of the door.

"Yes, well," said Abigail, "Heath told me that you had some photographs here and in the envelope I gave you that needed identifying as well as some other questions that only Lulu can answer, so I brought her here, knowing that if I left it up to the two of you, it would never happen."

Emmy surprised them all by laughing. "How did you get her to agree? And I hope a weapon wasn't involved." She stepped back to allow them both inside.

Lulu brushed past her. "Nope. She just said that we could talk about Jolene and the Web site while I was here."

Abigail sent Emmy an apologetic look as she walked past Emmy. "Heath wanted me to tell you that he's back from Atlanta."

"He is? It's been so busy at the store, I almost forgot that he was gone."

Lulu snorted but Abigail and Emmy ignored her as Abigail said, "He said he'll be here for a couple of weeks to finish all the electrical work for the new section at the store, and that he hopes you've been walking on the beach each morning like he told you because he's going to take you running."

Emmy took her time closing the door, unwilling to meet anybody's eyes. She'd gone to the top of the dunes twice with the intention of walking—she'd even worn her sneakers and the hat her mother had sent. But like finishing up with the stacks of books in her living room, moving forward onto the actual beach had been too much of a permanent step—a formal good-bye to something she was unwilling to name.

Abigail walked through the living room, giving only a cursory glance to the stacks of books; then she flung open the French doors at the back of the house. "Might as well let the fresh air in now while it's a bit cooler." She walked forward onto the screened porch and peered into the backyard. She clucked her tongue as she took in the half-built deck. "You and Heath and your unfinished projects. I'm sure that must mean something."

Lulu snorted again and Emmy shot her a pointed look.

Abigail continued. "You didn't tell me you had an osprey nest back here."

"A what?" Emmy came to stand next to Abigail, following her gaze to a tall pole with a platform that had been constructed near the half-built dock.

"Heath told me he'd built a nesting platform but he forgot to mention that he'd gotten a couple of the ospreys to nest in it."

"What do they look like?"

Abigail looked at her oddly. "They're pretty big—a lot of people confuse them with eagles. Except they're brown on top and white on the bottom, and their wings have a bit of a bend to them." She turned to face Emmy. "Sometimes, to get the fledglings to leave the nest, the parents will refuse to give them food." They both returned their attention to the empty nest. "And sometimes those same fledglings will go find another nest, where other adults will feed them until they're ready to leave on their own. Makes them seem almost human, doesn't it?"

Emmy wasn't sure how to respond, so she remained silent, watching the abandoned nest and how the afternoon sun created an orange halo over the sleeping marsh. "Where are the birds now?"

"Starting in August they begin migrating south, some to Florida, some all the way to Cuba or South America. But they'll be back in March to lay their eggs. They'll come back to this same nest—the same couple, too. They mate for life. Although when they migrate they might go to a completely separate continent, they'll always return to the home they share together."

Emily thought of the large birds leaving their nest and each other, secure in the knowledge that they'd see each other again in the nest they'd shared. "Not so human," she said, her breaking voice ruining her attempt to be flippant.

Abigail put a hand on Emmy's arm. "Give it time, Emmy. Just not too much time." After squeezing her arm, Abigail turned and went back into the house, as if knowing she needed to give Emmy a few moments to compose herself and accept that she'd been called a fledgling from another nest who'd just been told it was time to fly.

After a few deep breaths, Emmy followed Abigail into the house. "Can I get anybody coffee?"

She stopped, spotting Lulu sitting on a footstool in front of the pile of books Emmy hadn't searched through yet, a thick clothbound volume opened on her lap. Lulu's pale skin had whitened even further, and her hands shook.

Going quickly to Lulu's side, Emmy attempted to take the book from Lulu's hands but Lulu held on to it. "Are you all right?"

"What's wrong?" Abigail asked as she came to stand behind Emmy.

"I'm fine," Lulu barked, still clutching the book.

Abigail leaned over, seeing for the first time the words written in the margins. "What is it?"

"That's one of the questions I wanted to ask Lulu. In the box of books you sent to my mother's store, as well as in a bunch of the books stored here in Heath's house, I've found notes written in the margins of some of them. They appear to have been written by a man and a woman as an odd correspondence, although I have no idea of the chronology. There're no initials or signatures or anything to identify the writers, but from what I can tell, the handwriting looks the same in all of the notes."

"What kind of notes?" Abigail put her hand on Emmy's arm so she could get a better look.

Lulu hesitated, and for a moment, Emmy thought she might close the book and refuse to let them look. Instead, Lulu lifted up the book for the other women to read, her spine stiff and her attitude even harder to hurdle than usual.

Silently, Emmy and Abigail read, *"Love is a tyrant. Resisted." I must see you. When?*

"The first part is John Ford, from *The Lover's Melancholy*," said Abigail. "But who wrote that in the margins?"

"That's what I've been wondering, too. That's the woman's handwriting—the man's is different enough that you can distinguish between the two." Emmy took a deep breath, realizing that both Lulu and Abigail could be related to the writers and decided to leave out her suspicions that the lovers were involved in a clandestine affair. "They used these books to communicate with each other for some reason."

Emmy walked over to her laptop and picked it up to show Abigail. Handing it to her, she said, "I've been keeping a list of the books and notes I've found so far to see if I could put them in some type of order. As you can tell, they seem to be pretty random—except for the tone. Some of them are simply love letters, others are more desperate or angry, and a few are just eager for the next time they could see each other." She paused as she considered whether to continue, and her hesitation had as much to do with sparing the feelings of Abigail and Lulu as it did with her reluctance to simply let go.

Lulu continued to sit silently with her arms crossed tightly over her chest while Abigail read over the document on Emmy's laptop. When she looked up, Abigail's eyes were wide. "Where's that envelope of photos I gave you?"

Emmy thought for a moment, embarrassed to admit that she'd only glanced at the photos briefly before sticking them back in the envelope. She was pretty sure the envelope was on the kitchen counter, though, and she excused herself to go find it. Handing it to Abigail, she asked, "Why do you need them?"

Abigail sat down on a sofa and placed the laptop on the coffee table so she'd have both hands free to look at the pictures. "Well, as I'm sure the thought has already occurred to you, these books were Maggie's, so there's a good chance the woman's handwriting is hers. Since she wrote on the backs of the photographs, we can compare."

Carefully, Abigail slid the pictures out of the envelope onto her lap. The first was a picture of the same little boy Emmy knew was Abigail's husband, John. Emmy stood to retrieve the book Lulu still held, and when Emmy bent to get it, she again had the odd thought that Lulu wasn't going to give it to her. Instead, Lulu thrust the closed book at her. "Don't know why you want to dig up the dead. The dead should be left to rest in peace so the living can get busy with the business of living." Their eyes met and Emmy was certain that Lulu wasn't just talking about the unknown lovers.

Emmy brought the book back to Abigail, then flipped through it until she found the woman's handwriting. Abigail placed the photo of John wearing a cowboy hat, boots and holster on the page opposite and flipped it over where the words *Johnny November 5, 1944* were written on the back. They both bent over to look more closely, glancing up at the same time.

"They're identical," said Abigail. "Look at the way she curls the bottom of her lowercase *y*'s. And see here—" She pointed at the *r* in both the word *November* and *tyrant*. "They've both got a little curve at the top. It's very unusual—unusual enough to make me say that both of these samples were written by the same person."

"Maggie? Are you sure she's the one who wrote on the backs of all of these photos?" Emmy took the rest of the photographs and turned them upside down, sorting through them. All of them had something written on the back, and all in the same handwriting. She stopped when she saw the words *Our wedding day June 11, 1943.* Flipping it over, Emmy found a black-and-white photograph of Maggie wearing a smart skirt suit with hat and gloves next to an unfamiliar man wearing the uniform of a naval officer. She held up the photo to show Abigail.

"This is definitely Maggie, isn't it?" Emmy asked.

Abigail read the back, then took the photo before holding it up to show Lulu. "This is definitely Maggie. And this must be John's father. Is that right, Lulu?"

Lulu pursed her lips, tightening her arms across her chest. "I think Maggie would want us to stop prying into her business. She was a very private person."

Abigail rested her hands in her lap, still clutching the photograph. "But aren't you the least bit curious? I'm wondering if the man's handwriting is John's father's. I can ask John if he has any letters written by his father that we can compare. All I know about him is that he was stationed at the naval air station in Charleston during the war and met Maggie while dancing on the pier." She smiled. "That happened a lot back then. The high emotions of wartime brought people together a lot quicker than usual."

Lulu was staring hard at them, as if they'd missed something obvious, but she wasn't giving anything away. "I've got too much stuff to do today to take a trip down memory lane. Let's talk about your Web site."

Abigail held up her hand. "Hold on, Aunt Lulu. We need to look at these photos and the ones on the walls first. Emmy had a few questions." She took the photographs and spread them faceup on the coffee table so they could see them.

There were several of John in his cowboy outfit and boots, including one of him at the beach with the holster around his bathing trunks. Maggie appeared in most of the photos with John, always nearby, and in many of them, she had a hand on him as if she were afraid to let him go. She smiled in all of the photographs, but the expression in her eyes made Emmy lean forward, trying to see what it was in Maggie's eyes that seemed so familiar. With a start, she sat back, recognizing that what she saw was reflected every time she looked in a mirror: eyes with a muted light that looked out at the world like those of a caged bird.

Lulu was watching Emmy closely as if she saw it, too. "What do you want to know?"

Emmy lifted a photo from the table. It was a picture of the same man with the unusual eyes she'd seen in one of the framed photographs on the wall. She flipped it over to look at the back but there was nothing marked. "Who is this?"

With only a slight hesitation, Lulu said, "Peter. That was taken at the pier the spring of nineteen forty-two. Somebody gave Cat a camera for her birthday, and she went a little crazy taking pictures of everybody."

Abigail leaned closer. "I recognize the sand-dollar bracelet—is that Maggie's arm?"

Lulu shrugged. "Maggie's or Cat's—it's hard to say. It was Maggie's bracelet—she'd inherited it when our mother died—but sometimes Cat borrowed it. She borrowed lots of Maggie's things."

Emmy stood and walked over to the framed photograph. "It's definitely the same man—see the gold signet ring on his right hand? He sure doesn't look happy to be photographed."

"No, he hated it. That's why we only have two photographs of him."

Emmy jumped, unaware that Lulu had moved to stand behind her. Turning back to the four hanging pictures, she pointed at the wedding photo. "I believe this is Catherine, right? But who's her groom?"

A smile lit the corners of Lulu's eyes, as transforming to her face as the lifting of a veil. "Jim Brier. He was killed at Pearl Harbor."

Emmy studied the photo again, looking for clues of impending tragedy in the same way she'd studied her own wedding photos. But the faces were young and without guile, although her first impression that Catherine's expression was more of surprise and victory than of joy remained.

"How sad. Did they have any children?"

Lulu shook her head. "No. They weren't married very long before he was sent to Hawaii. She was very beautiful, wasn't she? Almost as pretty as Jolene."

Emmy frowned without responding, still trying to figure out what it was about the couple that made her uneasy, like considering sitting in a stuffed chair with visible springs. "Was Jim a local boy?"

"No. He was from Lafayette, Louisiana. He's the one who told me about the bottle trees."

Facing Lulu, Emmy said, "So, in a way, they're his legacy. Sort of like his own children that have lived beyond his years."

For a startling moment, Emmy thought Lulu would cry. Apparently, Lulu did too because she turned away and said gruffly, "Let's talk about the Web site."

"Fine," Emmy said, deliberately repeating Lulu's words, "what do you want to know?"

"When are you going to hire Jolene? I've seen what she's sent you and it's excellent work. You're costing me dollars here in potential orders."

Emmy raised her eyebrows. "Are you even prepared for more orders? It looks like you've got your hands full as it is."

Lulu mimicked Emmy's expression. "I've spoken with Janell. She's taking a class to learn how to bend metal in a controlled fire so she can make the tree trunks for me, which will make my turnaround a lot quicker. And I've got a stockpile of bottles that should last into the next millennium."

Abigail approached and put an arm around Lulu's shoulders. "Trying to rid the world of evil spirits one tree at a time, hmm, Lulu?"

Lulu snorted but Emmy hardly noticed. She was remembering the way Lulu had looked when they were discussing the photograph of Catherine and Jim. "How old were you when Jim married your cousin?"

"Why do you want to know?"

Abigail squeezed Lulu's shoulders before answering. "She was nine. Why?"

Emmy looked at Lulu, surprised to see her wearing a pleading expression. She swallowed her words, saying instead, "Just curious. I was trying to figure out how long this bottle-tree obsession of hers has gone on."

Abigail turned away, satisfied with Emmy's answer, but Emmy kept looking at Lulu, wondering why she didn't want a childhood crush brought up after more than sixty years.

"So why don't you go ahead and hire Jolene and get it over with already?" Lulu demanded.

Lulu's voice brought Emmy back to the present. "Because I haven't received any competitive quotes yet. And because she might be an alcoholic, which would make her unreliable. I can't afford that right now—especially with a new venture in this economy."

"Would you at least talk with her?"

Emmy studied Lulu for a moment. "I'm curious. Why is it so important to you that I hire Jolene?"

Lulu dropped her gaze, shaking her head. "You wouldn't understand."

"Try me."

Lulu's lips thinned as she glared at Emmy. "We both lost our mothers at a young age. It's an odd bond, but there it is. Other people don't understand what kind of a loss that is unless they've lost their mothers at the same age themselves. I knew why she couldn't continue to see Heath after he was diagnosed. I'm not saying that I thought she was doing the right thing, but I understood it—and I was the only one. I'm still the only one." She shot a quick glance at Abigail. "It makes her feel not so all alone, and I'm glad. Maggie did that for me, and maybe this is my way of returning the favor."

Emmy remembered what Abigail had told her, about how Jolene reminded Lulu of somebody she owed a debt to, and Emmy wondered if it could have been Maggie. But a niggling doubt remained, fueled by Lulu's antagonism and her reluctance to discuss the past and an old infatuation.

Emmy nodded her head, as if accepting Lulu's explanation. "I'll be happy to talk with Jolene. I wanted to before, but she went back to Atlanta. I'll admit her Web site pages are extraordinary."

"I'll have her call you and make an appointment, then."

"Fine," Emmy said. And then, as if somebody invisible had nudged, she added, "Thank you."

Abigail stood. "Well, I guess we should leave you so you can get back to your books." She led the way to the door, with Lulu and Emmy following.

They said their good-byes, and when Lulu and Abigail were almost down the steps, Emmy remembered one more thing she needed to ask. "Have you been able to locate that last box of books?"

Abigail turned around and shook her head but Lulu kept walking. "I've looked everywhere I could think of at the house and haven't had any luck. I'll keep looking, though."

"Thanks. I appreciate it."

Instead of turning around to follow Lulu, Abigail studied Emmy for a moment. "Don't spend too much time in the past, you hear? Sometimes you remind me of Maggie. I think sometimes she forgot that she had a life in the present."

Emmy stammered, too hurt and a little angry to come back with a response.

Lulu called back over her shoulder, "Or maybe she's just being nosy."

Ignoring Lulu, Abigail said. "I'll let you know if I find that box." Then with a wave, she turned around to join Lulu in the car.

Emmy closed the front door, remembering too late what Heath had told her about Maggie selling the house to Peter Nowak. For a brief moment, she considered running out to ask Lulu but decided she'd be better off catching her at work. Her interaction with Lulu had exhausted her, and she didn't think she could take another wayward glance or half-truth answer.

With her back leaning against the door, Emmy's gaze slid to the copy of *Mansfield Park* she'd placed on a side table before answering the door. Picking it up, she read the notation again: *This must end. I am near desperation—the kind of desperation that can drive a man to murder. I've been lying awake at night, trying to think of a way out of this intolerable situation. I need to talk to you. Meet me.*

She shivered again as a breeze blew through the opened French doors, bringing with it the pungent smell of the marsh and a whisper of music through the bottles in the bottle tree. They sang a song of unknown origin—a tune that tripped Emmy's memory and made her want to dance and cry at the same time. Emmy moved to the French doors and closed them, shutting out the marsh, the music, and the odd sensation that the world was conspiring to teach her steps to a dance she didn't want to learn.

CHAPTER 17

No light shone through the blackout curtains in Maggie's room, but she knew it to be near dawn by the sound of the birds outside. Her eyes stung from another night spent tossing and turning, listening to Lulu's breathing as she waited in utter darkness for morning. Peter had been gone for more than a week, and the temperature had risen quickly into the eighties, bringing with it high humidity that draped Folly like a wet sweater. Everyone seemed cranky, with news of more rationing and reports of even more ships falling prey to an accepted U-boat presence. Even though the Americans were finally claiming their own U-boat victims, with prisoners of one downed sub being sent to nearby Charleston, nobody could seem to shake off the persistent miasma that had settled on Folly along with the sudden change in season.

Maggie slid out of bed, careful not to wake Lulu; then she moved the blackout curtain to the side to let in enough light to see. After hurriedly washing and dressing, she headed downstairs. As she passed Cat's room, she noticed that the door was slightly ajar, although she knew Cat always slept with the door closed. Curious, she pushed the door open and peered inside, seeing the empty, unmade bed and Cat's nightgown left on the floor.

Maggie continued down the stairs, expecting to find Cat in the kitchen or parlor, a sick feeling settling in her stomach as she found the downstairs empty. She knew Cat wasn't patrolling the skies today because she was scheduled to work in the store and her spotter cards were still on the kitchen counter. Saturday was their busiest day and Maggie needed her help. But none of that explained why Cat wasn't in the house, or why Maggie's throat had become so dry.

She raised the blackout shades and straightened the parlor, eager to keep her hands busy. Restless now, and knowing she'd go mad waiting for Cat to come home, she grabbed a sweetgrass basket from a cabinet, slipped on her shoes, then headed out to the beach in search of turtle eggs. She'd make a nice breakfast for the three of them, and then hopefully she'd have a chance to talk to them about her plans to deed the house to Cat. If Maggie had to leave with Peter suddenly, she didn't want to have to wait or to worry about Cat. Lulu would go with them, of course, but Cat would need the house.

She walked slowly through the deserted streets toward the beach, swinging her basket by her side. May through August, the large loggerhead turtles lumbered from the ocean and laid their eggs on the shore before disappearing back into the sea. Since she was a girl, Maggie had come to the beach in the early morning to gather turtle eggs for breakfast, following the trail of gauged and ridged sand until it ended in a slight depression covered with sand and beach debris.

Her mother had taught her to take only as many as they would need and to re-cover the nest so that the rest would have a chance of hatching. Maggie had always wondered how a mother could leave her babies, never knowing if any of them would survive, and if the babies ever knew they'd been abandoned. She hoped they didn't. After her mother died, she'd lay her cheek against the sand and whisper into the nests that motherless babies could survive, even though the missing would never go away.

Maggie stood at the top of the dunes and breathed in the cooler morning air tinged with salt spray, her eyes spanning the empty beach. Farther down, to the west, she spotted the mounted-horse patrol too far away to wave. Leaving her shoes in the sand, she clutched the basket and scrambled down the dunes to the waterline and began her search for eggs and whatever treasures had been given up by the sea.

Long ago, when she was still a little girl, her mother had told her that what she found on the beach was just reminders that you weren't alone in the world. That she'd always find what she needed if she looked hard enough. It was a calming thought, and one that ran through her mind when she combed the beach. If she ever had a child of her own, she would make sure he or she would know that one little truth.

Ahead in the near distance, she spotted the telltale dips and sways in the sand and followed them up to the deeper sand of the beach. Kneeling, she placed the basket next to her and began to gently brush the sand away with her hands until she came to the round pearly-white eggs piled on top of one another by their mother and waiting for the call of the moon and the pull of the tides.

After gently taking six eggs from the nest and resting them in her basket, then re-covering the nest, she stood, eager to get back to the house before Lulu awoke but wanting to steal a few more moments of solitude on the beach. She almost wished she'd brought Cat's camera to capture the beauty of the morning.

Heading down the beach again, she walked near the surf, searching for sea glass. Her mother had called the bits of old glass washed in by the tides the ocean's jewelry—a treasure hidden in the sand and waiting to be found. As a child Maggie had loving finding the small bits of glass, imagining they'd once been part of a pirate ship or a king's yacht—a piece of the world outside of Folly Beach that she could hold in her hand. It was her first inkling that the world was much bigger than she could imagine, the sea glass her inspiration for studying world atlases and maps of the places she would one day visit.

She'd walked a good distance, lifting her head only when she heard what she thought was a seabird singing for its breakfast. With surprise, she realized she'd reached the pilings of houses on the east end of the beach, which had been washed away by the great storm of 1939, the storm in which the Folly River and the Atlantic Ocean had almost met in the middle of town. The pilings stood like silent sentinels watching over the ever-encroaching ocean, anticipating their fate.

Maggie heard the sound again, a wild plaintive cry, and swung around to see where it was coming from. A group of skimmers hovered over the water, swerving and dipping, calling out to one another like morning greetings over a back fence. But the sound she'd heard was different: a keening sound that she hadn't heard since she'd gone to Ethel Perkins' house to bring food after she'd received news that three of her four sons had been killed somewhere in France. It sent gooseflesh rippling over her skin, leaving behind the airless weight of dread.

She was about to turn back when she saw a flash of color in the sand behind one of the pilings. Slowly she walked closer until she identified the red of a woman's shoe, one heel hanging on to the bottom of the sole by a hinge of leather. She wanted to turn back, to pretend she hadn't seen it, to return to her ordinary world of searching for eggs and making breakfast. But since her mother's death, she had been the one in charge, the one people turned to because she would always do the right thing.

With her hand clutching the fabric of her dress over her heart, she approached until she spotted the hem of a matching red dress and the unmistakable fur jacket, now ruined with water and sand.

Still clutching her basket of eggs, Maggie rushed forward and knelt next to Cat, who barely resembled the woman Maggie had seen the evening before as she left to go dancing on the pier. Her hair was pulled out of its coiled curls, its golden mass in stringy waves over her mascara-stained face. Her red lipstick had faded to a pale pink, turning her face into the pinched underside of a starfish.

But it was her eyes, now a dull green with no hint of light behind them, that alarmed Maggie the most. If it hadn't been for the sound of Cat's crying, Maggie would have thought she was looking at a corpse.

Kneeling next to her, Maggie moved to put a hand on Cat's shoulder, but Cat flinched.

Surprised, Maggie sat back on her heels, resting her hands and the basket in her lap. "What's wrong, Cat? What's happened?"

Cat's sobs had become moans deep in her throat. Turning her face away from Maggie, she said, "Go away. You won't want to help me once you know."

"Know what, Cat? You're scaring me. Please tell me what's wrong."

Cat shook her head and Maggie saw that her hands were balled into little fists in her lap, a man's white linen handkerchief peeking out between her fingers.

Maggie's eyes widened with alarm. "Did Robert . . . Did he . . . Did he hurt you?"

Cat threw her head back and laughed, a sick choking laugh that had nothing to do with humor. Finally facing Maggie, she said, "No, actually. It's the other way around. I've hurt him in the worst way imaginable."

Maggie shifted on her knees. "You're not making any sense, Cat. What's happened? Tell me so I can help you."

Cat glared at her with her dead, dull eyes and shook her head. "You're so good and perfect, Maggie. Do you know how hard it is to live with you? To live with the shadow of your saintliness hovering over me every blessed moment of my day? You don't know, because you've never had a bad thought in your head."

Maggie wanted to tell Cat that she was wrong, that so many times over the years since her mother's death she'd had to cling to a deathbed promise to keep her from screaming out loud. Instead, Maggie reached for Cat, offering to comfort her in the same way Cat had done when they were children and Maggie was having bad dreams. But Cat pulled away again, and dread began its thick pulse through Maggie's blood. "That's not true, Cat, and you know it. Please tell me what's wrong. Please tell me so I can help you. There's never been a problem we couldn't work out together."

Cat struggled to a stand, her broken shoe making her twist her ankle in the soft sand. "God, Maggie, don't you see? You're so good that you can't see the evil in other people. You don't even suspect that it's there." She waved her hands at Maggie. "Go away. Go away before I tell you something you don't want to hear."

Maggie stood, too, being careful not to jostle the turtle eggs in her basket. She had the odd sensation that she was standing at the top of a long flight of stairs, knowing she could easily walk away or risk falling. Slowly she asked, "What did Robert do?"

"I'm warning you, Maggie. Stop asking or you're going to regret it." Cat wiped the back of her hand across her eyes, smearing mascara down her cheek.

Swallowing, Maggie asked again, "What did Robert do, Cat? You must tell me. Did he break it off with you?"

Cat pressed the heels of her hands into her eyes and let out a groan of frustration. "Yes," she shouted, loud enough to scare the group of skimmers and send them scattering. "Robert left me. He doesn't want to have anything to do with me."

Maggie marched toward Cat, ready to do battle for her cousin. "But why? It's so obvious he loves you."

Cat's lips turned into a thin sneer. "Because I'm pregnant."

Maggie stopped in her approach, surprised at Cat's answer. Of all the scenarios that had run through her mind, she'd not even considered this one. Cat knew how to avoid pregnancy; Cat had told her that when she'd married Jim. Maggie tried to hide her relief in finding out that it was news she could put in a box, could pack up and handle neatly. There was a convent near Charleston Cat could go to until the baby was born if Robert wouldn't reconsider. They could figure out all the details later. Right now she needed to get Cat home before anybody saw her, give her a bath, and feed her breakfast. Then they could talk about the rest.

Trying to hide her relief, Maggie said, "I'm sure it's just the shock of the news, Cat. From what I know of Robert, I'm sure he'll do the right thing by you. He's a good man. He wouldn't desert you—or his baby."

Cat shook her head, her green eyes never leaving Maggie's face. "He's not the father."

The words were delivered with such pointed accuracy that Maggie felt like she'd been shot. The sky seemed to dim, the water receding as her eyes focused on the woman in front of her in her ruined fur jacket and red heels.

"Then who . . . ?" Maggie couldn't finish the sentence. She seemed to be falling inside a red tunnel with only the sound of the ocean and Cat's voice as company.

"Peter."

The words were unadorned with maliciousness, making them that much harder to bear. The starkness of Cat's voice stripped away all the righteous anger that Maggie could conjure. Maggie stood still as her world spun out of control around her, afraid that if she moved she would break apart into sea glass. With a steady voice that surprised even her, she asked, "Does he know?"

Cat's voice rose. "Yes. I told him yesterday when he returned. He says he won't marry me because I'm not the woman he loves."

Maggie let her eyelids fall shut to block out the dead eyes and the red shoes. Without opening them she stepped backward and began walking, unsure of and uncaring where she went. She tripped and fell, her basket went sprawling, the eggs inside shattering against one another, their yolks bleeding yellow into the sand. She didn't stop but began crawling away until her legs could find the strength to stand again.

Cat ran after her, her fur jacket so incongruous on the beach that Maggie had the odd impulse to laugh, but knowing that if she started, she wouldn't be able to stop.

"But I know something about Peter that I'm going to tell everybody if he doesn't marry me and be a father to this baby. I told him I would shout it from the rooftops. But he said he didn't care, that he'd rather have you and be in prison than marry me." She was crying now, her voice near hysteria.

Maggie turned on her, unable to listen to another word. "Shut up!

Do you hear me? Shut up! I don't want to listen to any more. Go away. Leave me alone. I need to go someplace to figure this out, and I don't want you in my sight."

Cat stopped, swaying on her feet.

"Stay away from the house until I go to work. I don't want to see you until I figure this out."

Cat took a step forward, then stopped. "He has to marry me, Mags. I'm ruined if he doesn't."

Unable to remain in Cat's presence for another moment, Maggie turned away and began walking down the beach, unaware of the sharp edges of shells she crushed under her bare feet or the insistent rhythm of the breathing ocean that had once given her refuge.

⚬

LULU WATCHED AS MAGGIE SLID from the bed. Lulu pretended to sleep as she listened to the sounds of Maggie dressing. She wondered how long it would take Maggie to figure out that Cat hadn't come home the night before. Lulu had followed Cat again, the path made easier this time by the full moon and because Lulu had remembered to put on shoes.

Cat again had gone to the abandoned beach house, carrying her shoes as she waded to the steps. There'd been no flashing light this time, just the sounds of voices in the still night and of the door being shut, leaving behind just silence.

Lulu wasn't sure how long she waited but she'd fallen asleep, then was awakened by the sound of a man and a woman arguing. They were standing on the outside porch of the house and Cat was shouting loud enough that Lulu could hear every word and what she heard filled her insides with ice. It was only then that she figured out who the man was, and the recognition made her want to cry.

Cat left first, running down the stairs and not bothering to hold up the hem of her skirt. She was moving so fast that Lulu didn't have time to duck out of the way, not that it mattered in the end. Instead of going back down the street, Cat headed in the other direction, toward

East Ashley. Lulu thought for a moment that she'd follow but then the man left the house, too, getting in a car and driving away. Lulu had hidden behind a tree until he was gone, but by then it was too late to follow Cat. Lulu figured Nancy Drew and even Sherlock Holmes sometimes failed in their missions, but in the end, that was what always made catching the bad guys so much more exciting.

When she got home, Lulu was careful to wipe any sand from her feet, knowing that the last time she'd followed Cat, Maggie had asked about the sand in the sheets. She lay awake for the rest of the night, unable to sleep with the words she'd heard jumping around in her head like a rubber ball.

As soon as she heard Maggie leave and close the door behind her, Lulu left the bed and ran to the window and watched as her sister, with a basket on her arm, walked toward the beach. Lulu's stomach grumbled as she anticipated the turtle eggs Maggie would fry for her when she returned. At least it would give her time to figure out how much she should tell her sister, and to start making the bottle tree she knew Maggie was going to need.

Lulu was headed down the stairs when she heard the sound of one of the porch rockers being slid across the floorboards. Quietly, she tiptoed down the rest of the stairs and peered out the front window, not knowing she was holding her breath until she let it go in a gasp. Before she could step back, Peter had turned his head and was looking right at her. She stepped back, then ducked beneath the window, hoping he'd seen only his reflection.

They both sat within ten feet of the other for the next hour until Lulu heard the back of the rocking chair swing against the house as if Peter had stood suddenly. Peering carefully between the edge of the curtain, Lulu watched as Maggie approached the house. She didn't have the basket anymore, which was bad, but what really surprised Lulu was that Maggie was barefoot, her big toe on her right foot bleeding through the dirt and sand. In her whole life Lulu had never seen Maggie barefoot except on the beach, and even then she managed to keep her feet clean.

Maggie stopped at the bottom step and seemed to lean to one side when she saw Peter. "Why . . . ?" she started to ask, and then she began to fall like somebody had taken all the bones out of her legs. Peter caught her before she hit the ground, but his touch seemed to bring her awake again. She pushed herself away from him.

"Is it true? About Cat's baby?"

Lulu held her breath in puffed cheeks, waiting for the answer. But she could tell from Maggie's face that she already knew what it was.

Peter didn't look away, but stared Maggie in the face as he nodded slowly.

"I'm sorry, Margaret. It's not what you—"

Before he could finish talking, she raised her hand and slapped him hard on his face.

Lulu let out a cry, then put her hand over her mouth, knowing how thin the windows and walls were. But neither Peter nor Maggie seemed to have heard. She watched as Peter turned his head back to face Maggie again, a bright red spot on his cheek. Lulu had never seen Maggie hit anyone, and had always thought that maybe she didn't know how. Lulu wanted to look away, knowing that this would all be so much worse for Maggie if she knew Lulu was watching, but she couldn't stop. It was like when they had pulled Jimmy Fontaine out of the ocean after he'd drowned, and laid him on the sand. She'd wanted to make sure it was the same boy who sat behind her in math, so she had pulled away from Maggie to see.

Lulu still remembered what Jimmy had looked like, with all the color from his lips and face gone like it had melted in the ocean. And Lulu knew why Maggie hadn't wanted her to see, because Lulu still saw Jimmy's face sometimes when she closed her eyes to sleep, just like she figured Maggie would hear Peter's voice for a long, long time.

Peter stood staring at Maggie, and didn't defend himself when she lifted her arm to slap him again. Her eyes were puffy from crying, but now she was shaking so hard, Lulu thought it might have gotten cold outside again. In a voice that didn't sound like her own, Maggie said, "I'm not going to ask for any explanations because they don't matter.

The facts speak for themselves: you took advantage of a woman who is much more vulnerable than anybody could ever guess. She is weak, but you knew that. And now there's a baby to consider as well."

"Please, Margaret, I need to tell you—"

Maggie continued talking as if Peter hadn't said anything. "You will marry Cat now and become a member of this family, and I will accept you in it for the baby's sake. But that is all. There will be nothing but the most formal of relationships between us." She stopped talking, and for a minute, Lulu thought Maggie was going to faint because her hands were at her throat and she seemed to be trying to catch her breath.

Peter put a hand on Maggie's arm but she knocked it away, then began to walk up the porch steps.

His face was a greenish white, just like the color of an alligator's belly. "Margaret, I love you. You must believe me. There's so much you don't understand. . . ."

Without turning around, she shook her head as if to chase away gnats. "There is only one thing that's important here, Peter, and that would be that in less than nine months a baby will be born, and he will need a mother and a father to look after him."

Now Peter acted as if he hadn't heard what she'd said. "We can go away—just the two of us. To California. You've always talked about seeing Hollywood and meeting Bette Davis. And when the war is over, we could go to Paris. Or Rome. Or to any of the places we always talked about going." He put a foot on the bottom step but didn't go farther.

Maggie walked to the door, her back still to Peter. "I'll take Cat to see Father Doyle tomorrow to talk about the wedding. The sooner the better for everyone involved." Lulu watched as more tears dripped from Maggie's cheek, spotting her dress. "Can I trust you to at least do the honorable thing by Cat and the baby?"

Peter shook his head and looked at his feet. "Don't, Margaret, please. You must listen to me. There's something you need to know—

something much bigger than all of us. It won't excuse my behavior, but it might help you understand why. Please listen. I love you. You must believe me."

Maggie put her hands over her ears. "No more—do you hear me? I won't listen to you any longer. What's done is done. You've ruined everything, and I need to put the pieces of my family back together somehow."

Lulu remembered to duck behind a chair before Maggie ran through the door, slamming it hard behind her. As Lulu listened to Maggie's bare feet run up the wooden stairs, she peered through the window again, stifling a scream when her eyes met Peter's through the glass. He motioned for her to come outside, and she did, her heart slamming against her chest from surprise but not from fear. She'd heard his conversation with Cat and knew a lot more than he probably wanted her to, and as she'd learned from her books, it would keep her safe.

When she reached him, he sat down and ripped off a piece of notebook paper from the small pad he always carried in his inside coat pocket, and began writing something on it. She waited a few minutes until he stopped, then watched as he rolled up the paper like a cigarette and handed it to her.

His eyes met hers, and for a little moment, she felt sorry for him. She knew he loved Maggie as much as Maggie loved him, and Lulu began to feel as if she was seeing Jimmy Fontaine's body in the sand again, and she wished she could go back and stop herself from looking, because there are some things that will stick with you forever, whether you want them to or not.

She stuck out her palm and he placed the rolled-up note in her hand.

"Margaret told me that you put notes to your friend in your bottle tree. Could you put my note in one of the bottles? It's very important. Do you understand—*very* important." He stared at her hard, making her shift her feet.

"It's for Maggie but she's not ready to read it right now, or I'd ask you to give it to her. It's important nobody else sees it, so I don't want you hiding it in a drawer or anything. The tree is safer because everyone will assume it's yours."

She nodded, which was the response he seemed to be looking for.

"Tomorrow, let her know that it's there, all right? Do you understand?"

Lulu did understand, much more than he would ever know. She nodded her head again and closed her fingers into a fist around the note.

Peter stood and ruffled her hair. "I knew I could count on you. You're a smart girl, Lulu. Maggie's lucky to have you."

He picked up his hat from where he'd dropped it on the porch floor, and then he headed back down the steps. He turned around when he reached the bottom. "It's very important, all right? No one must read it but Margaret."

"I understand," Lulu said.

She waited until he'd driven away before she quietly let herself into the house and crept back into the hiding place between the window and the chair. Without thinking too hard about it, she unrolled the note and began to read.

My darling Margaret,

I need to talk to you, to explain everything. What I've done is despicable. But I need to tell you why—not to justify anything, but to keep you safe. Just give me this one last chance—that's all I ask. I want to take you far away from here, someplace you and I can start anew and leave this all behind us.

I promise that if you walk away after I've told you everything, I will never bother you again. And if you don't come at all, then I'll have my answer. I'll do what you ask, and marry Cat and be a father to the child, and I'll find a way to protect you from afar. But if you ever loved me as I still love you, you'll come. Meet me Wednesday night at our special place near the lighthouse at eleven o'clock. I'll be waiting.

Lulu read the note twice before rolling it up the way Peter had done. She stood, feeling like she was paralyzed, listening to the ticking of the clock on the kitchen wall. She couldn't let Maggie leave. She and Lulu belonged on Folly Beach. They always had and always would. And she definitely couldn't let Maggie go with Peter. Something inside of Maggie would die if she learned the truth about him, and just thinking that made Lulu feel stronger than she'd ever thought she could be.

Pushing back that voice in her head that always seemed to talk to her when she was doing something she knew she shouldn't be, she crept up the stairs and into her old room. The window blackout shades were still down, and she opened them to allow the light inside.

Then she knelt in front of her chifforobe and pulled out her treasure box, then set it on the floor and carefully opened the lid. Inside, the lace hair ribbon Peter had given her lay on top, and she felt a tiny stab of guilt at what she was about to do.

Sticking her finger inside, she moved back her special treasures to make room for the note and laid it inside next to the sand-dollar earrings and tortoiseshell barrette. She stared at it for a long time before finally covering it with the ribbon and quickly replacing the lid on the box. Then she slid it back into the bottom of the chifforobe and left.

She crossed the hallway and pushed open the door to the room she shared with Maggie. Her sister lay on the bed, her back to the door, but Lulu could tell by the way her shoulders shook that she wasn't asleep. Walking forward, she stepped in sand, then saw that Maggie hadn't wiped off her feet before climbing onto the bed. It was that one thing that convinced Lulu that she'd done the right thing. Lulu had come to understand since her mother's death that there was only so much truth and disappointment a person could take in life, and one more secret would be too much.

Without saying anything, Lulu slipped into the bed on her side and lay down, staring up at the ceiling and listening to her sister cry. Then she turned on her side and put her arm around Maggie just like Maggie had done for her when their mother died. She wasn't sure how long they both lay there, but by the time Maggie sat up, the sun had shifted in the sky and neither one of them had any tears left.

CHAPTER 18

This time when Emmy woke, the footsteps sounded so real that for a moment she wasn't sure she was dreaming. Throwing herself from the bed, she stumbled into the living room and looked around, half expecting to see Ben. Instead she heard the footsteps again, but they were coming up the steps outside toward the front door. In confusion, she raced to the front door and pulled it open, only to find a surprised Heath on the other side.

"Good morning," he said cheerfully. He wore an old gray T-shirt with cutoff sleeves and running shorts with the logo for the University of South Carolina emblazoned on the front corner. His knee was wrapped in a blue cloth brace and he had on serious running shoes. He looked at her closely as if wondering if she'd given herself the bedhead look on purpose.

She blinked at him a few times, still not fully awake. "Why are you here?"

His eyes flickered over Ben's shirt. "I hope you're not planning on wearing that to run in. It's so long, your feet could get tangled in the hem and you'd trip and fall."

His words jumbled past her brain, then reversed quickly before pausing on the word "run." "Run?"

"Yes—didn't my mother tell you I'd be here this morning?"

"I have no idea," she said, dropping her hand from the door.

"Do you want me to wait out here while you change, or can I come in?"

"You're serious about this, aren't you?"

He lifted his right ankle to his right hand and began to stretch his quad. "Yep. I'll give you five minutes before I'm coming in to get you. And don't forget a hat and sunscreen."

Still too groggy to wonder why she was doing this, Emmy quickly threw on a T-shirt, shorts, and sneakers, slathered on sunscreen, then grabbed a water bottle from the fridge before reporting to the front door, where Heath waited patiently. Belatedly, she went back to her bedroom, grabbed the visor she'd recently bought, and returned to Heath, breathing heavily from the exertion. He looked down at her shoes and frowned.

"I guess those will do for today since I'm only going to take you on a fast walk to get you started. But unless you want shin splints, you're going to have to get something else."

"That's assuming I survive the morning," said Emmy as she walked past him onto the porch. "Remind me why I'm doing this?"

"Because you've never done it before because you either never thought about it or maybe because your husband liked you pale and thin. Whatever. It's good for you."

She glared up at him. "You know nothing about my husband."

"That's right. But I know a little more about you, and you seem a little hesitant about doing new things or changing things up. I'm not being critical or anything. I just see you all pale and weak-like, and you've been living on the beach for some time now, and I have a sneaking suspicion you've only been on the beach once, and that was with me. Am I right?"

She stared at him for a moment longer, unable to tell him that he was wrong about her. About Ben. "Let's just go and get this over with, okay?"

Heath closed the door, and Emmy locked it behind them. His dog, Frank, sat patiently waiting for them, his red bandanna bright against his black fur. As they walked down the steps Emmy asked, "Why call a dog Frank? Why not Spot or Rover?"

Heath smirked. "He's named after my idol, Frank Lloyd Wright. I figured if my mother could name me after Heathcliff, I could name my dog after Frank."

They crossed East Ashley to the beach access with the clearly marked dog-leash sign, and emerged onto a nearly deserted beach at low tide. A lone beachgoer with a metal detector walked slowly at the water's edge, his detector hovering close to the sand.

"You mentioned before that your dad is a history buff who likes hunting for buried treasure." She indicated the man on the beach. "Is that what your dad does?"

Heath nodded. "Yep—but not at the beach because of his wheelchair. He likes going to battlefields and deserted plantations—that kind of thing. He's never found anything valuable—belt buckles and old shoes mostly but he really loves it. He'd love to take his metal detector to Morris Island—that's where more than twenty thousand Yankee troops were camped during the War of Northern Aggression—known to the rest of the country as the Civil War."

She glanced up at him and laughed at his mock seriousness.

"Unfortunately, most of it's underwater now." He reached down and snapped an expandable leash onto Frank's collar. "It's good to have a passion in life and keep at it. Unless it becomes an obsession." He glanced sidelong at her and she knew he was referring to the books that now littered every surface in her living room.

"We can beachcomb on the way back if you like," Heath said, picking up the pace. "Now, the object here is to take it slowly at first and then increase your speed so that you're giving your heart a reason to be up this early." He grinned. "But not too fast so that you can't talk, which is why I'm going to keep the conversation going so I can judge how you're doing."

"I was very happy in my warm bed, sound asleep. This just seems cruel."

"Yeah, well, I wanted to show you the other end of the island and this seemed to be as good a reason as any. Besides, you should take care of yourself. I'm a total believer in the mind-body thing. If you keep your body strong physically, it will help you mentally deal with everything else."

She sent him a sidelong glance, noticing how long his hair was, and that when it was wet, it probably reached his shoulders. It suited him, somehow, and it didn't bother her as much as when she'd first met him.

Focusing on the sand in front of her, she said, "Like losing a husband. Believe me, if I'd thought it was this easy, I'd have been running marathons long before this."

He continued to stare straight ahead. "I didn't say it was easy. I just said it would help. Maybe even more than escaping into the mysterious past of two lovers. Or spending every evening alone."

Emmy was breathing heavily now, but she wasn't sure if it was from exertion. "What makes you think that I wasn't that way before?"

"Maybe you were. I don't know. But you moved to Folly from Indiana, so that tells me that somewhere there's some wanderlust in you, some desire to see what's out there. Maybe it's time for you to become somebody different from who you were before."

She stopped, putting her hands on her knees so she could breathe better. "I will always be Ben's wife. I don't want that to change."

He stopped, too, but didn't say anything as if waiting for her to figure things out on her own. She wondered if that was how he designed buildings and neighborhoods, just stared at a blank page until the paper showed him the answers.

Heath began walking again. "Come on. You don't want to slow your heart rate yet." He turned to make sure she was following. "By the way, Liz wanted me to tell you that the babies' baptism will be on October twenty-fifth, and we're having a little party at my mom's to fuss over them. Lizzie was hoping you could come. They're pretty cute, and that means a lot coming from a guy. And since you're a girl, I'm sure you love babies."

Emmy thought for a moment, examining what the best way to answer would be, because the first thought that came to her was that babies meant loss and regret, learned both from her mother, and Emmy's own loss of missed chances. Instead, she said, "I haven't had any real experience with them, except from being around my friends who have them."

"Is that why you never had children?"

She squinted in the bright sunlight. "Ben and I wanted them, but decided to wait until he returned home for good."

"And you regret that?"

She turned to him, wondering how he managed to get her angry so often and why she still remained in his company. "Of course, I do. I would have had something that was a part of him to hold on to forever. Someone to share my life with. Maybe losing Ben wouldn't have been so hard if we'd had a baby."

They walked for a while in silence before Heath spoke again. "That's a little selfish, though, don't you think? That one small child would have to have some pretty big shoulders to carry all of your losses and expectations."

For a brief moment Emmy thought he was talking about her mother and how Emmy had never quite understood her own role of comforter and survivor. She stopped again, breathing so hard that she couldn't speak, much less shout at him.

As if he knew he'd said the wrong thing, Heath said, "I'm sorry. I guess that didn't come out the way it was supposed to. What I meant to say was that instead of regretting what might have been, you might consider that because you didn't have children you were free to cut anchor and move on."

She stared at him, trying to find her breath but glad, too, because no matter how hurtful and unfeeling his words were to her, she couldn't help but see the glimmer of truth behind them. Straightening, she took a deep breath. "This is that whole glass-half-full thing with you, isn't it?"

He'd stopped, too, but his breathing sounded regular, irritating her further. "Maybe. I just don't see the point of looking back when there's nothing you can do to change it."

She began walking away from him, his words stinging.

He quickly caught up to her. "I didn't mean that as a personal attack, so you can stop walking with such a stiff back—you'll hurt yourself."

Emmy stopped and glared at him. "Then what exactly did you mean?"

He stopped, too, and faced her. "I guess to sum it all up, I've been trying to tell you that I admire you. It was a brave thing to leave all your memories of your husband and your life together, your home, and your family and come to a place you've never been."

Brave. That word again. She felt such a resistance to it, as if it were the blades of the scissors cutting her life in two, separating it into "before" and "after" when she had no other desire than to remain whole.

She watched Frank straining at the end of his leash, eager to chase a seagull who'd found something to eat in a bed of seaweed. "Come on," Heath said, beginning to walk again. "Let's keep your heart rate up."

She followed silently behind him until he slowed down enough for her to catch up but wisely remained quiet. As they approached the pier behind the Holiday Inn, which bisected the beach into east and west, Heath asked, "Have you found anything interesting in the books since I last saw you?"

"Just the usual—a disjointed dialog between a man and a woman desperate to be with each other. There's nothing graphic—but sometimes I feel like I'm invading their privacy. Still . . ." She stopped.

"Still . . . what?"

She shrugged. "I get these feelings sometimes—like when I met Liz and told her that everything would be fine with her delivery. I'm not psychic. Just every once in a while, I find that I know something that I shouldn't. Like when Ben died. I knew it before they showed up the next day to tell me. But when I read those messages, it's like they're there watching me read. Waiting for me to figure it out."

He looked at her with a raised eyebrow, but left it at that. Finally he said, "I also wanted to ask you something. While I was helping you expand the children's reading corner, you kept mentioning that you needed more storage. Did you know that there's an attic storage area over Folly's Finds?"

"Attic storage? No. I had no idea. And I haven't seen any access to it, either."

"Yeah, well, apparently the contractor who renovated the store after Hugo sealed it up with drywall and forgot about it." He grimaced. "The good news is that the contractor's error is one of the inspirations I had to become a builder and architect, figuring I could do things better. The bad news is that I would have to saw through your ceiling if you want access to the attic and more storage space."

Despite the coolness of the morning, sweat was beginning to drip down her face, stinging her eyes. She wiped it away with the back of her hand, not feeling at all like the delicate bookworm girl Ben had known. She felt the pull of the muscles in her calves and thighs, the thought that maybe sweating wasn't such a bad thing floating in her head like a pesky mosquito. Pushing her legs harder, she said, "I'm dying for storage space, especially if my rare-book business becomes anything, I'll need a place for those books. Which means we'll need to make it an air-conditioned space, with built-in bookshelves and electricity."

He didn't respond, and when she glanced over at him to figure out why, she saw that he was smiling.

"What?" she asked.

"Nothing. I'm just amazed how a mention of sawing into your

ceiling has become an entire addition. Do you want me to draw up plans?"

She smiled broadly, tasting sweat. "Yeah, I think I do."

They'd reached the west side of Center Street, and Heath stopped, his hands on his hips and his breathing still annoyingly regular.

"Are we done?" she asked hopefully.

"Sort of. All we need to do now is go back." He wasn't smiling but his eyes were.

Emmy groaned and rolled her eyes, secretly glad that she hadn't actually died of respiratory failure, and that she was almost excited by the fact that she might even make it back without keeling over from exhaustion. "Can we at least wait until I catch my breath?"

"Just for a minute," he said. He turned to face the water. "There used to be a really great restaurant here: the Atlantic House. It was two old abandoned beach houses that somebody in the seventies joined together to make a restaurant. Everybody went there—except for us. For some reason that was never explained to me, Lulu hated the place and wouldn't set foot in it. I don't think it had anything to do with the food, because to my knowledge, she never ate there. My grandmother Maggie, too. She wasn't as vocal about it, but whenever I suggested we go there to eat, she'd always steer us somewhere else."

"What happened to it?" Emmy asked, trying to picture a building where now only water and sand existed.

Heath began walking back the way they'd come. "The same thing that happened to everything else in Folly Beach—Hurricane Hugo. Blew it away. With the newer zoning laws, the owner wasn't allowed to rebuild."

Emmy pumped her arms, finding it helpful in propelling her forward, although she still found that she had to take about two steps for every one of Heath's. She'd have to remember to mention that later, so he'd know that she'd had a much harder workout than he had. "That's a shame. A piece of history gone just like that."

"Yeah. I always thought the same thing even though I'd never set foot inside. But it was an historical building not just because it was old. During World War II they used it during daylight to spot enemy planes and German submarines. There's some other factoid associated with it that I can't recall—something else to do with World War II. But, yeah, something pretty historically significant gone just like that."

"They really thought the Germans were that close?"

"They were. Germany sent twelve U-boats in all to the U.S. They did a pretty good job of sinking ships along the Eastern seaboard for the first half of nineteen forty-two until the U.S. figured out how to fight back. It wasn't really realized, much less talked about, at the time how close we were to losing the war before we'd barely started. We had no oil reserves to heat U.S. homes for the winter, much less ship to our allies in England for the war effort, and we were losing oil tankers at a pretty fast rate. If Hitler had sent more subs, or if we'd been a little later in defending ourselves, we might be speaking German right now."

"You're kidding, right? I don't remember hearing any of this in history class."

"Oh, you probably did as a footnote. But that's in Indiana—here on Folly it was a little closer to home. There's even a spot outside the Outer Banks that they call the Graveyard of the Atlantic. It's a real hot spot for scuba divers because there're tons of wrecks including at least one U-boat. They even sent the survivors of one sunk U-boat here to Charleston."

"Well, at least they stayed in their subs. Can't imagine they'd get very far inland. I mean, even in Indiana there was a pretty big prejudice against anybody with a German last name—even if they'd lived there for generations."

He was looking at her oddly. "You should start reading some of those history books in your store, Emmy. There were landings by at least two groups of German spies—one in New York and one in Florida. They'd gone to spy school in Germany to learn how to speak English without an accent and fill it with American slang. They were

sent here with lots of cash, plans, maps, and all sorts of things to sabotage factories and the infrastructure here in the States."

"What happened to them?"

"By great stupidity on their part and sheer luck on ours, they were
captured before they could do any damage. Still, it's pretty scary when
you think about it. And those are only the spies we knew about. There
might have been more whose missions failed for whatever reason and
then sort of just assimilated into American life."

"That's amazing. What's scariest is that I didn't know. My grandfather's brother was killed in Normandy, but everybody knows about
the D-day invasion. And here this is, close to home, and I bet the av-
erage person you grab off the street—like me—hasn't a clue."

"Well, then, you learned something new today. You're welcome."

Emmy smirked at him. "Aren't you going to tell me that learning
something new means that I'm supposed to go on living or something?"

"Nope." Heath increased his pace and she nearly killed herself trying to catch up.

"Why not?"

"Because I was hoping you'd have figured that out by now on your
own."

If she'd had any air left in her lungs, she probably would have made
a snorting sound that would have made Lulu proud.

Heath seemed to take pity on her, and their pace slowed on the
way back, for which Emmy was grateful. Her calves and feet were
killing her, not that she'd ever tell Heath. Frank continued on his ex-
perimental dives into the ocean as far as Heath allowed the leash to go,
and then the dog sprayed them both with water every time he came
back and shook. The water felt too good to complain, and Emmy
found herself placing herself in the dog's path every time he emerged
from the water.

She'd passed the point of exhaustion and pain, since her muscles
were now blessedly numb, but lack of physical discomfort seemed to
make her brain function more clearly, or maybe it was the scent of the

ocean, which didn't seem so peculiar to her anymore: the potpourri of salt, sea life, and wind from faraway places that turned her mind inward. Recently, she'd found herself sleeping with the bedroom window open and enjoying the ocean's perfume, which reminded her of her mother's scent.

Emmy considered her conversation with Heath, and his seeming certainty that he knew what was best for her. Regardless of whether he was right or wrong, it still irked her that he could guess so much about her and be absolutely right.

"Why haven't you asked Jolene for Maggie's ring yet? If you don't believe in looking back, then you need to tell her. Waiting isn't going to help."

His face reddened under his tan. "It's different with her. She's . . . ill. I have to tread very carefully as far as Jolene is concerned. It's over, and she knows it. She just needs to wear the ring a little while longer."

Emmy's thumb found the gold ring on her own hand—the ring she hadn't taken off since the day Ben had given it to her—and she found that she had nothing else to say.

"I've found a good rehab place and paid a deposit, but I can't force her to go. And, not that you asked, but I think you should hire her for the Web site and marketing not just because she's really good at what she does but also because I think she needs this right now. Her interior-design business has shriveled with the economy, and if I can get her into rehab, then she'll have something to look forward to when she gets out."

They stopped near the beach access across from her house, and Emmy had to pause for a moment before she could find the air to speak. "For somebody who's so adamant about moving forward, the subject of Jolene is like quicksand to you, isn't it?"

His brows furrowed. "What do you mean?"

She looked at him, wondering if he really was that blind when it concerned his ex-fiancée. "Well, it's not like you've let her go, you know? You don't discourage her visits to Folly, and from what I can see, you're the only reason she comes here. She doesn't even own the house I'm living in, right?"

Heath nodded, still frowning.

"So why does she keep coming back?"

"Lulu, mostly. Lulu seems to need her as much as Jolene needs Lulu."

Heath turned his head and whistled, and Emmy watched as Frank returned to Heath's side. She was suddenly too exhausted to call Heath on his faulty reasoning, as if any reserves she had left after wallowing in her own problems had already been used up.

Bending down to scratch Frank behind the ears, Heath said, "I'm going to dive in for a quick wash off. I don't suppose you're interested?"

She looked down at her soaked T-shirt and wanted, just for a moment, to be the kind of person who said yes to swimming in her clothes, or parking on the grass, or wearing flip-flops to church. She'd made it to the beach, and had used muscles that hadn't been used in a long time, and figured she'd done enough for one day.

"No, thanks. I'll go take a shower at the house."

He bent down and began untying his shoelaces.

"Bye, then," Emmy said.

He nodded as he kicked off his shoes and stripped off his socks. She turned before anything else came off and began walking away before realizing she'd forgotten to thank him.

She turned in time to see his shirt hitting the sand. It was hard not to remember how Ben had always carefully folded his clothes, putting them away neatly. His neatness had been a quirk she'd grown to love about him, and something she'd adopted as her own. Until lately. She'd taken to letting her clothes drop where she took them off, picking everything up once a week when it was time to do laundry. It was almost like Ben was fading from her like a dream upon waking, his image gone as soon as she opened her eyes.

Concentrating on Heath's forehead, she said, "Thank you for the exercise. It wasn't so bad."

"You might want to hold judgment until tomorrow, when your muscles let you know how long it's been since you've used them." With a wave, he and Frank ran to the water and dove in, both of them disappearing into the surf. She watched them both for a moment, wanting to know what it felt like to go under like that, to completely let go enough to allow the waves to move you whichever way they wanted.

Emmy began walking away, trying in vain to remember the sound of Ben's voice. She waited for the panic to come, but felt instead only a dull throb around her heart. *Come back to me.* The words were there in her head, but she couldn't say them anymore. Because she had the sudden feeling that if Ben did come back, he might not recognize the woman she'd started to become.

She quickened her pace into a slow run, knowing that her muscles weren't ready and that she'd be regretting it tomorrow. But for now all she wanted was to feel the power of her own body propelling her forward, her feet pounding into the sand, to exhaust herself to the point at which she couldn't think anymore about Ben's absence in her life.

LULU TURNED HER HEAD AT the sound of running feet approaching on the gravel drive, expecting to see Heath and disappointed to see it was that Emmy woman instead. She thought about ducking behind a piling and avoiding her altogether, but realized she'd already been spotted.

Emmy was covered with perspiration, her oversized gray army T-shirt darkened with moisture, her face a bright red from exertion. Her eyes were wet, but Lulu wasn't sure if it was from tears or the running. Eyeing Emmy up and down, Lulu could see clearly that Emmy wasn't the running type, and she made a mental note to ask Heath what in the hell he thought he was doing.

Emmy stopped and put her hands on her hips, breathing heavily and staring back at Lulu. "Can I help you?"

Ignoring her, Lulu jutted her chin at Emmy. "Is that your husband's?"

Emmy looked down to see what Lulu meant, then nodded. "Yes. I don't own any T-shirts of my own."

The girl looked so small and fragile in the oversized shirt, her eyes wide in her reddened face. But there was something arresting about the eyes—something that made Lulu think of a battle between giving up and hanging on that reminded her so much of Maggie and the way she'd been after Jim. And Peter. "Are you still angry?"

Emmy's delicate eyebrows dipped, like the wings of a gull. "Angry? At whom?"

"Your husband. The army. The bad guys. The whole world, even. With your husband for leaving you."

Emmy looked at Lulu, pretending she didn't understand. But Lulu knew a lot more about grief than most people, and she recognized anger behind everything Emmy did: the way she walked with her chin jutting out, her avoidance of other people—not that there was anything wrong with that—and the way she still pretended as if she were here on Folly just as a visitor. An angry person would resent the need for change in the first place, would be mad at everyone who put her there. At least until she turned the anger on herself for ever letting him go. But maybe Emmy had passed all that already, and was just waiting for another emotion to take its place.

"I'm not . . ." Emmy began, then stopped before dipping her head. When she looked up, her eyes were clear. "How long does it take? How long before I'm supposed to stop missing him?"

Lulu was silent for a minute, her thoughts on Jim. "Long enough. You'll know when it's been long enough." Lulu scrutinized the younger woman, trying not to see so much of Maggie when she did. "Where'd they bury him?"

Emmy surprised Lulu by not crying as she would have done when Lulu had first met her. She still appeared delicate and fragile, but the girl had a backbone in there somewhere.

Sticking out her chin, Emmy said, "Back home, in Indiana. On his family's farm next to his grandfather, who was a World War II vet. Why?"

Lulu examined the amber bottle she held in her hand. "Curious, I guess. It's nice to have that, I guess. Cat's husband, Jim—the one in the photograph. They never did find him. Figure he was drowned or blown up on the *Oklahoma*."

"Poor Cat. How awful not to be able to bury her husband."

Lulu tilted her head back and laughed. "Don't ever say poor Cat out loud, or she's likely to come back and haunt you. She wasn't one who solicited a lot of pity—that's for sure. Except from Maggie." Her face darkened. "That's another one who was never found." She shrugged, studying the bottle in her hand. "But I think that's where she'd want to be, in the end."

Emmy stared hard at her. "What do you mean? Because she loved the ocean? Or because she had a thing for Jim?"

"Oh, we all had a thing for Jim." Lulu began to move past Emmy, already tired of the conversation. She heard Emmy's footsteps following.

"What do you mean? Did Maggie have an affair with Jim?"

Lulu swung around to glare. "Be careful which thoughts you decide to say out loud. Jim was true to Cat every day of their married lives, and that's all I'm going to say about that." She began to walk faster, already pulling out the keys to her golf cart.

"Why are you here?"

Lulu held up a bottle. "Needed this shade of glass for a tree I'm working on, so I substituted another one for Heath's tree. He won't mind. It was only stuck on there temporarily anyway. I'll be back to solder it on, once I've figured out that I'm done." She was already seated in the golf cart before Emmy caught up to her.

"I forgot to ask you this when you and Abigail came to the house. Heath told me that he found documents showing a sale of your house on Second Street to a Peter Nowak in February of nineteen forty-three. Is that the same Peter who gave you and Maggie the books?"

Lulu paused as she focused on sticking the key into the ignition, imagining she heard Maggie humming "String of Pearls." There was no trip down memory lane faster than riding a guilty conscience. She turned the ignition and listened to the motor whir.

"Yes, it's the same Peter." She turned the wheel and began to back into the street.

"Why did she sell it to him for only ten dollars—was it a gift?"

Lulu nodded without looking at Emmy, trying to focus on the road to see if anybody was coming. "Yep." She put the cart in drive.

"What kind of a gift?"

Lulu paused. "A late wedding gift. To Cat and Peter."

Lulu pressed the accelerator, not caring if she sprayed dust and gravel at Emmy. Maybe it would make her leave, make her stop asking questions that made the dead walk through Lulu's dreams at night.

Without looking back, Lulu headed down East Ashley, afraid to see Maggie's accusing eyes staring after her.

CHAPTER 19

The months that followed Cat's revelation became what Maggie would always think of as the sleeping time. She sleepwalked through her days, insulated from any emotion. She'd been this way after Jim was killed, too, but at least then she'd had a tangible grief to hold on to. What was she holding on to now? It didn't matter that she still loved Peter with a desperation that scared her. Peter's love had proven to be nothing but a fantasy, a romance from one of her favorite Bette Davis movies. Still, she clung to what she thought it had been, in the same way she imagined baby turtles clung to dreams of their mothers as they plunged into the foaming ocean.

She existed in a black-and-white world, as if she'd suddenly been struck with color blindness. Even noises seemed muted, tastes dulled. She imagined that life underwater must be like this, looking up toward the filmy surface from her liquid cocoon, and seeing the rest of a world that she was no longer a part of.

The only color that still existed in her world was Peter. When they were forced to share company, he was solicitous to her, even kind. The way a stranger might treat a stray dog. But his eyes—those beautiful amber eyes—shone with startling clarity as he watched. And he was always watching her, as if waiting, the way the wind waits for rain before a hurricane.

At least she'd been spared the wedding, as Peter had balked at being married in a Catholic church, adamant that a conversion would not be considered, so instead Cat and he had gone to Charleston and been married by a justice of the peace. Lulu had been sick, so Maggie stayed home, glad for the excuse to not attend the ceremony. She didn't know or care whom Cat had chosen as a witness instead.

Maggie and Lulu had moved all their belongings into Lulu's old room so that Cat and Peter could have the larger bed, and through the whole process, Maggie was glad of the numbness. As she tucked the corners of the fresh sheets on the bed where Peter and Cat would sleep, she felt nothing. Instead, she began to plan. She and Lulu would have to move. Not just to another house on Folly, but to another corner of the world. Not that it would matter, really. No matter how far away Maggie could go, she knew it would never be far enough. It reminded her of something Jim had told her—something like wherever you go, there you are. And she finally knew exactly what he'd meant.

She was glad to have Folly's Finds because Cat had stopped working there. The pregnancy was proving to be a difficult one, and most days she didn't get out of bed. It seemed that the mere act of placing her feet on the floor made her retch, and she'd lost so much weight that Peter had called the doctor to come to the house and demanded to know what was wrong. The doctor assured them all that nausea was common in early pregnancy and should be disappearing after the fourth month or so.

Shortly after the wedding, Maggie heard Cat crying out during the night. She pressed her pillow over her head until Lulu nudged her, telling her that Cat was calling for her. Maggie rose from her bed and threw on her robe and crossed the hall. Peter, still fully dressed, stood by the bed, his watchful gaze lighting from Maggie to Cat, then back again. Finally, he took a pillow and went downstairs. Maggie stayed for most of the night, trying to console a miserable Cat while wondering how long her mother expected her to keep a promise made so many years before.

She barely noticed her exhaustion at Folly's Finds the next day. The store had been busy with people eager to purchase newspapers because of all the news about the capture of the Nazi saboteurs who'd landed in New York and Florida. The war had finally come within the United States borders, and people were scared.

It was near dusk by the time Maggie made it home from Folly's Finds. No lights shone from the house as Maggie dragged herself up the front steps. None of the blackout curtains had been lowered yet, which meant Cat was lying up in her bedroom in the dark.

Peter was gone even more than before, and when he was home, he spent a good deal of time at McNally's on Center Street. When he came home, he was reeking of cigarette smoke but never of alcohol. And if it had been Maggie's business to question, she'd have wondered what he did for all those hours at Folly's biggest nightspot.

With trepidation, Maggie slowly climbed the stairs, pausing outside her old bedroom door, hoping Cat was asleep.

"Mags? Is that you?"

Maggie stepped forward into the room and went to the window. The room smelled of vomit even though Martha had been in earlier to clean out the basin. "Yes, Cat. It's me." She closed the blackout curtains, then turned on the small bedside lamp.

Cat lay on her back, her skin sallow against the white of the pillowcase, her small frame shrunken under the bedclothes. She looked like a scared child and not like a mother-to-be.

Maggie remained standing. "Why are you lying here in the dark?"

Cat attempted a smile. "Because I didn't want to catch sight of myself in the mirror. I know I'm a fright."

Maggie said nothing to reassure Cat. It wasn't out of animosity or any feelings, really, except that her gaze had strayed to the empty spot in the bed beside Cat.

"Have you had anything to eat?"

Cat shook her head. "Martha made some chicken soup but I didn't have the energy to get any. The doctor said I needed to eat so the baby will be strong and healthy, so I'm going to try." She licked dry lips, her hands with chipped red nail polish clutching at the sheets. "Since I've got nothing to do all day, I've been thinking of names. If it's a boy, I'm going to name him after your father. But if it's a girl, I'd like to call her Margaret. After you."

Maggie frowned as she studied the dip in the blankets where Cat's pregnant belly lay. It was the first time she'd associated a name with the unborn child, making it more real. A tiny person. Peter's child. "You have plenty of time to think about it, Cat. Besides, Peter might have other ideas."

Cat turned away. "Peter liked the idea of naming our daughter after you."

For a brief moment, Maggie was filled with hope until her eyes settled on the simple gold wedding band on Cat's left hand, and she was glad Cat couldn't see her face.

Cat turned back to face Maggie, her eyes wet. "You blame me for this, don't you?

Maggie quietly regarded her cousin, the once-beautiful gold hair now matted and dark with dirt. The question surprised her. In all of her internal battles, she'd only ever blamed herself for being so gullible. But now, staring into Cat's troubled eyes, Maggie thought she knew the answer. "No. I don't. I feel sorry for you, but I don't blame you. We should all share a portion of the blame somehow."

Maggie thought Cat would defend herself, never having been able to stand anybody's pity, especially not Maggie's. Instead she lay there like a wounded animal in the middle of the road, her eyes turned up in silent supplication.

"I did something horrible to Peter, Mags. Something you should know."

Maggie closed her eyes and shook her head. "No. I don't want to know. Because none of it matters anymore. What's done is done."

Their eyes met and held for a long time. Finally, Cat spoke. "Do you hate me?"

As a child, Cat had asked that often. Her childish pranks always held a hint of maliciousness in them, the hurt she inflicted not always repented—not at first. Eventually her conscience would bring her nightmares that had her calling out to Maggie. The need to comfort and be comforted had filled a void in each of them, carving a whole person out of two motherless girls. And always, there was Maggie's promise that bonded them together, regardless of the myriad hairline cracks that ran through it.

"No, Cat. I don't hate you."

"You should." She began sobbing as Maggie sat on the edge of the bed, clutching Cat's fists and trying not to feel the cold metal of the gold wedding band. "Peter doesn't love me, you know. He never has. It's all my fault. I just . . ." Cat was sobbing so hard that she began gasping for breath. Maggie put her arm around Cat's shoulders, the bones alarmingly prominent through her nightgown, and hoisted her cousin against the headboard. "I just couldn't stand having somebody not love just me. I don't know why I'm that way—I just am. It's like I see my father in all these men—and I want them to love me and stay with me. It killed me to see you with Peter, knowing he didn't know I existed when you were in the room. It blinded me until I couldn't see straight. And now . . ." She burst out in a fresh bout of sobs.

Maggie stared down at her cousin, remembering an old Christmas from their childhood. Their maternal grandmother had given Cat an extra gift: a set of two gold bangle bracelets. Maggie had always been suspicious that their grandmother loved Cat more because of her golden curls and bright green eyes, and that had been confirmed when her grandmother had brought out the box from Croghan's Jewel Box on King Street in Charleston. Maggie had even been hopeful enough to think that there was another box under the tree for her.

Doing her best to hide her disappointment, Maggie had begun to pick up all the torn wrapping paper and ribbons, her hurt growing with each crumpled ball until Cat stopped her by handing her one of the bangles. It had always been the small, unexpected acts of kindness that allowed Maggie to love her cousin, and to accept her shortcomings. Cat's maliciousness stemmed from a deep-seated insecurity that had begun to grow the day her father abandoned her; but her kindness came from a part of her heart that only a very few were ever allowed to see.

"Forgive me, Maggie," Cat said into Maggie's shoulder, her tears dampening the collar of her blouse. "I feel so sick, and I look a fright. But I know this is my just punishment for what I did. I just want to die."

Maggie shook her shoulders. "Don't say that, Cat. Do you hear? It's a sin to even think that. And you'd be killing an innocent child."

Cat wiped her hands across the blankets that covered her, as if cleaning up something no more meaningful than a messy spill. She began to sob harder. "I don't care. I don't want this baby. I want everything back the way it was."

Maggie watched her cousin cry, unable or unwilling to comfort her. "Stop it, Cat. You're only making things worse. Peter will be back any day now, so you've got to pull yourself together." A thickness formed in her throat, but she pushed it back as she'd learned to do from an early age. "I'm giving you and Peter the house as a wedding present, seeing as how you'll need the room once the baby's born. Lulu and I will be moving out to give you some privacy. I've written to Daddy's sister, Aunt Edith, in Galveston. Remember how I used to say I always wanted to visit? Maybe, if I like it enough, I'll want to settle down there. It's on the Gulf, so I'll have my beach. Won't that be nice?"

Cat went still, her bloodshot eyes staring up at Maggie. "No! You can't leave me! Not now—not after all we've been through together."

Like Jim? Maggie wanted to say but remained quiet, alarmed at Cat's state.

Cat continued, her voice pleading. "Dr. Brown said I shouldn't be exerting myself, that I need somebody looking after me. Martha already told me that she can't be here any more than she already is. And with Peter traveling, I'll be alone too much. What if I fall? Or start bleeding or something? What will happen to the baby if nobody's here to help me?"

Maggie looked down at the sapphire ring she still wore. She wasn't sure why she hadn't taken it off, but sometimes, as she lay in bed in the darkest part of the night, she'd begin to think that the best part of her life had already happened to her, and all that she had left to remember it by was the ring. She spun it on her finger, thinking about her plans to move to Galveston and how even now they seemed as transparent and fragile as a cobweb.

Her throat tightened, and she wanted more than anything to tell Cat that it was time she went after her own dreams. But her refusal warred in her head with an old promise, and with a sickening relief that she wouldn't have to say good-bye to Peter so soon. She hated herself for that, eagerly shoving that dark truth into the blackest part of her heart.

"Isn't there anyone else, Cat? I'll use some of the funds from the sale of Folly's Finds and pay someone to stay with you."

"They're not blood, Maggie. This baby is not their blood. What if I die in childbirth? Who will take care of the baby?"

Maggie stared into Cat's widened eyes, resignation creeping up inside of her like a choking vine, spreading beneath her feet and rooting her to the floor, while at the same time setting her free.

She stood and walked to the door, noticing the tiny rose wallpaper that peeled down from the corners of the room. She remembered her mother hanging it, and how she loved it still along with the scrubby grass outside and the peeling paint of their neighbors' houses, all worn and familiar as a favorite chair. She would stay for a while longer, at least until the baby was born. It was the only thing to do. But even as she made the decision in her head, a terrible dread loomed beyond her peripheral vision, the same way she could tell the approach of a storm by the color of the clouds.

Turning to face Cat, she said, "I'll stay. For a while. But if I do, you're going to have to try harder to make sure the baby is strong. You're going to have to eat—do you understand? Even if you don't feel like it."

Cat nodded, her relief a palpable thing that reached out and grabbed Maggie's heart, a small reassurance in an ocean of doubt.

"I'll go heat some soup for you and bring it up. I'll feed it to you if you don't feel like you can do it yourself."

Cat's voice made her stop. "Thank you, Maggie. Nobody has ever loved me like you do."

Maggie turned her head and met Cat's eyes. She tried to see the beautiful girl who'd been dancing and laughing with the officers the night on the pier when Maggie had met Peter. But all she could see was a pathetic woman who'd made the colossal mistake of getting what she'd wished for.

Without responding, Maggie left the room and headed downstairs, trying to pretend that she wasn't straining to hear the opening of a door latch and the sound of Peter's footsteps. Because still, after all that had happened, no matter how she tried, she couldn't forget her promise to wait for him, no matter what.

CHAPTER 20

On Sunday morning, Emmy squatted in front of the last batch of books in her living room, feeling oddly bereft to see the dwindling piles. She'd been organizing and shelving all of the books without notations written in them, categorized by the authors' last names like they would be in a library. She'd also prepared a worksheet that listed the books by title and author for quick cross-reference.

She wasn't sure who the list was for since Heath would have little interest in searching for any of the old books. There'd been a good number of first editions and hard-to-find books she'd unearthed, and these she indicated with an asterisk in the first column of the worksheet. In the back of her mind, she envisioned listing the books on her new Web site, with the option to purchase. She relished the research involved to come up with a fair price, and was almost excited over what other books she might find to add to the collection.

Her quads still protested every move she made as they had for the three days since her walk on the beach with Heath. She'd prepared herself to lie if he'd called and asked how she was, but he hadn't. Which was a good thing, she kept telling herself.

After situating herself, her laptop, and her coffee in front of the books, she slowly slid the first book toward her and began her search. It took her almost an hour before she'd reached the first notation, this one written in the man's handwriting:

I watched you today while you were at the beach, envious of the sun's touch on your hair and skin. Just once to be as it was before. We can change all of this—just tell me. You know where.

Emmy put the book aside and pulled out the next book, eager to find something more—something to fill in all the empty spots in this dialog. It was like watching a movie in which all the scenes had been switched around in no apparent order—a puzzle to figure out the beginning and the end and all the missing pieces in between. The one thing she was sure of was the buzzing in the back of her head, telling her that everything she needed to know was right in front of her; she only needed to figure out what it was.

She went through the few remaining books without finding anything else. Frustrated, she stood and poured herself another cup of coffee. Her limbs shook with restlessness, as if these strangers had become friends and were now leaving her. She didn't even know their names. She thought of Maggie and Jim again, and wondered if Lulu's denial about an affair between them had been too adamant. But how could an affair between two people who'd been dead for years be a taboo subject still?

Emmy moved out onto the back screened porch, sipping her coffee and watching the marsh move like a sigh under the morning sun, the tall stalks of grass bent gently as if in deep thought. A stack of wood waited its turn to be attached to the still-unfinished dock, reminding her of what Abigail had told her about Heath and his unfinished projects. She was impatient for the dock to be completed, still hesitant yet oddly eager to walk farther into the smells and sounds of the marsh, its beauty still an enigma to her.

Emmy paused with the cup halfway to her mouth, realizing it was the first time she'd thought of the marsh as beautiful and not simply strange. She straightened, studying the marsh at low tide with its mud flats and barren oyster beds bared to the sun. A hush seemed to hover over it, the summer sounds of insects and birds muted as the mud and river prepared for winter. It reminded her of the cornfields of home and the way the harvest signaled the end of yellow summer and the beginning of bleak winter. But Heath had told her that the marsh never died during winter, but remained always changing with the seasons, perpetually waiting for the outgoing tides to return and flood the marsh with new life.

She'd ask Heath to take her out in his boat and show her the marsh. Maybe then she could understand how something that seemed at first to be merely grass and water could be captivating enough to inspire songs and poetry, and make her stoic mother long for it in the silences of Emmy's childhood.

Emmy's gaze strayed to the bottle tree. She knew she'd find no more notes in it—she'd been dutifully informed by Lulu—but the fact hadn't diminished Emmy's curiosity. If anything, her interest in it and all of the trees Lulu created had become a sort of obsession. She'd even volunteered to take the digital photos of each tree that she'd planned to use on the Web site catalog so she could study them without Lulu shooing her away. Emmy hoped that by studying them through the lens of her camera, she might begin to understand Lulu's motivation for making them, and why the older woman worked so hard to keep the dark spirits at bay.

Emmy started to turn back inside, but stopped suddenly, sloshing coffee on her bathrobe. Quickly changing direction, she passed the dining table and placed her cup on top of it, then headed for the bedroom, where she'd brought all of the inscribed books from the very first box she'd opened from Paige's Pages that still hadn't made it to the shelves of Folly's Finds. They were in a small box by the door, and she picked it up and dumped the books onto the bed, sorting through them until she found *A Farewell to Arms*.

She quickly flipped to the back cover and found the sketch of the bottle tree—the same picture that had convinced her to leave Indiana and move to Folly Beach. Leaning over, she looked closely at the ink sketch, noticing something she hadn't seen before. Lodged inside one of the bottles on a lower branch was what appeared to be a rolled-up piece of paper. She sat up and chewed on her lip, staring at the picture. Finally, Emmy slid the book from her lap and reached for the phone, eager to tell Heath about her discovery and what she thought it meant.

As her hand touched the receiver, the telephone rang, startling her. "Hello?"

"Hi, Emmy—it's Heath. I hope I'm not waking you."

She glanced at her bedside clock and saw that it was nearly nine thirty. "You're just trying to make me feel guilty because I'm not walking on the beach, aren't you?"

"Not at all. I figured you'd be too sore to go back. Give it another day." She was about to contradict him when he spoke again. "How soon do you think you can get to the store?"

Emmy sat back on the bed. "The store? You mean Folly's Finds?" She glanced at the clock again. "About half an hour. Why? Is there something wrong?"

"Nothing's wrong. I've been here working on this attic access since about six o'clock this morning so all the messy parts would be done before you opened on Monday. Everything's on schedule—but I just found something that I think you'll want to see."

"Can't you just tell me over the phone?"

She heard the smile in his voice. "That wouldn't be a surprise, then, would it?"

"Fine. Because I have something to show you, too." She waited to hear him ask her what it was.

She could hear another smile in his voice as if he knew what she was waiting for. "Great. You can show me when you get here."

They said good-bye; then Emmy showered, dressed, and threw the book with the drawing into her purse. As she opened the front door, she saw a familiar car in her driveway, parked behind her own car so that she couldn't leave. After locking the front door firmly behind her, she climbed down the stairs looking for Jolene.

The car was empty, so after checking the street and in front of the house, Emmy walked to the back, wondering if she should have called Heath first. She felt guilty at the thought since every encounter she'd had with Jolene after the incident in the restaurant, although always on the phone, had been nothing but professional, and the work she'd submitted to Emmy so far was exceptional. But Emmy still had the image of Jolene on her couch, wearing an engagement ring for a wedding that wasn't to be, and she couldn't help but feel wary.

Emmy found Jolene on the finished part of the dock, looking up at the empty Osprey nest. Jolene turned as she heard Emmy approach. "Heath didn't tell me if the ospreys returned this year. I'm supposing they did but it would have been nice to see."

Emmy came to a stop at the end of the dock near the bottle tree. She wondered if Jolene would have known to check inside the bottles for the note Heath had left her, feeling relieved that it wasn't there anymore. "I don't know. I didn't even notice the nest until after they would have left."

Jolene turned her head back toward the marsh, her hands tucked into the pocket of a long, brocade coat.

"Did you need to talk to me about something? I love the design of Lulu's pages that you sent me this week. I think they're good to go without any changes. I'd actually planned to e-mail you today."

Jolene reached her hand up to push away hair that had blown into her eyes, the sapphire ring glinting in the sun. Emmy stared at it as a heaviness settled on her like a coat, its pockets filled with lost dreams and good-byes. Her thumbnail flicked the gold band around her own finger, feeling the weight of it on her skin.

Jolene nodded absently. "Good. I thought you'd like it. But I'm actually here today to see Lizzie and her babies. I've got a hotel room in Charleston, so I won't intrude on Abigail and John." She turned her head and sent Emmy a fragile smile. "They're kind to me, but I always get the feeling that they're waiting for me to leave."

Emmy glanced back at her car, confirming that she couldn't maneuver around Jolene's Audi without hitting the palm tree that sat by the driveway. "You're welcome to stay here for a while longer, but I'm actually on my way to Folly's Finds, and I can't move my car."

Jolene made no indication that she'd heard. Instead she turned her attention to the pile of lumber near the dock. "This is so typical of Heath. He's so exacting in his professional work, always finishing projects on time even if it kills him. But for his own projects, he can't seem to finish. It's almost as if he's afraid that when they're complete, he'll find himself having to deal with the real issues in his life." She turned around and began walking toward Emmy, stopping next to the bottle tree, and examining a squat cobalt jar suspended vertically like a blue angel. "Like our engagement. He's told me that we're not getting married, but neither one of us can quite believe it's true yet." She held her hand up and wriggled her ring finger.

Not knowing what to say, Emmy indicated the cars in the drive. "I've got to move my car and you're blocking me. Would you mind . . . ?" She stopped, catching the unmistakable scent of alcohol on Jolene's breath as the other woman studied the tree.

Jolene reached up and touched one of the bottles, the sun shining directly on her face and illuminating her bloodshot eyes and her lipstick, which appeared to have been applied with a shaking hand. "I guess I'd better be talking to Lulu about getting my own tree since it seems I need one."

Emmy laid her hand on Jolene's arm. "Look, I'm heading over to the store right now and Lulu's bound to be there. Why don't you come with me? I'll drive." She began leading Jolene back to the cars. "Just move your car out into the street so I can leave the driveway, and I'll wait while you take my spot."

Jolene nodded as she pulled her keys from her pocket. As she slid behind the wheel of her Audi, she looked up at Emmy. "How long are you going to wear your wedding ring?"

Emmy pulled back. "I don't know."

Jolene placed her hands on her steering wheel and stared straight in front of her. "I was hoping you'd know so you could tell me how long a person has to wait until she knows for sure that there's no reason to keep on waiting."

The thought of Maggie waiting through a hurricane flashed through Emmy's head, but before she could say anything else, Jolene had closed her car door and started the engine. Then she backed out into the street and instead of waiting drove away, leaving Emmy standing in the driveway, wondering how long was long enough.

ON THE WAY TO FOLLY'S FINDS, Emmy called Heath's cell phone, and when no one answered, she called Abigail and told her about Jolene. Abigail said she knew where to find her and would commandeer the car keys if necessary.

When she opened the door to the store, she was greeted by the ringing bell and the sight of her store wrapped in plastic sheets and covered with a coating of drywall dust. An aluminum ladder rose from the middle of the floor to a new rectangular hole in the ceiling. The only color in the room besides Janell's hand-painted sign for Folly's Playgrounds was Lulu's wall mural for the new children's corner. She'd painted the ceiling a midnight blue, then covered it with iridescent golden stars that mimicked the night sky. The walls above and between the low shelves—Lulu's idea to make them more kid-friendly—were filled with what appeared to be books falling from the sky. The titles and authors of popular and classic children's books were painted on the spines and splayed covers, and flitting around the books and shelves like ribbon were passages from some of the books. Emmy's favorite was from Nancy Drew: *Nancy, look out!*, which, according to Lulu, appeared in every single book in the series.

Emmy had taken photographs of the space and sent them to Jolene, and Jolene had used the colors and patterns as the wallpaper for Lulu's bottle-tree pages. Lulu hadn't seen them yet, but Emmy was anticipating the big unveiling. Emmy had yet to see Lulu smile in direct response to something she had said or done, and Emmy thought that maybe her waiting was about to pay off.

"Hello? Anybody here?"

Janell appeared from behind the counter of Folly's Playgrounds, where she'd been restocking cups and napkins, and waved before coming around and joining Emmy in the war zone holding two steaming mugs. Handing Emmy a cup of coffee, she asked, "So, do you like it?"

Emmy looked around at her nearly unrecognizable store. "I'm going to withhold judgment, if that's all right. I'm having a two-for-one sale for my 'more on Mondays' promotion tomorrow, so I'm hoping we'll be ready in time."

"Believe it or not, Heath said the messy part down here is done, and he'll have this cleared by this afternoon so it can be business as usual tomorrow. He's hired a cleaning crew to come suck up all the dust as soon as he's done."

"Good to know." Emmy took a sip of her coffee and looked around. "So, where is everybody?"

A thump from the ceiling answered part of the question. Janell tilted her head back and stepped away as if anticipating something falling through. Her green-and-blue beaded earrings jangled as she moved her head, reminding Emmy of the ocean. "Lulu was here earlier, but she seems to have disappeared. I just went outside to ask her about the next orders so I could get started on the metal work, but she wasn't there. Even checked in the shed but no luck. She doesn't believe in cell phones, so I couldn't call her." She took a sip out of her mug. "The last I saw her was about an hour ago, right after Heath showed her what he found."

"Do you know what it is?"

Janell nodded. "He knew you'd ask me, so he made me promise not to tell. But to be honest, I don't understand what's so exciting about it. He said you'd understand."

A voice called down from the ceiling hole. "Emmy? Is that you?"

Emmy moved to stand next to the ladder. "I'm here. Can I come up now?"

"Sure. Just hold on tight to the ladder, and I'll help you up when you get to the top."

Handing her mug to Janell, Emmy stepped onto the first rung and began to climb. When she'd reached about the fourth rung from the top, Heath reached down with both hands and held her arms while she climbed the rest of the way, thankful for his support as she stepped off the ladder and onto the dusty wood floor of the attic.

The space was lit by a half-moon window on the street side of the store, the sun picking up dust motes and plaster dust in its wedge of light. Lighter-colored studs stood out against darker wood, a testament to the hurricane repairs made after Hugo. At first glance it appeared that the attic was empty, until her eyes adjusted to the dimness, and she saw a box on the opposite end from the window identical to the box shipped to her mother in Indiana.

She approached the box, the back of her neck tingling. "Is this your surprise?"

"I'm thinking this is the missing box of books. I haven't gone through them yet, but I can't imagine what else they could be."

"It's them." Kneeling in front of the box, Emmy peered inside and lifted out the first book she saw: a travel guide to Paris from nineteen forty. Feeling out of breath, she looked up at Heath. "It's them," she said again.

Because of the dust and dirt on the floor, she had to resist the impulse to dump out the contents of the box. Instead, she stuck her hand in again and grabbed the first book she touched. Holding it up to the light, she read the title aloud: *"Around the World in 80 Days."*

Eagerly she flipped randomly through the pages, stopping when she spotted the bold black ink of the male writer in the upper-right-hand corner of a page in the middle of the book.

It will be cold, so bring something warm. Don't let her see you leave or we will never be free. I will wait for you, just as you once promised to wait for me.

Feeling breathless, Emmy held the book up for Heath to read. "What do you think?"

"Sounds like two overly dramatic teenagers to me."

Emmy pulled the book back and snapped it closed. "What did Lulu say when you showed her the box? Did she recognize it?"

Heath looked uncomfortable. "She didn't say anything, actually. She just glanced at the box, then went back down the ladder."

Their eyes met. "I have something to show you, too, that might be connected." Emmy slid her purse off of her shoulder, then pulled out the copy of *A Farewell to Arms* with the bottle-tree sketch, and opened it up to the inside back cover.

She stood, then turned it around to show the drawing of the bottle tree to Heath. "Look really closely at the bottle on the lowest branch. What do you see?"

He squinted at the drawing, his eyes widening when he spotted the note in the bottle.

"What do you think this means?" Emmy asked.

"I have no idea." He raised an eyebrow. "But I bet the librarian does."

Emmy smiled back even though he'd called her a librarian. "Remember me telling you that of all the messages I'd read, not once was there any specific time or place mentioned? I guessed that the information would have been placed elsewhere, so if anybody stumbled upon one of the notes, the whole gig wouldn't be up."

"You mean, like this was some sort of secret affair."

She bit her lower lip. "Yes."

"And you think the notes were stuck in a bottle tree."

"Yes, I do." She looked steadily at him, waiting to see if he'd arrive at the same conclusion she had. When he didn't say anything further, she said, "Who do we know who's made a lifelong habit of tucking notes in bottles?"

Heath sobered. "Aunt Lulu. But she can't know anything about the messages. She would have said something already."

Emmy gave him a dubious look, not feeling so convinced. "I know the handwriting isn't hers—I've seen it enough on her orders, unless she's deliberately changing it." She looked up at Heath again, remembering something Lulu had said about Cat's first husband, Jim. *We all had a thing for Jim.* "Do you think Lulu and Jim . . . ?" She shook her head. "Never mind. Jim was killed in nineteen forty-one when Lulu was eight. And these notes were definitely not written by a nine-year-old."

Standing, Heath brushed his hands against his jeans. "They're probably just notes between my grandparents. Maybe they liked a bit of drama. By the way, my dad found a sample of my grandfather's handwriting. You can look at it to compare when you come to the party."

Emmy stood, too, and slipped the book back into her purse. "I'd like the chance to examine all of these. Could you help me bring them down the ladder and put them in my trunk?"

"Sure." He didn't move right away. "Although I'm thinking you're taking all of this a little too seriously." Absently, he rubbed the scar on the side of his head the way Emmy imagined a pilgrim would rub a relic. "Maybe you'd be better off focusing on your business right now. Jolene told me that your ideas for Internet expansion are amazing. It would seem to me that somebody looking to move forward would leave all this stuff in the past, where it belongs."

"There's nothing wrong with what I'm doing. There's a story here, and I don't know the ending. I can't let it all go just like that." She eyed him curiously. "Are your objections because all of this most likely involves your grandmother?"

"Well, how would you feel if somebody found out something in your family's history that wasn't exactly what you'd been led to believe?"

She paused. "Look. I understand. And I promise you that if I find anything, I'll tell you first. All right?"

"But then it would be too late—I'd know the truth even if nobody else does."

She frowned at him, thinking, and realized there was something more to his objection. "Maybe your resistance is because you like things to be perpetually waiting to be finished." Bending over to lift the box, she added, "You can still die even if you have unfinished business. Believe me, I know."

When she straightened, he took the box from her, and when he spoke, his voice lacked the geniality she'd begun to associate with him. "Stand at the top of the opening and hand me the box when I get halfway down the ladder."

She moved into position and took the box again, then did what he asked. When she reached the bottom of the ladder, Heath had already made it to the back of her truck. In silence, she opened up the back and waited for him to slide the box inside. He closed the door carefully, then turned to her.

"E-mail me your ideas of what you need in terms of storage and space in the attic, and I'll do some measurements and draw up plans. I have to go to Atlanta for work for a couple of weeks, but I can e-mail you my ideas for you to look at. I'll be back for the party and we can go over things then."

Emmy folded her arms across her chest. "I guess you don't want to ask Aunt Lulu about the sketch, do you?"

Heath looked past her head. "No, not really. I don't think this digging is good for anybody. Finding the truth isn't going to make you forget your troubles for more than a few minutes at a time, much less bring your husband back."

"Fine," she said, digging her car keys from her purse. "I guess I'll just ask her myself."

His eyes narrowed. "Lulu's an old woman, Emmy. Be careful what you say."

"What's that supposed to mean? Do you think I would deliberately hurt her?"

"I didn't say that. What I meant is that I don't think Lulu wants this to go any further. I figured that out when she hightailed it out of here after I showed her the box. I even almost called you to keep you from coming over, but figured I couldn't stop you."

"No, you're right. You couldn't have." She had the irrational urge to stomp her foot. "I wish you wouldn't fight me on this. It would be a lot more fun if I didn't have to do this all by myself."

"I thought you preferred to be left alone." His eyes weren't mocking and she relaxed.

"I don't. It's just been . . . easier."

Heath shoved his hands in his pockets. "Yeah, well, I've never found 'easier' the best way to go." He began to walk toward the store. "Call your mother. She's a bookseller, so she must be a lot like you. Bet she'd love to help."

Emmy stared after him as he climbed the steps and entered the store, letting the door slam shut behind him.

Slowly, she got in her truck and started the engine, suddenly confused as to what direction she needed to go in. Glancing in her rearview mirror she caught sight of the box of books and felt reassured, somehow. She was nothing like Paige, but it might not hurt to call anyway.

She took a different route home, down East Cooper Avenue instead of East Ashley, visually scouring the yards for bottle trees. She told herself it was for researching an idea she had to directly market the trees to Folly residents, but after she'd passed the third tree, the sun glinting off glass like exposed treasure, she'd begun to wonder, yet again, what evil spirits Lulu was trying to keep away.

CHAPTER 21

L ulu stood facing Maggie, jumping up and down. "So can I have it? She never wears it anymore, and if I bring it in, I'll beat Sheila McKowskie. I'll get a whole pound of sugar if I win—so it'll be helping you out, too. Sheila's brought in the most tin cans but nobody's brought in a fur coat. They're using them to line the coats of merchant marines."

Maggie stared at Cat's ruined coat as if it were a dead animal, feeling again the panic and pain of the day on the beach. It had hung in the closet, untouched, for three months until Martha had discovered it and taken it outside to beat out the sand and hang in the sun. It was unwearable now, but still Maggie hesitated to say yes.

"Let me see it," she demanded, holding out her hand.

Hesitantly, as if she were expecting Maggie to take the coat and not give it back, Lulu handed it to her sister, releasing it only when Maggie tugged. The fur was coarse in places, and still smelled of Shalimar, Cat's perfume. Opening up the coat, she examined the lining for the manufacturer's label, curious as to where it had come from. But instead of a label, all she found was stitching in a rectangular pattern where it looked like somebody had carefully cut one out.

Maggie was about to hand the coat back to Lulu when she noticed a slight bulge in the lining. On closer inspection she discovered a slit pocket inside the right breast. Reaching inside, she pulled out a wadded handkerchief, her hand stilling as she remembered Cat clutching one on that disastrous morning on the beach. It reeked of Shalimar, its sickly sweet smell reminding Maggie of red shoes and smeared mascara and the unforgiving ocean.

Maggie handed the jacket to Lulu, and then the handkerchief. "And you can have this, too. I don't care what you do with it."

Lulu took the handkerchief and stared at it intently before shoving it into the pocket of her skirt. "Aren't you going to ask Cat first?"

"No. She can't wear it, regardless. Besides, she's got other things on her mind right now, and I'd rather not upset her." Cat had been confined to bed for the past month on doctor's orders. It scared Maggie because instead of becoming difficult, Cat had instead retreated inside her bones, each joint pronounced under her skin and only the protruding ball in her stomach to show there was a baby inside. Cat's hair and skin had lost all of their luster, leading Martha to say that the baby must be a girl since it was stealing all of her mama's looks.

"Maggie?" Cat's pitiful voice crept down the stairs.

"I'll be up with your breakfast in just a minute, Cat." Maggie glanced down at the breakfast tray with the buttered toast swimming in the runny yolks of the fried turtle eggs. She turned her head, barely able to look at them. Since the day she'd found out about Peter and Cat, she hadn't been able to stomach them. She hadn't even been back to the beach, but sent Lulu out instead to gather eggs. She'd begun to number the days until she and Lulu could leave, and she could start rebuilding the dead spot inside of her.

Maggie opened a silverware drawer and took out a fork and knife, then wrapped them in a napkin for the breakfast tray. She rubbed her shoulders, dreading another trip up the stairs.

"Can I help?" Lulu asked, looking sincere.

Maggie smiled. "No, sweetheart. But thank you for asking."

Lulu picked up a copy of *A Farewell to Arms* that Maggie had left on the counter and put it on the breakfast tray. "Maybe this will keep her busy so she's not always asking you for things."

"Thanks." Maggie studied Lulu's face, noticing the freckles on the bridge of her nose and realizing that like Maggie, she'd never be a great beauty. It hurt Maggie, wishing things could be different for Lulu.

Maggie placed the utensils and napkin on the breakfast tray on top of the book. "I've waited to talk to you about this, but since Cat's time is getting near, I figure now is as good a time as any." She pulled out the letter from Aunt Edith and opened it carefully.

"You know I've been corresponding with Aunt Edith in Galveston, and she's found us a house to rent. If I can sell Folly's Finds, we should have enough money to get us through for a little while, or at least until I can get a job. She says the schools there are real good, so a smart girl like you shouldn't have any trouble fitting right in."

Lulu looked at her sister with wide eyes as if she were speaking in a foreign language. "What do you mean? You want us to move—like Amy? And never come back?"

Maggie's arms fell to her sides. "Oh, Lulu, I know this is hard for you. It's hard for me, too. This is our home. But it's . . . I can't live here with Cat and Peter. It's . . . complicated. One day, when you're older, you'll understand."

Lulu swallowed hard, her eyes moistening, and Maggie wished she'd waited for a better time to bring up the subject. She glanced at the eggs, hardening now as they cooled.

"I don't want to move, Mags! I don't know any other place. Folly Beach is the only place I ever want to live."

Maggie felt tears gather in her eyes, too, but she blinked them away, trying to be strong. "I know, Lulu. But I don't have a choice." She reached for the breakfast tray and lifted it.

"It's because Peter married Cat, isn't it? I wish we'd never met him. He's ruined everything."

Maggie gripped the tray tighter. "Don't say that, Lulu. Don't say those things out loud because somebody might hear you."

"But it's true, isn't it?"

Maggie closed her eyes. "You're too young to understand. . . ."

"No, I'm not. You just said I'm smart, remember? I know a lot more than you think I do."

Exasperated, Maggie put the tray down and turned to face Lulu. "Just because you read mystery books all day long doesn't make you more knowledgeable about adult matters, all right? Now go get that jacket out of my sight. I've got to be at the store in half an hour, and I still need to feed Cat her breakfast."

Lulu's lower lip was trembling as she turned to go, dragging the jacket on the floor behind her. Then, just as she reached the door, she turned around and ran back to Maggie. "I know why Jim stopped asking you to go get ice cream and started taking Cat instead."

Maggie picked up the breakfast tray again and began carrying it to the stairs. Lulu had a vivid imagination, and Maggie could only guess at what story Lulu had concocted. She put her foot on the first step. "Why, Lulu?"

"Because Cat told him that you didn't want to see him anymore. That you only went out with him because you felt sorry for him because he was just a dumb old hick. And that you were in love with Frank Ferriday from church and were going to get married as soon as he came back from the war. Then she kissed him on the mouth and used her tongue."

Maggie stumbled, and the book and the glass of juice fell over the side of the tray, spilling on the steps and splashing the whitewashed walls. Leaning against the wall, she looked down the steps at Lulu. "That's a horrible thing to say. Why would you say such a thing?"

But Lulu's eyes and mouth were open as if in shock, reminding Maggie of when she'd had to tell Lulu that Jim had been killed. It was the look of a person who'd seen the thing that lurked behind doors and under beds. And Maggie didn't need Lulu to say anything for her to know the answer. *Because it's the truth.*

Dropping the jacket, Lulu ran out the door, slamming it behind her as she left. Maggie slid down the wall until she was sitting on the step and still clutching the tray with the ruined breakfast.

"Maggie? I'm hungry. Are you coming up?"

Maggie gazed up the stairs, but couldn't find the air to speak.

The front door opened and Maggie moved her head to see if Lulu had come back to tell her that she'd been lying, that she was trying to hurt Maggie because Maggie wanted to leave Folly Beach. Instead, Peter walked through the door as if summoned, his eyes brightening when his gaze settled on her.

Stepping over the coat without a glance, he rushed over to the steps, kneeling in front of her. "Margaret—are you all right? Did you fall?" He took the tray from her frozen hands. "I saw Lulu running but she wouldn't stop when I called her."

Maggie shook her head, wondering if she was dreaming. "No. I . . . I had to sit down, that's all."

"What's wrong?" He looked at her the old way, and she felt herself beginning to thaw.

She stared at his beloved face, remembering each line, each crease, the way his hair swept his forehead. "You said . . . you said before that you needed to talk to me. I'm ready. I'm ready to listen now."

He glanced toward the top of the stairs, then looked back at her. He shook his head. Whispering, he said, "I'll write you another note."

Frowning she whispered back, "Another?"

A look of realization swept over his face.

"Peter? Is that you?"

They both looked up. Shaking his head again, Peter stood with the tray. "Yes, Cat. I'm back."

"Could you please ask Maggie to hurry with my breakfast? I'm hungry."

The book, which had fallen from the tray and had been leaning against the step, fell over, its back cover opened to one of Lulu's ink drawings of her bottle tree.

"There," he said quietly.

Their eyes met and it was as if the intervening months hadn't happened, as if there were no Cat and no baby and Peter belonged to Maggie again. Peter called upstairs, "I'll bring it." Without another word, Peter headed upstairs with the tray, looking back only once as he entered the bedroom.

B

LULU WATCHED FROM THE DARKENED kitchen window as Peter left the house from the back door and quickly crossed the backyard to her tree. She hadn't been to it since the morning Peter had given her his note to put in the tree because looking at it made her feel sick with guilt. As Maggie would have told her, keeping the note had been the sin of omission, and seeing her tree only reminded her of it.

Two of the bottles were missing, and the whole tree leaned to the side, like it was tired of holding up all that guilt. And now Peter was heading right toward it, and she sat up and squinted, glad for the full moon. He'd been sleeping on the downstairs sofa for a while now because of Cat being so sick, and Lulu might not have heard him except that she had gotten up to go to the bathroom and heard the creek of the sofa springs.

She watched as he took something out of his pants pocket and stuck it into the neck of the amber root-beer bottle on the bottom limb. When he turned around, she ducked back, but not before she'd seen his face clearly in the moonlight. He was smiling, and his eyes glittered like sea glass in the sun, scaring her a little. Even though she knew he couldn't see her, she would have sworn he was looking right at her, and the thought sent goose bumps all over her.

Peering out again, she saw that he wasn't heading back to the house at all, but was turning up the side yard. Rushing to the front window, she very carefully moved the blackout curtain aside and peered out, watching as Peter emerged into the front yard and continued walking to the street. Even though he wasn't supposed to because of the blackout, Peter pulled what looked like a pack of cigarettes from his jacket pocket. A few seconds later a match flared, and Lulu ducked, waiting for a German torpedo to find that one source of light in all of Folly Beach.

When nothing happened, Lulu peered out of the curtain again

and watched Peter head down the street, keeping to shadows made by fences and trees, and heading toward the beach. She watched the orange circle of his lit cigarette until it grew too small to see. Lulu remembered the handkerchief Maggie had found in Cat's jacket. She'd flattened it out and found three initials that didn't make any sense because they weren't Peter's. It had taken Lulu a while to figure it out, but she still needed proof. The handkerchief was hidden in her box with her other treasures, and she had no intention of showing it to anyone. Yet.

As soon as Peter was out of sight, she rushed to the back door and quietly let herself outside. The note almost glowed in the moonlight, making it easy to see. She slid it from the bottle's neck and brought it inside to the kitchen, where she found Maggie's flashlight in a drawer and flipped it on. After waiting a moment to hear if anybody else was awake, she slowly opened the note with one hand and began to read: *Our picnic spot. Two o'clock a.m. The horse patrol comes at one and three, so be careful.*

Lulu shut off the flashlight and replaced it in the drawer, then held the note in the palm of her hand until the clock struck the hour. She wished Amy was there to talk to, to remind Lulu that she had hidden the first note only because she didn't want Maggie to leave her. Even though now it seemed it didn't matter what she did—Maggie was going away with Peter and leaving her behind. It was just like Jim had said to her—no bad deed ever went unpunished. He was right, she knew. She only wished that the punishment didn't hurt so bad.

Quietly, she let herself out of the house again and made her way through the moonlight to the tree. Very carefully, she placed the note exactly where Peter had left it for Maggie to find.

Then she headed to the street to follow Peter, thinking she knew where he was heading and half hoping that she was wrong.

CHAPTER 22

FOLLY BEACH, SOUTH CAROLINA
October 2009

Emmy looked down at her new jogger's watch, which sprouted buttons she still didn't know what to do with, and picked up her pace from a walk to a slow jog. Her new running shoes slapped at the pavement, the sound insulated by the low-lying clouds, muffling her progress as if they, too, wanted to keep her secret.

She had parked her car at the store around five thirty, and gone over Heath's final plans for the attic while she waited for the sun to rise. Then she'd headed down the west end of the island, hoping to make it all the way to the gates of the county park and back without stopping.

Emmy chose the streets this time instead of the beach, deciding it was time to explore her new home. She ran up Center Street and passed the pink city hall building, where the indomitable Marlene Entridge worked as the city clerk. Emmy had quickly found that if she needed an answer to any question about Folly, or about permits, or about anything, Marlene would either know the answer or know who would.

As she slowed back down to a walk, she passed larger, newer houses with manicured lawns and professional landscaping tucked between the older Folly cottages that Emmy had overheard a tourist at Taco Boy calling fraternity houses. She'd almost turned around to tell them to go to Kiawah or Seabrook if they wanted a different beach scene, but had held back when she realized that she'd thought the same thing when she first arrived.

But now, after living here for just a few short months, she'd begun to appreciate the charm of the town, and how different it was from the other sea islands that surrounded Charleston. It would never give airs of pretension or exclusion: what you saw was what you got, and there was something reassuring about that, especially for a person who wasn't really sure who she was in the first place.

She made it down West Arctic and passed the house where George Gershwin had lived while writing *Porgy and Bess*, the house now completely surrounded by a high wooden fence. Marlene had told Emmy it was because of all the tourists who kept knocking on the front door looking for a tour.

Breathing deeply, Emmy smelled the salt of the ocean and the pluff mud of the marsh, and neither seemed so foreign to her. The air in Indiana at the beginning of October was full of the promise of the coming harvest, crisp and yellow with waiting corn. But here the air carried with it the weight of water filled with teeming life that lay hidden until you looked close enough to see.

Emmy made it all the way to the county park, walking more than she jogged, but she figured it was at least a start. Without pausing, she turned around in front of the park's gate and headed east, crossing back over Center Street to East Ashley, passing Bert's twenty-four-hour market with the handwritten sign that read *"We might doze, but we never close!"* on the door, then finally turning left to return to Folly's Finds. She circled her truck several times, trying to catch her breath and feeling a lot older than she was. The old Emmy, Ben's wife, wouldn't have exerted herself like that. She wasn't sure why; Ben would have loved her regardless. It had more to do with the roles they'd played for each other, and how she still felt lost, like an actress without a script.

Her gaze rested on the box of books in the back of her truck. They'd been in there for a week, yet she hadn't done anything with them. Nor had she asked Lulu about the sketch of the bottle tree in the back of one of the books. She knew she was close to the end now, but the closer she came, the more she backed away. Maybe she was a lot like Heath and his unfinished projects, avoiding finishing something because he was too afraid to face what came next in his life. But Emmy wasn't afraid; she was simply lost.

With determination, she unlocked the car, fished for the store's keys from under the seat, and pulled them out. After opening the door, she grabbed the box and brought it back into Folly's Finds, dumping it on the floor with a loud thump. It was Sunday and the store was closed, so she could spend as much time as she needed to get through this final box.

She didn't have her laptop, so she grabbed a pad of paper and a pencil, then sat down next to the box with her back against the checkout counter and began the familiar ritual of pulling books from the box, then methodically scanning each page from cover to cover.

These books were similar to the rest inasmuch as they were an eclectic grouping like one might find in a person's home book collection. Except most of the books appeared new, without any creasing of the spines. And several of them were duplicates, as if purchased without much thought; or as if reading them hadn't been the intended use.

Emmy's head throbbed with anticipation, scaring her with its sudden intensity. There was something important here, something she couldn't miss. It was only after she'd opened the first five books that she realized the biggest difference in this box of books. Every single one of them had at least one notation in the margins, like these books had been collected and put together in a box for just that reason. But these notes weren't love poems; these notes had taken on a completely different tone. Pulling her notebook onto her lap, she copied: *I have a plan.* That one had been written in the man's handwriting.

She finished thumbing through that book, and picked up the next one, a late edition of Faulkner's *The Sound and the Fury*. Peering into the box, she spotted at least two more identical copies and her head throbbed with renewed intensity.

The next seven books held similarly cryptic messages from both the man and the woman. Staring down at her notepad, she studied what she'd written, then scrambled them around until she'd arranged them in some kind of order, alternating between the man and woman like a fluid dialog.

I can't. She's in a bad way tonight and I must stay with her.

Where were you?

It's too soon. She's still so weak.

I can't wait much longer. Things are changing that I can't control.

She's too young to be left behind—even for just a few short months. She needs me.

Now, darling. It must be now. You'll understand later, I promise.

I don't know if she'll believe me if I tell her. I'll be back for her.

I have a plan.

Emmy felt as if she were eavesdropping on a conversation she could only hear part of, reminding her of the game she'd played as a child in which a secret was whispered around the circle of children until the secret had been distorted so much it barely resembled the original.

After pulling off the fifteen books on top, she saw that the rest of the box was filled with old atlases and maps. On closer inspection she saw that they all showed the world as it had been prior to World War II. The boundaries of Western Europe looked strange to her, and she imagined she could see the Germans standing eagerly at Poland's borders, ready to march.

The atlases and travel guides were like new, just like the books, without any sign that they'd been read more than once or at all. And after thumbing through the first layer and not finding a single note, she began to feel discouraged. Her neck tingled as she stared at the assortment of travel books, remembering how Abigail had told her that the travel section in Folly's Finds had been Maggie's favorite.

With a deep breath, Emmy reached into the box and lifted out as many as she could, stacking them on the floor next to her to make her perusal of them a little easier. When she leaned in to reach for the next stack, she spotted a dark navy blue linen binding of what looked like a hardcover book.

Getting down on her knees, she lifted everything off of it and discovered a pristine copy of *Gulliver's Travels*. When she held it in her hands, she realized that the cover was warped slightly, but the book didn't seem to have any water damage. Tilting the book to view it from the top, she saw a slim space between the pages in the middle of the book, as if something had been stuck inside.

Gingerly, she placed the book on her lap and allowed it to fall open, the pages misshapen by memory automatically opening to the right spot and revealing a single sheet of paper, folded in thirds. It was pale blue, and thin, definitely not the heavy stock of today's printer paper. The edges were folded crisply and cleanly and very straight, as if whoever had folded the letter had allowed their fingers to pinch the crease over and over as if in deep thought.

Emmy lifted the letter from the pages, momentarily surprised by how light it felt in her hand, somehow expecting it would bear the weight of the words within. She stared at the letter for a long moment, wondering if she could put it back and close the book, and never open it, understanding a little about how Heath felt.

Her thoughts turned to Ben, and the last time she'd seen him and how they hadn't said good-bye. She nudged that thought the way a person might press a bruise to see if it had healed, wincing slightly because it wasn't quite gone. When she thought of Ben and pictured his face, it was always that last scene in the doorway of her parents' house, the way they'd said everything except good-bye. She closed her eyes, trying to get her troubled mind to see more clearly, to remember their final parting and to see the truth, no matter how hard it was.

Emmy listened to the quiet of the room, her temples beating with her pulse. She let out a breath of air as light seemed to penetrate the small space, forcing her eyes open. Staring at the folded letter, she remembered again in startling clarity the last time she'd seen Ben. Maybe that was why she kept hearing his footsteps; their incomplete parting had been like an unopened letter, and he was waiting for those final words. Maybe all of her indecision since then stemmed from that one omission.

She wiped her eyes with the backs of her wrists, and then, swallowing heavily, she opened the letter, unfolding each third until she could see all of it. The handwriting was one she hadn't seen before, and she allowed her eyes to scan to the bottom of the page to see the signature. *Catherine.* Returning to the top of the page, Emmy began to read:

I know the truth. I've always known that you were never really mine, but I thought if I tried hard enough, we could be happy. I've not given up, but I know that you have and it's made me angry and heartbroken until I don't know what to feel anymore. I have no desire to live without you and you have no desire to live with me. which leads me to believe that we are both better off with me dead.

I think I really loved you, at least for a little while. I hope that is some consolation to you for all that I have wronged you. Forgive me.

Emmy read the note again, her mouth dry. Her first thought was to call Heath, but after remembering their last conversation, she knew she couldn't. But then she recalled his parting words about calling her mother.

Carefully refolding the letter, Emmy took her cell phone from her pocket and dialed her parents' home number. Her mother picked it up on the second ring.

"Emmy. This is a nice surprise." The tone in Paige's voice made Emmy believe that she was telling the truth. "Your father and I were just talking about you this weekend. We took a road trip to the Smokies to see the changing of the leaves. We had a lovely cabin but without cell phone coverage. We were wondering if you were missing the change of season in Folly."

Emmy thought of the migrating ospreys and the sleeping marsh, and the way the colors of the cord grass had begun to change from green to yellow as its seeds clustered, then blew at the whim of the wind, and she realized she hadn't missed the flame orange and russets of the trees she remembered from childhood.

"Maybe," she said, trying to recall the last time her parents had ever gone anywhere. "The last few times I called, I ended up talking just to Dad, but I wanted to make sure that he passed on my thanks for the clothes you've been sending."

"Yes, he did." Paige's voice seemed different, her Southern accent less pronounced and more flattened almost. Or maybe it was the same but Emmy had grown used to hearing the accent in its true original form. "Have you worn the bathing suit yet?"

Emmy paused. "No. Not yet. It just shows more skin than I'm used to."

Emmy could hear the smile in her mother's voice. "Give it time. Just make sure you wear a T-shirt and shorts over it if you decide to go mattress surfing."

"What?"

"Oh, just something we used to do as kids—figured they probably still did it as long as the cops aren't around. You tie a mattress behind a car or truck on the beach and try to hang on."

Emmy tried to picture her mother doing something like that, and only drew a blank. "Okay. I'll try to remember that." She shook her head, wondering what else her mother had never told her about growing up on Folly, and why she'd waited so long.

"You sound good, Emmy."

"I feel good," she said, not even having to think about it. "Things are . . . better. I've starting jogging. Well, half walking really. I hope to be running soon."

"Really? You used to make fun of people who ran for exercise."

"I know. Abigail's son, Heath, he pretty much forced me. I've been going almost every morning and can do about three miles in a half walk, half run. It feels good."

"I hope you're wearing sun protection."

Emmy smiled. "You sound like Ben." They were both silent for a moment as if realizing that it was the first time she'd said Ben's name so casually. They both seemed to wait a moment for the crush of grief to overwhelm her. Emmy still felt it, but it was softer now, the edges rounded by the life she'd begun to explore on Folly.

"Do you want me to go get Dad?"

"No. I actually called to speak with you about something."

"About the store? Shoot."

"No, actually. About the Reynolds family. I know you weren't born until much later, but I was hoping you'd remember your mother or neighbors talking about something that happened here a long time ago."

"About what?"

"You said you knew Maggie, Abigail's mother-in-law, who used to own Folly's Finds."

"Well, I knew *more* of her, to be exact. I'd go in her store all the time as a child. I knew Lulu better because she was a lot younger."

"Do you remember Maggie's cousin, Catherine? They called her Cat."

"I remember hearing of her, but never knew her—she died before I was born. During the war, I think." Paige paused for a moment. "I seem to recall that there was something tragic about her death. She was very young—that could be it. But that's all I remember. Abigail might know. Lulu definitely would, since she's related to Catherine. Abigail didn't move to Folly until high school. Why? Does this have something to do with the notes in those books?"

"I don't know. But I found a letter stuck inside one of the books.

It's signed by Cat, and the handwriting is very different from the woman's handwriting in the margin notes."

"What kind of letter?"

Emmy took a breath. "Let me read it to you and you tell me what you think." Slowly, she read the letter into the phone.

There was a long pause before her mother responded. "It's a suicide note. There's no doubt."

"That's what I thought, too. Could that have been the tragedy that you remembered?"

"I really don't know. It happened so long ago, but I suppose my mother might have mentioned . . . something. You'll have to ask someone else."

"I'll ask Abigail first. Lulu tends to be a bit elusive around me. Not one to give off the warm and fuzzies, you know?"

Paige chuckled, an unfamiliar sound to Emmy. "She's always been that way. When she used to work in the store with her sister, she'd scare all of us children with the way she'd look at us without smiling. But I remember her sneaking me candy when my mama wasn't looking. And she used to save books she thought I might like at the front counter for whenever I came in. They had a little lending library there for a while. I remember she was really into Nancy Drew. My mama told me that when Miss Lulu was younger, she'd go around Folly Beach with a magnifying glass and a flashlight, pretending she was a junior detective just like Nancy. I was never afraid of her after Mama told me that."

Emmy frowned. "She's never said anything to me about knowing you when you were a girl. I wonder why."

Emmy imagined Paige shrugging. "I was married and living here then, but I remember people telling me that she went real into herself after Hugo—when her sister died. She was always quiet before, but she became almost a hermit. If it hadn't been for Abigail and John and their kids, I don't think that she would have made it."

Emmy thought of Lulu in her bottle-tree garden, asking about Ben and telling Emmy that she was brave. There was so much about Lulu she didn't know, had never even tried to know. The barrier Lulu had erected around herself was very effective. But surmountable. If only someone cared enough to try.

With renewed determination Emmy said, "I'll talk to Lulu."

"Would you let me know?

Emmy paused for a moment. "Sure."

"You sound surprised that I'd be interested."

"Well, I am. You never really looked beyond your store and house before."

"Yeah, well. Things are . . . different since you left. It's your father, mostly. He's been bitten by the travel bug. We've been doing little weekend trips, but now he's thinking about a visit to the Napa Valley. And then maybe Europe. We'll see. But it's been . . . reviving. I know that's an odd word, but that's how it feels. Like I've been taking shallow breaths for years and finally learned how to fill my lungs."

Emmy understood. She'd felt the same way the first time she'd started running. "You could come back to Folly for a visit."

There was silence on the line, and Emmy pictured her mother staring out the kitchen window at her bottle tree. "Yes, I know. We've . . . talked about it."

Emmy leaned back against the checkout counter, remembering the jar of sand and the way it had smelled like the ocean. "Why have you never come back, except for funerals?"

The pause was long enough for Emmy to hear the slow progress of a car on the street in front of the store. "I don't know, really. Maybe I figured if I returned, I'd realize how much I missed it, and how I'd want to stay. But returning forever was never an option. It would have felt like defeat, almost, to return—like I'd be forgetting all those babies and the good parts of my marriage. I didn't want your father to know that I was tempted. There's something so healing about being near the water, isn't there? Makes you forget all the bad parts. But I couldn't go back."

"Was it all bad, Mama?"

"No, sweetheart." There was a slight pause, the silence filled with Emmy's heartbeat. "Because I had you."

Emmy squeezed her eyes shut, trying not to think of how long she'd been waiting for her mother to say that. Swallowing heavily, she opened her eyes and her gaze rested on the letter in her lap again. "I need to go show this letter to Abigail. And I guess I need to find Lulu to see what she remembers about Catherine."

"You do that. It was good talking to you, Emmy. And don't forget to let me know what you find out."

"I won't. And call me if you think about anything—anything to do with Folly Beach or anybody who once lived here. It might help."

"I will. Good-bye, Emmy."

Emmy said good-bye, then ended the call and considered why she didn't feel so far from home anymore.

LULU STOOD IN THE DOORWAY to her shed behind Folly's Finds, blinded momentarily by the brightness outside so that the interior of the shed seemed like an endless hole. She almost wished she could step inside and fall forever, like Alice from one of her favorite childhood books.

Lulu had awakened that morning after a fitful sleep, finally knowing what she had to do. Today was the party for Lizzie's babies, and that Emmy woman would be there, asking her questions and thinking she needed to find the answers for herself and to solve her own problems. She just had no idea.

And the whole time Lulu had lain in the bed wondering what she was going to do. While she was remembering everything that had happened all those years ago, it hadn't been Maggie's eyes she'd seen, but Heath's. When he'd shown her the box he'd found in the attic, he'd known—known that he'd pierced a hole into her past that nobody was ever supposed to find.

His eyes were understanding, but somehow wounded, too, accusing her of deliberately keeping her secret from him so he wouldn't understand just how dangerous leaving your past open-ended could be.

She stepped inside the shed, blinking as if that would help her see. As she reached out blindly, her hand struck the row of hoes and rakes leaning against the interior wall, knocking them to the ground with a large crash.

Her heart burned in her chest, and she stumbled backward, trying to catch her breath. Her fingers tingled as she reached again, finally grabbing hold of the short spade she'd hung on a nail on the wall. Forcing her fingers around the handle, she lifted the spade, then staggered from the shed.

Leaning against the door, she squinted in the sun as she struggled to fill her lungs with air, the burning in her chest getting strong enough that she swore she could smell smoke. She didn't think she could make it up the short flight of steps to go through the store, so she focused on cutting through her bottle trees without knocking anything over, then fumbling through the closed gate of the fence that let her out into the side yard by Folly's Playgrounds.

Janell stood outside emptying a coffeepot full of water on the camellia bush. She straightened when she saw Lulu.

"Haven't see you for a while, Lulu. Emmy said you've got lots of orders waiting. I was hoping we could talk so I know how much metal—"

Lulu kept walking, putting a lot of effort into standing up straight. "Not right now, Janell. Maybe this afternoon." She waved her hand and headed to the front yard.

She almost shouted with relief when she spotted Abigail's car parked at the curb, the driver's side open and the engine running as if she'd just dashed into the store for a quick moment. With a quick glance around, Lulu slid into the driver's seat, plopping the spade on the seat next to her and belatedly noting the cake from the Cake Stand done in the shape of matching pink and blue booties, on the floor of the car.

Pressing her hand against her chest, she leaned forward and shut the door, then put the car into drive. The pain was insistent now, so much so that she could barely find the strength to press the gas pedal. It was early October, too late to be worried about tourists crossing the street in front of her.

When she made it to the empty lot, she didn't have the time or energy to try to park parallel to the curb, so she drove up on the property with her front tires sinking into the sandy soil.

She rested her head on the steering wheel with the air-conditioning blasting as sweat prickled her face. Her right arm felt numb, and she had the alarming thought that she'd have to dig with her left hand.

Using her whole body to push open the door, she fell out of the car, barely catching herself on the side window. She stared across the empty lot, calculating how far it was to the cross at the back of the property. Taking a deep breath, she focused on putting one foot in front of the other until she'd reached the cross. Then, her eyes blurry with pain, she made the twenty paces to the right and stopped.

She knew if she got down, she might not be able to get up again, but she had to try. Carefully, she went down on one knee, then the other, wincing from the pain in her chest and knees. Then, awkwardly gripping the spade in her left hand, she tried to dig. But now her left hand wasn't cooperating either, and she succeeded only in scraping away the smallest amount of dirt and dead grass.

Her eyes dimmed, and she looked up, expecting to see a cloud covering the sun. Instead, the blue sky illuminated the world around her, the sun shooting halos of light around her peripheral vision. And then, inexplicably, she saw Maggie. She was walking toward her from the direction of the ocean, and she was shaking her head.

Lulu closed her eyes tight, knowing that her punishment was near. She waited for what seemed like a long time, then opened her eyes again, wanting to see Maggie's face just one more time. The pain vibrated through her body now, radiating down her arms and legs. But none of it mattered; she was going to see Maggie again.

But when she opened her eyes, all she saw was darkness.

CHAPTER 23

As Maggie finished rearranging the shelves of her lending library one more time, she listened with only half an ear to her daytime drama, *Against the Storm*, on the radio she'd brought from the house. She'd been spending so much time at Folly's Finds since Cat's marriage that she'd lost track of some of the story lines. It was Lulu who'd suggested she bring in the radio, and it was only then that Maggie realized how much time Lulu was spending in the store instead of at the house, too. It was almost as if Lulu thought Maggie would disappear if Lulu let her sister out of her sight for a moment. Maggie supposed it was natural for a young girl who'd lost both parents at an early age to fear separation. But a part of Maggie—the part aware of Lulu's secretive nature and dark, private thoughts—wondered if Lulu's fear stemmed from something else entirely.

Maggie stood back, examining the shelves. Her favorite books—the ones Peter had given her and most of her travel books—were already moved to the very top. But now they were also pushed back to the wall so that the spines weren't visible to anyone standing below. She'd even gone as far as to place dictionaries and reference materials—books she was sure no one would ever willingly borrow—haphazardly in front.

This had been Peter's idea, whispered in her ear the first time they'd huddled together in their coats and blankets in the sand under the stars and listened to the ocean breathe. The blood rose in her cheeks as she remembered their stolen time spent together cocooned in each other's arms, and all the times since. She tried not to think what her mother and father would think, or anybody else she knew. Despite Folly's past, which included a vacation home for prostitutes, she would be scorned if her friends and neighbors knew her secret.

Mostly, she tried not to think about her own conscience, or the consequences of her sin. She was shamed, but somehow defiant, too. It seemed that her entire life she'd spent doing the right thing, being everyone's constant; a jetty deflecting others' sorrows at the expense of her own. She had let Jim go so easily, and even Peter—at first. But she wasn't that same girl anymore. Lulu's revelation had awakened something that had been festering since she'd promised her mother to protect Cat. It was an unnamable thing between resentment and loyalty, a truth she'd tried to deny her entire life. She had passions, and wants, and desires—all the things she'd kept hidden. Until Peter. And Peter loved this new and brave Maggie, and that was who she now chose to be.

"I was hoping you'd have something for my niece." Maggie redirected her attention to Lillian Rhodes, an attractive blonde whose family had owned the same summer home on East Arctic since the turn of the century. "She's coming to stay with me until the war is over. They live in Cape Hatteras, and my sister is just petrified that the Germans are going to invade. There have been so many ships sunk right off the coast there, and two weeks ago an Eagle Scout patrolling the beach found a dinghy that had been hidden behind the dunes. They think it was used by spies from a German U-boat. Who knows where they are now? My sister just didn't want to take any chances with Rebecca."

"I'm sure she'll be safe here, Mrs. Rhodes. Our patrols are pretty thorough, and we haven't seen anything out in the water for months now—not since Mrs. Knutson thought she saw a German sub while she was on lookout duty. They've probably all gone north because they know they can't get to us here on Folly without being seen."

Mrs. Rhodes widened her blue eyes. "That's exactly what I said. So Rebecca will stay with me until the end of the war. I'd like my sister to come, too, but she wants to stay put for her husband. He's a merchant marine, and when he gets leave, she wants to be there."

"I understand." Maggie changed the subject. "So how old is Rebecca and what types of books does she like?"

As they talked, the bell over the door rang. Maggie didn't go look, knowing that most of her customers would come find her or leave the money on the counter if they just needed a newspaper or some other item they could grab themselves. She was reaching up for a copy of A. A. Milne's *When We Were Very Young* when she heard the sound of a coin hitting the bottom of the can behind her.

Her neck tingled, like it had been brushed with an unseen kiss. She had to pause for a moment to catch her breath, feeling the heat begin to pool behind her knees. Schooling a professional smile on her face, she turned around.

"Peter, what a nice surprise. Welcome home. Cat must be so happy to see you since the baby's due any minute now."

He took off his hat and held it in his right hand. In his left, he held a book. "Good afternoon, Mrs. Rhodes. Margaret." He nodded to each of them, his eyes meeting Maggie's briefly. "I haven't seen Cat yet. That's my next stop. I wanted to return my book first before I forgot."

He handed it to her, and Maggie took it, briefly glancing at the title: *Romeo and Juliet.*

Mrs. Rhodes eyed it, too. "Is that Shakespeare? I think Rebecca might enjoy that. She's very advanced for her age."

Maggie held the book close to her chest. "I'm not sure it would be appropriate, Lillian. How old did you say Rebecca was—fourteen? I think it sends the wrong message to young girls, not to mention it has such a sad ending. Especially in these times, I think a more uplifting book would be more suitable."

Mrs. Rhodes knitted her eyebrows, not looking entirely convinced.

Maggie turned back to the shelf, her eyes rapidly scanning the books. She tipped back the binding of the first book she found, and pulled it off the shelf. "Has Rebecca read the Betsy-Tacy stories? This one is the first in the series—but there are two more. Every girl is reading them right now."

Lillian took the book and opened it to the first page, reading silently to herself. Smiling she said, "You're absolutely right, of course. I can see how this type of story would be much better for a young girl like Rebecca. Do you have the other two in the series? That way, if she likes this one, I can come back and get the next two."

Maggie hoped she hid her relief. "Why don't you take all of them now to save you a trip? I promise you, she'll love them. Lulu read them all in two days and is eagerly waiting for the next one." She turned back to the shelves and quickly found *Betsy Tacy and Tib,* and *Betsy and Tacy Go over the Big Hill.* "All you owe me is a single nickel." She indicated the can. "Just drop it in there, and take one out when you return the last book."

"Thank you, Maggie. I do appreciate it. I'll send Rebecca back so you can meet her."

The bell rang, and two men in uniform entered, the last one holding the door open for Mrs. Rhodes as she left. Peter's eyes held Maggie's for a moment before Maggie turned to greet the two men.

She returned to Peter, her eyes meeting his as the spot behind her left ear began to ache. Forcing her voice to sound normal, she said, "I have a book I thought you might like. I'm holding it behind the counter for you."

Maggie felt his gaze on her as she walked to the shelves under the cash register, where she kept her pocket book and lunch pail, and slid the slim volume toward him. "Do you like plays?" She turned and handed him the book with the green linen cover. "This is a series of plays by John Ford. My favorite is *The Lover's Melancholy.*"

He took the book from her, his fingertips lingering over hers, making the spot at the base of her throat tingle with a remembered kiss.

"I'll look forward to reading it." His eyes held hers for a long moment until the two customers approached to pay for their purchases.

The door opened abruptly, shortening the ring of the bell. Lulu ran inside, her face red and covered in perspiration despite the chill outside, one of her pigtails loose from its ribbon. "Maggie! Martha told me to get here just as fast as I could—she said Cat's started her pains and they're coming real fast."

Clutching the book tightly, Maggie said, "Go get Dr. Brown and tell him what you just told me. I'll go right home."

The two customers left and Maggie ducked to pull out her purse. "Peter's back—and in the nick of time, I would say."

Lulu stood facing Peter, breathing heavily as she scrunched her nose. "Just now? But I saw you . . ." She stopped, her face going slightly paler. "Never mind." Turning on her heel, she ran back out the door without another word.

Maggie grabbed her purse and coat, and as she flipped the *Closed* sign in the door before opening it, she realized that Peter was still staring after Lulu.

ß

As it turned out, Dr. Brown beat them to the house by about five minutes. Lulu had run into him coming out of McNally's and they'd taken his car to the house. Peter and Maggie rushed past the doctor's car on the curb, stopping abruptly inside the door as a loud scream rumbled down the stairs. Turning to face Peter, Maggie said, "Keep your coat on and wait on the porch. I'm hoping there's still time to take her to the hospital, but be prepared to wait just in case there isn't."

His gaze strayed to the staircase behind her, then settled back on her face. "All right. I'll wait there. Just let me know if . . . if she asks for me."

Maggie's eyes slid away as she nodded, his hand squeezing hers as she turned to run up the stairs just as another jarring scream exploded from upstairs like a sudden tidal surge. Lulu leaned on the wall outside Cat's bedroom, her color back to normal and looking a lot calmer than Maggie felt.

Just as Maggie reached the top step, Martha opened the door with a bundle of towels wrapped in a sheet. Maggie clenched her teeth when she saw the blood on one of the towels, watching as it stained the sheet in a growing circle of crimson.

Martha handed the bundle to Lulu. "You go take this and throw it on the back porch, then rush right back up here with more clean towels, you here? And be quick about it." Her brown eyes settled on Maggie. "You get in here fast—she been askin' for you. Doctor say it won't be long."

Lulu stopped at the top of the stairs, holding the bundle as far away from her body as her arms could reach, and turned her face away. Through gritted teeth, she said, "I'm never having babies. Not ever." Then she ran down the stairs, managing to get down them without tripping.

The stench of blood and sweat hit Maggie as she entered the room. Dr. Brown was draping a sheet over Cat's upraised knees, and he turned toward Maggie. "That baby's ready to come. No time to get her to the hospital." He approached her, his gray eyes serious behind his glasses. "Where's your phone? I need to call my office and have my nurse bring me what I need. And whatever you do, don't let her push until I get back."

Maggie sent the doctor to the kitchen while Martha stood by Cat's head, mopping her forehead with a damp rag. Maggie moved to the side of the bed, hardly recognizing the Catherine she knew in the swollen, shiny face of the woman on the pillow. The large mound of her stomach protruded under the white sheet like an exposed secret and Maggie found she couldn't look at it. Instead she took Cat's hand, the skin clammy and cold. Cat gripped her fingers tight enough to break them, like they were a drowning victim's last hope.

Maggie glanced up at Martha, who'd given birth six times and had helped bring four grandchildren into the world. "Thanks, Martha, for staying. Does everything . . . ?" She swallowed, unsure how to phrase her question. "Does everything look all right?"

Martha gave her a weary smile. "So far. Baby coming real fast, is all."

Cat began to thrash on her pillow, squeezing Maggie's hand even tighter until Maggie could feel the bones rubbing against each other, the band of her ring cutting into the flesh on the inside of her finger.

"Don't you push, Miss Cat. Doctor ain't ready for you to push." Martha held the cool cloth on Cat's forehead, pressing on it as if to hold in the pain.

Cat screamed, raising the hair on Maggie's scalp. "I have to. I have to." She began to groan, and Martha dropped the rag to use both hands to hold Cat's legs down until the urge had passed.

"I've got to see what's taking Lulu so long with them towels. Miss Cat be fine for a moment with you here, okay?"

Maggie nodded at Martha's reassuring glance.

Cat was breathing heavily, her eyes bloodshot from the strain. "Open the window, Mags. It's so damned hot in here."

Maggie stood, rubbing her hand to renew circulation as she approached the window and pulled up the lock. With an easy shove on both sides, the casement windows opened, allowing a cool breeze and fresh air to penetrate the pall of the room. Forcing a light tone, she said, "I wish the window in my room would open so easily."

"Mags?"

Reluctantly, Maggie returned to the side of the bed and reached for Cat's hand with her right one. "Yes, Cat, I'm here."

"I need you to promise . . ."

A heavy stone of dread rolled into place in the pit of her stomach. "Promise what, Cat?"

"I need you to promise me . . ." She licked dry, cracked lips. "I want you to take the baby. If I die. I want you to raise this baby as your own. You'd be a much better mother—we both know that." She clenched her eyes, her hands flying to her protruding stomach, her fingers arched like claws. "Promise me."

Panic seized Maggie as she squeezed Cat's hand between both of hers. "Everything's going to be fine. You're not going to—"

"Promise me." Cat's voice was urgent, her head beginning to toss on the pillow as another contraction gripped her frail body.

Martha, carrying a bundle of clean towels, entered the room at the same time as the doctor. She approached the bed while Dr. Brown went to the window, closing both sides with an irrefutable snap. "It's too cold in here—we'll all end up with pneumonia."

Cat began to writhe again, but her eyes settled on Maggie's face. "Promise me," her mouth formed but no words came out.

Slowly, Maggie nodded, making another promise that would bind her to someone else forever. She imagined the stone in the pit of her stomach growing moss, reminding her how permanent the bond of a promise made could be: as delicate as a spiderweb, but just as impossible to extricate yourself once the words were spoken. Maggie stepped back from the bed, feeling already the soft filament of a web forming around her.

CHAPTER 24

Emmy found a spot close to the Reynolds house on West Hudson, and parked her car. The party wasn't scheduled to start for another fifteen minutes, but Heath had said he and his dad had found something to show her, and he'd asked her to get there a little early.

Juggling two gift bags with coordinating pink and blue helium balloons, she made it up the stairs of a modest bungalow. It looked like a Folly Beach original that had been updated without losing the character of the house—a straddling of the line that Emmy was growing accustomed to that separated the traditionalists from the newer residents of the island.

She was surprised to find Jolene sitting on a joggling board on the front porch, nursing a tall glass of something cold. Before she could ask, Jolene answered, "Sweet tea, that's all. I was feeling warm, so I asked for something cold."

Emmy nodded. It was about fifty-five degrees and she wore a sweater, but she could see a sheen of perspiration on Jolene's upper lip and her hands trembled slightly as she held the glass.

"Are you all right?"

"I'm fine. It's just that . . . I'd like a drink. Real bad. But Lulu said she'd knock me into next week if she found out I'd had a sip."

Emmy frowned. "She wouldn't really, would she?"

Jolene's mouth twitched. "No. At least I don't think so. But I figured it wasn't such a bad idea anyway. I'm still afraid of her, though."

Emmy nodded. "Do you want to walk back in with me?"

Jolene shook her head. "No, but thank you. I'm waiting for Lulu." Her lips turned up in a wry smile. "I feel . . . more comfortable when she's with me. This sounds stupid, but she's been sort of my surrogate mother through all this mess with Heath. She doesn't mind me leaning on her, and I need somebody to lean on right now. I can only hope that I can return the favor someday."

Again, Emmy nodded, but didn't go inside right away. "I love what you did with Lulu's pages on the site. The pictures of her bottle trees displayed like a storybook with changing pages is really brilliant. I've gotten a lot more hits since her pages went live. We're actually getting a backlog of orders. Janell told me that she wants Lulu to teach her how to make the tree branches so that she can help. Which means we might need to do another page to introduce Janell soon, too."

"Great." Jolene's voice was flat, as if she hadn't really been listening.

"Is something wrong?" Emmy asked.

A furrow formed between Jolene's delicate eyebrows. "I don't know. Abigail arrived on foot a few minutes ago saying somebody had stolen her car with the cakes for the party. She thinks it's just a teenage prank and she'll get her car back—she's just worried that the cakes might get ruined. And Lulu should be here by now."

Joe, Lizzie's husband, pushed opened the door. "I thought I saw balloons. Come on in, Emmy. We've got plenty of food." He reached for the two bags. "Glad you could come."

Jolene shot them a tentative smile. "I'll be there in a bit."

Emmy nodded and entered the living room, where a few people, early like herself and most of whom she knew as customers at Folly's Finds, stood or sat in comfortable-looking chairs and a pair of couches upholstered in bright yellow slipcovers. Heath's father, John, and his wheelchair were in the center of a group of people who let out a laugh at something he'd just said as Emmy approached.

"Emmy!" he said, holding out his arms. She bent down and gave him a hug and a kiss on his cheek, his enthusiasm at seeing her making her smile.

"Hello, Mr. Reynolds. Congratulations on the birth of your first grandchildren."

Abigail came up behind him holding a tray of what looked like hush puppies. "He says I've gone gaga over them, but he should see himself fussing over them. He's already told Lizzie and Joe that he's ready for the next one."

She extended the tray to Emmy, who took a hush puppy and a napkin. "I can't wait to see them."

"Oh, don't worry. You will. Lizzie's in the back bedroom feeding them, and as soon as they're done, she'll be out to show them off." Abigail moved away to another group, holding out the tray.

Emmy swallowed her hush puppy and was looking around for a familiar face when she felt someone touch her arm. She turned and smiled at Heath, aware of how glad she was to see him. He smiled, too, but his eyes were serious. "You ready?"

"Sure." Curious, she followed him down a narrow hallway to a room at the back of the house. He opened the door and stepped back, allowing Emmy to walk inside first; then he closed the door behind them.

The room was set up as an office, with a large desk and a conspicuously empty spot where a chair would be. A framed American flag, torn and dirty, dominated one wall, while all sorts of military paraphernalia—medals, swords, bullets, and belt buckles that spanned more than a century of battles—were framed or displayed on every wall and available flat surface.

"Your dad's office, I'm guessing?" Emmy asked, her eyes going back to the flag.

"Yes." He followed her gaze. "My dad brought that back from Vietnam. So he wouldn't forget, is what he tells us but I think there's a lot more to that story. That's one area of his life he doesn't talk about."

Emmy's gaze didn't drop. "Ben didn't either." The grief this time came to her like the unfurling of a flag, soft and fluttering as it settled around her. It no longer dulled her vision, or stole her breath, but it was still there. She supposed it always would be, but maybe she could live with it the way a person learns to live with sidetracked expectations.

"It hurt me, the way he wouldn't talk about it." This was the first time she'd ever admitted that to anybody, but she wasn't surprised that it had been to Heath. There was something reassuring about him that inspired confidences.

Heath watched her closely. "It's normal. It doesn't mean that he didn't love you any less; it meant that he loved you enough to want to protect you."

She looked down, feeling her eyes well up. It was the first time she'd ever looked at it that way, and she felt some of her grief give way to relief. It freed a part of her inside, allowing her to let some of it go. "Thank you," she said.

Heath moved to the other side of the desk and opened up the top drawer. "My dad pulled this out for you to look at."

Glad for the change of subject, Emmy joined Heath and peered down at the two handwritten letters. The handwriting was male, but completely different from the writing in the books. Her gaze traveled down to the signature at the bottom of the page. *Robert.*

She faced Heath. "Who was Robert?"

"My grandfather. He and Maggie were married in June 1943." His eyes were soft as he regarded her, like he understood her sudden vulnerability, as if the shedding of grief left a person raw. "Does this help you with anything?"

"Sort of. I know that Robert's not the writer of the margin notes. The handwriting is completely different."

Heath opened the drawer again and pulled out a stack of letters tied in a faded red ribbon. "This is where Dad found the letters from my grandfather—with all of these. They're letters between my grandparents written during the war."

Emmy's eyes widened. "Maggie? You have Maggie's letters?"

"Apparently. These have been in a box since Hugo, and my dad forgot they were here until he went looking for a writing sample from his dad. He's glad he did. Feels like it's an important part of our history that shouldn't be kept hidden in a box."

"But you're not a history fan."

"Not personal history, no. I've never seen much point in reliving the past, as you know."

"So what's changed?"

"I don't know. Maybe it's the pictures on the walls in my house— how I didn't know who those people were. And Lulu . . ."

"What about Lulu?"

"Well, she's not here yet, which is strange. She's usually the first one at any gathering, helping out behind the scenes, staying on the periphery to watch people. Something has happened, and it has to do with those damned books you found." His eyes darkened as he looked at her. "She's seventy-seven years old. How does a person get to be so damned old and still be afraid that the past is going to catch up to her?"

Emmy studied him closely, wondering if he was still talking about Lulu. Glancing down at the letters, she noticed the woman's handwriting, recognizing it from the dozens of times she'd already seen it. "Not that I needed any further confirmation, but it's the same, Heath. Maggie's handwriting is the same I've been reading in the book margins and on the photographs in your house."

His jaw hardened. "I'm not surprised. There're some interesting tidbits in the letters. My father and I read them for the first time last night."

She looked at her watch. "It's still early. Would it be all right if I read them now?"

Heath indicated an old leather couch pressed up against the wall under the flag. "Go ahead. We figured you'd want to."

She settled down on one side of the couch while Heath sat next to her, his arms folded as Emmy began to read.

The letters started in August of 1943, apparently after Robert's deployment overseas. It was hard to tell exactly where because it was never mentioned, most likely for fear of censorship, but they talked about his being far from home and wanting to eat a hot dog again.

She looked up. "When did you say they were married?"

"June 1943. Why?"

Emmy shrugged. "Because these don't seem like the letters from a newlywed, that's all. I remember Ben's letters to me. They were full of mundane stuff, too, but there were . . ." She paused, remembering how she used to sleep with Ben's letters pressed against her chest, and how the paper wilted, as if mourning his absence. Emmy continued. "But there were the emotional aspects, too. There's none of that stuff here."

"It was a different time. Maybe men were pressured to be more stoic."

She shook her head. "I don't know. History is full of letters from soldiers writing home. Have you ever heard about the Sullivan Ballou letter from Ken Burns' Civil War series? It makes you weep, it's so beautiful. He wrote, 'My love for you is deathless.'" She looked down at the letter in her hand. "I think it makes sense that men facing death have a better insight into their hearts."

"Sometimes." Heath looked at her, an understanding passing between them, like two soldiers on the same battlefield. "So what happened to Sullivan Ballou?"

"He died a week later. I always thought how grateful his wife must have been to have that letter from him. But after Ben . . . I don't know." Emmy shook her head. "Maybe it would have been easier for her if she hadn't known how much he loved her. So she wouldn't know how much she had lost." The words seemed hollow to her, not quite ringing true anymore.

The leather of the couch creaked as Heath leaned forward. "I'm thinking Ben was a lucky man to know he was loved by you. And that he died knowing that."

Emmy didn't say anything for a long moment, the handwriting in front of her swimming through blurred vision. Like when she was called brave, Heath's words had cracked open something inside the dark part of her grief, like a curtain being raised halfway to let in the light.

"How do you know so much?" Emmy kept her gaze focused on the letter.

"Look who raised me. Besides my mother and father, who are pretty amazing, I had Maggie and Lulu. Pretty strong women all around."

Emmy nodded, still unable to look at him. She continued to read the letters between Maggie and Robert, all signed with love, but the triviality of the contents belying the word. There was certainly affection, but nothing that would indicate the hell of two lovers being separated by a war.

When she was done, she handed the letters back to Heath. "Thank you for sharing these with me."

He looked at her oddly. "What aren't you telling me?"

She was silent for a moment. "I don't think you're really going to want to hear what I have to say."

Crossing his arms across his chest, he said, "Why don't you start, and I'll tell you if I need you to stop?"

"All right." She leaned back. "The big question is to whom Maggie was writing the notes in the book margins since it wasn't her husband. And Lulu tells me it wasn't Jim, either—although she could have been lying. But Jim died in nineteen forty-one, and some of the books have a nineteen forty-two copyright date, so that wouldn't work. The only other man is Peter, and I'm pretty sure the handwriting doesn't match. Unless, of course, he deliberately disguised his handwriting to be different from his signature in the books to Maggie and Lulu. But why do that if he was already taking such pains to hide the notes?"

Heath's jaw tightened and Emmy was reminded again of his reluctance to deal with the past or the future. But it seemed to her that his insistence on living in the present was the same as putting blinders on a horse: you missed a lot of what was going on in the world around you. If it hadn't been for the notes in the books, she'd still be sitting in the back of her mother's store, unaware of the change of seasons or the way the sun seemed to melt like butter as it settled over the marsh at dusk. Or that ospreys mated for life and that alligators didn't swim in the ocean.

Heath stood and moved to the window to look out on the street below. "So what are you going to do now?"

"I'm not sure. But there's something else. It's a letter from Cat, Maggie's sister. It was hidden inside a book in the box you found in the attic at Folly's Finds."

He faced her, his eyes uncertain, like those of a man about to step onto a tightrope wire suspended high between two buildings. "Who's it addressed to?"

"It doesn't say. But I read it to my mother, and we both seemed to think the same thing."

"Is it something that could hurt Lulu?"

"It might be. Although it also might be something she already knows about."

"Then I'm ready to stop there. I think we've dug up enough of the past for one night."

"Fine." Emmy stood, too, feeling somehow disappointed that Heath could see her path clearly but be so blind about his own. "Thanks for letting me see the letters. They've raised as many questions as they've answered, but thanks."

Heath straightened. "There's one obvious thing you haven't mentioned, and I'm only going to bring it up because it will probably occur to you in the middle of the night and wake you up. I figure I might as well spare you now."

Emmy raised an eyebrow. "What is it?"

"The dates of my father's birth, and Maggie's wedding to Robert. Apparently, they were married when my father was six months old."

Emmy thought for a moment. "You're right. I probably would

have figured that out sooner or later, but thanks. Just another puzzle piece to throw on the table. I just have no idea where it fits."

They began walking toward the door. "Do you think your father knows?"

"He never mentioned it, but I have to assume that he probably figured it out at some point."

Emmy turned to face him. "You know, if it's true, then that could be why Lulu's been so secretive about all of this. Out-of-wedlock babies were scandalous back in the forties."

Heath's eyes were serious. "And have nothing to do with us now, and could only upset an old lady."

Emmy was about to tell him that they both knew that Lulu wasn't a shrinking violet who shunned scandal—especially one that had happened more than sixty years ago—when the door flew open. Abigail stood in the doorway, her face pale and her chest rising and falling rapidly.

"They found my car—it's over at the old property on Second Street." She pressed both hands across her chest. "They found Lulu there, too. She might have had a heart attack and is being rushed to Roper Hospital downtown."

"Oh, no." Emmy hugged Abigail. "Is she going to be all right?"

"I don't know. She's very lucky. A woman walking her dog saw her fall over and was able to call for help on her cell. The ambulance was there in about five minutes, and they were able to start treatment." She swallowed. "Thank God that woman was there."

"Let's go—I'll drive." Heath began shepherding the women through the door. "We'll take the van so Dad can come, too."

"What was she doing there?" Emmy asked, trying to sound calm.

"We don't know. She had a spade with her, like she was going to dig something up." Abigail choked back a sob and Emmy put her arm around her.

"It'll be okay. We'll all get through this together." She squeezed Abigail's shoulders, surprised at how much she meant the words.

Then they walked through the quiet group of partygoers and followed Heath out the front door. Emmy stopped for a moment, breathing in the cool fall air, which still smelled of salt and the browning marsh, and wondered what Lulu could have been digging up, and if her past had finally caught up to her.

CHAPTER 25

FOLLY BEACH, SOUTH CAROLINA
May 1943

Maggie stood barefoot in the summer grass, her feet and night-gown damp from the misting rain. She waited a moment before venturing too far into the yard, waiting to hear any movement or voices. But the warm night slept, the hum and croak of unseen things muted by the mist.

Slowly, she walked toward the bottle tree, where she unhooked the cobalt blue bottle from the lowest limb and slid the note into the neck. This had become routine, but no less frightening each time she placed a note inside a bottle. She and Peter had agreed on the meeting location in their previous meeting, and she'd left a book at the store for Lulu to give him when he'd returned home that afternoon from another business trip. All he needed was the time, and her note in the bottle would tell him. She'd long since stopped thinking about the guilt, remembering instead what Lulu had told her about Cat and Jim, and how she needed Peter the way that the tides needed the moon.

Maggie stepped back, listening again and watching as a swift dark shadow flew overhead, a night heron in search of supper. She made her way back to the house and quietly entered the kitchen through the back door. She locked the door, cringing at how loud the snap of the lock latching into place sounded in the quiet house.

As she turned around, she stifled a scream as her eyes made out a dark shape in front of her. A cold hand touched her arm. "Mags—it's me, Lulu."

Maggie could hear her heart thumping in her ears. Forcing herself to keep her voice calm, she whispered back, "What are you doing up?"

She could feel Lulu's eyes fixed on her. "I need to tell you something."

Maggie's fear quickly subsided into exasperation. Since the baby's birth, Lulu had become even more secretive and less communicative. She was now ten years old, still too young to be studying the world around her with such quiet, knowing eyes. "Can't it wait until morning?"

"No," Lulu whispered, the word coming out as a hiss.

"Then quickly tell me what it is so that we can both go back to bed."

There was a long pause as Maggie shivered in her damp nightgown. "The last time you left in the middle of the night, Cat came into our room and went to your bed. She sat down and stayed there for a long time while I pretended to be asleep."

Maggie tasted the roast they'd had for dinner in the back of her throat and for a moment thought she was going to throw up. "And then what did she do?"

"She went back to her room and closed the door."

Maggie nodded in the darkness, knowing there was nothing she could say.

"I thought you'd want to know."

Maggie stared at her sister, where the darkness made her eyes and mouth into pools of shadow, feeling incapable of being both mother and father to Lulu, and how she'd failed in so many ways.

"Thank you," she said, hearing the baby upstairs starting to fuss.

Maggie made her way quickly to the stairs, hoping she could get to the baby before he woke Peter and Cat. When Peter was home, Cat moved the crib into the upstairs hallway so he wouldn't awaken Peter, which was fine with Maggie since she was the one who would hear his cries long before his own mother.

In the blackness inside the shrouded house, Maggie felt her way along the wall until she fumbled around and found the small lamp she'd set up next to the rocking chair she'd moved from the porch. Standing over his crib, she looked down at the flailing arms and legs, noticing how the baby quieted when he spotted her.

"Sweetheart," she said, lifting his tiny body with the baby blanket she'd knitted for him. She'd unraveled a shawl Peter had brought back from one of his trips for the yarn to make the blanket since she knew she could never wear it again.

Cradling him in the crook of her arm, she sat in the chair and began to rock. "I just fed you, little man, so you can't be hungry. Were you just lonely?"

He stretched, then smiled up at her, fully contented. Lulu came up the stairs and sat down on the floor next to the chair, leaning her head against Maggie's legs as if to make sure that Maggie wasn't going anywhere.

Maggie watched as the baby's eyes drifted closed, the warm weight of his body against hers making her feel full like the ocean at high tide. Her heart tightened, remembering Peter's latest note. *I have a plan.*

She knew parts of it, of course. They'd been discussing it for months. She'd even written to Aunt Edith asking her to come stay with Cat, saying she was going on a trip and Cat would need help with the baby. She'd also asked Edith to take Lulu back to Galveston with her, promising to come back for Lulu as soon as she could. Without telling Cat, she'd sold the house to Peter so that Cat, as his wife, could claim ownership and always have a home for herself and the baby.

Still, the pain of being separated from Lulu and the baby caused Maggie to hesitate, to question Peter's sense of urgency. *Trust me,* he'd said, and she did. She had so many reasons not to, but her heart was blind to all of them. Even the untold secret, the one she'd refused to listen to that awful morning on the porch, did nothing to make her question him. He'd since told her it was too dangerous now for her to know, that he would tell her everything as soon as they were far away and safe. And that they would return for Lulu as quickly as they could.

Maggie secretly guessed he was working on a project for the government, and she felt proud and honored to be under his protection. It was a new and unexpected feeling, having somebody else have all the answers, being sheltered from unpleasant things. She reveled in it, and didn't push against its boundaries for fear it might break.

In his sleep, the baby opened his mouth, seeking, and Maggie guided his thumb where he greedily latched onto it, the urgent sucking sounding loud in the darkened hallway. Reaching down, she rested her hand on Lulu's head. "It's time to go back to bed."

Lulu nodded sleepily and stood, then waited by the bedroom door as Maggie carried the baby back to his crib, as if afraid that Maggie might not follow her into the bedroom. Maggie would have to tell Peter what Lulu had told her about Cat, and that they needed to be even more careful than before. She knew that the news would only increase his sense of urgency, and shorten the time she'd have with the baby and Lulu, and her heart squeezed again.

Maggie lowered the baby into the crib and tucked his blanket around him, watching him as he slept and sucked his thumb, and wondering if she could have loved him any more if he'd been hers. She stayed there for a long time, listening to the sleeping house and trying to remember back to when her parents were alive and life didn't require so many compromises.

Lulu yawned, reminding Maggie that they both needed to go back to bed. She placed the backs of her fingers against the baby's cheek, marveling at the soft roundness, the perfect innocence of his face. "Good night, Johnny," she whispered before turning back to Lulu and heading into their bedroom, closing the door quietly on the night while the house continued to sleep.

LULU LISTENED AS HER WAGON hit another rock in the road and thudded over it, its worn rubber wheels now scraping metal against the ground. It was loaded with all kinds of tin—from cans and chewing gum wrappers to anything else the housewives she visited could give her and that hadn't already gone to Sheila McKowskie. Lulu also had a bag of tomatoes from Mrs. Walker's victory garden. It was the only thing the older woman had learned to grow, and she ended up supplying half of Folly with what she was able to pick before they fell off the vines. Maggie felt sorry for Mrs. Walker, and usually sent Lulu with peas or collards from their own victory garden so it would seem like more of a trade.

It was suppertime, and most of the families were sitting down to eat, so the streets were pretty deserted. She stopped suddenly on the corner of Tenth Street and East Cooper, aware of the man crossing the street two blocks ahead of her. She stayed still in the shadow of a palmetto, looking away so he wouldn't feel her eyes on him. It was Peter. Even if she hadn't seen his face, she could tell it was him from the stiff way he walked, like the soldiers she'd seen in the movies at the theater in Charleston, where their neighbor Mrs. McDonald would sometimes take her.

Lulu often went to Mrs. McDonald's house to collect scrap metal. Mrs. McDonald always gave Lulu a cookie and made her sit down for a while. Mr. McDonald had died before Lulu was born, and Mrs. McDonald's son was fighting in Europe somewhere. Mrs. McDonald hadn't heard from him in a long time, and Maggie said that his plane had gone missing over the English Channel. Lulu figured Mrs. Mc-Donald needed company, so she always sat for as long as she could, knowing that sometimes just being in the same room without talking could make you feel better.

When Peter was out of sight, Lulu left the noisy wagon parked on the corner and hurried to see where he was headed. He'd left early that morning, telling Cat that he was off to Washington on business and would be back in a week. *So why was he still here?*

Sticking to the shady side of the street, she followed about a block behind him until it became clear that he was heading toward the end of East Arctic, where the road and houses had been washed away by the last big storm. Lulu knew at low tide kids drove cars down on the beach there, making it a game not to hit any of the tall wooden pilings of the houses that had once been there. But that was at night. In the daytime not many people went there because of all the stuff still stuck on the beach that made it difficult to lie down on a towel or dig in the sand.

She waited until Peter had disappeared over the dune, then moved forward, ducking down as she approached the top. Spying through tall blades of nutgrass and watching out for sandspurs that could cut her feet, she spotted Maggie sitting on a large rock and staring out to sea. Maggie turned to Peter although Lulu was pretty sure Peter hadn't said anything at all; then Lulu watched as Maggie's face began to shine as she ran to Peter and let him hug her and put his mouth on hers.

Lulu ducked, and not just because she was embarrassed but because she'd just realized how close they were to her. She glanced around her and spotted a rotting wooden walkway through which the wind had poked a big hole in the sand beneath it. Lulu figured that if Peter and Maggie turned and started walking toward her, she could crawl toward the hiding place under the walkway, praying the whole time that they wouldn't look in her direction.

"Margaret, we can't. Somebody might see."

Lulu took a chance to peer through the grass again, and watched as Maggie stepped back and put her hands to her sides, yet seemed to lean toward Peter like a sea oat pushed by the wind.

"There's nobody here."

"But we can't take any chances. Especially not now. Not when we're so close. Not after what you told me about Cat going to your room when you were gone."

Maggie turned away toward the ocean, her hair blowing into her face. "I know, Peter. It's just been weeks since we've been together, and now you're going to be gone for a week. I don't know if I can stand it."

"You will. This will be the last time, but I have to go. I need to make arrangements for us. And when I return you need to be ready to leave with me."

"It's so soon, Peter. What about Johnny? And Lulu? You know Cat can't take care of them by herself."

"Cat's a lot stronger than anybody really realizes—you know that, Margaret. You've always known that."

Maggie looked down. "I know. But it's not her I'm worried about. It's the children. Aunt Edith can't get here for another month."

"We don't have another month. Each day that we wait, it gets more and more dangerous for me. For you. For all of us."

"Peter, tell me. Maybe if I understood the danger, it wouldn't be so hard to leave. You tried to once, remember? I'm stronger now. I can face anything now because I know that you love me."

Peter looked past Maggie to the water behind her, squinting his eyes as if he expected to see something. Facing Maggie again, he said, "I know, darling. But for now you're safer not knowing—and so are the children. I don't want to put anybody in jeopardy. You just need to trust me a little bit longer, all right? I promise that as soon as we are away from here, I will tell you everything." He touched Maggie's cheek with the backs of his fingers, then quickly dropped his hand again, almost as if he knew someone was watching.

"Promise?" she asked, her face sad even though she was smiling.

"Yes," he said. "We're good at making promises to each other, aren't we? You haven't forgotten yours, have you?"

"No, Peter. Never." She lifted her chin and the wind blew her hair back from her face. "I will wait for you to come back for me. However long it takes."

"Good." He smiled. "And I promise you that as soon as it's safe, we will come back for Lulu, and to see Johnny. I'll miss him, too, you know."

Maggie nodded, even though her eyebrows were wrinkled in the middle like she was frowning to herself. "I'll talk to Martha about her moving in. With the extra cash you gave me, I think we should have enough to pay her to do that at least until Aunt Edith gets here. And then we should be back in about six months, right?"

He nodded quickly and Lulu wondered who he was trying to convince, Maggie or himself. "Yes. Ask Martha, and if she can't, then tell her to ask her friends. We can do this, Margaret. Together. But we need to hurry." He looked down at his wristwatch, then allowed his gaze to swiftly scan the area to make sure they were still alone. Then he put his hands on either side of Maggie's face and pulled her closer.

"I love you, Margaret O'Shea. I always will." Their lips touched, but this time Lulu couldn't look away. Of all the secrets Peter kept and the lies he'd told, Lulu could look at his face and know that this wasn't one of them.

"Come back for me. I'll be waiting for you."

Still holding Maggie's face close to his, Peter rested his forehead against hers. "I'll be back a week from Wednesday. Be ready. Leave your suitcases where we discussed. I won't come to the house first, but I'll write a note in *Gulliver's Travels* to let you know where and when. And I've already put a little note in *Around the World in 80 Days* just to lift your spirits. Can you do this?"

Maggie was crying quietly, but she nodded.

"You're strong. I know you can do this or I wouldn't have asked. This isn't forever. But if you're not ready, I'll have to go alone. There's no turning back."

He kissed Maggie on the forehead and slowly backed away from her. Ducking behind the dune again, Lulu began quickly crawling toward her hiding place and made it there by the time she heard the crunching of sand under shoes as Peter walked by. He was close enough that Lulu could have reached out her hand and touched the leg of his trousers.

Lulu waited a long time for Maggie. When it began to grow darker, she carefully emerged from her hiding place and crawled back to the spot behind the dunes and peered through the sea grass again. Maggie sat in the sand with her legs pulled up under her chin, staring at the ocean as if it was answering a question she'd asked. Lulu could tell she'd been crying because of the hair stuck to her cheeks, and the sight of her made Lulu want to cry, too.

Slowly, Lulu ducked out of sight again but stayed where she was in the sand, looking up at the sky as it turned from blue to purple then black, and the stars began to poke holes in the night, all the while knowing that if Maggie left Folly, she'd never come back. Lulu began counting the stars, numbering them with the reasons why Maggie couldn't leave with Peter until the stars blurred above her.

She hid in the dark as Maggie walked over the dune near her and headed home. Lulu waited until Maggie was out of sight, then followed. It wasn't until she'd reached the front door of the house that she realized she'd left her wagon behind.

CHAPTER 26

Emmy stood at the farthest end of the unfinished dock, watching the marsh at dawn and marveling how still it was on the surface. The crabs were gone, searching for warmer water, and the grass, its yellow seeds long since blown away by the wind, seemed to be bent in sleep as if it, too, was waiting for the spring sun to make it bloom again.

The letter in Emmy's hand flapped in the early-morning breeze. She turned to block the wind, pulling her sweater closer, and noticed a dark blue pickup truck pulling into her driveway. She watched as Heath stepped out of the cab, his hair still wet, like he'd just showered but hadn't taken the time to dry it. He walked to the top of the driveway, hesitating at the bottom of the back-deck steps as he looked around the backyard.

He spotted her before she could call out to him, and she waited for him to approach. His face was serious, but she still felt a warm rush of anticipation at seeing him, and it no longer startled her. He stopped next to her and stared out at the marsh without speaking.

"Is Lulu . . . ?" She couldn't finish.

Finally, he looked at her, his brown eyes turning an unusual amber from the glow of the morning sun. "She's still in ICU but they're pretty sure she won't be staying there long. She's lucky she was found so quickly. They don't think any permanent damage was done."

"Thank God." Emmy closed her eyes, the sun bright behind her eyelids, and felt the relief flood through her.

"She's asking for you."

"For me?"

Heath nodded. "Yeah. You'll have to wait a couple of days, though. No visitors outside of family. Jolene already tried."

"I wonder why she wants to talk to me. It's not like we're . . . close."

"Yeah, well, she's asking for you. I'll go with you, if you like."

Despite his seriousness, Emmy smiled. "Why? Do you think she'll bite?"

Heath smiled back. "You never know."

The wind blew harder and Emmy brought her hands up to the neck of her sweater, forgetting she held Cat's letter. It rustled like a whisper, drawing Heath's attention.

"Is that the letter from Cat?"

Emmy nodded. "I've been carrying it around with me for some reason. I suppose I was thinking that if Lulu died, this would die, too. And I was just trying to be okay with that."

"Were you?"

"No. I like to think that everything has a reason. Finding Maggie's notes in those books led me here, and I'm so grateful to her for that. I've been thinking about how much we have in common—our love for books, owning the same store, each of us marrying a soldier. I even work behind the same oak counter she must have." *And when I look at her photograph, her expression reminds me of that of a caged bird, and I see myself.* She kept this last thought to herself, not ready to admit it, even to Heath.

Emmy continued. "I feel compelled to learn her story, almost as if she's prodding me to. And I'm sorry if that sounds selfish to you, but I have to think that her story is meant to be told, that maybe it can shine light on something relevant today." She looked up at him, unable to read his expression. "But after finding this note, it was like hitting a dead end, and the only person who can help me is Lulu. Yet I'm afraid that you're not going to let her."

Heath didn't say anything for a long moment as they both watched the sun rise higher over the marsh and the lighthouse beyond like a glowing benediction. "I'd like to read the letter." When his eyes met hers, Emmy saw that he no longer looked angry.

She pushed back her feeling of hope. "Why? Why now?"

He looked down at his feet for a moment. "After seeing Lulu in the hospital, I couldn't help but think about her dying and how neither one of us is ready for that. And it's more than just me not being ready to lose her. She's been hiding something all these years, since long before I was even born. The only reason I could think of for somebody to hide something for so long is guilt. Or fear of punishment." He shook his head. "I don't want her to die without forgiveness."

She touched his arm because she couldn't think of anything to say to that—anything that would comfort someone who knew what dying with unfinished business was really like. She handed him the letter and watched him as he read.

His expression changed from expectation, to relief, then confusion. He read it twice, then looked up at her. "So what does this mean?"

"My mother and I are pretty sure it's a suicide note. Unfortunately, your dad was too young to remember Cat, and the only person I know to ask is in the hospital in ICU."

"What makes you think this has anything to do with Lulu?" He seemed almost hostile, but Emmy knew enough now not to take offense. He wasn't arguing with her; he was fighting the vagaries of fate and how death happened whether people were ready or not. Emmy had already learned that lesson, but secondhand. She imagined that staring it in the face would be a lot like seeing your own ghost.

"Lulu played her disappearing act as soon as you discovered the box of books. She's the one who put them there, so she had to know what was in them. Your mother told us that Lulu was the last person to see Maggie, and Maggie gave her a box of her favorite books before Lulu evacuated with your family. So it had to be her who put them in the attic before it was sealed sometime during the restoration process. Nobody else knew about the box."

Heath shook his head. "It's just that Lulu was a little girl when Cat died—and I can't imagine her being ashamed of a suicide in the family when she had nothing to do with it. There has to be something else."

"There might be. Your mother said something about where Lulu was found on the old lot. She had a spade in her hand as if she were digging something up."

"I know, but I can't imagine what could be buried there. After Hugo, my dad went out there with his metal detector and shovels to find if anything valuable was left. We found a few things—kitchen pans and utensils mostly—but not much. Hard to believe we missed anything."

"Unless it was buried afterward."

"But why would she bother? That was nineteen eighty-nine."

"You said she was the last person to see Maggie. Maybe they talked about something then—something that convinced Lulu that whatever secret she'd been hiding needed to stay secret."

Heath frowned at Emmy. "You're good at this, you know?"

Emmy took a deep breath, trying not to smile. "I once traced a single document to the library of a remote castle in Scotland for one of my mother's customers. Nothing is too improbable for me." Serious again, she said, "But this is your family, not mine. And if you want the story to end here, it will. I figure it got me here to Folly, and that should be enough." She shrugged as they both recognized the lie. "Or I could make it be enough."

"It could be." He looked down at the letter one more time before handing it back to her. "But if Lulu was digging something up, then I'd have to guess that she didn't want it to be buried anymore." He rubbed his hands over his face, his shoulders sinking in resignation.

Walking back toward his truck, he called over his shoulder, "Come on. Let's go get my dad's metal detector and see what we can find."

"Now?"

"Unless you feel like waiting."

"Not at all," she said, relief and excitement running through her in equal measure. She followed Heath to his truck, sensing the calmness of the marsh behind her and thinking of Maggie again, of how she had died and whom she had been waiting for.

B

THE SUN HAD DESERTED THE sky when they reached the vacant lot, and dark plump clouds nestled against one another on the horizon like the paws of a pouncing cat. The air was heavy with moisture, the palmetto trees and even the grass seeming to droop with dampness.

"The EMT said she was found about six feet away from the cross." Heath pointed to the white painted cross in the middle of the yard. "Lulu put that up for Maggie when we figured we'd never find her."

Emmy nodded, saddened by the sight of the small memorial, a tangible reminder of Lulu's sister. Twenty-one years was a long time to wait for the grief to go away.

Heath flicked a switch on the metal detector. "I'll start at the cross and move in a gradually growing circle. If I get some kind of signal, I'll start digging."

He began hovering the rounded coil of the detector low over the ground, sweeping it back and forth like a vacuum cleaner. The telltale prickling began at the roots of Emmy's scalp, slowly tiptoeing down her spine just in case she'd missed the message. Without asking, she went back to Heath's truck and took out the shovel he'd brought with them.

She didn't sit down or place the tool on the ground, sensing they were very close to whatever it was they were supposed to find. When a beeping sound came from the metal detector, Emmy almost laughed out loud.

Heath stopped the sweeping motion and began to be more specific with his placement, stopping when the beeps became a constant line of sound. "Whatever it is, it's less than a foot below the surface." After flipping off the detector, he laid it on the ground behind him and reached for the shovel.

"What can I do?" Emmy asked, impatient to see what lay hidden under the grassy dirt.

Heath pretended to contemplate the question for a moment. "You can either stand back and let me dig, or you can dig by yourself. I don't think this will require both of us."

He'd taken off his sweatshirt and stood in the cool wind in just jeans and a T-shirt. She eyed his biceps and thought of her own pitiful attempts at running. "You go ahead. Let me know if you need me to wipe your brow or anything."

"Will do." His face serious again, he stabbed the earth with the tip of the shovel and began to dig.

Heath made shallow scoops of earth, the dirt softened by an overnight sprinkle. The tingling that had started at the back of Emmy's neck now raced up and down her arms, and she had to force herself to stand still instead of dance with anticipation.

He'd only been digging for about ten minutes when the shovel made contact with something hard. He sent a glance of warning to Emmy. "Don't get too excited—it could just be a rock."

"It's not. It's what we're looking for."

He leaned his hands on the shovel. "You know, huh?"

Emmy bit her lip. "Yep. And I'd bet money that you're about to find whatever it is Lulu was looking for."

With a dubious look, he continued taking shallow layers of dirt out of the hole he'd made until he uncovered what appeared to be the smooth top of a small wooden box.

Their eyes met over the hole. Without a word, Heath began to use the shovel tip to loosen the dirt around the edges of the box, pulling enough away to make room for a hand to slip down the sides and lift the box out of its prison.

Indicating the box, Heath said, "Stick your hands in and let me know if you can feel the bottom edge of the box. I'm thinking it's only three to four inches wide, so the hole should be deep enough."

Not caring about the damp ground, Emmy eagerly knelt and wiggled her fingers into the space Heath had created with the shovel. "It's good," she said as she concentrated on digging her fingers under the box to give her enough leverage to lift it out.

She was able to place her thumbs on top of the box and the rest of her fingers underneath, and the box lifted easily as if it had been waiting for her. Emmy had expected it to be heavier, and the unused force jerked her back into a sitting position next to the hole, the box held in her hands.

Carefully, she brushed the dirt off of it, revealing a rectangular box with a metal latch and hinges, and a lacquered surface with hand-painted flowers decorating the lid. She looked up at Heath. "I think it's a jewelry box."

Heath lay the shovel aside and squatted next to her. Suddenly unsure, her eyes met his and she said, "It's your call."

He took the box from her, and for a moment, Emmy thought he was going to replace it in the hole in the ground. Instead, he very gently opened the lid. A faint scent of perfume wafted from the red velvet interior and then was gone as soon as it had appeared, making Emmy wonder if she'd imagined it. Heath sat down next to her as they both peered inside to find out what Lulu had thought important enough to bury.

"Go ahead," Heath said, offering the box to Emmy.

Carefully, Emmy lifted out a roller-skate key. She turned it over to see if it had any markings, surprised at how cold it felt in her palm. She placed it on the ground next to her, then reached in and pulled out sand-dollar earrings and a tortoiseshell barrette, a long strand of brown hair still caught in the clasp. Fighting back her disappointment at finding such inconsequential things, she pulled out the last items in the box, an old penny, a handkerchief, and a lace hair ribbon, the fabric soft and yellowed like an old photograph.

She studied the penny with the familiar Lincoln bust, then flipped it over to see two wheat sheaves bordering the words *one cent* and *United States of America*. "It's a 1933 penny," she said holding it up.

"That's the year Lulu was born."

She placed the penny on the ground with the other items, then smoothed the handkerchief over her leg, noticing the monogram in the corner. She wrinkled her nose at the smeared lipstick and makeup that stained the fine linen. "Who's PWK?" She rubbed the black thread of the embroidery and its unfamiliar letters as if they could tell her something. "P could be for Peter, but his last name was Nowak."

She dropped the dirty handkerchief in her lap, not wanting to touch it anymore, and picked up the penny again. "I can't believe this is all there is."

"What's that?" Heath asked, indicating the spot where the ribbon had been.

Leaning over, Emmy noticed a small, rolled-up piece of paper that had been wedged between the bottom and sides of the velvet lining. Using her fingernail, she pried it out, then held it between two fingers. "It's rolled small—like a person would do if they wanted to stick it in a bottle."

His eyes met hers and she knew he'd been thinking the same thing. "You read it. I feel enough like an eavesdropper on your family."

He surprised her by not arguing, trading the box for the rolled piece of paper. Slowly, as if to avoid tearing it, he unrolled it and flattened it against his palm. He squinted to see the tiny handwriting before reading the words out loud.

My darling Margaret,

I need to talk to you, to explain everything. What I've done is despicable. But I need to tell you why—not to justify anything, but to keep you safe. Just give me this one last chance—that's all I ask. I want to take you far away from here, someplace you and I can start anew and leave this all behind us.

*   I promise that if you walk away after I've told you everything, I will never*

bother you again. And if you don't come at all, then I'll have my answer. I'll do
what you ask, and marry Cat and be a father to the child, and I'll find a way to
protect you from afar. But if you ever loved me as I still love you, you'll come.
Meet me Wednesday night at our special place near the lighthouse at eleven
o'clock. I'll be waiting.

Heath looked up. "It's not signed." He handed it to Emmy so she
could get a better look.

Her blood seemed to flow more slowly in her veins as she stared at
the familiar handwriting. "I know who wrote this."

He raised his eyebrows in question.

"Peter. I recognize his handwriting from the inscriptions in the
books to Maggie and Lulu. I wouldn't except the capital M and the
lowercase g are unusual enough for me to have noticed them and
remembered." She indicated the capital M in Margaret's name. "See
how there's a tail before the first leg and after the last? And how the
g doesn't just have an umbrella handle at the bottom but actually
duplicates a typewritten g? I noticed that right away—it's one of
the criteria I used when I determined that the Peter who inscribed
the books to Maggie and Lulu hadn't written the notes in the book
margins."

Heath pulled back. "Then who did? I can't picture my grandmother with multiple lovers. She wasn't like that."

Emmy touched his arm. "I know. But maybe Peter did write both.
And for some reason disguised his handwriting in the inscriptions.
Which would make sense . . ." Her words trailed off as she realized
what she was about to say.

"Go on," Heath said. "We've gone too far to quit now."

"Well, I was saying that it would make sense that he was disguising
his handwriting if he were having an affair with Maggie and didn't
want Cat to recognize the handwriting if she should ever find one of
the notes."

"But who is Cat's baby? And what did Peter do that was so
despicable?"

Emmy studied him silently for a moment. "And why did he need to keep her safe?"

Heath nodded, staring at the lone white cross that rose out of the dirt like a question. "There's only one person who can answer any of this."

After picking up all the items from the grass, Emmy stood. Handing the empty box to Heath, she said, "It's up to you to decide what to do next. I'll understand if you don't want to upset her."

Heath was silent as he considered her words. "It's been long enough," he said. "I think Lulu knew it, too, and that's why she was trying to get to the box. A lifetime is a long time to live with unfinished business. Or guilt."

Closing the box's lid, he turned it upside down to study it more closely. A short thunking sound came from inside, surprising them both.

"I thought the box was empty."

"Me, too," Heath said as he flipped the box again and the heard the same sounds. He opened the lid and they both looked inside, seeing only the red velvet lining.

"Switch with me." Emmy gave him the items she held while she took the box and pressed her fingernail into the small crevice where she'd found the note. Then squeezing her two fingers together, she tugged and was rewarded with the lining pulling out of the box, revealing a small cavity between the lining and the bottom of the jewelry box. Turning the box on its side, Emmy hit the corner and a gold ring clattered out of the box and into her opened palm.

She held it up for both of them to examine. It appeared to be a man's signet ring, plain yellow gold with a flat black onyx square at the top and the initial *K* in gold standing out in bold relief against the onyx.

"I've seen this ring before," she said. "In a photograph of Peter, he's wearing it on his right hand. It's definitely the same one."

"But his last name was Nowak. Where does the *K* come from?"

Emmy frowned. "Maybe it was a gift or something. Or an inheritance."

"Possibly," Heath said, not sounding convinced. "Of course, this gives the monogram on the handkerchief new meaning, too."

A drop of rain landed on the box, and they both looked up at the sky. "Come on," Heath said. "Let's put everything back and go find out how soon we can see Lulu."

They replaced the earrings, barrette, skate key, handkerchief, ribbon, note, and penny, but Heath held on to the ring. It began to rain harder as they ran back to the truck, both of them sodden by the time they'd closed the doors.

Heath started the engine just as Emmy's cell phone began to ring. She looked at the number and saw it was from Paige's Pages.

"Mama?"

"Hi, Emmy. We're swamped and I only have a minute, but I wanted to tell you something before I forgot."

"What is it?"

"Remember how you told me to call you and let you know if I remembered anything about Folly's residents or its history?"

"Yes." Emmy looked at Heath and shrugged.

"Well, I thought of a few things that I thought you might find interesting. They probably don't have anything to do with what you're looking for, but I thought I'd tell you anyway."

"Sure—go ahead."

"Let's see. . . . Did you know that Folly Beach was first called Coffin Land? It was because all the ships heading toward Charleston harbor had to drop off their sick passengers so no sickness would be spread in the city. When the ships came back to pick them up, most of them had already died."

Emmy raised her eyebrows in Heath's direction. "That is interesting. Anything else?"

"Now I know this one is definitely too late for your time frame, but did you know that Folly Beach had its own serial killer? A man abducted and murdered three teenage girls in the early seventies and buried their bodies. They did catch him, thankfully."

"That's awful. Again, not pertinent . . ."

"Oh, I know. And there're other tidbits, too, like how it's rumored that Elvis Presley vacationed there before he was a star, and how some big gangster was arrested in the fifties by FBI agents on the corner of Erie and Center Street. Or was it East Ashley and Center? Oh, never mind. You did ask."

Emmy smiled into the phone. "I did, and thanks. It's all entertaining and I appreciate hearing about Folly. Please let me know if you think of anything else."

"I will. Oh, wait. There was one more thing. I was talking with your father this morning about Folly Beach and how my favorite restaurant when I was a girl was the Atlantic House, which isn't there anymore because of Hugo."

"I know. Heath told me. What about it?"

"I remember a local historian coming to talk to us in grade school, and he mentioned that the old house that eventually became the restaurant was an abandoned structure during the forties, and that some thought it was used by Nazi spies to signal out to the U-boats offshore. It probably has nothing to do with anything, but I thought I'd tell you just in case since we're talking the same time period."

"Thanks, Mama. I don't know yet if it will be any help, but I'll let you know."

"You're welcome. And there's one last thing."

"Yes?"

"I wanted to tell you that your father and I are planning to come for a visit." They were both silent for a moment. "Your dad tells me it's been long enough, and I think he's right."

Emmy stared out at the mismatched houses on the side of the road, which had become as familiar to her as the cornfields of Indiana, watching as the rain made patterns on her window. "Mama?"

"Yes, Emmy."

She traced a rivulet of rain with her finger as it made its journey down the glass. "How do you know when it's been long enough?"

Emmy could sense her mother smiling into the phone. "When you realize that love doesn't have a time span. Only pain does. I think sometimes it's hard to distinguish between the two, so we just hold on to both of them like they're inseparable."

"Really?" Emmy frowned into the phone, not sure she understood. "Well, I'm glad it worked for you. And I'm glad you and Dad are coming."

"Good. Somebody just walked into the store. I'll have your daddy get in touch with the details."

"Okay. Good-bye." Emmy waited for the sound of her mother hanging up before she closed her cell phone; then she returned to staring out the window and thinking about what her mother had said, and how much longer she'd have to wait until she understood.

CHAPTER 27

FOLLY BEACH, SOUTH CAROLINA
May 1943

Maggie opened the downstairs front windows wider, inviting in the cooling breezes and the sounds of the band from the pier. She imagined the crush of people and the brightly colored dresses of the women as they swished their skirts under the hanging moss from the rafters, dancing to "Don't Sit Under the Apple Tree" and "I've Got a Gal in Kalamazoo."

Her feet remembered the steps as she went from window to window, pulling back the curtains and raising the blackout blinds at least until the night came and all light and sounds had to be hidden again. The music kept her mind too busy to think about the packed suitcase and the notes to Lulu and Cat that were hidden under her bed or the letter from Aunt Edith saying she was on her way. Or that the house she loved that held all the memories of her mother was no longer hers.

Her humming stilled in the back of her throat as she peered out the last window, recognizing a familiar figure clad in service khakis on the street in front of the house. He seemed to be hesitating, deciding on whether to move up the steps to the porch or continue walking past. Without really thinking why, Maggie raised her arm and waved to him. "Robert—hello."

His eyes drifted to where she stood and he smiled without moving. "Hello, Maggie. It's been a while."

She ducked back inside and went to the front door and opened it. With a quick glance up the stairs, she stepped out on the porch and closed the door quietly behind her. "Hello, Robert. This is a nice surprise." She hadn't seen him since before Cat's wedding, not blaming him for avoiding Folly Beach and all of its associations. Maggie had found that she'd even missed Robert's easygoing manner and sense of humor as he'd once been a frequent enough visitor that she knew how he took his coffee and that he liked vanilla better than chocolate.

He removed his hat as he approached, his smile warm but his face and eyes weary. The sounds of laughter and shrieks from the carnival punctuated the Glenn Miller melody from the pier, creating its own summer music, which Maggie imagined she'd remember long after she'd left this place.

"You're looking well, Maggie."

"Thank you." She indicated a rocking chair. "Why don't you come sit and I'll get us some iced tea so we can catch up? It's cooler out here than it is inside."

His face turned serious. "This actually isn't a social call." He frowned down at her. "Is Cat at home?"

"She's sleeping. The baby has a summer cold and was crying all night long. I told her to nap when the baby did." She didn't add that she'd been the one up all night rocking him after Cat gave up trying to quiet him and returned to her bedroom with a pillow over her head.

He nodded. "That's fine. It's actually you I wanted to talk to." His eyes flickered toward the front door as if he were half hoping that Cat would appear. "I need to ask you a few questions."

Maggie's heart seemed to freeze in her chest. *He knows I'm leaving.* Forcing herself to remain calm, she made her lips smile. "But we can at least sit and be comfortable, can't we? And I'm dying of thirst— won't you please join me in a glass of iced tea?"

Robert paused just for a moment before nodding. "Sure, Maggie.

That would be fine." He removed his hat as he stepped up on the porch and remained standing until Maggie returned with two full glasses of freshly brewed sweet tea. When she handed him his glass, she hoped he couldn't see the way her hands shook.

They sat and Maggie held her glass with both hands to keep them still. "What can I help you with?"

He took a long sip of his tea, and Maggie wasn't sure if it was because he was thirsty or because he wasn't sure how to start. Finally he said, "I don't know if you've heard, but a courier sent from the naval air station was found murdered near Myrtle Beach last Sunday. He'd been stripped, and all identification and classified materials were removed from his person. The only way we were able to make a positive identification was because he was a native of Myrtle Beach and somebody was able to make a positive ID on the body."

Maggie's hands stopped shaking, relieved to know that Robert wasn't there to ask her about the suitcase under her bed. "That's terrible. Was it somebody I know?"

"I doubt it. His name was Richard Kobylt. Ring a bell?"

She shook her head. "No. Should it?"

"I was hoping it might. Because of your store, you get to meet a lot of people and hear a lot of talk. I was hoping you might recall the name, maybe tell me who else you might have seen him with in your store. He'd been stationed at the air base for about six months, and I know he traveled to Folly often for the dancing and the girls." They avoided eye contact as if they were both thinking about Cat and the night Robert met her on the pier.

"Do you have a photograph?"

He nodded and slid out a small photo from his breast pocket and handed it to her. She studied it closely, seeing a young man with a smooth, round forehead and dark curly hair. He was smiling, a nice, easy smile, and it saddened her to think that he was now dead.

She handed the photo back to Robert, shaking her head. "I'm sorry. He doesn't seem familiar to me at all."

Robert regarded her carefully, trying to determine if she was telling the truth. "Thanks, anyway. It was only a hunch." He sat back in his chair. "So how are you, Maggie?"

"I'm fine, thanks. The store's doing well despite the shortages, and Lulu's had top marks in her class at school last year. The baby's real healthy and has a strong set of lungs on him that he's not afraid to use." She smiled, somehow feeling the need to erase the crease of concern between his eyes.

Robert smiled back. "I love babies. I know that sounds stupid coming from a man, but I always pictured myself with a household full of them." He looked away. "Don't know if I'll get the chance now."

Maggie leaned forward and put her hand on his arm. "I know what you mean. Believe me, I do. But don't give up hope. I've learned that sometimes if you don't give up, you can make things happen."

He looked at her closely, as if really seeing her for the first time. "You're a good person, Maggie." He put his hand over hers on his sleeve. "Maybe I went after the wrong girl that night. Think how different our lives would be."

She felt the tears prick the back of her eyes, allowing herself one second to imagine Peter with Cat, and herself with Robert and how she wouldn't have to leave everything behind. "Don't say that, Robert. There's no going back, ever. And it will make you crazy thinking that you can."

He was silent for a moment before dropping his gaze from hers. He took a long swallow of his tea and placed the empty glass on the porch railing before standing. "If you need anything, anything at all, please don't hesitate to ask me. I'll do whatever I can to help."

Maggie placed her hands in her lap. "I will, Robert. Promise. And thank you."

"I've got to go," he said, pulling on his hat again. "Thanks for your time. And the tea."

Maggie stood, too, wondering why he wasn't moving.

Finally he asked, "How is Cat?"

"She's . . . she'll be fine. Motherhood has been a huge change for her, and she needs more time to get used to it, that's all."

He looked away. "Is she . . . happy?"

Maggie held back all the words she wanted to say. "You'd have to ask her that yourself."

His eyes narrowed as he nodded. "Yes, well, thanks again for the tea." He headed down the steps but paused on the last one, turning back to her as if with an afterthought. "By the way, Maggie, do you by any chance know where Peter is?"

She shook her head. "No. He travels so much for his father's business that he doesn't always know where all he's going when he heads out." She thought for a moment before deciding that Robert was a safe person to tell. "I know that he was going to Washington, D.C., first, but after that, I have no idea. I think he's due back sometime next week. Why?"

He paused for just a second before answering. "Oh, just thought that with all of his traveling, he might have run across Richard Kobylt—maybe have something to add."

"I'll tell him to get ahold of you when he gets back."

"Thank you, Maggie," Robert said, replacing his hat. "I'd appreciate that very much." He sent her one last look, which she couldn't quite decipher; then he left, his shoes crunching on the unpaved road. She watched him for a few minutes as he approached a jeep he'd parked down the road despite the empty spaces in front of the house, wondering briefly why he'd parked so far away.

She picked up the glasses and opened the front door and paused, not sure if she'd imagined the sound of footsteps in the upstairs hallway. After placing the glasses on a table, she tiptoed up the stairs and past the crib in the hallway, where Cat had kept it even after Peter had left. Maggie noticed that Cat's door was cracked open slightly. Putting her cheek against the door, she peered inside, her eyes widening in surprise to find the bed empty. Opening the door fully, she examined the empty room. The bed was unmade, and the clothes Cat had worn the day before were thrown on the floor.

A soft thud sounded from the bedroom across the hall, and Maggie walked quickly to the door and thrust it open. Cat was crouched on the windowsill, her hand on the latch. She looked up at Maggie, her face blank. "It's so damned hot in this house. I'm trying to get a cross-breeze going."

"Please don't, Cat . . . ," Maggie said, stepping forward. But she was too late. Cat had already bumped the stuck window with her hip, managing to catch herself on the sill at the very last minute to keep herself from falling.

"I wish you wouldn't do that."

Cat shrugged, jumping down from the ledge and brushing her hands together. "It worked, didn't it?" She strode past Maggie to the door, keeping her eyes averted and leaving no doubt that she'd heard Maggie speaking with Robert.

The baby began to fuss, and Maggie followed Cat into the hallway, surprised to find that Cat had scooped up the baby and was attempting to soothe him by patting on his back. Maggie knew that Johnny preferred to be cradled instead of being held over the shoulder, but she kept silent.

Maggie wiped her hands on the front of her dress. "Well, since you're awake, I'm going to head off to Folly's Finds. I'll be back by six to start dinner."

She turned to head down the stairs but stopped when Cat spoke. "How did you know when Peter said he was coming back? He only told me."

Maggie didn't turn around, not knowing if she could trust her face. "He must have mentioned it at dinner."

"No. He didn't. He only told me when he kissed me good-bye and you weren't there."

"He must have mentioned it in passing, then." Maggie took another step.

"That must have been it."

Maggie continued down the stairs. "I'll see you at six, then." She reached the bottom without turning around, trying not to hear the cries of an inconsolable baby and feeling Cat's knowing eyes on her back the entire way.

ℛ

ON WEDNESDAY EVENING, LULU LOOKED at the clock on the wall behind the cash register for about the thirteenth time in the past twenty minutes, relieved to see it was finally five o'clock. All day long she'd been waiting for Peter to come back, like he'd promised Maggie, and the entire time Lulu wished very, very hard that he wouldn't. A bad storm was coming up from Florida, and as she watched the growing clouds and felt the thick, warm wind, Lulu couldn't help but hope that Peter would change his mind and not return at all.

She began to do the closing duties Maggie had taught her: sweeping, counting the money in the register before locking it, reshelving any out-of-place items. She was only ten, but Maggie said she was mature for her age and could be trusted to do the things she'd been watching Maggie do for as long as Lulu could remember.

Maggie hardly ever let Lulu close alone, but all day long Maggie had been fidgety, dropping things and calling customers by the wrong names. And every time the bell over the door rang, she'd rush to see who it was. It made Lulu sick to her stomach because she hadn't figured out a way to stop Peter from taking Maggie away without letting Maggie know that he wasn't the person she thought he was. Sometime in the last week, Lulu had figured out that keeping Maggie on Folly wasn't really about Lulu at all: it was about protecting Maggie from a truth that would hurt Maggie so much she might never get better.

When Maggie finally left the store, she said she was going to the beauty parlor and, if anybody came by looking for her, to tell them that was where she was. Lulu knew she was talking about Peter but had to pretend that she didn't.

As Lulu bent below the counter to find her book, the bell over the door jangled and her whole body froze. She even thought about staying where she was and pretending nobody was in the store but before she could even make up her mind, she heard Peter's voice.

"Lulu."

She looked up and saw that he'd come behind the counter and stood about two feet away from her.

Swallowing, she grabbed her book and stood. He was without a hat, and his hair was messy, as if he hadn't had time to comb it. His shirt was untucked, his shoes dusty, and his tie loose, and he was sweating like he'd been running. She wondered if he was sick because he didn't look like Maggie's Peter at all.

"Hello, Peter. Maggie's not here. She's at the beauty parlor." Lulu clutched her book tightly in front of her, her fingers sweaty.

"I know." *Of course he knew.* His voice sounded dry and she almost asked him if he wanted a Coca-Cola, but she didn't want him staying that long.

"I need you to give her something." Peter's eyes narrowed, and Lulu thought that maybe she should be frightened. "Not like that note I told you to put in the bottle tree a while back. Maggie told me she didn't get that one." He took a step forward but Lulu didn't move. Nancy Drew wouldn't have either.

He handed her a thick book, and when she looked down, she read the title *Gulliver's Travels.*

"Something very bad could happen to you if Margaret doesn't get this—do you understand?"

Her mouth had gone so dry that she was surprised when words managed to leak out. "Yes, sir."

He straightened. "You want your sister to be happy, don't you?"

Lulu nodded.

"Then don't interfere again. This is an adult situation that you can't understand. But I love Margaret and she loves me. That's all you need to know, all right?"

"Yes, sir," she managed again.

They both looked toward the door as footsteps approached. Peter ducked out of sight from the door's window as Mrs. Rhodes came up to the door and turned the handle. Peter must have locked it behind him when he came in because the door didn't open and Mrs. Rhodes turned and walked away, her footsteps gradually disappearing down the wooden sidewalk.

Lulu glanced back at Peter and saw him watching her. "You go on home now and give that to Margaret when she gets back. Don't tell anybody where you got it from." He began to walk toward the back door but stopped when he was next to her with just the counter in between them. "You forgot to hide your wagon the other night." He looked right at her, and his eyes seemed to get darker as she watched. "I don't know what you've heard with all your sneaking around, but you need to forget it all. Saying one word about any of it would be the same as killing Margaret. Or baby Johnny. You don't want that to happen, do you?"

Lulu shook her head, her pigtails flying; she knew not to even attempt to make any sound.

"Good. So give Margaret the book and keep quiet. Because I know how to find you. Remember that."

Lulu flinched as he walked back toward her, then reached behind her to the closed cabinet against the wall, where they kept supplies and where Maggie kept her purse. Lulu watched as Peter pulled out Maggie's suitcase and a small train case that had once been their mother's. Tucking them both under his arm, he turned and made his way past her to the back of the store.

"Don't forget what we talked about, Lulu."

Lulu tried to answer but no words fell out of her mouth. She waited for a full minute after hearing the door open and shut before she raced to the door and locked it. Crouching down next to the door, she opened the book looking for a note in the margins like all the others she'd found. It hadn't been hard to do since Maggie kept all of Peter's books on the top shelf, where she thought nobody else could reach them.

Wetting her finger, Lulu began turning each page. She'd made it only to page twenty before she found Peter's handwriting. When she'd first found the writing inside one of the books, she'd wondered why he'd made it so different from the handwriting he used in signing her Nancy Drew book for her, but she understood it all now.

Smoothing down the page, she read what Peter had written: *Finally, darling! Tonight. 7:00. I'll be waiting.* Lulu rested her head against the door and closed her eyes, squeezing them tightly so the tears wouldn't come out, but they did anyway. She didn't want Maggie or the baby or anybody to get hurt. But she couldn't let Peter leave with Maggie, either—and while Peter had been talking to her, she realized that it was because of so much more than just Maggie or Lulu. It was because of Jim and Amy's father and Mrs. McDonald's son. It was because it mattered that they had died.

A large gust of wind slammed against the store, and the bell over the door jangled. Lulu shut the book and rested her forehead on top of it, clenching her eyes as she tried to think. She remembered the time at the beach when she'd been pushed under by a large wave, the water holding her under until Maggie grabbed her and pulled her up. And the whole time she'd been trying to find the air, she'd been amazed at how heavy something like water could be. She felt that way now, how all the thoughts in her head could weigh so much.

By the time the next gust shook the store, she'd decided that the only thing she knew she could do would be to tell Maggie everything, no matter how much she didn't want to. Maggie would know what to do, who to tell. And she'd stay here on Folly, with Lulu and baby Johnny, and everything would be all right.

Grabbing the keys, Lulu left the store through the front door, her hands shaking so badly that she could hardly fit the key into the lock. She ran all the way home, not even noticing the heat or the way her sweat made her clothes stick to her body or how scared she should be of the black shelf cloud that sat on the horizon like a blanket, ready to roll over all of Folly Beach.

Lulu ran into the house, calling Maggie's name and hoping she'd be back from the beauty parlor by now. She took the stairs two at a time and flung open the bedroom door, then stopped, not quite understanding what she saw. Cat, wearing a bright yellow robe over her slip, sat in the middle of Maggie's bed with Lulu's treasure box from the chifforobe turned upside down and all of Lulu's favorite things spread over the bedclothes. The rolled note that Peter had meant for Maggie lay open on her lap as Cat read it. The window was closed, making the room even hotter than it was outside. Little drops of sweat stuck to Cat's upper lip and nose, and her hair over her left ear was twisted with a little rag strip to curl it since they'd given up all their bobby pins to the war effort.

Cat looked up at Lulu but didn't move, almost as if she'd been expecting her. "You've been very busy, haven't you?"

Lulu frowned, not wanting to give anything away. "That's my stuff. You had no right to go snooping."

Cat pretended she didn't hear Lulu. Instead she reached down and picked up Peter's note. "Where did you get this?" She slid off the bed and took a step forward, then shook the note in Lulu's face. "Where?"

Lulu began to cry. She needed to find Maggie, to tell her about Peter, but now Cat was here messing up everything. "That's mine," she wailed, not caring that she sounded like a baby.

Cat grabbed Lulu's arm and shook her hard, making the girl bite her tongue. "Where did you get this?"

"Peter!" she screamed. "Peter gave it to me to give to Maggie." She hadn't meant to tell Cat that. There was no reason to. Cat couldn't help her because she already knew about Peter and hadn't said anything to anybody. But Cat let go of Lulu's arm and stepped back, allowing Lulu to move out of reach.

Cat nodded, her face matching the white paint on the walls. In a calmer voice, she asked, "When? When did he give this to you?"

Lulu remembered exactly. Like any good detective, she had an excellent memory. "The day you ruined your fur coat on the beach. Peter came to talk with Maggie, but she didn't want to talk to him.

So he gave me the note to put in the bottle tree for her to find. But I didn't."

"The bottle tree?"

Lulu looked down at her scuffed shoes and realized that it didn't matter anymore. "Yes." She didn't say anything else because she didn't want Maggie to get in trouble. Lulu figured she'd let Cat try to put the pieces together herself.

Cat sat down on the edge of the bed. "They've been passing notes to each other for a long time, haven't they?"

Lulu looked away, not wanting to lie to Cat's face. The room seemed to grow hotter as sweat dripped from her forehead into her eyes, making them sting. She glanced over at the window, wishing the wind outside would push it open and blow at her face. Even Cat seemed wilted, like a flower without water.

"Oh, Lulu, what are we going to do?"

Lulu looked at Cat with alarm at her use of the word "we."

Cat rubbed the back of her wrist against her forehead. "We have to stop them from seeing each other." She glanced up at Lulu. "Oh, don't look at me that way. It's not to hurt Maggie. I've already done plenty of that. It's to help her. And us. He's already ruined my life—although I can't say he did it all on his own. But we can't let him ruin hers."

Cat stood suddenly and walked across the room to the window; then she pulled up the latch and pushed on the glass. The window stayed closed. "Damn. I can't stand this heat one moment longer."

She slapped the window with the flat of her hand before turning to Lulu again. "You and I both know that Peter can't stay here much longer. They're looking for him now."

Lulu started to cry again. "Cat, they're leaving tonight. Peter came and got Maggie's suitcases at the store, and they're meeting tonight at seven o'clock."

Cat looked angry for a moment and turned her face away. Her voice was quiet when she spoke again. "Maggie has no idea who he really is, and it would destroy her to know the truth. But it would be too late then. She'd be ruined and she couldn't come back home. And that would kill her. You know that, right?"

Lulu nodded, her knees feeling weak as she realized that she didn't have to fight alone, that somehow she and Cat were on the same side. "So what should we do?"

"I don't know." Cat slapped her hand against the glass again. "It's almost too hot to think." Cat began walking around the room, talking to herself. "Peter has to leave tonight, so all we need to do is find a way to make sure that Maggie doesn't go with him—and that she doesn't try to find him." She stopped in the middle of the room between the beds, her hands on her hips and her gaze focused on the box of stationery in which Lulu kept all of her bottle-tree orders and spying notes. Cat's eyebrows rose as she grabbed the box and the pencil sitting next to it. Without saying anything else, she sat down on the bed and began to scribble something on one of the blue sheets of paper. Lulu didn't say anything even though it was rude to borrow a piece of paper without asking for permission.

Cat folded the paper in thirds, then pinched the creases closed over and over again before handing it to Lulu. "This is a suicide note. No, don't worry. I'm not going to kill myself. But we need Maggie to think that I am. Here, take it." She wiggled it in front of Lulu until she took it.

"Give this to Maggie, and tell her that you found it on my bed. If Maggie believes that I'll kill myself if Peter leaves me, she'll stay. He'll leave, and her heart will get hurt—but not as badly as if she ran away with him and learned the truth then."

"But what will happen when you don't kill yourself?"

"It doesn't matter—just as long as she *thinks* I'm going to do it. We need to keep the truth from Maggie, whatever it costs. Do you understand?"

Lulu nodded, and embarrassed herself by crying again. But this time it was just because she was so happy that she didn't have to do any of this alone.

"I'll go to a friend's house in Charleston to make it look good. All you have to do is show Maggie the note when she gets home."

"Okay." Lulu swallowed and quickly wiped the tears from her face, hoping Cat hadn't seen them. She'd never seen Cat like this, standing up for somebody else, although she wasn't completely sure that Cat wasn't taking care of herself, too.

"If we're lucky, he'll just disappear because he can't afford to wait. And then it will be just the three of us again. And Johnny."

Frowning, Lulu said, "But that would mean that he doesn't care about you."

Cat pulled back her shoulders, and she didn't look so wilted anymore. "He never did, at least not in the way that he cares about Maggie. But that doesn't matter. What matters is that Maggie never finds out the truth about Peter. If he leaves without her, she'll never know." She placed her hand on Lulu's head, the first time Lulu remembered her touching her on purpose. "You're a smart girl, Lulu. I trust you to do this. For Maggie."

Cat walked quickly back to the window. "I can't stand this heat anymore. I know a storm's coming, but I've got to open this window." She jumped up on the ledge as Lulu had seen her do a million times; then she put a hand on the window and the other on the lever. Lifting a hip, she pushed against the window until it gave way. But this time, maybe because of the wind, Cat leaned too far outside as the window snapped back against the house and Cat was suddenly left with nothing to hold on to.

She seemed to hover for a moment as her hands circled in the air, looking for something to grab on to, her green eyes looking at Lulu as if she was about to ask a question. Lulu started to take a step forward, but before she could even move, Cat disappeared from the window.

Lulu screamed and raced to the ledge to look out, wind and sand pelting her face and making it hard to see. When she finally managed to open her eyes, she wished that she hadn't. Cat lay on the ground below, so still and beautiful that she looked like one of the mannequins at Berlin's. For a moment, Lulu had the small hope that Cat might be sleeping because of how pretty she looked lying on her side in the grass as the wind blew her gold hair around her face. But when the hair lifted, Lulu could see the wide-open eyes that saw nothing, and the small line of blood that spilled from the corner of her mouth.

The rain began to spit softly, dotting the dirt and darkening Cat's yellow robe with circles that looked like fingerprints. Lulu began to shake, unable to move back out of the window as she stared down at Cat's body. When she felt she might throw up, she ducked back inside and slid down the wall, not caring that the rain came in through the window, wetting her, the curtains, and the floor.

Her gaze fell on the copy of *Gulliver's Travels* that Peter had given her, which she'd left on the dresser when she'd entered the bedroom. She stared at it for a long time as the sky got darker and darker. She was on her own again, and Cat was dead. But she still needed to save Maggie, and baby Johnny, and herself. There was nobody else to do it.

She turned her face up to the rain, letting it wash back the tears, and began to think as hard as she could. She remembered what Cat had said: how the most important thing was to not have Maggie find out the truth about Peter, and how they needed to make sure Peter left tonight without Maggie. And she needed to figure it out soon because Maggie was on her way home.

Lulu rubbed the heels of her hands into her eyes until she saw stars, trying to think what Nancy Drew or Sherlock Holmes would do. When the idea came to her, it scared her at first, made her think that she couldn't do it. But then she remembered how much she loved and needed Maggie, and how she needed to do this for her.

Trying not to think of what lay outside in the backyard, Lulu slowly stood and moved toward the bed. Picking up the book, she opened it and stuck Cat's letter into the middle of the book and hid it under her bed. Then she picked up all of her treasures and put them carefully back into the box and stuck it back in the chifforobe so no evidence was left behind. But she left the window open, afraid to get near it again, because she needed Maggie to find it that way.

Johnny began to fuss in his crib, and Lulu went to him and picked him up and soothed him, wondering if he was crying because he knew his mama was dead. She waited for him to settle down, then placed him back in his crib. She didn't want to leave him alone, but she couldn't bring him with her, and Maggie would be back soon.

She touched his soft cheek and whispered, "Don't worry, Johnny. Everything's going to be all right." He began crying again but Lulu tried not to hear and instead raced down the steps and out the front door, hoping she wasn't too late.

CHAPTER 28

Emmy heard the footsteps in her sleep again, awakening when she dreamed they'd stopped by the foot of the bed as if waiting for her. Sitting up, she listened to the soft patter of rain that had continued into the night, and breathed in deeply, hoping to smell Ben. Instead she felt the darkness around her and a gentle tingling in her spine. And all around her, she sensed him there, waiting.

The battery light from her laptop glowed a bright green from the small desk she'd brought into the bedroom, even though she was pretty sure she'd turned the laptop off the previous night. She'd been going over all of the messages she'd entered into the database, trying to put them in a logical order. She'd gotten frustrated by the whole exercise, finally stopping when she realized that the order wasn't as important as the meaning, and that the meaning was perfectly clear: Peter and Maggie had loved each other and had planned to go away together. From what Emmy understood so far, something had interrupted their plans. Emmy found herself left with too many questions. What had happened to Peter? And to Cat? They'd have to find a death certificate to see her cause of death, and if it listed suicide. Why had Maggie married somebody else? And Lulu—what role could she have played in any of it?

Slowly, Emmy got out of bed and moved to the desk, opening up her laptop as she sat. Without turning on the light, she clicked on the Safari button on the toolbar, watching the monitor flicker blue as her fingers hovered over the keyboard. The clock in the right-hand corner of her computer registered three twenty-four a.m., but she was wide-awake now. She pointed the cursor on her browser and hesitated only a moment before typing in the name Peter Nowak. Pausing only for a moment, she hit the enter key.

The name appeared several times in soccer-related articles and other miscellaneous listings, but after searching three pages Emmy gave up trying to find something of relevance to her own search.

Not yet ready to give up, Emmy began typing in miscellaneous names and events that might trigger something. She used Cat's name and Robert's, even Maggie's and John's, turning up nothing pertinent. Then she began doing searches about Folly Beach and its history. Her eyes burned from the brightness of the monitor in the darkened room, but she wasn't ready to give up. She knew there was something she was missing—something right in front of her if she only knew where to look.

And then she remembered her conversation with her mother and what Paige had told her about the Atlantic House restaurant. Small static shocks erupted on the back of Emmy's neck as she typed in the name and then began scrolling down the listings, many of them referencing a book about the island's history written by a local writer. Emmy made a mental note to get a copy for herself, then kept scrolling down the list.

She was about ready to accept defeat when a short entry caught her attention. *Former site of Atlantic House restaurant linked to Duquesne spy ring. Thirty-three Nazi spies captured. . . .* It then listed a URL, and Emmy eagerly clicked on it, unaware that she was holding her breath until she let it out.

It appeared to be the introduction of an article on the official FBI site about historical cases. Emmy eagerly read about the thirty-three spies who were living and working in the United States prior to Pearl

Harbor whose purpose was to glean information about American life and the best ways to sabotage American infrastructure.

She scanned the article for mention of the Atlantic House restaurant or of Folly Beach and found nothing. But at the end of the article was a link that read *Read the full story*. Dubious now about finding anything relevant, she clicked on it with a promise to herself that she'd go back to bed as soon as she'd finished glancing at the site.

The page was similar to the first with a graphic of the American flag at the top and a listing of FBI links on the left margin. But this page contained a list of names of all the spies cited in the Duquesne spy ring, and each name was a link. She began to halfheartedly scan the names and was about to close her browser when her gaze fell to the bottom of the list, where the final name, separated by several spaces from the rest, was one single name: Peter Wilhelm Koehler. *PWK*. She could almost feel the embroidery on the dirty handkerchief between her fingertips.

With a shaking finger, she clicked on the link and stared at the picture of the man staring back at her. She didn't need to go check the photograph on her wall to make sure. One look at the odd, light-colored eyes told her she was looking at the same man.

She scanned the article, finding the words *Atlantic House Restaurant* in the final paragraph. Quickly skipping to it, she read it twice.

Peter Koehler, a Berlin native with family in Iowa, was the only spy not apprehended. He disappeared in 1943 from South Carolina, where he'd been placed as a traveling salesman near Charleston. He was suspected in the death of a courier carrying pertinent naval intelligence from Charleston to Virginia Beach, Virginia. Had the information been turned over to the Germans, the war could very well have had a different ending. Luckily for the United States and her allies, the papers were never found, and Koehler disappeared shortly afterward. His whereabouts remain a mystery today.

Emmy's hand immediately went to her cell phone to call Heath before she remembered it was close to four o'clock in the morning.

She leaned back in her chair and stared at the familiar face in front of her, and waited as the puzzle pieces began to slide into place.

EMMY HATED HOSPITALS. SHE SUPPOSED it was because she'd been to one so many times as a child to visit her mother after each miscarriage. They reminded her of forced smiles and lost expectations, and stale lollipops given to her by well-meaning nurses.

Roper Hospital was no different. Despite the different-colored walls and tiled floors, layout, and artwork, it was still a hospital, and Emmy found it hard to shake the feeling of having been there before.

At the main desk, she asked for directions to the floor where Lulu had been moved; then she made her way to the waiting room, where Heath had told her he'd be with his parents and Lizzie. In the end, she hadn't told Heath what she'd found out about Peter. She'd already stepped too far over the line, and she'd rather keep Peter's secret for the rest of her life than cross that line. Her only goal in speaking to Lulu this morning was to find out about what had happened to Maggie and Peter. That way, Emmy told herself, she would know the end of their story and could move on. As to where, or what, she had no idea.

Heath stood as she entered and greeted her first before Emmy made the rounds of hugs and kissing cheeks, finally settling into a chair next to Lizzie. After sitting down, she noticed Jolene standing in the corner. Her color was slightly better than when Emmy had last seen her, her eyes clear but sad. Emmy remembered what Heath had told her about Jolene's mother, and realized that Jolene had an even greater reason to hate hospitals than Emmy did. Jolene gave Emmy a small smile before finding a seat on the bank of scratchy cloth chairs beneath the window. Close enough to the family but not too close.

Emmy touched Lizzie's arm. "How are you? How are the babies? I guess I'm going to have to make the drive over to Mt. Pleasant soon to actually see them."

"We're fine. Thanks for asking. Joe's with them now, which means I can't stay long—you know how men are when they're required to multitask." She rolled her eyes at her father's grunt.

Turning to John, Emmy asked, "How's Lulu?"

"A lot better than she should be, apparently. Still as crusty as ever and no permanent damage to her heart. They say she'll be able to go home in a few days. There will be some adjustments with her diet which she won't be happy about, but we'll work on it." He sent a quick glance to his wife. "Right now she's refusing to talk to anybody but you. And she wants to see you, Heath, and Jolene together."

Emmy glanced up, meeting Heath's eyes before they both turned to Jolene, who looked just as surprised.

"Well, then, we'd better go see her." Emmy stood and began walking toward the door, her flip-flops slapping against the tile floor.

"Emmy," Abigail called to her, "flip-flops in October?" She smiled, her perpetually browned skin creasing.

"Well, it warmed up today, so I figured I might as well."

John let out a chuckle. "Careful, there. The more you start dressing like a tourist, the more you start looking like a native."

Emmy paused at the door while Jolene and Heath joined her. "I think I've heard that before." With a smile, she allowed Heath to hold open the door as she and Jolene passed through and made their way to Lulu's room.

The room had two beds, but the other bed was unoccupied, and the partition separating them was pulled back. Heath set three chairs by the bed and they sat down, Emmy by herself on Lulu's left side.

Lulu watched them, her glasses lending her face an odd normality, considering the oxygen tubes coming from her nose. Without greeting any of them, she turned to Emmy. "So what do you know?"

Used to Lulu's abruptness, Emmy didn't answer. Instead she said, "I'm glad you're doing better. John tells us that you'll be coming home in a few days."

Lulu's lips twitched as if she was trying not to smile. Serious again, she repeated, "What do you know?"

Emmy leaned forward. "Jolene and Heath are here. Is that all right?"

"I asked them to come, didn't I?"

Emmy blew breath out of her lower lip, blowing her bangs out of her eyes. "Are you sure? I only know bits and pieces—which could be more dangerous than knowing the whole story. . . ."

"I'm old, Emmy, but not yet dead. I know Heath and Jolene are here because I can see them with my own eyes. So when I ask you to tell me what you know, it's because I want them to hear it. All of it."

Without glancing at Heath or Jolene, Emmy nodded. "All right then." Leaning back in her chair, she kept her eyes on Lulu as she spoke. "The messages in the books were between Maggie and Peter, although Peter's handwriting was different from the inscriptions in your book and Maggie's. I believe that was deliberate, as he didn't want anybody connecting his unsigned margin messages with him." She stared hard at Lulu to see if the last part had any effect on her, but Lulu's expression remained the same.

Emmy continued. "Cat married Peter in June nineteen forty-two, and seven months later, she had a baby. I'm assuming that's John, Heath's father, since the birth date matches."

"Go on."

Emmy glanced at Heath and Jolene, who looked as confused as she felt. "That's really all, except . . . except for Peter's real name." She waited for a moment to see if Lulu would stop her.

"Yes?"

Emmy drew a deep breath. "It was Peter Koehler, wasn't it?"

Lulu's face appeared to soften, to smooth out its wrinkles and age spots as if the weight of years was being lifted. "And what else?"

Again Emmy glanced at Heath, but his face remained blank. "He was a German spy, embedded on Folly to collect information and send it to the U-boats that were off the coast here and farther north. He was part of a larger spy ring that was mostly apprehended in nineteen forty-one—all except for him. He disappeared in nineteen forty-three." She swallowed. "That's all I know."

Lulu's eyes were closed and Emmy thought she might have gone to sleep. She'd started to stand when Lulu's hand shot out and grabbed her forearm, her grip surprisingly strong. Lulu's lips were thin and colorless, but her eyes were a rich hazel behind her glasses. "I want you to know the rest of the story. But at the rate you're going, I don't think I'll live long enough for you to figure it all out by yourself."

Emmy sat back down. "Don't say that, Lulu. You're going to be fine."

Lulu frowned but didn't pull away. "I didn't mean today. But I'm not going to live forever, and at the rate you've been going, I'd have to." She sent a cursory glance to Heath and Jolene. "It's time to tell the truth." She took a deep breath, her eyes closed. "It's time to tell the story of how I killed the one person I loved most in this world."

Emmy leaned forward, the puzzle pieces she'd so neatly placed in her head beginning to scatter. "Who, Lulu? Peter?"

The old woman shook her head, her eyes searching out Heath's. "No. It was Maggie. I killed my Maggie." She closed her eyes then and said, very softly, "I'm going to start at the very beginning, on the night when Maggie first met Peter on the Folly Beach pier." Then, after a deep breath, she began to tell her story.

CHAPTER 29

—

The rain fell hard on the dirt road, each drop like a little slap. Lulu knew she'd never be able to listen to rain again without seeing Cat lying in the backyard and feeling so scared she thought she might actually die.

She ran to the end of the street, where the Healy family lived. They had five boys and all of them had bikes. Lulu figured they wouldn't miss one for a couple of hours, especially since it was raining.

She took the first bike she found leaning against a palmetto trunk near the end of the driveway. As she pedaled away, she realized it must belong to Harold, the oldest boy, because she had to stand to pedal it since the seat was too high up.

It was hard moving the bike through mud and puddles, and she could hardly see because of the rain blowing in her eyes. She knew she was crying, too, but none of it mattered. She needed to get to Peter before Maggie did, and that was all she needed to be thinking about.

She passed no one, taking back streets just in case, and moving toward the farthest end of East Ashley. She spotted Peter's car pulled up on the side of the road, partially hidden by scrub brush, but she'd been looking for it. It was empty, as she'd been hoping, and the final part of

her plan fell into place. Allowing herself to sigh with relief, she began
to feel a little less worried that her plan wasn't going to work.

She dropped the bike in the sand as she neared the beach and continued on foot, noticing that the rain had let up and was coming
down now in a constant drizzle. But the waves were white-tipped and
angry-looking, splashing up over the rocks of the groin that extended
out into the ocean. Lulu eyed the lighthouse, reassured to see there
was still enough island surrounding it. She'd checked the tide schedule
that morning—a habit started when her father was alive and they'd sat
down for breakfast together. She'd been very small, but it was the only
time she ever remembered having his attention.

Looking up at the sky, she figured it was around six thirty, and
high tide would be coming in about an hour, although the storm
seemed to be pushing it in early. Lulu crossed her fingers like Amy
had taught her to do, and made a wish that everything would happen
now like it was supposed to.

At first, she wasn't sure she'd heard her name being called or if it
had just been the wind echoing against the deserted stretch of beach.
But she'd been expecting to see Peter, so she didn't scream when he
touched her arm.

Rain poured off the brim of his hat, and his raincoat and pants appeared black from the rain.

"Lulu," he said again and she made herself not step back, "did you
give Maggie the book?"

She nodded, and when she spoke, she remembered to shout so he
would be sure to hear her over the rain. "Yes. But there's a problem.
The police came to the house looking for you. They want to know
where you are. Maggie's afraid that they're watching for your car all
over the island."

He drew back, his eyes looking black behind the rain. "Isn't she
coming?"

"Yes. She's definitely coming. But she's coming by boat. And don't
worry about her—she knows the water and has been out in a boat

in weather worse than this. She wanted to make sure you knew that so you wouldn't worry. She's going to borrow a neighbor's boat and pick you up at the lighthouse. She's got it all figured out. She can't get close to the beach with the currents and everything, so that's the safest place. After she picks you up, you'll head to Sullivan's Island, where she's arranged for a car."

He narrowed his eyes. "Whose car?"

Lulu didn't flinch as she quickly ran through possible answers in her head. "She didn't tell me. She said it would be safer for me if I didn't know."

His shoulders relaxed under his soaking raincoat. "When will she be here?"

"She told me no later than seven thirty. There are people looking for you all over Folly right now, and you need to head to the lighthouse to hide before the creek gets too deep."

He glanced over at the creek, which separated Folly Island from Morris Island, then at the ocean beginning to swell the creek's banks as it did at every high tide. Lulu crossed her fingers tighter, hoping he'd believe her and not ask her any more questions.

Looking back at her, he asked, "How do I know you're telling me the truth?"

She stared at him, knowing that it was all over, that he was about to guess everything. But then the words came to her lips, exploding from her mouth before she even had time to figure out what they were. "Because I love my sister. And Maggie loves you no matter what and wants to be with you." She knew she sounded convincing, because for the first time that night, she'd told him the truth.

Lulu held her breath as he continued to stare at her. Finally he said, "All right." Cupping his hand over his wristwatch to protect it from the rain, he added, "Tell her I'll be waiting at the lighthouse door." He frowned. "Are you sure she can handle a boat in this kind of weather?"

Looking him straight in the eye, Lulu answered, "She's visited or lived on Folly Beach for most of her life. There's nothing she doesn't know about the ocean or how to handle a boat." She looked behind him to the creek. "You need to hurry. The creek is rising fast."

"Thank you, Lulu. You're a good sister." He unbuttoned the top of his raincoat and reached into an inside pocket. But before the raincoat fell back into place, she saw the canvas bag that was slung over his shoulder. A canvas bag that looked like the kind used by couriers in the few war movies Maggie had allowed her to watch. Lulu pretended she hadn't seen it and instead accepted what he was offering her.

She took it, not realizing it was a chocolate bar until he'd already started to walk away in the direction of the lighthouse. "Thank you," she called out to him, but the rain and wind pushed the words back to her. She watched him until he'd waded across the creek; then she turned around and began to walk away, unable to watch him anymore.

When she'd reached the road, where she'd left the bike, she stopped, unsure what to do next. Maggie would be home by now and wondering why Johnny was alone. She'd be worried, and might even check the backyard and find Cat. Lulu squeezed her eyes tight, hoping the storm would keep Maggie inside the house.

She sat down on the bike, trying to tell by the sky what time it was, but the clouds had long since created an early nightfall, making it impossible to even guess. She wondered if Peter had figured out by now that Maggie wasn't coming, and that the door leading up into the lighthouse was bolted shut, allowing for no escape from the water that was only going to get higher. She closed her eyes, trying to shut out the picture of Peter slipping under the waves. But there was another picture, too: a picture of Peter managing to swim back to shore.

She heard herself groan, knowing that she needed to go back, to be sure that Peter was gone and Maggie was safe. Or else she would spend her entire life wondering.

Despite the mugginess of the air and the pelting rain, she shivered as she began running back to the beach she'd just left. The creek was impassable now, and if she tried to cross it, the strong currents would take her out into the ocean with no hope of getting back. She walked along the edge of it on the Folly Beach side, her saddle shoes sinking into the sand and filling with water with each step.

Squinting into the rain, she gazed over at the lighthouse, which was now completely surrounded by water. She stared harder, hoping to see some sign of Peter just so she would *know*. She was about to give up when she spotted him on top of the cofferdam that Jim told her had been built around the foundation of the lighthouse to protect it from falling into the sea. The storm was pushing the waves up over the edge, covering the lone figure with water. Lulu couldn't be sure, but it looked like Peter was staring back at her.

Her eyes stung from the rain and she blinked, and when she looked back, he was gone. Scrambling down the beach to where the rocks of the groin met the shoreline to get a better view, she stared out at the almost-black water and began to shake. It wasn't that she hadn't known it would happen, or that it had to happen to keep them all safe. She'd just never expected it to be so *real*, not something she read about between the covers of a book. And he was going to die because of her.

"Peter!" she screamed because she couldn't think of anything else to say. Then she spotted him, a black dot in the white-tipped waves, halfway between the lighthouse and the rocks, and all of her thoughts of protecting Maggie seemed to fade. She saw only a person struggling in the water who needed help—someone who wouldn't be there if it hadn't been for her. She stood tall and waved her hands, hoping he could see.

She studied the direction he was moving, and how fast, and realized that he'd be going past the tip of the groin, and if she could get there in time, she'd be able to reach out and grab an arm. If only she could get there in time.

Being as careful as she could on the slippery rocks, she began to make her way up the groin, stopping when a huge wave pushed at her and covered her with water. Her eyes stung with the salt and the rain, but she no longer felt any pain. She could only focus on the tip of the groin and getting there as fast as she could.

Somehow she managed to reach the farthest rocks, which were now nearly submerged. She'd lost a shoe and her hand was bleeding, but when she looked at the blood, it seemed that it was somebody else's hand. Lifting her head, she looked out toward the ocean again, relieved to see the figure in the water was exactly where she'd thought it would be.

"Peter!" she called again, and she could tell he'd heard her because he looked up. She couldn't see his eyes and she was glad. Leaning over as far as she could without falling in herself, she stuck out her arm and waved it back and forth to make sure he saw it. "Over here," she screamed, just in case he could hear her.

He lifted an arm and then another as if he was trying to swim, but even Lulu knew that was useless. Her father had lectured her about the currents here, how dangerous they were and how the best thing would be to let the current carry you away until help could reach you. Otherwise, you exhausted yourself and drowned. She could tell by how slowly Peter was moving that he'd been trying to swim to shore and that he didn't have much time.

"Peter!" She waved again, and he was close enough this time that she could see his eyes, and they were hard and cold, and she knew she would see those eyes again in every nightmare she'd ever have for the rest of her life. His head sank beneath the waves and she stretched farther, figuring he was moving so fast that she probably had only one chance to grab his arm.

He drifted closer and closer, and his hand rose out of the water and reached for hers. She stretched her arm so far, she thought she could hear her shoulder popping, already feeling his cold, wet hand in hers. That was when she realized that she still held the candy bar that he'd given her in her hand, soaked and melted from being squeezed in her fist, but somehow still intact even though she'd managed to use that hand to help her climb over the rocks. His eyes got really wide as they both realized that she couldn't grip his hand tight enough.

The candy bar dropped, and she braced her feet so she wouldn't fall as she reached out her left hand to grab his other arm as he swept by. This time just their fingers touched, but he was too far away, and she wasn't braced enough to be able to put any strength into her hold.

She managed only to grab hold of his ring finger, and as the current pulled him away, she felt his gold ring slowly slide off into her fist. She watched, helpless, as he drifted farther and farther away, still watching as his head disappeared beneath the waves. She continued to stare at the ocean for a long time, afraid to blink in case she missed him coming up again, but he never did.

She continued to watch for him until her feet were submerged in water, and she knew it was time to go. Not really knowing why, she put Peter's ring on her finger and closed her hand in a fist so she wouldn't lose it; then she carefully made her way back to the shore and toward home. When she got there, she would tell the first of many lies to Maggie, then put away her Nancy Drew books and everything else that belonged in her life before, when she had still been just a child.

B

FOLLY BEACH, SOUTH CAROLINA
October 2009

EMMY REACHED FOR LULU'S HAND and held it tightly. Jolene was crying softly while Heath rubbed his scar absently, his eyes troubled. "What happened when you got home? What did you tell Maggie?"

Lulu's eyes seemed to refocus on the world around her, like those of a swimmer returning to the surface. "I told her that Peter was a murderer, and that he'd run away to escape the law."

"But who . . . ?" Emmy looked up and saw Jolene with her beautiful green eyes watching her carefully. "Cat. You told Maggie that Peter killed Cat so that Maggie wouldn't go after him. That's why you hid the suicide note."

"I didn't know what else to do. But in the end, none of it really mattered. I killed her, just the same as if I'd thrown her into the ocean myself."

Emmy worried a torn fingernail, unable to look across the bed at Heath and Jolene as the last niggling thought rubbed its way to the surface. "Did you ever tell her the truth?"

Lulu's chest rose under the pale blue blanket. "I did. But not for more than forty years. Years where I watched her waste away her life, waiting for somebody who was never coming back." She let out a lingering sigh. "You see, Maggie made a promise to Peter that she would wait for him to come back for her, no matter how long it took. That's why she never left Folly. She was waiting for him to come back, for him to ask for her forgiveness. To explain what had happened to Cat so that Maggie and Peter could be together again. Over the years she'd begun to believe that Cat might have been partially to blame— anything to justify in her mind her reason for wanting him to come back. So she waited."

Heath's face was shuttered, obliterating all emotions. "But you knew. Why didn't you tell her?"

"In the beginning, it was easy not to say anything. So many people had been killed or damaged in some way by the war, and knowing the truth about Peter would have made Maggie feel responsible for so much of the pain. She'd had one too many disappointments, and was so delicate then. Even I could see how fragile her mind was, and I knew she couldn't take knowing the truth. I knew I was right because Robert never told her, either. I never knew if he realized I knew the truth, too, but we each kept silent thinking we were protecting her."

Emmy thought for a moment. "She married Robert only a month later. Why?"

"Robert had told Maggie that if she ever needed something to ask him. She was crazy with grief about Peter and Cat and I was so worried about her. So I found Robert and asked him to come." Her forehead puckered. "I think they both found something in the other they needed, some kind of substitution for what had been denied to both of them. And with Robert being sent overseas, I guess it just seemed the most logical thing for them to do.

"And then the years passed, and Maggie was busy raising Johnny, and then I saw how knowing the truth could hurt that bond, make her reject him in some way. I knew what the loss of a mother was like, and I didn't want to risk that happening to that innocent little boy. I told myself that Maggie was happy with her life, and that I didn't need to bring up the past. Sometimes, I would even begin to think that she'd forgotten her promise to Peter because she'd seem content with Robert. But then I'd see that ring on her finger, and know what I'd always known: that a promise to Maggie was binding forever. She never took that ring off her finger."

Heath sat up, his face dark with confusion. "Until Hurricane Hugo. She took the ring off then, didn't she? And gave it to you. But why? Why would she change her mind then?"

The room was silent except for the beeping of a monitor and Jolene's quiet crying, but Emmy sensed the heaviness of the air as if it were filled with the years of blind longing and a sister's guilt. Her eyes met Lulu's, and Emmy suddenly knew the answer.

Lulu blinked, a tear escaping down her cheek from behind her glasses, as incongruous to Emmy as Lulu's smile. "John and Abigail were all packed up, ready to leave with the children, but nothing any of us said would make Maggie leave. I knew that she was afraid that if she evacuated, it might be months before she could return, and that was too long for her. She was so afraid that Peter would come that one time she was gone."

Lulu seemed to run out of breath. Emmy touched her hand and watched as Lulu's fingers held on tightly like a blind person lost in her own darkness.

Lulu continued. "Maggie hadn't evacuated in nineteen fifty-nine for Gracie, either, so she said there was no need to go. But Hugo was going to be so much worse. They were already predicting that it would be the storm of the century. So I . . ." She shuddered and

Emmy watched as Heath took her other hand. "So I told her the truth about Peter, and how he'd died. And about Cat. After more than forty years, I finally told her the truth, thinking that it might make a difference." Her eyes clenched shut, but she opened them again quickly, as if she'd seen a part of her past she wanted to forget. "She didn't believe me at first. But in the end, I convinced her."

Emmy glanced up at Jolene, who was pressing tissues to her eyes. "But she still wouldn't leave."

Lulu shook her head. "No. I wanted her to be angry with me for ruining her life—not just for what I'd done to Peter, but for letting her hope all those years. But she didn't. She just sat there, twisting that ring on her finger over and over."

Jolene had stopped crying, but the monitor continued its incessant beeping, bringing Emmy back to the present.

"The police were going door to door, telling people to evacuate, that parts of the island were already beginning to flood. John called and I told him to leave with Abigail and the children. I had my own car and would be all right. Then Maggie gave me that last box of books and even helped me put it in the car, and I thought that meant she'd changed her mind. But when I got in the driver's seat, she just stood there in the rain, twisting her ring."

Lulu's breath caught and Emmy moved closer, holding the older woman's hand with both of hers, as if that might somehow make it easier.

"I rolled the window down, to tell her to get in, and she leaned toward me and kissed my cheek instead, then held out her hand to me. When I took it, she dropped something in my palm. It was the sapphire ring—the one Peter had given her. I started crying but she just walked back to the house and shut the door without looking back. Not once." A sob broke from her throat. "And I never thought to ask for her forgiveness for all of those years she'd wasted. Robert had grown to love Maggie, but she could never make room in her heart for him because of Peter."

Her gaze traveled to the three faces around her. "So I killed her, you see. If not that day, I killed her the day I let Peter drown."

Emmy shook her head, trying to sort through everything she'd just heard and all the words that needed to come out. "No, Lulu. Everything you did, you did because you loved your sister and were trying to protect her. Don't you see that? Maggie made her own choices. She chose to wait her whole life for somebody who was never coming back. She had a husband and son who loved her, yet she chose to put that life on hold."

Lulu's eyes were wide behind her glasses. "But she died because I told her the truth too late."

"You're wrong, Lulu. Maggie died because she didn't know when she'd waited long enough. She was going to die that day, regardless, because she wasn't evacuating. But it was her choice. And, Lulu—" Emmy swallowed back her own tears, knowing how important her next words would be. "Lulu, you didn't have to ask for forgiveness. She'd already given it to you."

Lulu frowned, an expression so familiar to Emmy that it almost made her want to smile with relief. "What do you mean?"

"She kissed your cheek when she said good-bye, right? And then she gave you her most precious possession because she trusted you with it. Because she loved you and knew that you loved her. And that you're trustworthy and honorable and you did the right thing, regardless of the consequences. She knew that, and that's why she gave you the ring."

Lulu stared solemnly through her glasses, and Emmy saw the glimmer of hope shine through before Lulu quickly looked away and swiped at her face with the sleeve of her hospital gown. Emmy's gaze fell to her gold wedding band on the third finger of her left hand, making her recall what Lulu had said to her the first time they'd met.

Emmy leaned toward the bed, taking Lulu's hand again in both of hers. "That night on the beach with Peter, you saved the lives of a lot of people who never knew you to thank you." Smiling softly, she added, "You're a real hero, Lulu."

Their eyes met, both of them understanding more than most what it meant to be brave. Lulu's face softened, the lines of regret that had formed around her mouth seeming to diminish as if forgiveness had the power to erase the years.

Heath's gaze settled on Emmy with an odd light as he mouthed the words *Thank you*. Leaning forward, he rested his forearms on the bed. "You're really quite brilliant, Aunt Lulu. Think about it. You were ten years old but managed to take down the remaining spy in a notorious spy ring. You should be writing mystery novels."

Jolene and Lulu exchanged a glance before Jolene spoke. "Actually, she has been. For years."

Heath and Emmy both focused their attention on Lulu as she waved her hand dismissively. "Just scribblings, mainly. Jolene's been going through them to see if she can make them readable."

Jolene squeezed a wadded tissue in her hand. "They're really good. I have a friend from college who's a literary agent in New York. When they're ready, I'm going to send them to see what he thinks."

Emmy felt a nearly imperceptible and almost completely inexplicable glimmer of relief. It certainly clarified a little of Lulu's loyalty to Jolene. But then her gaze fell to Jolene's left hand, where Maggie's ring still shone, and things weren't so clear anymore.

Heath's face was unreadable when he spoke. "So Cat was my real grandmother, and my grandfather wasn't Robert Reynolds at all. He was a Nazi spy named Peter Koehler."

Lulu nodded. "Biologically, yes. But Robert couldn't have loved your father any more than if he had been his own flesh and blood. And Maggie thought the sun rose and set over Johnny's head. They were good people, and good, loving parents, regardless of the other troubles in their lives."

Turning to Lulu again, Emmy asked, "So what did Maggie tell everyone had happened to Cat? The only thing people here seem to remember about her is that she died tragically young."

Lulu sighed. "Despite everything, Maggie still loved Peter. She knew she couldn't be with him, but she wanted him to be free. And in the end, it all worked out." Lulu's eyes darted from each person around the bed as if she were a child with a secret. "She told everyone that it was an accident, that Cat fell out of the window while trying to open it. Which, of course, was the truth."

Lulu reached a hand toward Jolene. "You reminded me so much of Cat. I remember the first time Heath brought you home, and everyone was so struck with how pretty you were, and all I could think about was how you and Cat had the same eyes, and how you both understood your power over men."

Jolene blushed and looked down in her lap, her right hand covering her left so the ring was hidden. Lulu continued. "That's why I wanted you here today, so I could tell you that. You have become like a daughter to me, but in the beginning, I used you to make myself feel better about how Cat died, and how Maggie never knew how Cat had tried to save her. I wanted to somehow make things work for you the way they hadn't for Cat. I kept you coming back here long after I knew it was bad for Heath. Bad for both of you. And I'm sorry." She took a deep breath. "But I guess guilt's a bit like quicksand: the harder you struggle to get free of it, the more you get stuck."

Heath stood slowly, then moved to the window. "But why have you decided to tell all of this now?"

Lulu looked exhausted all of a sudden, as if the retelling of the past had made her relive it—something her seventy-seven-year-old body wasn't prepared for. Softly she said, "Because I'm tired. I'm tired of waiting for forgiveness. I finally realized that sixty-six years is too long to wait."

Emmy's eyes met Jolene's over the old woman on the bed, and Emmy knew they were both recalling their conversation in Emmy's driveway, about how long a person had to wait before she knew it had been long enough.

A familiar expression crossed Lulu's face, allowing Emmy a moment of preparation before Lulu spoke. "And I'm tired, too, of people making the same mistakes Maggie and I made, as if nobody has learned anything." She pointed at Emmy's wedding band, the gold reflecting the fluorescent lights of the hospital room. "How long are you going to pretend that Ben's coming back to you? You're living like you expect him to walk in the door any minute."

Before Emmy could react, Lulu turned her head to face Jolene. "And you, with all your beauty and brains—you still insist on banging your head against the one man who won't have you. You've got so much going for you, don't waste it on somebody who's not for you."

Lulu closed her eyes, bright spots of color on her cheeks a startling contrast to the bleached white of the pillows. "I'm being harsh, but that's my way. I wish I'd been that way with Maggie before it was too late. She might have had a better life if I had."

Jolene stood abruptly. "Excuse me. I need to . . . I have to go." She leaned over and gave Lulu a kiss on the forehead, then walked quickly to the door, her heels tapping against the tiles as she left without a backward glance.

Heath moved as if to follow her, but Lulu spoke, holding him back. "Don't, Heath. She needs to fight her own battles, and she can't do it if you keep rescuing her. She's not one of your unfinished projects." She closed her eyes and relaxed against the pillow. "Let her go."

Heath's eyebrows knitted as he stared at the door for a long moment. Shaking his head, he turned to Lulu. "I'm sorry. I just can't do that." He gave Lulu a kiss on her cheek, then left, promising to come back.

Emmy felt herself trying to shrink back in her chair, still stung by Lulu's words. "You're exhausted, Lulu. I should go so you can rest."

Lulu grasped the sheets near Emmy's chair. "No. Not yet. It's your turn to talk."

Emmy stared at her, not understanding.

"I want you to tell me about Ben."

Emmy waited for the hurt and loss to overwhelm her, for the grief to take hold of her breathing again. But all she felt was the warmth of her feelings for her lost husband, of all the love they'd shared in their brief time together.

"Where would you like me to start?"

"At the beginning. When you met. And when you're done, I'll tell you about Jim."

Emmy raised her eyebrows. "Jim—as in Cat's first husband?"

Lulu nodded. "Yes. I fell in love with him when I was nine years old, and I never found anybody else just like him. But that was my mistake. There would never be anybody just like him—but there must have been plenty more who were just as good." She closed her eyes before Emmy could try to read what else Lulu wanted to say.

"All right, then. Just tell me when you want me to stop." Emmy poured herself a glass of water and began to tell the story of Ben and her, starting with standing on her mother's porch when he'd kissed her for the last first time.

CHAPTER 30

—❧

The honking of a car horn woke Emmy from a sound sleep. She sat up, disoriented, as she looked at her bedside clock and realized it was after ten o'clock in the morning.

She splashed cold water on her face and dragged a toothbrush over her teeth before running to the front door and pulling it open to find her parents just climbing the front steps. Her father enveloped her in a bear hug first, patting her back with his large farmer's hand and making her feel like a little girl again.

"You're looking good, Emmy," he said, studying her face closely. "The warmer weather must be agreeing with you." Smiling broadly, he added, "If this is what October in South Carolina is like, I might have to consider retiring here."

When he let her go, she was left to face her mother, and they stood awkwardly regarding each other. Then they both took a step forward and wrapped their arms around each other, the feeling as unfamiliar as running in heels. But as Emmy made to draw back, her mother held her harder, making it easy for Emmy to lay her head on Paige's shoulder and imagine what it had been like once, when the love Paige felt for her only child overcame the pain of her grief. It had been there all along, but it had just taken the bridge of months to make them both realize it.

Clearing her throat, Paige stepped back and looked up at the house. "It's beautiful. And you say that Abigail's son designed and built it?"

"Yes. Heath built it for his fiancée, before she broke off the engagement. Since he's still working part-time in Atlanta, he spends his time on Folly with his parents instead of here—for obvious reasons. I've enjoyed staying here."

"I bet it's got a lovely view of the marsh," Paige said, sounding hopeful.

Emmy walked to the door and opened it wider. "Come on in, and I'll show you."

Her dad said, "I'll go ahead and unload the car and bring things in while you and your mother talk shop."

Both women smiled at him as they walked through the door. Paige sent an admiring glance at the soaring ceiling and windows before pausing in front of the photographs Emmy had finished framing and hung on the walls.

Paige lifted her hand and touched the photograph of Maggie and Robert on their wedding day. "Is this the rest of your story?" she asked, studying the faces in the old picture.

"Pretty much. I'm sleeping better, if that's what you mean." Emmy frowned to herself as she looked closely at Maggie's face, knowing now why she had always thought there was a sadness in Maggie's smile. She glanced at the next picture, of Peter sitting at a table, looking annoyed to be photographed. She saw now Heath's profile and nose, wondering why she hadn't noticed it before.

She stopped for a moment, considering. "I haven't dreamed about Ben in a while, either. Not since I had that long visit with Lulu, and she asked me to tell her about him."

Paige just nodded, then continued walking straight through to the back of the house to the rear porch, which overlooked the small backyard and the marsh beyond it. Paige's eyes softened as she stared into the distance as if seeing a long-lost friend she'd never expected to see again. "It's still the same," she said, her gaze brushing over the light-house and the muted autumn shades that hovered over the river and the wet marsh that surrounded it. "I think I'd like to paint again, and this would be the first thing I'd paint."

Emmy looked at her mother, remembering the sheet-shrouded easels in Paige's attic, and all the dried-up paint, forgotten over the years. She smiled. "I think that would be a very good idea."

Paige indicated the dock area with her chin. "Is that one of Lulu's bottle trees?"

"Yes. It was there when I got here. It even had a message in it." She thought of the words now—*Come back to me*—seeing the emptiness in them, the impossibility of wanting something that was never meant to be; the naïveté of believing that if a person waited long enough, the words would come true.

"A message?"

"Yeah, something Lulu started long ago, sort of as a way of re-membering someone or some place you loved."

Paige raised her eyebrows but didn't say anything. "Where's your boat?" She was glancing down at the unfinished dock.

"Don't have one, and haven't thought to borrow one, either. The closest I've gotten to the marsh is the dock. I've been putting it off, although I'm not really sure why."

Paige pulled back to get a better look at Emmy. "Because its beauty and mystery will pull you in and never let you go." She returned her gaze to the glare of sun off the ocher-colored water. "You probably realized that at some point, it would make it hard for you to leave." She drew in a deep breath. "It stays with you. Even the smell of the pluff mud. I smelled it coming over the bridge, and I knew that I'd come home."

The corner of Emmy's mouth lifted. "I thought home for you was Indiana."

"Oh, I figure home can be several places. I've got my jar of sand to remind me of that. Ben knew that, too, you know."

Emmy stared at her mother, noticing how thick and brown her

hair still was, with sparkling silver strands interspersed throughout. "What do you mean?"

Paige regarded her daughter with eyes the color of Emmy's. "Before he left, that last time, he came to see me at the store when you weren't there. He told me . . ." She stopped for a moment, as if trying to remember the exact words. "He told me that if something should happen to him, he wanted you to make a new life for yourself someplace else. He wanted you to follow your dreams, wherever they would lead you, and start a new life without memories of your life together holding you back."

Emmy blinked away the sting from her eyes. "Ben told you that?"

Paige nodded, her eyes bright. "He did. He loved you that much."

Emmy felt the old familiar anger burn beneath the surface. "But why didn't you tell me this before?"

"Because you weren't ready to hear it. You would have fought me about leaving even harder. But I think you're ready now." They were both silent for a moment as they watched a hawk glide low over the water, hunting for something only it could see.

Emmy studied the scene, and the Morris Island lighthouse in the distance, until her eyes became blurry with unshed tears. She thought of Ben, and the words he'd meant for her, and her anger dissipated, leaving behind only a warm glow and a certainty that she'd ended up where she was supposed to be. "I haven't dreamed of his footsteps for almost a week now."

Paige remained silent, as if waiting for Emmy to figure out on her own what her words meant.

"I think I'm going to be okay now, Mama."

Paige spoke softly. "I know. I wouldn't have let you go if I didn't think you would be."

The old familiar knowing whispered on the back of Emmy's neck as they allowed a smile to pass between them before returning their gazes to the autumn marsh, where the water nourished the tall grasses, and no more words were needed.

ß

AFTER HER PARENTS LEFT TO go see Abigail, with a promise to meet at Folly's Finds in a few hours, Emmy returned to her desk in the bedroom and sat staring at nothing for a long time, thinking about Ben and what he'd told her mother, and what Lulu had told her about facing the truth that he was never coming back.

Emmy pushed her laptop aside, then drew out a small notebook from the drawer and ripped out a page. She paused with a pen in hand poised over the paper, thinking of all the unsaid words between Ben and her, the two words she regretted never saying, and began to write. When she was finished, she very carefully rolled up the note into a tubular shape, making sure it was small enough to fit inside the neck of a bottle.

Emmy began to walk away, but stopped and returned to the desk, her attention drawn to her reflection in the mirror on the wall. Leaning closer, she saw that her eyes were clearer now and she'd lost the caged look that had reminded her of Maggie's photograph. She looked down at her hand, remembering the day Ben had placed the ring on her finger, finally understanding what her mother had meant about only pain having a time span and not love.

Slowly, she removed the gold wedding band from her left hand and placed it in the drawer, closing it softly and moving away from the desk before she could change her mind.

She threw on her running gear, tucking the note into her jacket pocket, and was jogging down the front steps when she recognized Heath's truck pulling into the driveway with a kayak lying in the open truck bed. Frank let out a bark from the cab before bounding out of the open window and running toward her, barely stopping in time to avoid knocking her over.

Scratching Frank behind the ears, she stood waiting for Heath as he climbed out of the cab and headed toward her, and suddenly she felt shy. She hadn't seen him since he'd left Lulu's hospital room to go find Jolene and hadn't asked Abigail or Lizzie what had happened next, not really sure why but feeling it had something to do with being afraid to know.

Heath stopped in front of Emmy with his hands tucked into his front pockets. "Going for a run?"

"I wouldn't call what I do 'running,' but it works. How are you?"

"Better. Thank you. I've been in Atlanta."

"I know. Your mother told me. And Lizzie. And Lulu. And your dad. It's like they all want to make sure that I know where you are."

He smiled, looked away. When he faced her again, his eyes were serious. "I was with Jolene. She said she was ready to consider rehab. I found her a place that didn't remind her of hospitals so much." He dug the toe of his sneaker into the sandy grass that struggled to grow between the two cement tire runners. "She wanted me to tell you something."

"Really? About what?"

"That Aunt Lulu was right. About it being long enough." He reached into his back pocket and pulled out a wad of tissue. He unwrapped it slowly, revealing a ring with a blue stone that winked in the sunlight. "She gave me back Maggie's ring."

Emmy stared at the sparkling stone, sensing Heath's relief and sorrow that the inevitable had happened, forcing him to consider a different future. "I'm sorry."

"And she also wanted to let you know that you've inspired her."

"Me?"

"After she gets out, she's moving to California. She's hoping a change of scenery can work for her, too."

"Me, too. And I'm glad she wasn't forced to go kicking and screaming like I was." Emmy grimaced, forcing a smile from Heath.

"She also says not to worry. She can continue managing your Web site—that's the beauty of the Internet. If you'd like her to, of course. She said she'll call you as soon as she can to talk about it."

"Good. It seems like you're both okay with things. I know it wasn't easy."

Frank trotted up to Heath with an old tennis ball he'd found in the neighbor's yard and dropped it at his feet. Heath picked up the ball and threw it into the backyard, and they both watched Frank spring into action.

Eager to change the subject, Emmy asked, "How's Lulu? I visited last week, and she was still a little wobbly on her feet."

"She was up and around this morning, bossing my mother around her own kitchen, so I guess she's back to normal. Kept calling poor Janell at the store asking about orders, so I finally took the phone away from her."

"Good call. Janell's doing a great job of filling bottle-tree orders. Maybe it's time to reorganize—put Lulu in charge of design, and Janell in charge of the physical work. And I'll let you and Abigail suggest it. I'll make sure I'm on vacation that week."

Heath threw back his head and laughed, making Emmy smile. "That's probably a good call on your part."

"Has Lulu decided what to tell your father?"

"Yeah. She's going to tell him everything. I think we've all learned what hiding the truth can do. And you know my dad—he's a pretty tough guy. It might take some getting used to the idea that he's the son of a Nazi spy, but he's been through worse. He's such a history buff that I can even see him writing a book about it. I mean, the last Duquesne spy discovered after sixty years—it's pretty interesting stuff, whether or not history's your thing."

"True." Emmy stuck her hands into her pockets, feeling the note she'd written earlier, measuring its weight between her fingers. "And I'm sorry. I never meant to turn your family upside down. I hope you know that if you wanted me to drop it, I would have."

He grinned wryly. "I know that. But actually, I should be apologizing to you. And thanking you. I think the radiation must have warped my thought processes for a while. All I wanted to do was focus on the future and ignore any of the messes I'd left behind. Like none of that mattered, including Jolene. And once you told me about the books, it was like none of those people—Maggie, Lulu, Cat—mattered, either." He rubbed his scar, probably something he'd do for the rest of his life. "All of my indecisions—about my job, about Jolene, about the old lot, about this dock—were just roadblocks I'd set up so that I couldn't see the future too clearly. I figured if I waited long enough, they'd all clear up on their own."

Frank lay down on Emmy's feet, preventing her from moving. "Give yourself a break, Heath. You almost died."

He studied her closely as he spoke. "I'm glad I didn't. Leaving things undone—or unsaid—would be the hardest thing to accept, I think. So I'm glad you found Maggie's books and started this whole thing. You've made me think more clearly again, and made an old woman very happy."

Emmy looked down at Frank, who'd fallen asleep, as her hand again found the rolled note in her pocket, and she allowed her fingers to fold over it. *Leaving things unsaid.* His words reverberated in her head, settling with a surety she hadn't felt in a very long time.

"Speaking of your family, your mother finally admitted to me that she has no interest in retiring and would like to continue working part-time at the store. I pretended to think about it before I told her yes."

Heath grinned. "Good. It'll give her an excuse to keep an eye on Lulu, and keep her too busy to get involved with my personal life."

Emmy raised her eyebrows, then squinted up at him, the sun in her eyes. "Your mother also mentioned that you were finally working on a house plan for the old lot."

He grinned. "I'm going to build a modest cottage, a sort of up-to-date replica of Lulu's old house but with better plumbing and central air. And I'll let her live in it for as long as she wants. I figure Folly Beach doesn't need another McMansion, but it could use a little re-minder of its history."

Emmy's spine tingled, making her focus intently on Heath. "You made the right decision. And I couldn't imagine a better one."

He raised an eyebrow. "And you know this for sure."

"I do." She lifted her eyes to the sky, embarrassed as she usually was to discuss it. "Call it woman's intuition, except mine is always right." Changing the subject, she asked, "So what are you going to do with this house?"

Meeting her eyes again, he said, "Sell it to you, I hope."

His words surprised her, making her speechless for a moment. "I . . . I don't think I can afford it."

"Aha. At least you didn't say that you weren't planning on staying. So that's a start."

Emmy stared at him, the words finally spoken out loud. "Yes," she said slowly, "I suppose I am."

A wide, easy grin split his face. "Great. My mom will be thrilled, and so will Lulu, although she'll never admit it. And don't tell her I said that, either."

Emmy crossed her heart with her forefinger. "Promise." They avoided looking at each other as if each were waiting for another obvious name to be added to the list. Finally, Emmy looked back at the house. "Lulu once said something about hurricanes coming every thirty years on the nines. Does that mean the next big one will hit in two thousand nineteen?"

"Yep. But believe me, this house could withstand another Hugo. And that's not intuition." He winked. "I know the builder."

Emmy studied the house, remembering how vulnerable she thought it was the first time she'd seen it, perched between the crouching Atlantic and the flowing Folly River. But now, considering it again, she realized how deceptive the thin pilings were, and how the beauty of the joists and beams belied the strength of the house. She could imagine it bearing the wind and tidal surge of a big storm, emerging bruised, but stronger somehow, too.

Glancing back at the truck, she asked, "What's the kayak for?"

"To show you the marsh. It's about time you started to learn your way around. Once you know how to kayak and not get lost, I'm going to teach you how to shag. You can't live in South Carolina without knowing the state dance. It might even be illegal."

"Really."

Heath nodded. "And once I finish the dock, I thought I could leave the boat here, if that's all right with you."

"Sure." She looked at the kayak with apprehension. "I've never actually been in one before. But I'm game if you don't mind a beginner."

"Come on, then. Help me unhook it and you grab the paddles, and we'll go see if it floats."

Emmy looked at him with alarm.

"I'm kidding. Of course it floats. I've been in it at least a dozen times and never even got wet."

Reassured, she did as he asked and followed him to the end of the solid docking. She helped him place the kayak in the water, then stowed the oars inside.

"One second," she said. "I'll be right back."

Emmy ran to the edge of the dock, where the bottle tree stood sentry. Sticking her hand in her pocket, she pulled out the note she'd written to Ben, then carefully placed it inside the bright blue bottle, making sure it was in all the way before stepping back. A breeze from the marsh blew at her, bringing with it the scent of the pluff mud as she stared at the rolled-up note, now blurry and distorted from the blue glass of the bottle. The scent was less foreign now, more like an old and favorite perfume trapped inside a winter scarf, remembered still after seasons of forgetting.

Migrating geese called from the azure sky, making their annual trek from the north in an age-old ritual of following an unknown sense of home. The wind rustled the tall grass, making each reed whisper so the whole marsh erupted with conversation. Emmy thought of all the time that had passed since Ben's death, now knowing it as her waiting time, and she gave a silent thank-you to Lulu and Maggie for teaching her how to know when it had been long enough.

Emmy placed her hand on the bottle, its surface warmed by the bright sun and reflecting its jeweled light like sea glass on the beach. Then taking a deep breath and closing her eyes, she said good-bye to Ben for the last first time.

Author's Note

SEVERAL YEARS AGO I WAS in the Outer Banks of North Carolina for a family wedding. While there my family and I took a sightseeing tour of the famous Cape Hatteras lighthouse. It was on that tour that I learned of a German U-boat sunk right off the coast from where I was standing.

I've always considered myself a history buff, but couldn't recall ever learning in school anything about Germans being that close to the United States mainland. I was fascinated, and continued to mull over that factoid until the right book came along.

I chose Folly Beach because of its reputation during the nineteen forties as being *the* place for fun. The Folly Beach pier attracted top-notch entertainers, and it's rumored that the famous South Carolina dance, the shag, was first performed there. Folly was a spot of light during a dark time in our nation's history, and thus the idea for a book was born.

Before writing the book, however, I had to educate myself on the history of "Operation Drumroll," the German code name for the initiative to send a handful of U-boats to our Atlantic coast. It began in January 1942, catching the U.S. completely unaware. In the first six months of 1942, the Germans sank 360 merchant ships and oil tankers—more than had been put down in the Pacific by the Japanese from Pearl Harbor to Midway.

If Hitler had granted his own admiral's request for more U-boats to be sent, or if the U.S. had delayed even more in establishing a naval defense, blackouts, and convoys through our eastern seaboard shipping lanes, it is completely conceivable that the U.S. would have lost the war before we'd barely begun to fight. As the great statesman Winston Churchill said, ". . . the U-boat attack was the worst evil. It would have been wise for the Germans to stake all upon it." Thankfully, for us and the rest of the world, they did not.

It was in the course of researching the U-boat invasion that I also came upon two other fascinating historical events that I was also ignorant of—the Duquesne spy ring and the landing of German saboteurs on American soil. By sheer luck on our part and general stupidity on theirs, the spy ring and saboteurs were apprehended before too much damage could be done. But for the purposes of this book, I had to ask myself the what-if question: what if they hadn't all been caught? And so the story of Folly Beach in the nineteen forties and the real history of World War II melded into *On Folly Beach*, as told through the eyes of Lulu O'Shea, who is nine years old when the story starts in 1942.

To faithfully portray Lulu's story, I had to do a lot of research—a lot more fun than it sounds! I found the following books very helpful and interesting, and highly recommend them to those of you who'd like to learn more:

Torpedo Junction, by Homer H. Hickam, Jr.

Saboteurs: The Nazi Raid on America, by Michael Dobbs

Folly Beach: A Brief History by Gretchen Stringer-Robinson

Folly Beach: Glimpses of a Vanished Strand by Bill Bryan

The Humours of Folly photographs by Frank Melvin Braden, words by Ellie Maas Davis

For those of you who'd like to learn even more, Folly Beach offers plenty of summer rental homes for your own "research."

Karen White is the award-winning author of eleven previous books. She grew up in London but now lives with her husband and two children near Atlanta, Georgia. Visit her Web site at www.karen-white.com.

On Folly Beach

KAREN WHITE

This Conversation Guide is intended to enrich the
individual reading experience, as well as encourage us to
explore these topics together—because books, and life,
are meant for sharing

A CONVERSATION
WITH KAREN WHITE

Q. *The idea of the bottle trees is really interesting—how did you learn about them?*

A. A friend of mine is from New Orleans, but now lives in Memphis. On a recent visit, I saw that she had a bottle tree in her backyard. She explained what it was, and how she'd bought it in New Orleans and brought it to her new home as a sort of reminder. Like everything in my life, her explanation sparked a story idea.

Q. *Do you know anyone else who has a bottle tree, and do you have one yourself?*

A. I don't have one—yet. But since I first saw one at my friend's house, I'm seeing them more and more. While looking through a pictorial coffee table book, *The Humours of Folly,* I saw a picture of a bottle tree in a Folly Beach backyard that cemented my idea to set the book on Folly.

Q. *What inspired you to write* On Folly Beach? *Was it visiting Folly Beach?*

A. I knew I wanted to set part of the book during World War II and in the South Carolina Lowcountry. I didn't have to dig very deep to discover that Folly Beach was *the* hot spot for dancing and fun during the nineteen forties, and pictures from the era were a wonderful inspiration. I visited Folly Beach after I'd started writing the book, renting a house there for a week during the summer for additional research.

Q. *One of the themes of the book seems to be the power of literature over the imagination—both positive and negative. Do you think if Lulu hadn't read Nancy Drew mysteries, she would have been less likely to spy on others? And is her spying really a bad thing, since she may have prevented a Nazi invasion?*

A. I was a voracious reader in my teens, and I can cite specific examples of how particular books changed my way of thinking, or acting, or perceiving the world around me. Yes, I really did have a "Scarlett O'Hara period" during middle school. I do think Nancy Drew and the other books Lulu read definitely had an influence on her, and I hesitate to say that her spying was "bad." Trying on new identities is part of growing up, after all. And luckily for the citizens of Folly Beach and the rest of the country, Lulu's "spy period" happened at just the right time.

Q. *The idea of leaving secret coded messages in books is intriguing— is this something you've done yourself? If not, how did you come up with the idea for Maggie and Peter to communicate?*

A. A few years ago, a friend of mine loaned me an old

out-of-print book she'd acquired from a used bookstore. Inside was a handwritten letter dating back to the nineteen forties from a person in Australia. The contents of the letter were mundane, but I was fascinated by the identities of the sender and the recipient.

Of course that sparked a book idea—what if the contents weren't so mundane? What if they were from two lovers instead—lovers who had something to hide? And that was how Peter and Maggie's story began.

Q. *How did you come up with the framing device of using two different wars to tie together the two different stories?*

A. Since the whole history behind the German U-boats off the U.S. coast was one of the idea sparks for this story, I knew I needed something current to counterbalance those events. That was how I thought of two women personally affected by war, but sixty years apart, with a Folly Beach bookstore as a touchstone for both of their stories.

Q. *You've played with different points of view in your previous novels, and in* On Folly Beach, *you decided to stay with third person throughout. Why did you decide on this particular point of view for* On Folly Beach?

A. I always let the characters in my books "decide" on how they want me to tell their stories. Maggie and Lulu were adamant about not telling their stories in flashback, which made it necessary for me to jump back in time with them to tell their stories as they happened.

I chose not to write any of the women's points of view (young Lulu, old Lulu, and Emmy) in first person because that would have made one story more prominent over the others, and I saw them all as being equally important.

Q. *The planned Nazi invasion of the eastern seaboard is a fascinating footnote in history. Why do you think this isn't something that is discussed much in school?*

A. I wish I knew the answer to that question! I always thought that I had a pretty good education, both from my schooling and from my dad, who is a definite history buff, so it was a surprise when I first heard about it several years ago while on a trip to the Outer Banks, North Carolina.

I think the main reason why the whole episode has been relegated to history's footnotes is because the worst that could have happened didn't. In other words, if the D-day invasion hadn't been the success it was in turning around the war, we would only be hearing about some big plan to end the war that was never actualized and then move on to the events that *were*. If the Germans had sent over more U-boats and effectively blockaded our coasts in 1942, we wouldn't have been able to help England and her allies. That could have been the end of the war, which would, of course, have made it into the history books as more than a footnote. And those history books would probably be written in German, too.

QUESTIONS
FOR DISCUSSION

Please note that some of the following questions reveal important plot points. Readers who have not finished the novel may want to stop at this point and return afterward.

1. Although Folly Beach, South Carolina, is a real place, "folly" also describes some of the mistakes the characters make throughout the story. What are some of these follies?

2. The story of the planned Nazi invasion of the East Coast is based on historical fact—is this something you already knew about before reading *On Folly Beach*?

3. Did you find Lulu a sympathetic character despite her habit of spying as a child and her abrasiveness as an adult?

4. Do you think Lulu can be held responsible for Peter's death?

5. Despite Peter being a Nazi spy and a murderer, do you think he deserved to die? Was he truly a "bad" man?

6. Why do you think Maggie refused to evacuate her home before Hurricane Hugo hit?

7. Were Lulu and Robert wrong to not tell Maggie the truth about Peter being a Nazi spy for so many years? Do you think Maggie suspected the truth since she never wanted to go to the Atlantic House restaurant?

8. How many times did Lulu misinterpret what she observed, or do you think she was always correct in her interpretation?

9. Do you think Cat seduced Peter, or did Peter seduce Cat to not betray his secret?

10. Do you think Peter really loved Maggie? Do you think Maggie would have still left with Peter if she had known the truth about him?

11. Why do you think Lulu finally decided to tell the truth about the past to Emmy and her family?

12. Emmy and Lulu are linked with two different wars, and the effects of war on the homefront. What are some of the similarities between what they experienced because of war?